EMPYRION:
THE SEARCH FOR FIERRA

BOOK ONE

EMPYRION:
THE SEARCH FOR FIERRA

BOOK ONE

STEPHEN R. LAWHEAD

Crossway Books • Westchester, Illinois
A Division of Good News Publishers

Other Books by Stephen R. Lawhead

Fiction

Dream Thief

In the Hall of the Dragon King

Warlords of Nin

The Sword and the Flame

Non-Fiction

After You Graduate

The Phoenix Factor: Surviving and
Growing Through Personal Crisis,
with Dr. Karl Slaikeu

Rock Reconsidered

Turn Back the Night: A Christian
Response to Popular Culture

The Ultimate Student Handbook,
with Alice Slaikeu Lawhead

Empyrion: The Search for Fierra. Copyright © 1985 by Stephen
R. Lawhead. Published by Crossway Books, a division of Good News
Publishers, Westchester, Illinois 60153.

Book design by K. L. Mulder.

First printing, 1985.

Third printing, 1988.

Printed in the United States of America.

Library of Congress Catalog Card Number 85-70476

ISBN 0-89107-358-2

And though the last lights off the black West went
Oh, morning, at the brown brink Eastward,
    Springs—
Because the Holy Ghost over the bent
World broods with warm breast and ah! bright
    Wings.

                     G. M. Hopkins, God's Grandeur

PRELUDE

V1: [Static] We're down! And it's beautiful! Wonderful!

V2: It's heaven! It really is.

V1: All probe data confirms observational analysis. Geoscience Officer Tovardy will dispatch a brief preliminary report.

V2: Okay—

V1: Keep it short, Ben.

V2: Right—just the highlights. Atmosphere is thin, but friendly—high oxygen and nitrogen content; other gas ratios well within normal tolerances—except for minute levels of rardon ionization in the inert sectors. No idea at present what effect that will have on freebreathing; we'll check that out. Weather—there's no weather to speak of here! It's Hawaii everyday. No observed cyclonic disturbances; projected climatic variation: negligible. Flora and fauna? This is a fairly complex environment. It's going to take time to sort everything out properly. At present no known pathogenic lifeforms identified. No sentient life either, for that matter. Like I said, the place is an absolute paradise! That's it for now. Full report to follow.

TEN SECONDS SILENCE

V1: Okay, let's take a look . . . How long ago did this happen?

V3: Three minutes maybe . . . not more.

V1: Ground control, we've got a situation here. We're not sure . . . [static—two seconds] . . . event monitors have picked up electromagnetic disturbances that could indicate . . . [static—four seconds]—anomaly in singularity region. Don't know what it means. We'll stay on it at this end. Next dispatch will be at our regularly scheduled time. This is Empyrion Colony Com—[static—five seconds]

END OF TRANSCRIPT

ONE

The body staring up through the translucent green of the nutrient bath might have been dead. It floated beneath the surface, open-eyed, its face becalmed, a snaking nimbus of dark hair spreading like a black halo: a saint embalmed in emerald amber.

Presently a small bubble formed on the rim of one nostril, puffed up bigger, and broke free, spiraling to the surface. Plick! This was followed by another slightly larger bubble, which also spun up to the surface of the bath, drifted momentarily, and burst. Plick!

A whole fountain of bubbles erupted and boiled up, and in the center, rising with them, the head of Orion Tiberias Treet, sputtering and inhaling great draughts of air, like a whale breeching after a long nap on the ocean floor.

Two broad hands came up, dashing liquid from two dark eyes, pushing ropy strands of hair aside. Treet snatched up a watch from the rim of the white marble bath and held it before his face. "Six minutes!" he shouted triumphantly. "A new record."

"I'm impressed."

Treet glanced up quickly and saw a stranger sitting on the edge of the bath opposite him. The stranger had a needle gun aimed at his throat, and, contrary to his word, did not seem at all impressed with the new submergence record. Besides himself and the gunman, there was not another person in the public bath.

"What do you want?" Treet asked, the skin at his throat tingling beneath the aim of the needle gun.

"I have what I want: you," replied the gunman. Cool menace clipped his words efficiently. "Get out of the soup and get dressed."

Orion Treet glared dully at the slim needle gun in his abductor's hand as he rose slowly from the bath, took up the

fluffy white bath towel the attendant had given him upon entering, and began drying his limbs and torso with exaggerated care
in order to give himself a moment to think. By the time he was
fully dressed he had concluded that it was probably no use
trying to talk his way out of whatever it was this stranger with
the gun wanted to do with him—he looked like a man who was
used to having his way, and was not overly shy about how he got
it.

"You have been a problem, Treet," the man was saying. "I
don't like problems. In my line of work, problems cost me
money, and you've cost me plenty. It's over now, so you might as
well relax and put that brain of yours in neutral for a while. I
don't want you taxing yourself over how to get away this time.
Just stand easy, do as you're told, and you'll likely live that much
longer. You like living, don't you, Treet?"

Treet had to admit that he did indeed like living; it was,
after all, one of the things that made life so worthwhile. But he
did not share this observation with the man training the needle
gun on his jugular. Instead, he just glared and tried to look
dutifully irritated.

The man took a short step closer. The gun did not waver.
"I almost had you in Cairo, and then again in Addis Ababa,
Cologne, Zurich, Salzburg, Milan, Tokyo, and San Francisco.
I've got to hand it to you, you're a shrewdy. I don't know when
I've enjoyed myself more, but it's over."

"As long as it's over," replied Treet evenly, "maybe you
won't mind telling me why you've been trailing me all this time.
What do you want?" He had known since Zurich that he was
being followed, but was unsure why, though several possibilities
sprang to mind. Still, he felt entitled to an explanation. Wasn't
that a victim's prerogative?

"I don't mind telling you at all, scumbag. There are some
peopl. who want to talk to you. They seem quite anxious, in
fact. Personally I don't give a rat's hind end. I'd just as soon drop
you where you stand."

At least this meant the man would not kill him outright.
But who were the people so desperate for conversation? Treet
ran down a list of former employers, angry innkeepers, outraged
restauranteurs, and offended debtors of various sorts, but the
effort proved futile. He could not come up with anyone who
would go to this amount of trouble to reach him. "So?"

"So, bright boy, we lockstep it to the nearest teleterm. I'm going to report in. Keep your hands where I can see them; turn around slowly and move. Outside there's a terminal directly to the right. If you so much as deviate one millimeter from the course, you're dead. Understand?"

Treet understood. They turned and marched from the spa and out into the main corridor of Houston International Skyport. Travelers, not a few of them free-state refugees by the tattered look of them, jammed hip to thigh, swept along the moving walkway before them, and Treet entertained the notion of jumping on the conveyor and worming himself into the crowd—a trick he had used in Salzburg. He started to turn his head, but felt the needle gun's sharp nose in the small of his back.

"Try it, slime ball. Let's see how you look with a cyanide tattoo." The voice behind him was disconcertingly close.

"Don't get your hopes up." Treet saw the triangular sign with the distinctive blue lightning bolt on a white oval screen and stopped in front of the booth. Passengers sliding by on the walkway ignored the two men as they squeezed into the booth together.

The gunman jammed a card into the slot above the keypad, and the screen flicked on. A line of blue numbers appeared in the upper right hand corner of the oval screen. Treet watched as his captor entered an alfanumeric code; the screen blanked. Instantly another code came up in the center of the screen. With one hand the man typed in two words: GOT HIM.

For a moment nothing happened. Then as Treet watched, hoping for some clue to the identity of the person or persons on the other end of the linkup, the words HOLD FOR PICKUP appeared below the gunman's entry. With that, the gunman tapped a key, the screen cleared, and his card ejected from the slot. "Okay, move it."

"Where to?"

"Heliport Six." The man jerked the gun upward toward Treet's chin. "Let's take our time, shall we? There's no hurry, and I wouldn't want you to get overheated."

They exited the booth and shunned the peoplemover, walking instead to a bank of escalators. They jumped on an escalator labeled TO HELIPORT SIX and rode up three levels to the rooftop. Through the tinted bubble, the sky glowed dark green-gray and the sun shone a nauseating chartreuse. Radiating out from the bubble were at least a dozen landing platforms on the end of walkway tubes. Helicopters sat on two or three platforms, their rotors spinning idly.

"Number three platform," the gunman whispered in Treet's ear. He underscored his words with another nudge from the needle gun. When they reached the tube entrance, the gunman shoved Treet into a sculptured foam chair and said, "Sit."

Treet sat, his hands atop his knees, his knees beneath his chin. "Who's coming to pick me up?"

"You'll see soon enough."

"How much are they paying you?"

"Trying to figure out how much you're worth? Forget it— you're not worth that much."

"I'll pay you more." Treet thought he saw a glimmer of interest flit across the man's pinched features.

"How much more?"

"How much are they paying you?"

"Thirty-five thousand in metal, plus expenses. I have a lot of expenses." The man with the gun watched him slyly. "Well?"

"I'll give you forty thousand." Treet tried to sound as if that were in some way possible.

"You lying filth! I ought to drill you for jollies."

Treet shrugged. "If you don't want to be reasonable—"

"What makes you think I'd let you go for any amount of money? You pus suckers are all alike."

"You won't let me go?"

"Never. I'd kill you first, and that's a fact."

"Why? I've never done anything to you."

"Principle. How far do you think I'd get in this business if my clients couldn't trust me to deliver the goods? Besides, you've made me look very bad in front of a very influential client. I don't like that—bad for business."

"You've got me now, don't you?"

"I've got you all right. But I lost a double bonus along the way."

Treet could tell he was getting nowhere and decided to wait and take his chances with whoever showed up on landing pad number three. He slumped back in his chair and tried to think who might value his company at thirty-five thousand plus expenses—and in precious metals, yet. He was still trying to produce a name when he heard the muffled sound of approaching rotors.

"On your feet, grunt-face." The gunman held his weapon

level and pointed down the tube to where the helicopter was dropping onto the pad at the other end. "After you."

Treet got slowly to his feet and shambled down the tube, watching as the copter's sidehatch opened and two men, dressed in dark blue paramilitary uniforms, scrambled out. They came to stand on either side of the tube exit and waited. Outside, the air was warm and rather humid. As Treet stepped from the tube, a hot wind from the helicopter's twin jets hit him in the face. The uniformed men grabbed his arms and led him forward without a word.

A third man inside the copter held the hatch open. Treet turned. "I guess this is good-bye," he told the gunman.

"This is good-bye all right." The gunman raised the needle gun, and his finger pressed the flat trigger.

Treet cringed away from the impact as a little puff of vapor issued from the sharp muzzle. He did not feel a thing. Was the gun unloaded after all?

He glanced down and saw a tiny needle sticking out of his stomach, its red cap pulsating, pumping poison into him. His hands reached for the dart, plucked it out, and threw it before his guards could stop him. Momentarily free, he turned and dived away from the helicopter, hit the rubber surface of the landing pad, rolled to his feet, staggered once, and fell backward with arms outstretched, his head bouncing off the pad on impact. Treet stared upward at the clear blue Texas sky as his eyesight dimmed and the leering faces above him diffused and disappeared.

T W O

aves crashed in his head and his stomach heaved, as with the ocean's swell. Somewhere nearby someone was moaning, and Treet wished they would shut up—until he realized it was him. Well, perhaps moaning was called for, then.

After several long minutes, the ocean effect subsided and he battled his eyelids open. But the light hurt his head, so he closed his eyes again and listened instead. The moaning—his moaning—had stopped, and silence lay thick and artificial. A synthetic silence, he decided, as if the quiet had been manufactured in some way and layered over the noise that was going on all around him just to prevent him from hearing it.

He sniffed the air and smelled the heavily filtered, oxygen-enhanced stuff typical of a sealed building. Wherever they had brought him, it was at least up to code. But that could be any relatively modern structure anywhere in the Northern Hemisphere. Nevertheless, he guessed there was a good chance he was still in Houston. The copter—had there been a copter?—yes, he remembered something about a helicopter—had come from somewhere close to the skyport. No more than four or five minutes away.

Of course, they could have taken him anywhere after that. He had no idea how long he had been out. A few hours, most likely; less than a day. His stomach gurgled, reminding him he had not eaten in quite a while. Orion, he thought, you've really done it this time.

Close on this thought came a question: *what* had he done? He still didn't know. If he hadn't tried to escape, he would have found out by now. No, that pinhead gunman had shot him *before* he had tried to escape. At least the needle hadn't carried the promised dose of cyanide. His hand went to the spot on his stomach where the dart had stuck him. The wound, though tiny, throbbed mightily and was inflamed.

He was still taking physical inventory when he heard the sigh of a door opening automatically. "Up and at 'em, tiger," called a cheery female voice. "They're waiting for you upstairs." She gave the word *upstairs* a subtle rising inflection—as if Upstairs was the name of a foreign territory not altogether friendly to the interests of the sovereign state of Texas.

Treet kept his eyes closed and feigned sleep. The ruse did not work. "I've been monitoring you on my video, Mr. Treet. I know you're awake, although you probably feel a little rocky. The best thing is to be up and moving around. The drug will leave your system that much quicker."

Whoever owned that dreadfully cheerful voice was now standing directly over him. He could hear her breathing down on him, and then felt a cool touch on his forehead. He opened his eyes to see a rather severely pretty redhead looking down at him. She wore the white-and-blue shift of a nurse. "Temperature and blood pressure normal," the nurse announced, withdrawing her hand from his head.

"Where am I?" Treet made a move to get up, and his stomach rolled dangerously. The nurse expertly slipped her arm under his shoulders and levered him into a sitting position.

"All will be explained, Mr. Treet. I'm to see that you are up and around as soon as possible."

"And nothing else. Is that it?"

"I wouldn't want to spoil the surprise now, would I?" She gave him a quick professional smile. "Swing your legs over the edge and try to stand."

Treet did as he was told. He had a feeling that the boys in the blue uniforms were hunkered nearby, ready to pounce on him if he needed pouncing on again. He decided to go along peacefully for the moment. Keeping his options open was how he described it to himself.

Leaning on the nurse's arm, Treet managed to stagger, like a sailor making landfall after a long storm-tossed voyage, across to the door of the small, single-bed infirmary. The door slid open once again and admitted them to a brightly lit foyer done up in pleasant greens with blue and yellow foam chairs clustered around the cylindrical screen of a holovision: a doctor's waiting room.

"You're doing very well," said the nurse amiably. "I won't be a moment. Walk around if you like." She ducked behind a counter and into a cubbyhole. Treet heard her voice speaking

low—into a teleterm, he guessed—saying, "He's ready, Mr.
Varro. Yes, I will. You're welcome."

Varro? Varlo? He didn't know anyone named Varlo. The
name did not connect. At the opposite end of the waiting room
was a window. Treet walked over nonchalantly, pulled the green
curtain aside, and peeked out. He looked down several stories
into a square courtyard. Blank windows from four facing walls
stared into the same courtyard, and none of them gave any clue
to where he was. The sky, what he could see of it, was cloudless
and greenish with a tint of orange.

"Mr. Treet?" The nurse called him pleasantly. "Your escort
is here."

He turned to see another blue uniform approaching—a
different blue uniform than the one worn by the men in the
helicopter. Theirs had been dark blue with flashy yellow insig-
nias on the upper arms. This man wore lighter blue, with a white
collar and a black belt around the middle. Attached to the belt
was a flat brown pouch which, Treet supposed, contained a
needle gun or stunner of some sort.

The man beckoned to Treet with a jerk of his head. Treet
joined him, fell into step, and was conveyed down a wide, low,
vacant corridor, across a pentagonal lobby, and finally down
another, shorter corridor to a waiting elevator. The elevator was
open; they stepped in, and the guard pressed a button. The
doors slid closed, and the elevator rose. There was, Treet noticed, only one button on the panel, marked OPEN/CLOSED.
Which meant that the elevator was designed to be run from
somewhere else. From upstairs, Treet guessed.

As the elevator rose, Treet weighed the advantages of striking up a conversation with his guard. Since no one else he'd met
this day—if it *was* still this day—seemed inclined to enlighten
him as to the nature of his predicament, he doubted whether a
holstered elevator attendant would be the one to start giving
away free information. So he stood and gazed at a point on the
ceiling just over the elevator doors and waited to find out what
sort of fate would greet him on the other side.

The elevator ride was longer than he guessed it would be.
But finally the doors slid back to reveal a lushly carpeted receiving room of goodly size. Live plants in beaten brass pots lined
softly glowing walls. Airy hangings of fabric and metal dangled
from the ceiling, which slanted upward just slightly. From some-

where the sound of water splashing in a fountain-pool reached Treet's ears.

The guard lifted a hand like a doorman and ushered his passenger out of the elevator. Treet stepped out onto the cream-colored carpet. The elevator door closed behind him, and he was left alone. He stood waiting for something to happen, but nothing did or seemed about to, so he began looking around.

Large wooden doors—black teak, floor to ceiling, ridiculously expensive—stood on either side of the room. Neither door had any markings. Straight ahead were equally large double doors, but these were studded with gold or brass and were painted bright colors. Closer, he could see that the colors formed a design: two winged men, one on each door, faced one another with outstretched arms—one arm shoulder-high and the other raised over their heads. The images had long hair, braided into a single braid down their backs. They wore long robes or gowns, flowing as if in the wind; the robes were marked with spiral designs and symbols in red, blue, violet, and gold. The men's wings were gold, with long, broad feathers spreading out behind them the length of their bodies. Their faces were in profile—straight, angular faces with large, dark eyes. Upon their chests they wore some kind of copper-colored amulet on a chain; the amulet was in the shape of a symbol or a letter from some alphabet Treet did not recognize. Between the winged men and above them a very round and rosy sun cast down golden rays that wiggled like snakes. The sun was divided equally, one half on each door, and its wriggling rays slanted down across the surfaces of both doors, which Treet could now see were bound in leather.

"You're awake sooner than expected." The voice behind Treet did not take him completely by surprise. This had been a day for people sneaking up behind him, and he had come to expect it.

Treet turned to see a stiff, round-headed man approaching with hands folded behind his back. A fringe of short-cropped gray hair accented the roundness of his head, as did full cheeks that were thickening to jowl. The head perched on a short neck over sloping shoulders and overlooked a sturdy, short-limbed body.

"I see you appreciate fine things." The man smiled, glanced at the handsome doors with the approval and detachment of a museum curator, and then offered his hand. "I am Varro, and I am pleased to meet the famous Orion Treet."

Treet did not know whether he should shake the man's hand or throttle him, but considered that he would gain nothing by being belligerent, so took it, though a little less cordially than he might have under ordinary circumstances. Varro evidently sensed the restraint and responded, "I *do* most heartily apologize for the misunderstanding at the airport."

"Misunderstanding? Was that what it was?" Treet pulled a face that was meant to convey concern, and also anger under civilized restraint. His tone, however, was bewilderment.

"I am afraid so." Varro shook his head, as if deeply regretting what had taken place. He stepped close to Treet and took his arm, leading him a few steps aside to a nook. One wall of the two-walled cranny was glass; another was flat slabs of irregular stone down which a pleasant cascade of water trickled into a pool somewhere below them. "Please sit down, Mr. Treet. I'd like a word with you before we go in."

Treet glanced out the window and saw that they were atop the building. Green forested hills stretched out into blue misty distance. There was not a single sign of Houston, or any other city—at least not from this view. Treet sat down on a polished wood bench facing an opposite bench on which Varro settled himself. "I'd like a word with you too, Mr. Varro. The first one being why—why have you people been following me?"

Varro smiled again, showing very small fine white teeth. "Nothing sinister, Mr. Treet, I assure you. Perhaps I'd better explain."

"Perhaps you'd better. No one else seems inclined to, and I'm becoming testy. I get that way when abused."

"It isn't what you're thinking."

"I'm not thinking anything. I haven't done anything—as far as I know. Have I?"

"We're not the militia, Mr. Treet. But I'm not aware that you have done anything you ought to worry about. We don't particularly care one way or another. It is none of our concern."

"You're just concerned with drugging innocent citizens and kidnapping them in broad daylight." Treet looked down at his sore stomach and rubbed it distractedly.

"Please, I am sorry for that unfortunate incident. As I have said, it was a misunderstanding. The man responsible has been severely . . . ah, reprimanded." Treet wondered what the clown at the airport had suffered for popping him with the needle. Varro did not give him time to wonder for long, but continued. "Now then," brushing all unpleasantness behind him, "I assume you have heard of Cynetics Corporation?"

"I've heard of it," replied Treet coolly. Who hadn't? It was one of the six or eight largest multinationals on the planet. Maybe *the* largest, for all anybody knew. Corporation law prevented anyone—especially the government, as long as a company paid its tribute—from finding out just how big it really was. But Cynetics holdings were thought to include whole countries, several independent corporate states, and not a few colonies. "What does Cynetics want with me? I take it we're on Cynetics property somewhere?"

"Yes, Mr. Treet, we are. North American headquarters just outside Houston." Varro glanced back at the leather-bound doors quickly. "I'll try to explain briefly. We haven't much time. I wanted to speak to you first before we went in. We can talk at length after we have seen him."

"Him?"

"Chairman Neviss." Varro spoke as though Treet should have known instinctively who he meant.

"Oh," Treet said. Ordinarily he would have been honored by a private interview with one of the most powerful men in the known universe, but today the prospect did not exactly send a thrill through his viscera. Under the circumstances, he felt he was being extremely magnanimous to even consider an interview.

"He is intent on seeing you, Mr. Treet. He is convinced you are the man for a special assignment he has in mind."

"Which is?"

Varro made an impatient movement with his hand. "I'll let him tell you about it. What I want you to understand is that he is not at all well. Please, I am asking your cooperation. Do not excite him or cause him anguish in any way."

"How would I do that?"

"By refusing him."

"You mean I'm supposed to agree in advance to whatever he wants? What's the point of even going in there?"

"No, no. Nothing like that. I just meant—well, if you like what he offers, accept by all means. If not, just tell him you will require time to think it over. He'll understand that. He won't like it, but he'll understand it. However," Varro brightened once more, "I think you will find his proposal attractive."

"I'll play along." Treet shrugged. Why not? He had nothing to lose.

"Good. I knew I could trust you. Shall we?" Varro got up and moved off toward the painted doors, and Treet followed him. This time, as they approached the threshold the panels swung inward on silent hinges, and the two men entered a gallery decorated with pottery and alabaster carvings displayed on metallic pedestals, each with a light shining down upon it from the ceiling as in a museum. All of the pieces were pre-Columbian Aztec. It was an impressive collection.

At the end of the gallery another set of doors opened to reveal a young woman, dressed incongruously in a long white robe—much like the two winged men on the outer doors. Her hair was jet, like her eyes, and bound in a single braid down her back. Her skin was light bronze and porcelain smooth, her cheekbones high, her lips dark. She was easily the most beautiful woman Treet had seen in a very long time. He could not help staring.

"Miss Yarden Talazac," said Varro, "his executive administrator."

She offered Treet her hand and said demurely, "Welcome. I'm glad to know you, Mr. Treet. This way, if you please."

"My pleasure," replied Treet sincerely. For the pleasure of being in this radiant creature's company, Treet was willing to forgive whatever grievances he had been nursing to this point. Even his punctured stomach did not feel so bad anymore.

The stunning Miss Talazac conducted them into a cavernous domed room whose ceiling was dark and winking with artificial starlight like the ceiling of a planetarium. There were no windows, but at intervals around the circumference of the dome lighted niches contained statuary.

Before them, on a dais served by a long sloping ramp next to a very large and old-fashioned wooden chair, stood a smoking brazier on a tripod. The smoke was scented—like flowers, but delicate and airy, not oppressive. Treet felt as if his senses sharpened upon entering the room and wondered whether the incense had anything to do with that impression.

In the oversize chair facing him sat a man whose age could not be determined. This, Treet assumed, was Chairman Neviss.

Though his very ordinary features were expressionless, he appeared alert, and Treet thought something like mirth played at the edges of the full, fleshy lips—as if the Chief Officer of Cynetics were enjoying some amusing private observation.

"Chairman, may I present Mr. Orion Treet." It was Miss Talazac who spoke rather than Varro.

Slowly, almost painfully, the Chairman rose and, with a condescending nod of his head, diffidently offered his hand to Treet. Treet approached the dais and accepted the handshake. The grasp was dry and cool, and Treet felt bones beneath the flesh of the palm. "I'm glad you're here, Mr. Treet. I have been looking forward to this meeting with some anticipation."

Treet did not know what to say, so mumbled something about being honored and privileged to find himself in such exalted company.

"Please be seated, gentlemen." The Chairman indicated chairs, and Treet twisted his head to see that chairs had appeared where there had been no chairs before. Varro, no doubt, had produced them. Miss Talazac, on the other hand, had disappeared.

Treet sat down and rested his arms easily on the armrests. Now that he was here, he suddenly felt very nervous, very intense—almost excited. What was this all about? Why the intrigue? What did they want?

Chairman Neviss looked at him dryly, and then his mouth opened in a wide grin. "Orion Treet," he said, shaking his head, "this is indeed a pleasure."

"I'm honored, sir."

"Do you know that I have been following your writings for thirty years? From the beginning, in fact. You have a style, sir. Lucid. Astute. I like that; it shows a clear-thinking mind. Your grasp of the interconnected events of history is simply astounding. I envy you your abilities, sir—and there is not much in this world that I do envy."

It took Treet some moments to realize that it was indeed himself that the Chairman was talking about—he always had that reaction to praise. "Thank you, sir," he muttered.

"No. Thank *you*, Orion Treet. I have learned a great deal from you. I respect you as a man of keen intellect and sensitivity. Also a man to be trusted. Rare these days to find that, I'm sorry to say. Very rare, sir."

Treet wondered whether the Chairman knew that his honored guest had been pursued across three continents and then abducted by a contract nab artist in order to make this cozy meeting possible. Likely not—though he might be interested to know. Treet decided not to play that card just yet.

"I can't think, however," Chairman Neviss continued, "that writing monographs on history—excellent though they are—would offer much of a living for you."

True, true. No one had much use for history anymore; the present was enigma enough. And though his work was on laser-file with every major library in the world, as well as available through several global datanet services, his royalties from sub-scriber fees were barely enough to cover necessities. "I manage," Treet allowed.

"I'm sure you do. But I am in a position to help you, Mr. Treet. I have a proposition I think you will want to consider."

"I'm always willing to listen."

"Of course." The Chairman's smile flashed again, but this time it had a forced appearance. They were getting down to business.

"Empyrion, Mr. Treet. Ever heard of it?"

"Yes, of course. From Ptolemy's theory of the five heavens. The fifth and highest heaven, the empyrean, is a realm of pure, elemental fire. The home of God and His angels."

Chairman Neviss nodded as he listened, obviously enjoying the recitation. When Treet finished, the Chairman said, "It is also our newest colony—a planet in the Epsilon Eridani system."

At first this remark did not register with Treet. He did not believe he had heard correctly. Then, when he saw that no one was laughing, he figured the "illness" Varro had mentioned was mental. Now the warning made sense.

The Chairman leaned forward and said, "You perhaps did not hear me correctly." A response was necessary.

"But that . . . that," Treet stammered, "would be the first extrasystem colony. Epsilon Eridani is more than . . . what?—ten light-years from earth. It's—" Don't get him riled up, he remem-bered. He'd been about to say something that could upset a man of unstable bearing.

"Impossible? Was that the word you were looking for?" The Chairman seemed to be taking this in good humor. "I always say that a secret is no good unless you can tell someone, eh Varro?"

"Yes, Chairman." Varro, too, was smiling at Treet, apparently enjoying his befuddlement.

The Chairman raised his hand in an open gesture. "Now you know, Mr. Treet. I won't trouble you with a recitation of the details, although with a mind like yours, I'm sure you would find them fascinating. Only myself and a select number of Cynetics board members know of Empyrion's existence."

"Why tell me?" He did not mean the question to sound so terse. It just came out that way.

"The proposition I have in mind has to do with this colony. I want your help in solving a problem there."

Treet's next question was just as terse as the one preceding it: "Why me?"

From nowhere the Chairman's beautiful administrator appeared and handed him a laserfile reader. Chairman Neviss held it in his hands while it spooled information across its black screen, then began reading what he saw there: "Orion Tiberias Treet . . . son of Magellan Treet, noted historian and astronomer . . . conceived *in vitro* at Spofford Natal and engineered by Haldane Krenk on December 30, 2123 . . . graduated from Blackburn Academy in April, 2149 . . . received your first degree in anthropology from Nevada Polytechnic in March, 2160 . . . second degree in history from the Sorbonne in June, 2167 . . . third degree in journalism from Brandenburg Institute in August, 2172 . . . joined the staff of the *Smithsonian,* rose through the ranks and, as a result of an unfortunate dispute over editorial philosophy, left as editor-in-chief in May, 2200 . . . became food critic for Beacon Broadcast System, and quit in 2216 . . . taught philosophy at the University of Calgary until 2245 when the school was closed due to failing enrollment . . . have spent the last thirty-two years traveling and writing—mostly about history."

Here the Chairman paused and looked up. "Our information, as you can see, is quite extensive. I could go on, but you get the idea."

Treet nodded, although such information was readily available from any of several sources if someone cared to spend the time assembling it—which apparently they did. It still did not answer his question, but he let it go.

"In short, you are the man for this special assignment. I want you to go to Empyrion, Mr. Treet. I want you to study the place and write about it. I want you to find out all about it—how it's developing economically, culturally, philosophically. And I want you to send back reports, Mr. Treet."

Although stated quite reasonably, the idea struck Treet as preposterous. He had to suppress an astonished laugh. "You want me to *write* for you?" he asked incredulously. "That's why you have had me followed, drugged, and brought here?"

The Chairman made a deprecatory gesture. "Varro has informed me of the unfortunate incident at the airport—an overzealous agent who will no doubt think twice before exceeding himself next time. He was to have simply contacted you and persuaded you to accompany him here. I gather he had considerable trouble locating you and lost his patience."

"He thought I was some kind of criminal," scoffed Treet softly.

The Chairman glanced quickly at Varro, who shifted his eyes uneasily. "He was mistaken. A misunderstanding, as I said." The Chairman coughed suddenly, a deep, wracking cough that rumbled in his chest with a hollow sound. This brought on a fit of coughing which doubled the Chairman in his seat. Varro stood and started forward, but his boss held up a hand. "No, I'm all right; but I must rest now. Please, Mr. Treet, you are to be my guest this evening. I have requested a private apartment to be prepared for you. The building service will supply you with anything you need, and there is a very good restaurant on the nineteenth floor."

Varro got up from his chair and gave Treet a look which indicated that he was to follow. Treet rose reluctantly, still vaguely unsatisfied by the answers he had received to his questions. "Thank you, Chairman Neviss, I'm sure I will be quite comfortable."

"And think about my proposition. I've instructed Varro to answer any other questions you may have. He will also attend to any contractual arrangements which you may agree on." He smiled briefly, and Treet saw that his eyes had gone a little glassy—from pain?

"I will give it most careful consideration, Chairman. Thank you."

Treet was hustled from the old man's presence so quickly he felt as if the coughing spasm had been staged—a prearranged signal to bring the meeting to a close. But he said nothing as they left the domed room and walked back through the gallery.

Once outside, when both sets of doors had closed securely behind them, Treet turned, put a hand on Varro's arm, and spun the round-headed man around to face him. "Okay, Varro, what's this all about?"

THREE

Feet propped on a handsome and no doubt costly antique walnut table, hands atop his head, reclining in a comfortable, well-made, and also excruciatingly expensive leather couch, Treet ignored the holovision before him and instead replayed his conversation with Varro a few hours earlier. It played no better this time than it had originally. "Something is not right," he said aloud. He often spoke to himself; some of his best thinking was done aloud.

What he was thinking now was not some of his best. Try as he might, he could not come to any substantial conclusion about what it was that Cynetics was up to and why it should involve him.

"The Chairman has read your work; he respects your talent and ability. He'd like to see you on our team," Varro had told him when they had settled in the round-headed man's office—more an apartment or luxury suite than an office.

"Whatever the Chairman wants, the Chairman gets—is that it?"

"Something like that." Varro put on a wry smile. "You've met him. You see how he is. He's explained to you his reasons for wanting you."

"Yes, he explained. But why don't I believe him?"

"What is it that you find so difficult to believe?"

"That I should have been hauled in here like a wanted man, for one thing."

"But you *are* a wanted man, Mr. Treet. Chairman Neviss wants you."

"Your *agent*," he said the word with some contempt, "told me he was being paid thirty-five thousand in metal for finding me. Isn't that a lot of money to arrange a simple job interview?"

Varro simply shook his head. "No, it isn't. Not when you're the Chairman of Cynetics Corporation. Chairman Neviss is a man who is used to—"

"Used to getting what he wants—so everybody keeps telling me." What Treet wanted was to grab the smarmy man and pummel him. He forced the lid back down on his anger and tried a new approach. "For another thing, I find this proposal highly suspect. It was all I could do to keep from laughing in His Highness's Royal Face, if you care to know the truth."

"What exactly is your difficulty?" Varro blinked back at him; his round gray eyes held genuine puzzlement.

"Don't let's be coy, all right?"

"I don't see a problem, Mr. Treet. Perhaps if you'd elaborate—"

"Certainly I'll elaborate. Setting aside the fact that it is well nigh impossible to even get to Epsilon Eridani from here, it would be equally impossible to keep an extrasystem colony a secret. Why keep an achievement of that magnitude secret in the first place? And then there is the problem of wanting me to go there to write about it. Why me in particular? You must have dozens, hundreds, a thousand people equally or better qualified for such an assignment already on payroll. Why bring in an outsider? Why do it at all? If you want to know about Empyrion, why not go there yourself and find out? Better still, why send anyone? Why not have someone who is already there write back to you? Shall I continue?"

Varro laced his fingers beneath his chin and nodded slightly. "That is quite enough. I'm beginning to see it from your point of view, I think. Yes, looking at it that way it might seem rather odd."

"Odd? Oh, I wouldn't say odd. It's raving lunacy!"

"But you do not fully appreciate our situation here." Varro continued as if Treet's outburst had not occurred. "What you have been told is true. Cynetics has, as you know, several extraterrestrial colonies. Mining is an important part of our business. Empyrion is a colony like any other—it just happens to be on a rather more distant planet."

"One that just happens to be in another star system."

"Undoubtedly Chairman Neviss would prefer to visit Empyrion himself, but that is out of the question. As Chairman, he must remain here where his services are most needed. And then there is the matter of his health. He is simply not well enough to make the trip."

"What's wrong with him? He didn't look all that ill to me. And if he is, why isn't he in a hospital?"

"I am not at liberty to discuss his medical condition with

you. But he *is* being cared for, around the clock. The entire floor below this one is a private hospital. Small, but one of the best in the country, I'm told."

"All for him?"

"He is the principal recipient of its services, yes. But anyone may use it. Any Cynetics employee."

"What about the secrecy?"

Varro leaned forward in an attitude of perfect candor. "Have you any idea of the legalities involved in creating a colony?"

"I imagine there is a certain amount of red tape," Treet allowed.

"Mountains of it. Not just here in the United States, but in every other nation and paranation as well. Colonies are considered free states under international law—countries in their own right. We lose a certain amount of control as soon as the colonial charter is ratified in the League Internationale."

"You create a colony, finance it, and then give it its freedom. So? That's the cost of doing business, isn't it?"

"Of course. But an extrasystem colony would be an entirely different matter. First of all, there would have to be scientific studies carried out by the LeIn and when they were through tramping around, trying to determine whether we had any right to be there, it would go to debate in the House of Nations, and then new legislation would have to be written, voted, enacted, and so on. Decades would pass before we saw a charter, Mr. Treet. If ever."

Treet had nothing to say to this. He had simply never thought about it before.

"Now then, suppose *you* were in a position to establish such a colony, what would you do?"

"I don't know."

"I think you do. You are an intelligent and practical man; you would choose the path of least resistance."

"And form an illegal colony?"

"Not illegal, Mr. Treet. Extralegal. There are no laws to govern this situation; they do not exist as yet."

Treet granted the point, then asked what had been uppermost in his mind all along. "But how do you get there? Even traveling at the speed of light—which we'll never get anywhere close to—it would take over ten years just to reach Epsilon Eridani."

"What would you say if I told you the trip could be made in slightly less than twelve weeks?"

Treet did not let his jaw drop, though he felt like it. "Are you telling me you have a vehicle that can travel faster than lightspeed?"

Varro smiled broadly. "I don't believe anyone has suggested that at all, though we are working on it. No, we have discovered something quite different."

"But you're not at liberty to tell me what it is, am I right?"

"If I told you and you declined the Chairman's offer, I'm afraid that would put us at something of a disadvantage."

Something told Treet that Cynetics was seldom at even the slightest disadvantage. "I see."

"Let's just say that it might be possible to make the distance between points a good deal shorter."

Treet ran his hands through his hair and rubbed them over his face. He didn't know what to think. There were theories that such a thing as telescoping space might be possible under certain circumstances—black holes, for example. Anyway, no one had ever gotten close enough to a black hole to find out exactly what did happen, nor was anyone likely to in the near or distant future.

Still, suppose what Varro was telling him was absolutely true. What then? "Are you saying that this whole scheme is merely the whim of an eccentric, wealthy old man?"

"I wouldn't use just those words, but yes, that's the sense of it. But don't give me your answer just now. Think it over; sleep on it. We'll talk again in the morning."

Varro showed Treet out and led him to the private elevator. The uniformed attendant was there waiting for him. "Enjoy your evening, Mr. Treet. I'll be looking forward to seeing you again."

As he sat in his luxury apartment, thinking about all that had taken place in the last twelve (or however many) hours, it occurred to Treet that he could make no sense of the situation because he had not eaten in at least that long. His brain cells were shrieking for nourishment.

He rose, somewhat dizzily, and made his way to the window that formed a wall of his apartment. He was somewhere in the middle of the building, judging from the height as he had estimated it from the top story (if Neviss' floor had in fact been the top story). A violet twilight, thick with faintly luminous haze, trailed across the landscape—mostly hills dense with short round trees: live oak and mesquite. Away toward the east (he presumed it was the east since he could not see the sunset at all), the faint glimmer of lights smudged the horizon. There was not enough to be seen from his vantage to tell if they were the distant lights of Houston or someplace else.

Treet gazed out upon the scene as the twilight deepened. The sky had clouded up during the latter part of the afternoon, and these clouds hung as if they were steel wool, rusted in spots and suspended on wires from an iron firmament. He looked on until he realized that he was staring but no longer attending to what he was seeing; his eyes were simply open to the view with nothing taken in.

He turned, put his shoes back on, and left the apartment, feeling the key in his pocket on his way out. Oh well, he thought, walking back to the private chauffeured elevator along a quiet, deserted, and well-lit corridor, if nothing else, he would have a good meal and a free night's lodging out of the deal. What could be so bad about that?

FOUR

"I am so glad you could join us, Mr. Treet. I do hope you will come back again very soon." The *maitre d'* placed the silver coffee urn on a warming cradle, tilted his head, and nodded as he backed away from the table. "Enjoy your dessert."

Glazed strawberries the size of hen's eggs swam in thick, sweetened cream in a chilled bowl on a silver tray before him. Spoon in hand, he stared thoughtfully at the luscious extravagance, but he was not thinking about the strawberries. He was instead puzzling over something that had been going on all during his meal: a polite but incessant stream of diners had made their way to his table to introduce themselves to him and make his acquaintance as if he were a holovision celebrity.

How did they all know his name? Was he so conspicuous that every Cynetics employee—he supposed that the thirty or so other diners in the restaurant were all Cynetics employees—knew who he was on sight?

Obviously they had been told of his arrival and instructed to greet him. But why? Was it really *that* important to the Chairman that he feel welcome? He imagined an order that may have been issued:

Executive Memo
To: All Cynetics Division Heads
Re: Arrival of Orion Treet

All employees using the restaurant facility this evening are instructed to extend every cordiality to Mr. Orion Treet, who is visiting at the special request of Chairman Neviss. Anyone found not in compliance with this directive will be terminated immediately with total forfeiture of all company benefits.

Varro

The thing that bothered Treet about all this, besides the interruption of one of the best meals he had eaten in nearly three years—not counting that dinner with the uranium heiress in Baghdad eighteen months ago—the thing that needled him most was that the lavish attention he was receiving was all out of proportion with the proposed assignment. In his mind Treet had begun calling it the *supposed* assignment; he felt that uncertain about it.

Treet spooned thick white cream over the ruby berries, sliced one in half with his spoon, and slipped it into his mouth as he turned the problem over in his mind, letting out a little sigh of pleasure as the strawberry burst on his tongue. The easy answer was that, as Varro had suggested, Chairman Neviss was an extremely—no, make that *unimaginably*—powerful man who was accustomed to having his slightest whim satisfied instantly and in spades.

He wanted Treet, and Treet he would have at whatever cost. The expense did not matter; it was not a factor. Money itself had no meaning to a man like Chairman Neviss. He wanted what he wanted; the money simply made it happen. For some quirky reason—perhaps all those spoony history articles he had written over the years to finance his wanderings and keep his brain from ossifying—Treet had struck the Chairman's fancy; so here he was.

Treet ate another strawberry and, with eyes half closed in gastronomic ecstasy, decided that perhaps he was being unduly moronic not to take the Chairman's proposal at face value. Besides, here was a chance to make some money. How much money? A seriously large amount of money; a sum quite radically excessive in the extreme. More, at any rate, than he was prepared to imagine on the spur of the moment.

For the first time since being surprised in the public bath at Houston International, Treet began to relax and warm to the idea that there may be something to this enterprise after all.

He was basking in this sunny notion when he heard an inviting female voice utter in a throaty whisper, "I hope I'm not disturbing you, Mr. Treet."

"Uh—Oh!" His eyelids flew open. "No, not at all." The woman standing next to him bent slightly at the waist as she slid onto the edge of the empty chair to his right.

"They *are* delicious, aren't they." She indicated the bowl of strawberries, now half full.

"An unparalleled pleasure . . . Miss, ah—"

"My name is Dannielle." She held out a slim, long-fingered hand and smiled. "I always have them with a nice Pouilly-Fuisse. It's a wonderful combination."

The girl was stunning. "I am happy to meet you, Dannielle. I much prefer a Rheinpfalz myself."

She glanced around the table. "But you're not drinking wine tonight?"

"No, just coffee. I wanted a clear head to think."

"Is that what you were going to do tonight? Think?" Dannielle folded her hands under her chin and gazed at him from beneath dark lashes.

Treet felt a sudden emptiness in his stomach, or a lightness in his head—he couldn't decide which. But he knew what the feeling meant. He heard himself reply, "Yes . . . think. That is, unless something more sociable turned up." He made a show of looking around the room. "I don't see your table. Were you with someone?"

"No, I was alone." She smiled languidly. "Until just a moment ago."

"In that case I insist you join me."

"Only if you order wine."

"Of course." Treet had only to look up and the *maitre d'* was there. "We'd like a bottle of Pouilly-Fuisse," he said, and then added, "One of your best please."

When he turned back to his unexpected companion, she had settled herself in her seat and had drawn it closer. Her perfume—something light and provocative—drifted to him, and he spent the next few moments trying to think of a suitably uncorny compliment he might pay her. Dannielle merely smiled and gazed at him with her liquid green eyes and rubbed a shapely hand up the smooth bare skin of an equally shapely arm.

"I understand you are something of a traveler," Danielle said. "I've always wanted to travel."

"It's what I do best," replied Treet. "When I'm not thinking."

"Oh, I bet there are *lots* of other things you do very well, Mr. Treet."

"Please, my friends call me Rion."

"Rion, then. I'm told you are a writer. What do you write?"

"History mostly. And the odd travel piece. The trouble is that the market for travel and history has all but dried up.

People have no use for history, and why read about travel when it is so easy to do? There's no place on Earth a tourist can't get to in less than four hours these days. But tell me something, Dannielle . . ."

"Yes?" She leaned closer, and he caught another enchanting whiff of her scent.

"Is everyone here at Cynetics so deliriously charming to all visitors, or is it just me?"

She lowered her head and favored him with that throaty whisper once again. "Haven't you heard? It's Be Kind To Visiting Dignitaries Day—an official Cynetics holiday."

"I was beginning to wonder. And I am a visiting dignitary I take it?"

"The only one I've seen all day."

"How is that you all know who I am?" The banter had gone out of his voice. He really wanted to know.

The girl was saved from having to answer by the appearance of the sommelier with a bottle of wine in his hand. Without a word he produced the bottle for Treet's inspection and began peeling the seal preparatory to uncorking. Dannielle reached over, took Treet's hand, and rose gracefully from the table.

"Steward, we'd like this sent to Mr. Treet's apartment," she said, then tugged Treet to his feet. "We'll enjoy it all the more." She laughed and took his arm, guiding him willingly from the restaurant.

At Treet's door he fumbled for his code key while Danielle, having pulled his free arm around her waist, nuzzled the side of his neck. The empty, light-headed feeling was back in force. Treet felt adrenalin pumping into him furiously as he jammed the plastic key into the lock.

They tumbled into the semidarkened room in full embrace. Dannielle's mouth found his, and she pressed herself full-length against him. Treet returned the kiss with every ounce of sincerity in him, devoting himself to it exclusively.

"Ahem."

A polite cough from a darkened corner of the room brought Treet's head around. Still holding Dannielle, he turned partway toward the sound. A shape emerged from shadow. "Varro!"

The round-headed man stepped apologetically forward. "I *am* sorry to interrupt, Mr. Treet."

Danielle turned and glanced at Varro, and Treet thought he saw a sign pass between them. She stepped away, saying, "I see that you two have business."

"No," protested Treet. "I don't—"

She planted a kiss on his cheek. "Maybe I'll see you tomorrow."

Treet found himself staring in stunned disbelief at the closing apartment door. He turned and faced Varro unhappily. "We were going to have a drink," he explained, and then wondered why he was explaining.

"Of course," sniffed Varro sympathetically. "I am sorry, but something's come up. We must talk."

"It couldn't wait until tomorrow?" Treet whined, still reeling from his loss.

"No, I am afraid it couldn't wait. Please, sit down." Varro seated himself in the leather armchair, so Treet took the couch.

"Whatever it is, it better be good."

"I promise you won't be bored."

FIVE

Treet drained his glass in a gulp and poured another before plunging the bottle back into the ice bucket. The wine spread its mellow warmth through him from his stomach outward to the extremities. Varro's glass sat on the table between them, untouched.

"So, what you're telling me is that I have to make up my mind right now. In that case, the answer is no—I won't do it." Treet swilled the Pouilly-Fuisse around in his long-stemmed glass for a moment, and then added, "Not for any amount of money."

Varro frowned mildly—more from concern than from any apparent unhappiness. Treet noted the frown. It, like all of Varro's movements, gestures, and expressions, was finely-tuned and rehearsed. Did the man spend his spare time posing in front of his mirror in order to get such precise effects? Was each of his actions so perfectly controlled?

"I don't think you should dismiss our proposition quite so hastily, Mr. Treet. I'll admit that this probably seems a little sudden to you, and that you'd no doubt rather have some time to think things over—"

"A week or two would be nice. I could straighten out my affairs, settle some old accounts, tie up a few loose ends."

"Then the idea of accepting our proposal is not entirely out of the question."

Varro was one slippery negotiator, but they were now heading in the direction Treet wanted to go—toward money. "Well, not entirely out of the question, I suppose."

"Then it's really a question of time—in this case, time to make up your mind."

"You might say that," allowed Treet. "Call it peace of mind."

"Yes, peace of mind. How much is your peace of mind worth to you, Mr. Treet?"

"Frankly, Varro, I don't know. I've never had to price it

before. As a man of some principle, however, I'd have to say that it doesn't come cheaply."

"No, I'm certain that it doesn't, Mr. Treet." Varro pressed his hands together and touched his index fingers to his lips. "I want you to understand that this is as awkward for me as it is for you."

"So you've said." Treet doubted that anything was ever awkward for Varro.

"But let me tell you, Mr. Treet, that in tracking you down we found that your prospects are . . . shall we say, minimal? Isn't it true that you have been dodging bill collectors of one type or another for several years now?"

Damn the man! Varro knew about his dismal financial prospects—that would bring the price down somewhat. Treet parried the thrust as best he could. "Occupational hazard." Treet shrugged. "Writers get behind occasionally. Slump seasons, and all that. So what?"

"What if I could guarantee that you'd never have to dodge another bill collector or suffer another slump season the rest of your life? Would that change your mind?"

"Perhaps. But I'd have to see the guarantee." Treet swallowed another sip of wine, eyeing the bottle carefully. Should he order another one? The first had arrived almost the instant Danielle left and was now nearly empty. He dismissed the idea: negotiating the deal of a lifetime while piffled on fine wine was not exactly in his own best interest. He placed his glass on the table, saying, "Why don't you just come right out and tell me what kind of terms we're talking about here?"

"Very well." Varro leaned forward slightly. "One million dollars in any currency you prefer. One third paid to you upon signature of a standard Cynetics service contract, one third paid to you upon completion of your assignment."

"And the remaining third?" Treet felt like pinching himself—a million dollars! Since the Currency Revaluation Act a few years ago, a million dollars was worth something again.

"The remaining third will be placed in an interest-bearing trust account in your name, payable upon your return."

"I see. And if for some wild reason I fail to return, you keep the money, is that it?"

"Not at all. Let's just say that it is an incentive for the swift completion of your assignment and a speedy return. In any case, you can designate a beneficiary."

Treet stared across the antique table at Varro. Was he telling the truth? There was absolutely no way to tell; the man's face gave away nothing. Treet decided to see how far he could push it. "No," he said softly. He let silence grow between them.

Varro only nodded. "You have another figure more to your liking, Mr. Treet?"

"Three million," he said slowly, watching Varro carefully. He saw no flinch, not even the slightest blink at the enormity of the figure, so he continued. "Plus a million in trust."

Varro got up from his chair and headed for the door. Treet felt panic skid crazily over him. He'd misjudged the situation and had insulted Varro by naming such a ridiculous figure; now Varro was leaving, and he'd be thrown out by security guards any minute. His mind spun as he frantically tried to think of something that would bring Varro back to the table. But before he could speak, Varro paused at the door and said, "I hope you understand, Mr. Treet, that since time is short, I have instructed the contract to be prepared." The door opened, and a man held out a long white envelope. Varro took the envelope and came back to the table. He sat down and snapped the seal on the envelope, drawing out a pale yellow document. "I need only fill in the amount agreed upon, and—with your signature, of course—this contract is binding." He handed the sheaf of paper to Treet.

"Ordinarily my agent would handle all this," Treet mumbled, taking the document. For several minutes he silently scanned the contract, reading all the pertinent clauses and subclauses—especially those having to do with forfeiture of payment for breach of contract. All in all, it was a fairly simple, straightforward agreement; Treet had read far more obtuse and difficult publishing contracts. But then, he reminded himself, Chairman Neviss was not interested in actually publishing the material, merely reading it. Besides, Cynetics probably had a flock of sharp-beaked legal eagles who did nothing but slice, dice, and fricassee fools who thought they could waltz through a loophole in one of their contracts.

"I think you'll see that all is in order, Mr. Treet," Varro said after a suitable time. "Will you sign now?"

"Yes, it's all in order. You've thought of everything." Treet handed the contract back. "Fill in the amounts and I'll sign."

Varro already had a pen in his hand. "Three million upon

signing—" He scratched on the pale yellow paper. "Three million on completion of your assignment, and two million in trust."

"That's eight million!" Treet couldn't help shouting. Had Varro lost his senses?

"Yes, I am aware of that, Mr. Treet," Varro explained. "I have been instructed by Chairman Neviss to double any figure we agree upon as a demonstration of our goodwill—also, as a token of the Chairman's high regard for your abilities. He is very pleased that you are undertaking this assignment for him."

Treet swallowed hard. Eight million dollars! It was a blooming miracle! He stared open-mouthed at Varro, who looked up from his writing. "Was there something you wished to say, Mr. Treet?"

"N-no," Treet said, licking his lips. "It's fine. Everything's fine."

"Good. Now then, if you will sign here—" Varro slid the contract toward him and placed the pen in his hand.

After only a brief pause to remember who he was, Treet managed to scrawl his full name. Dazed, he stared at the signature on the document and at the figures Varro had neatly inscribed. Eight million!

"We're almost finished," said Varro. He flipped to the last page of the contract and pulled a piece of tape from the paper, revealing two shiny squares of about six centimeters each side by side. Varro pressed his thumb firmly in the middle of one of the squares, and then initialed the box. "Your turn, Mr. Treet."

Treet pressed his thumb onto the second shiny box and saw that when he removed it, the film had recorded a precise duplicate of his thumbprint. He looked up at Varro and said, "Now what?"

Varro folded up the contract and stuffed it back into the envelope. He glanced at his watch and rose quickly. "It is nearly time to go, Mr. Treet. We'll have to hurry, I'm afraid."

"What? Hold on!"

"Please, as I have explained, time is short."

"Yes, but I thought . . . you mean I'm leaving tonight?"

"Right now. You're boarding within the hour."

Treet sat stubbornly. "But—"

Varro looked at him sharply. "I assumed you understood. That's why I came here this evening."

"You don't give a guy much of a chance to enjoy his good

fortune. When do I get my money, by the way?"

"It will be waiting for you at the shuttle. Shall we?" Varro gestured toward the door.

"I haven't packed or anything. I'll need—"

"I don't recall that you arrived with any luggage. Did you?"

"No," Treet admitted, remembering the way he had been shanghaied in the skyport. Not that it much mattered—he was, after all, wearing his entire wardrobe. "No luggage."

"Just as I thought. Therefore, I've taken the liberty of arranging for suitable kit and clothing to be provided. You'll find everything waiting for you aboard the shuttle." The round-headed man glanced quickly at his watch again. "Now, we really must be going."

Treet stood up and looked around the apartment one last time as if he were being evicted from his childhood home. Then he shrugged, picked up the bottle of wine and his glass, and followed Varro out.

Treet expected a quick flight back to the skyport and a lengthy preboarding passenger check which would culminate in a seat aboard a commercial shuttle to one of the orbiting transfer stations where he'd join a Cynetics transport heading secretly for Epsilon Eridani.

Instead, he and Varro took a long elevator ride down—so far down that he imagined the bottom had dropped out of the elevator shaft—eventually arriving at a subterranean tunnel where two men in standard Cynetics uniforms awaited them in an electric six-wheeler. Stepping from the elevator the moment the doors slid open, they climbed into the cart and were off, humming along the wide, low corridor whose illuminated walls cast bright white light over them.

The driver kept his foot to the floor the entire trip, and Treet, with the bottle between his knees, held onto the passenger handgrips and watched the smooth, featureless interior slide by. He felt like a bullet traveling through an endless gun barrel. No one said a word; both attendants kept their eyes straight ahead, and Varro seemed preoccupied with thoughts of his own. Twice he glanced at his watch, and then returned his gaze to the tunnel ahead.

At last the cart slowed as it rounded a slight curve and came to a gateway—a squatty set of burnished metal doors, guarded by a tollbooth arrangement and two more uniformed men who carried unconcealed stunners on their hips. Varro waved and one of the guards hurried forward with a press plate, which Varro took, pressing his hand flat to its black surface.

Instantly the right-hand door slid open just wide enough to admit the six-wheeler. With a jerk, the driver bolted through the gap and they entered another corridor, slightly larger than the first. This tunnel wound around a tight corner and unexpectedly opened into a gigantic cavern of a room.

Treet blinked in surprise as the cart rounded the last turn

and sped into the enormous chamber. Lights—red, yellow, blue—burned down like varicolored suns from a ceiling seventy-five meters above, forming great pools of light on the vast plain of the floor. Across this plain they raced, gliding in and out of the pools of light. First red, then blue, then yellow—plunging through light and shadow like minidays and nights until at last they came to a slope-sided metal bank which rose up from the floor.

Around this bank swarmed several score men and women—each dressed in an orange one-piece uniform. They were, Treet noticed, entering and emerging from the bank by way of numerous passages cut into the face. Some of these workers pushed airskids loaded with duralum cargo carriers, while others dashed here and there with mobiterms in their hands.

The driver parked the cart in a recharging stall near one of the passages, and Varro turned, saying, "Here we are, Mr. Treet. And not a moment too soon. Shall we?"

Treet got out of the cart, handed his bottle to the driver, and followed Varro through the passage. On the other side, glittering in a bath of white light, looking like a dragonfly poised for flight, a shuttlecraft stood on its stilt legs. The vehicle was smaller than a commercial craft by more than half, Treet estimated; but it was far more graceful and streamlined than the stubby, rotund taxis of the airlines.

The heatcones of two large engines swelled the skin of the craft on the underside near the center, then flared gracefully along the belly to end in a bulge at the rear of the vessel. Thin, knifelike wings slashed out from grooves along the upper back. Once in space, the wings would be retracted and solar panels affixed in their place. Along the side and beneath the wings, lettered in bright sky blue, was the shuttle's name: *Zephyros*. An escalator ramp joined the main hatch, which was open.

"Some boat," remarked Treet, but Varro was already striding toward the ramp, across a tangle of cables and hoses snaking to the shuttle from every direction. At the ramp Varro turned and waited for Treet, allowing him to mount the moving stairs ahead of him—less from courtesy, Treet decided, than from caution. Varro did not want to take any chances that Treet would get cold feet at the last minute and bolt.

As the escalator took them up into the belly of the gleaming, silver shuttle, Treet gazed all around him at the hurried activity below. Controlled chaos, he thought. They're obviously pushing a tight schedule. Why the rush?

The interior of the shuttle was divided into compartments of various sizes, and along one bulkhead a row of staterooms. "I think this first one's yours, Mr. Treet." Varro pressed a button, and a door folded back.

Treet dipped his head and stepped into a small room with curving walls. In the center of the room, dominating it, sat a wide couch, flat, with a panel at one side. It looked like a slightly more generous version of a dentist's chair. There was a closet of sorts next to the door; in a corner across from the couch, a small holovision with a few dozen cartridges on its carousel; opposite the closet, a sanitary stall; diagonally across another corner, a desk with terminal, screen, and chair all molded from a single piece of white plastic; directly above the couch overhead, a tiny oval window.

"I am certain these will fit, Mr. Treet," Varro said, dipping into the closet. He brought out a new singleton in light green with darker green boots and sleeves—the latest style. "Your measurements were taken while you were sleeping off the effects of the drug."

"Oh?" Treet cocked an eye. "Pretty sure of yourselves, weren't you? How did you know I would accept your offer?"

"Chairman Neviss is a remarkable judge of character, Mr. Treet. He is also a man who doesn't—"

"Doesn't like to lose. Yeah, I know."

"What I was about to say was that he doesn't mind spending a little money in order to smoothe things out. Speaking of which—" Varro reached into the closet and turned, hefting a bulging, zippered bag which he tossed to Treet. "Your stipend, Mr. Treet."

Treet caught the silver bag and tugged the zipper down. Inside were notes, banded and stacked. He withdrew a stack. "Five hundred thousand!"

"In platinum notes of twenty-five thousand. There are six bundles—three million dollars. As agreed?"

"As agreed." Treet breathed an inward sigh of relief. Up to this very moment he had doubted he would ever see the money. Now he realized that he had been told the truth. Crazy as it sounded, it was the truth.

Just then a man with a gold, long-billed flight cap stuck his head in the door. "Oh, Captain Crocker," said Varro. "Come in, I'll introduce you to your passenger. This is Orion Treet."

The man, tall, loosely knit, blond-haired, and slightly sun-burned, ducked easily into the compartment. He wore the easy, breezy manner of the old-style Texas natives, and a generous portion of the legendary cowboy charisma as well. "So this is the VIP we're taking up tonight!" The Captain smiled and offered his hand. Treet zipped the bag shut and tucked it under his arm, extending his hand to grip that of the Captain's. "Welcome aboard the *Zephyros,* Mr. Treet."

"Thanks. You fly this route often, I take it?" asked Treet.

"Have you ever been in space before, Mr. Treet?"

"This is my first time, although I've done a fair amount of suborbital travel."

"It's exactly the same. We're going to have a good trip, so don't you worry 'bout a thing." He turned to Varro, smiled, and said, "Well, I've got a flight check in progress, so I best get back to business." He touched the bill of his cap and disappeared.

"Captain Crocker is Chairman Neviss' personal pilot, so I'm certain you'll be in good hands," said Varro. "And now I'll leave you to get settled." He brought up his watch once more. "You're scheduled to lift off in three minutes."

Outside a klaxon sounded, and the lights switched from white to red. Hoses were disconnected and retracted as the orange-suited army scurried for safety. Treet followed Varro back to the hatch. "We're looking forward to hearing from you soon, Mr. Treet. I think you'll find this a most extraordinary assignment."

"I'm looking forward to it," Treet said somewhat mechanically, then realized that with three million dollars in platinum certificates tucked under his arm he actually *was* looking forward to it. "You can tell Chairman Neviss that I won't disappoint him."

"Good. I'll tell him. Good-bye, Mr. Treet." Varro offered his hand, and Treet took it. "Bon voyage!"

"Thanks." Treet watched the back of Varro's round head as the slump-shouldered man rode the escalator down. A man in orange, standing on a platform beneath the moving stairs, drove the stairway back. Treet watched his last tie with the earth disappear, and then turned back to examine the interior of the shuttle.

"Two minutes, Mr. Treet." Crocker's voice sounded from a

hidden speaker overhead. Treet guessed that Cocker was in the cockpit already warming the engines, or whatever pilots did in the last seconds of preflight. "You'll want to get strapped in now. Think you'll need some help?"

"I can manage. Thanks just the same." Treet, back in his compartment, glanced at the console next to the couch and saw that a red button had lit up. He punched it and with the buzz of electric motors, the bed tilted up and scrunched in the middle, forming itself into a lounge chair. Pouches opened in the sides of the couch, and Treet drew out a single strap which he fastened across his hips as he lay back.

"Ninety seconds, Mr. Treet. All set?"

"Ready!" He clapsed the zippered bag between his hands over his stomach and lay back in the chair as if basking in the bright sun of his incredible fortune. Who could have imagined that before this day was over he would be a millionaire! And who could have foreseen that this fledgling millionaire would be winging his way to a distant star system to write about a secret corporation colony!

The thrum of rocket engines seeped up through the floor-plates, sounding like the distant rumbling of an earthquake. Treet felt the deep sonorous vibration in his diaphragm, and realized simultaneously that he had not the slightest idea how the shuttle would escape the underground chamber. The thought made him frown.

"Thirty seconds, Mr. Treet." The Captain's calm voice fell from above. "Would you like to watch the liftoff?"

"Uh, sure—if it's no trouble."

"No trouble at all. I'll switch on the holovision."

A second later the holoscreen blipped on and Treet, swiveling his chair with the aid of a button on the armrest, saw a view of the cavern ceiling opening to a sky pitch-dark, devoid of moon or stars.

"Some cloud cover, as you can see. But all things considered, a pretty good night for flying. Fifteen seconds," Crocker's voice intoned. "I'll be a tad busy for the next few minutes. I'll talk to you when we've locked in our trajectory. Until then, relax and leave everything to me."

Treet felt the shuttle tremble and sensed slight movement around him. The holovision revealed that the ship had angled up—the floor beneath them had become a steep incline to give them a straight shot away. The thrum of the engines became a boom and then, with only the merest suggestion of a bump, the craft rose from the floor.

He watched the holoscreen and saw the cavern slide away slowly. Then they cleared the ceiling—the lights, now pointing skyward, flashed momentarily—and he glimpsed dark landscape spreading out around them. Treet felt himself grow heavy in the chair, sinking down into the cushioned material as the shuttle took on speed.

Faster and faster the ship climbed. There was nothing to see; the screen showed a dark, formless expanse of empty sky. Gravity pressed him down with a heavy hand. His eyesight darkened, as if the light in the compartment had dimmed, and his limbs became sluggish and lethargic. It took too much effort to shift his arms. Suddenly tired, he closed thick eyelids and allowed sleep to descend upon him.

Treet awoke—seconds, minutes, hours later, he couldn't tell which—to see through the oval window above him a slice of bright-spangled starfield. He sat for a moment without moving, then, feeling strangely light and buoyant, lifted his hand to open the catch on the seatbelt. The hand flew up and tugged him away from the chair. They were in orbit.

He retrieved his floating moneybag, stuffed it into a drawer under the seat of his couch, unbuckled his belt, and let himself drift up over the chair, then kicked off toward the door. Treet learned next why the walls of his stateroom were covered with a spongy padding, for he had misjudged the angle of his flight and piled into the doorframe. The door, evidently pressure-sensitive, folded back automatically, and he grappled his way through the opening and into the main compartment where he collided with someone just emerging from the cubicle next to his.

The body was male and pear-shaped, with hips slightly wider than shoulders. An overlarge fuzzy head, sporting jug ears, wobbled on a thin-pencil neck as the stranger richocheted toward the nearest bulkhead. "Hey!" he cried. "Watch it!"

"Sorry!" Treet said. "You okay? I don't quite have the knack of this yet."

His fellow passenger raised his arm and spun around like a diver making a slow-motion pirouette. "It's easy, once you learn how. Zero-G is a blast!" The man smiled. His glasses flashed in the light, and Treet realized that he was, despite the antique metal-framed glasses, much younger than he looked—half Treet's age at least. "You're overcompensating, that's all. Just take it easy."

Treet tucked his legs under him and pushed off, using about half as much muscle power as he thought he should. He drifted closer to the stranger and extended his hand. "Thanks. I see what you mean. My name is Orion Treet."

"Asquith Pizzle, here. Glad to meet you, Treet. By the time this flight is over zero-G will be second nature to you."

"Oh, I don't expect I'll get the chance to become an expert."

"Of course you will. After all there's really nothing else to do for the next twelve weeks." The young man drew his lips back in a goofy, toothsome grin which made him look like a bookish gnome.

"Twelve weeks? I'm getting off at the transfer station in a couple of hours. I—" Treet stopped. "What's the matter?"

Pizzle looked at him quizzically. "Are you sure you're on the right bird?"

"Of course! This is a Cynetics shuttle heading for rendezvous with a corporation transport." Treet's voice sounded thin in his ears.

"This is no shuttle, Treet. This *is* the transport. We're on our way."

SEVEN

"You're joking!" Treet glanced around him. The jerk of his head sent him gliding off at an angle to Pizzle. A ripple of panic fluttered his stomach. "We're going in *this?*"

"Righto mundo! This is a transport. Scaled down, of course—by about sixty times."

"But . . . I . . . thought . . ."

"Not to worry. Crocker is a champ. He could fly a washtub to Mars if it had hydrodrive. He'll get us to Empyrion with starch in our shorts."

"You're going too?" Treet's mind flip-flopped. Surprise made his voice whine. "I mean—I assumed I was alone." On second thought, there was no reason for that assumption. Varro had not mentioned any other passengers, but then again, he hadn't said there weren't any others. "Is anyone else aboard?"

"One other. I don't know who. He's in his compartment, and I haven't seen him. Then there's Crocker, of course."

The irrational fear ebbed away as Treet got used to the idea of traveling into deep space in such a small and apparently crowded craft. He wondered what else Varro had neglected to mention. "I, uh—got a little nervous just then. See, I was under the impression that we'd dock and transfer to a regular Cynetics transport. I guess not, huh?"

Pizzle shook his head. "Nope. This is it. Hey, but this is one elegant vehicle—a Grafschoen carbon-tempered titanium, hull with twin sealed Rolls-Bendix plasma engines. There's not a better-made ship anywhere—you can bet your biscuits on that."

"You an engineer?" asked Treet. Pizzle shook his head again. "A physicist?" Another shake, ears wobbling. "What then?"

"I'm a TIA man." Pizzle grinned proudly.

"What's that?"

"Trend and impact analyst."

"You're an accountant?" Treet asked incredulously.

Pizzle's face fell a fraction. "Not exactly. TIA is more than statistics and balance sheets." He brightened again. "My branch is social integration of economic operants: SIE for short."

"Oh." Treet still had not the slightest idea what Pizzle was talking about—something to do with marketing, he figured. "I see."

To break the silence that followed, Treet asked, "How come you wear glasses?"

"You mean instead of corneal implants or permatacts?" Pizzle placed a thumb to the bridge of his nose and shoved his steel frames back into place. "Nostalgia. These belonged to Z. Z. Papoon—one of my favorite authors. We have the same astigmatism."

"Z. Z. Papoon? I don't believe I've ever heard the name."

"He wrote a long time ago—futuristic fantasy mostly. Marvelous characters: Beeno the Beast-Stalker—that was one of his. People tell me I look like somebody from one of his books, so I guess it's only right I should have his glasses."

"Only right."

"Why did they pick you?" Pizzle asked.

"Sorry?" Treet bobbed in the air, drifting off to one side.

"Here, kick your legs together like in the water—that'll straighten you out. I meant, what's your specialty, Treet? How'd you convince them to give you one of their precious berths aboard this tin cricket?"

"Oh, I'm a writer mostly. History is my specialty, but I also do the odd travel piece. I guess the Chairman liked one of my articles, so here I am."

"You must be some writer. Ever write any science fiction?"

"Strictly nonfiction."

Pizzle looked incredulous. "I had to fight to get on here. I was one of five hundred applicants. They narrowed it down to a hundred a week ago, and this morning I was chosen."

"You don't say. I was more like kidnapped." Pizzle acted interested, so Treet went on to elaborate the details of his day, leaving out the part about the eight million dollars. "But tell me, Pizzle," he said when he had finished, "what's your assignment on Empyrion? You mind my asking?"

"Not at all. It's long-range forecasting. Specifically, to prepare probability studies on the effects of high-production vibramining on the social and environmental infrastructures of the Empyrion colony." Pizzle made a gesture as if to say it was all in a day's work, then said, "Are you hungry? I could eat a brick. Let's get some breakfast."

Pizzle gathered himself into a ball and then whirled his arms; he tumbled end over end slowly toward the nearest bulkhead where he kicked off toward a console overhead. He grabbed the padded handring on the consol's pedestal and pulled himself around.

"Yo, Crocker!" he said, punching a button.

"What's on your mind?" Crocker's voice answered from a speaker somewhere below them. The ceiling had temporarily become the floor.

"We're hungry."

"I could use a bite myself."

"How about giving us a little thrust? It's a putch trying to eat in zero-G."

"We're scheduled for a little OA and A burn in about thirty minutes. I could give you some now and take it off the other end."

"Thanks. I'll get the coffee perking." Pizzle shoved away from the pedestal and spun in the air. "Follow me," he called to Treet. "The galley is this way."

Treet slouched in a basket-shaped foam chair, gum-soled boots propped on the edge of a retractable table, sipping black, pungent Tasmanian coffee. Both he and Pizzle were listening to the Captain explain the intricacies of space navigation.

Crocker had joined them earlier, wolfed down some eggs and a few slices of Texas ham, and now sat puffing on a very long, green aromatic panatela, saying, "Of course, ground control computers handle all the really tricky maneuvers. Our onboard system is nothing to sneeze at, though. We've installed the Cynetics Cyclops in place of the usual Hewlett StarNav equipment. That bugger is nearly a hundred times faster and smarter than anything commercially available. It's made solely for LeIn's peacekeeping forces." He smiled broadly. "But we got a special deal."

"Why such a powerful computer," asked Treet idly, "if ground control can handle everything?"

"Just plain good backup," shrugged Crocker, his sunburned face creasing in a conspiratorial wink. Then he leaned forward and said, "Thing is, nobody really knows what happens when you get that close to the event horizon. And once inside the wormhole, we're on our own."

Treet blinked back at him. Had he heard right? "Wormhole, did you say?" He exchanged a bewildered look with Pizzle.

"Uh-oh." Crocker nodded slowly, took the cigar out of his mouth, and tapped the ash off into an empty mug. "Ol' Horatio has stepped in it again. I thought you fellas knew."

"Are you saying we're reaching Empyrion via wormhole?" asked Pizzle, visibly awed at the prospect.

"Well, let's just say we don't have provisions for a fifty-year trip, so we're taking a shortcut."

"Fan-super-tastic!" Pizzle rocked back in his chair, beaming. Crocker smiled broadly.

"I'm glad you're both so delighted," said Treet sourly. "Just what in blue-eyed blazes is a wormhole exactly?"

"Well, it's—nobody knows what it is *exactly,* but—" began Crocker.

"Let me tell him," offered Pizzle cutting in. "It's like a tunnel in space, only elastic, sort of . . . " His voice trailed off when he saw that Treet was frowning. "A hole in the space-time fabric, you know?"

"Something like a black hole, you mean?" Treet felt that sinking feeling in the pit of his stomach again. What had he gotten himself into? "Are we talking about a black hole?"

"Yes, sort of," said Pizzle. "Um . . . but not exactly. They're distant cousins, maybe."

"What kind of answer is that?" Treet kept his temper down, barely.

"It's a phenomenon on the level of a black hole," said Crocker. "Very difficult to describe."

"Apparently," puffed Treet indignantly. "Am I supposed to believe that we're going to fly through some *phenomenon* to get to the colony? Like diving through a hole in a wedge of Swiss cheese?"

"That's it!" Pizzle nodded vigorously. "But more like pinching Jello. Say you had a block of Jello—that's space, see?" His hands described a large cube. "You pinch it in the middle and push the two opposite sides together—collapse the center, see?" He brought his index fingers together through the imaginary Jello. "Well, the distance you have to travel decreases the more you pinch, see?"

"And since in space," added Crocker, "distance and time are one and the same thing . . . *Voila!* Decrease distance and you decrease time, see?"

Treet was silent for some moments, looking from one to the other of them and back again, a dark frown lowering his brow and pulling his mouth down. "I see," he said finally, "but I don't like it."

"Take it easy," Crocker soothed. "It's perfectly safe."

"How do you know? You just said nobody knows what happens inside a wormhole."

"Our best guess it that you just pop on through—like riding a trolley through a tunnel. Only you've carved about forty or fifty years off your travel time."

"I don't believe this," said Treet softly. "Both of you are crazy. You can let me off right here. I'll walk back."

"Look," said Pizzle, "it'll be all right. There's a book I can call up for you that'll tell you all about wormholes—what there is to tell, that is."

A chime sounded over the speaker system. "Back to the bridge," said Crocker, jumping up, obviously glad for an excuse to leave. "You read that book, Treet, and we'll talk again later."

Treet watched the pilot pull himself hand-over-hand up the wall toward the cockpit. Even at one-quarter gravity, Treet doubted he could have managed the feat. Feeling Pizzle's eyes on him, he turned and glared at the gnome. "Well?"

"Nothing. I was just thinking that it's going to be a long trip. We might as well be friends." He paused, waiting for Treet to say something polite, like: *Oh, of course, let's by all means be the very best of chums.* When Treet said nothing, he continued. "You play Empires?"

"No," Treet said coldly. "I detest games of chance."

"Oh, there's no chance involved—all intellect. It's a lot like chess, only bigger and more subtle." He grinned his snaggle-toothed impish grin again. "I'll teach you. How about it?"

Treet shrugged, getting up. "Some other lifetime perhaps. If you'd call up that book for me, I'd appreciate it." He turned and bounded from the table, leaving Pizzle to clean up.

"That slime devil Varro," Treet muttered, "better have a wonderful explanation for all this, or there's going to be a mutiny!"

EIGHT

"I am sorry, Mr. Treet, but as I have already explained, Mr. Varro is in Maracaibo for at least three weeks. He cannot be reached due to the recent severance of diplomatic relations. No calls are being transmitted between Venezuela and League countries."

Treet felt his temper rising dangerously. He wanted to reach through the screen and shake the smug young lady on the other side. "Then I must have a word with Chairman Neviss. It concerns a matter of utmost importance. Life and death," he added. "Please, you must let me speak to him."

"Mr. Treet, you know I would like to help you. I cannot. No one may speak to the Chairman without clearance."

"Get me clearance!"

"I would love to arrange for clearance, Mr. Treet, as soon as you give me your personal identification code. As you refuse—"

"Refuse! I don't *have* a code, dammit!"

"Anger won't help you, Mr. Treet. Perhaps you would like to call back when you have calmed down."

"Wait, don't hang up. Look, there must be someone there who can authorize clearance without a PI code—"

"Only Mr. Varro—"

"Besides him. Who else? There must be some other way."

"Well," the young lady paused, "I could have Chief of Security do a PSP on you—that's a Personnel Security Probe. Upon completion of the PSP you would be issued a personal identification code, but—"

"Do it."

"But—"

"But nothing. Just do it."

"Mr. Treet, it takes six weeks to do a thorough PSP."

"Grrr!" Treet growled and slammed his fist down on the EOT button on the console, ending the transmission. Instantly he regretted the move. There were still several things he wanted to say to the officious young witch on the other end.

Due to sunspot interference, it had taken him the better part of thirty-four hours to get a call through to Cynetics. All that time the *Zephyros* streaked ever closer to rendezvous with the wormhole, and with every passing hour the possibility of turning back diminished even further.

Not that there had ever been much chance of turning back in the first place. But Treet had at least hoped to scorch Varro with a few well-chosen words. Apparently even that was impossible. He had begun to think that Varro had caused the sunspots in order to avoid being contacted. And as far as Treet was concerned, the story about Varro's trip to Maracaibo was an out-and-out lie. The scumbag just didn't want to talk to him. It was the oldest tactic in the executive manual: don't call us, we'll call you.

Treet sat with clenched fists and teeth, grimacing at the empty screen. He knew now that he had been tricked, and that Varro also knew that he knew and was therefore avoiding him. That more than anything else angered him: the impotence of playing the dupe.

He shoved back his chair, gliding halfway across the room with the force of his movement. They were under thrust most of the time now, flying perpendicular to the orbital plane of Earth—that was as much as he had been able to get from Crocker about their route—and the acceleration created a comfortable one-half G, which allowed them near-normal conditions.

He was still sitting in the center of his compartment when he heard a muffled thump—a sound he had come to recognize as someone knocking on the padding around his door. "What do you want?" he hollered.

"Can I come in?" Pizzle yelled back.

"No!"

The door folded back regardless. "Sorry, Treet. I feel silly talking to closed doors. Let me in, okay?"

"It seems I can't keep you out!"

"Look, I brought you something."

Treet still stared at the blank computer screen across the room. "What is it?"

"It's that book I told you about. Some of it, that is. I only printed up the pertinent chapters. Here, take it."

"Go away. I'm not in the mood."

Pizzle put the book on the bed and took a seat there himself. "I was wondering if you've seen our fellow passenger yet."

"No, I haven't. So what?" Treet turned and looked at his guest for the first time.

"Well, I haven't either. And it's going on two days now. Don't you think that's strange?"

"Not particularly. He probably just wants to avoid having to play that stupid game with you."

"You said you *liked* Empires. You almost won last time."

"I lied. Besides, you let me almost win just so I will keep playing with you, which I won't."

"Two days though. That's a long time. One of us should have seen him."

"Did you ask Crocker?"

Pizzle nodded. "Sure. He said he didn't know who it was, but that he wasn't concerned and furthermore it was none of my business."

"There you are. It's none of your business."

"But two whole days, Treet. What if something happened to him? Maybe he had a heart attack on liftoff or something like that."

Treet thought about this. "What do you want me to do about it?"

"Be a spy with me. Help me find out who it is."

For a moment Treet considered this. "It *does* seem a trifle strange, as you say. But then," he added grumpily, "it wouldn't be the first strange thing about this trip."

"Like what?" Pizzle sat cross-legged on the bed, elbow on knee, resting his receding chin in his hand.

Treet got to his feet. "You really want to know? Okay. First, there's the supposedly oh-so-secret nature of this trip. Only I find out from you in casual conversation that you were one of five hundred applicants. Seems like everybody and his mother knows about this colony but me. Secondly, how come I've never heard of this wormhole business? I'm an intelligent person; I've been around a long time, and I've never heard mention of the alleged phenomenon. Thirdly, why were they so anxious to get me aboard this crate? The ink wasn't even dry on the line when I was hustled aboard. Why the big hurry? And why won't Crocker tell me anything? What more is there I'm not supposed to know? Shall I go on?"

Pizzle shrugged. "You're making more of this than there is, really. I can explain everything."

"Go ahead; be my guest. I wish you would."

"Well, the mission *is* secret. Sure, they took applications, but that's standard for any transfer situation. I knew only that there was a hefty pay bonus and a promotion for going. I'd been looking for a way out of the Northwestern Hemisphere Division for over a year and when the chance came up, I grabbed it."

"Even though you didn't know where you were going or what your assignment would be?"

"Didn't matter to me. Anything was better than NH under Oberman, not to mention there were at least seven guys ahead of me in line for promotion. I'd have been eighty-five before I joined senior staff!"

"Still, you knew about it. Varro told me it was a secret."

"It was for me too, up until the time I boarded the *Zephyros*. There was a confidential packet waiting for me in my cabin: length of trip, our destination, my assignment, that sort of thing. I'd never heard of Empyrion Colony either, until after I read my packet."

"What about wormholes?"

"Sure, I know about them. The concept has been around a long time. I'm surprised you haven't heard of them, really. But then again, they're not exactly common knowledge. In fact, they were entirely a mathematic speculation until Cynetics discovered one lurking on the rim of our solar system. On second thought, maybe you wouldn't have heard of them unless you read astrophysics abstracts or professional journals."

"How did you get so chummy with them then?"

"I read old SF novels." Pizzle's close-set eyes gleamed impishly.

"Sci-fi, huh?"

"Speculative fiction, if you please. There were some great books written about wormhole travel just before the turn of the century. Great stuff! *Timeslip* is a classic. My favorite, though, is *Pyramid on the Thames*."

"Okay, so I'm out of touch," Treet sniffed. "Now, why the big hurry to get me on board? Was that so I wouldn't change my mind?"

"Well, if you know anything about wormholes at all—"

"Which I don't."

"—you'd know that one of the major theories is that they are not a constant event."

"Meaning?"

"They come and go. They change. They move around. One might appear one place for a while and then disappear, only to reappear somewhere else. They're sort of elastic, like I said. Where a black hole is a fixed phenomenon, wormholes—displacement tubes or dilation tunnels, as they're sometimes called—are more unpredictable."

"Therefore?"

"Therefore, you have to move when there's one open or you miss your chance. Obviously—"

"Cynetics found out the wormhole was open now and didn't want to lose the opportunity."

"Righto mundo! Who knows when it might come again." Pizzle took off his glasses and polished them on his shirt.

"You just said they move around."

"Relatively speaking. As far as anyone knows, they usually occur in the same general vicinity of space. Whatever kind of force or disturbance creates a wormhole operates in a localized region—you know, like a whirlpool in a river. It swirls around, opens, and closes, sometimes deeper, sometimes shallower, stronger one time, weaker another, and so on. That's how it is."

"And we're going to dive through the eye of this whirlpool."

"Banzai!"

Treet gazed balefully at Pizzle, his brow wrinkled in thought. "Granting for the moment that what you say is true—which I intend to check out thoroughly—but say that it's true, just how did the first transport know that they'd reach Epsilon Eridani by jumping through this wormhole? How could they know that?"

"My guess is they didn't."

"Great heavens! You mean they dove in blind?"

Pizzle shrugged lightly. "It was a colony ship, remember. They were outfitted to start a colony, which they were intent on doing anyway, so what difference would it make where? They were pioneers. Someone had to be the first."

"But how do we know they made it?"

"You've got me there," Pizzle admitted. "Ask Crocker; maybe he knows something."

"We could be diving into . . . well, *anything*. Or nothing. There might be a sun at the other end and we'd burn up, or maybe an asteroid field and we'll be smashed to cosmic dust. What happens if the wormhole closes while we're still inside? What then?"

"Look, what do you want from a bookworm? Nobody has ever done this before, so we'll just have to wait and find out."

"Wrong. The first transport found out, didn't they?" Treet huffed. "Well, where are they now?"

Treet sat hunched on a folding stool in the crowded cockpit of the *Zephyros*. Pizzle sat next to him with his elbows on his knees, trying to take up less space. Crocker swiveled in his captain's chair, twirling his hat in his hand. After their discussion, Treet and Pizzle had gone directly to the Captain to find out what he knew of the fate of the first colonists.

"Epsilon Eridani," Cocker said, "is an extensive system. We know that it has at least thirteen planets in the OLZ—that's Optimum Life Zone."

"How do you know that? How do you know that the colony ship even reached Epsilon Eridani, let alone started a colony?"

"We had communication, of course. I have read all the transcripts myself. There were three communications received— one month apart for the first three months, Earth-time. The first one came when the ship reached the system—we know that they got through the wormhole without any problems. The second was sent when they identified Empyrion—that's what they named it—and decided to settle there. The third and last came when they had finished their survey of the planet and had started raising the environment dome."

"And then?"

"Nothing after that."

"What happened?"

"The wormhole closed. No more signals could be sent through the conduit, so to speak."

"No doubt they're still sending signals," offered Pizzle, "but without the wormhole it takes a whole lot longer. We just haven't received them yet."

"Maybe the signals stopped because they all *died!*"

"Possible," Crocker allowed, "but highly improbable."

"But why? You said anything could happen. Anything!"

"Theoretically yes. But you have to figure that once they reached the planet they knew what to expect. Colony ships are prepared for the unknown. Empyrion is uninhabited by any thinking creatures, and has little second-order animal life—certainly nothing to worry about. The probes would also have verified atmosphere, weather patterns, and climatic trends. There were no surprises there."

"Microorganisms, viruses, bacteria—what about those? Maybe they got down there and succumbed to a killing virus."

"Maybe, but I don't think so. They would not have disembarked until the environment dome was raised and the air and ground beneath it sterilized. Only then would they have actually set foot on the soil."

Treet remained silent. He had exhausted all his objections for the moment. He looked around at Pizzle, who sat nodding. "It's just like the IASA colonization manual recommends."

"Right by the book. All contingencies foreseen."

Crocker looked at Treet's unhappy face. "Look, it's going to be all right. Believe me. I read the transcripts. By all reports the planet is an absolute paradise. You'll love it. When we get there you'll see what I mean. An absolute paradise." Crocker spun in his huge, padded chair as an electronic chime sounded. "Now if you two will excuse me," he said, "I've got a little housekeeping to do."

Treet stood. "Thanks, I feel so much better," he said without meaning it. "See you later."

Pizzle rose and followed Treet out of the cockpit. They clambered into the connecting gangway and through the forechamber along to the passenger compartments. At Pizzle's door they paused, and Pizzle yawned. "I'm going to get some sleep. Maybe you'd better, too. It might be a long night."

Treet glanced up quickly. "Huh?"

"We're spying tonight, remember? You said if I went with you to talk to Crocker, you'd help me spy tonight. Well, I went with you, didn't I?"

"But you were on his side. You were supposed to be on mine."

"His side? There were no sides. You had some questions and we got answers. What more do you want?"

Pizzle had him there: what more did he want? Why was he

still not satisfied? "All right," Treet agreed reluctantly. "I'll help you spy." He turned and went into his stateroom.

"Good," called Pizzle after him. "I'll come and get you when I'm ready." He watched Treet disappear into his room and the door sigh shut behind him. "Loosen up," he called. "You'll live longer."

NINE

Pizzle's idea of spying was to hide in some cramped place and wait long hours for the quarry to show up. He reasoned that unless separate supplies had been stocked in the mysterious stranger's cabin, which he doubted, then the man must eat when the others were sleeping. So far he had seen no evidence that anyone had been surreptitiously using the galley, but then as long as the person cleaned up after himself, there was no way anyone could tell.

So Treet and Pizzle crouched in a cramped cubbyhole for dry stores, waiting—an eternity it seemed to Treet—for the stranger to materialize. The galley lights had been turned off so they could observe the mysterious stranger without themselves being observed, and they had been taking turns watching. It was Treet's turn to put his eye to the crack in the partition, and he was ready to call it quits.

"I don't see why you need me at all," complained Treet, not for the first time. "This is a big waste of time."

"I need you to verify the sighting."

"You make it sound like we're waiting for a UFO." He craned his neck around and saw the metal rims of Pizzle's glasses glint in the dim light. "Phew! It's stuffy in here. I'm getting out before I'm hunchbacked for life."

"Shh! Quiet, will you? If anybody *was* out there, you'd have scared him off by now."

"Whoever it is is probably fast asleep in bed, and that's where we should be. Look, why can't you rig up a few motion detectors or proximity switches or something. Anyone messing around in the galley would trip the alarm and you could come running with your little Panasonic holocamera and catch them flatfooted in the act."

"Yeah, and get nothing for my trouble but pictures of you or Crocker sneaking food from cold service while I'm trying to sleep."

"Why is this so important to you, anyway?" Treet asked. "This guy just likes his privacy. So what? *I* should be so lucky."

"It isn't natural, that's why. And I'm curious—that in itself is enough reason for me."

"Well, I'm not that curious. I don't know why I agreed to this lunatic scheme of yours anyway. I'd feel silly if I wasn't so sore." Treet shifted his weight and banged his head against a shelf. "Ow! That's it—I'm getting out of here."

With that he pushed aside the partition and climbed out. "You coming?"

Pizzle glanced at his watch. "Might as well. Time's nearly up anyway." He crawled out of the cubbyhole on his hands and knees. "If he was coming tonight, he'd have been here by now."

Treet walked back to his compartment and Pizzle followed, pausing at the entrance to the stranger's quarters to press his ear against the door. Treet cast a disparaging look back at him; Pizzle shrugged and shuffled along to his room. "G'night, Treet."

Treet stood on the threshold of his compartment with the door open. When he heard Pizzle's door close, he tiptoed back to the stranger's compartment and listened. He heard nothing, so pressed his ear against the door. He was about to turn away when, to his surprise, the door folded back and he stood staring into two jet-black eyes. The eyes—set in an exquisite, bronze-colored face which was surrounded by a fall of shining black hair—regarded him coolly. His first impression was that he'd seen that face before, but in a very different context.

"Miss Talazac!" he said, recovering himself. "I didn't recognize you without your braid."

"Mr. Treet," she replied crisply, "is this one of your perverse habits—listening outside people's doors?"

"Not at all." Treet received the strong impression that she had expected him to be there. "I was just . . . well, curious. We wondered about you—I mean, about the person inside. We hadn't seen anyone, and it's been several days. We thought something might have happened to you."

"You need not have concerned yourself. I am, as you see, quite all right. If you will excuse me—" She made a move to pass by him, and Treet stepped back.

"I'm sorry if I disturbed you," he said, more for something to say than from any real regret.

She turned and faced him, holding his eyes with her own, her face expressionless. Treet felt ridiculous, as if he were floundering in shallow water. He wanted to look away, but her eyes held his and he could only stare back blankly. "I'm sorry," he murmured and the spell was broken.

She turned from him without a word and moved silently off along the gangway toward the galley. Treet watched her slender figure glide away. He realized his scalp was tingling all over and his palms were sweating.

He thought to himself: There goes one weird lady . . . or a vision.

Treet did not see her again for five weeks. What she did in her compartment, how she avoided all the others, and why he could but wonder, and did often. Why did she hole up like that? Why did she refuse to join the others? Certainly it was not because she feared them—the only woman on a ship full of men, that sort of nonsense. No, whatever the reason, it wasn't fear. Treet's manly intuition told him that Yarden Talazac would be more than a match for any male.

He did not tell Pizzle about the midnight meeting. Somehow he knew that Talazac would not want him to mention it. At the same time he felt silly carrying around his secret—especially since Pizzle continually nagged him to rejoin his espionage program. Treet refused, knowing somehow that she would not be caught again. Actually, he decided, she had not been caught at all. She had revealed herself to him alone; it was of her choosing.

But why? Why him? Why in that way?

Treet wondered about these things in idle moments, and he attempted to fix her face in his mind but could not. Every time he tried to remember what she looked like, he drew a blank. All he saw on his mental screen was a stock representation of a human face—vaguely Asiatic, or perhaps Polynesian, no distinct features, just a sketch. This both puzzled and frustrated him. Why could he not remember what she looked like?

He told himself that, after all, he'd only met her twice, and then fleetingly. But he also reminded himself that he had no difficulty remembering faces of people he'd met just as briefly: the Cynetics nurse who had helped him up when he awoke from the drug, the elevator attendant, the driver of the cart—all of them he could see in his mind's eye as clearly as if they stood before him.

But, Yarden . . . all he had of her was an impression: smooth, honey-colored skin, a deep darkness that was eyes or hair, slim, molded limbs, and a sense that she floated rather than walked. That was all.

Trying to remember her became something of an obsession with Treet. And when he wasn't wracking his brain in the futile attempt to conjure up a picture of the phantom woman, he thought about their meeting and tried to recall every word and nuance that had passed between them that night, to understand the meaning behind it. In this he was largely unsuccessful too. Despite his efforts, and long hours musing on it, he could discover no hidden purpose or explanation. Pure chance, it would seem. And yet, was it?

Treet was reasonably certain that very few things happened by chance where the mysterious Miss Talazac was concerned.

Another mystery occupied him as well—the mystery of wormhole travel. In the second week of the flight he had picked up Pizzle's book and begun reading, tentatively at first because the book began at the seventh chapter—Pizzle hadn't printed up the whole thing—and much of the terminology was astrophysics jargon. Clearly Belthausen's *Interstellar Travel Theory* was a book written for a select group of academics. There were, Treet decided, probably not more than seventy people in the whole world who could fully appreciate what Belthausen was getting at. That Pizzle should apparently be one of them surprised him.

But with little else to do besides eat and sleep and play Empires with the gnomish Pizzle, Treet made reading Belthausen a religious duty—struggling mightily with the interminable paragraphs made up of awkward sentences running on for pages freighting words whose meanings could only be guessed at or approximated in context and then only on second or third reading.

Belthausen was no William Shakespeare, but he seemed to know what he was talking about. Treet sensed as he read that the man grasped whole realms of possibility and feasibility that heretofore had been only hinted at, if considered at all. If he labored to bring his ideas into clear focus—and the signs of monumental labor were everywhere visible in his ungainly book, at least to the professional eye of another writer—it indicated that these were fresh ideas, concepts born of deep insight and creativity whose birth had cost the author something. He might not have been the Bard, but he wasn't chipped beef either.

So with increasing admiration, Treet slogged along, feeling like a foot soldier trudging under full field pack, following a commander whose orders he could scarcely comprehend. Along the way he also learned something about wormholes—among other things.

And what he learned disturbed him utterly.

Treet lay on his couch with the printout of Belthausen's book propped on his pillow while he sat cross-legged, tearing open rubbery capsules of dermal nutrient he'd found in his sanitary stall and smearing the viscid green emollient into his skin. It wasn't a proper nutrient bath, but considering he was several million miles from the nearest public spa, the little capsules were the next best thing.

So, smoothing the sticky substance over his face and chest and arms, he read, for the fourth or fifth time, a passage about time distortion in connection with wormholes—one of the more disturbing sections of the book for Treet—when he became aware that his scalp was tingling again. He stopped reading and tried to think where he had experienced that sensation before. With a start he remembered: Yarden!

At the same instant he glanced up and there she stood, framed in the open door of his compartment. He jumped up, opened his mouth to speak, but could not. What does one say to a vision?

"Mr. Treet," she said, less a greeting than the recitation of a known fact. "May I come in?"

For a moment Treet could only stare at her. Then he realized he had been addressed and asked a question. "Y-yes! Please come in. I wasn't expecting anyone. I . . . would you like to sit down?" He whirled around and picked up the foam chair at the terminal desk

"Thank you, no. I sit entirely too much as it is. I imagine we all do."

"Yes." He stared at her, trying to fix her face firmly in his mind this time.

"Mr. Treet, I won't keep you from your reading. This will only take a moment." She glanced around the compartment, which in six weeks Treet had managed to make look like the dayroom of an asylum for the criminally untidy.

With her standing there, he suddenly became aware of just how shabby the place looked. "I've been meaning to do some cleaning."

"It doesn't matter. I wanted to speak to you."

He waited. She looked at him curiously, full in the face, expectantly, as if there were some formal response he must make before she could continue. "Yes!" he said at last.

"Are you a sympath, Mr. Treet?"

It was a simple question, and Treet had heard the word before, knew what it meant, but her use of it caught him unawares, and for a moment its meaning evaded him. "A sympath?"

"Remote intelligence receptor. Surely, you are familiar—"

"Oh, yes! Yes, I know what it means. It's just that I didn't expect you to ask me that, of all things." He made an awkward gesture and realized he still had the foam chair before him. He put it down, saying, "No, I'm not a sympath. I've never had the training. Or the inclination for that matter. Why?"

She went on looking at him in that intense, engaging way and then said finally, "Some people are natural adepts and do not know it, Mr. Treet. You could be one of them." She said this last as if it were a challenge or an indictment, he couldn't decide which.

"I think I'd know, wouldn't I?" He smiled, trying to break through some of the high seriousness of the young woman. She seemed not to notice, but nodded slightly to herself as she backed away a slow step.

"Look, don't go," he said quickly. "It's a little . . . I mean, I'd like to get to know you a little better."

But she was already in the gangway. "No, Mr. Treet," her voice called back as she disappeared again, "perhaps you *wouldn't* know."

TEN

*O*rion Treet now had two things to be deeply disturbed about: wormhole time distortion, and the suggestion— no, the *insinuation*—that he was a sympath without his knowing it. About the former he had every right to be upset, but why the latter should bother him, he couldn't say. Except for the simple fact that he was a man who arranged his life like one of his essays: direct, uncluttered, balanced.

The insane expedition, as he now considered it, removed what little balance he had achieved of late. It had certainly eliminated the delicate equilibrium between penury and pelf (although the three million dollars stashed away in his flight kit had theoretically removed penury from the picture, his startling new wealth had yet to produce any tangible effects for him). Then there was the wormhole: how was it possible to find meaningful direction when at any moment *anything* might happen? The wormhole loomed as a monstrous, undulating question mark on his personal horizon, throwing unforeseen kinks in his ability to direct his fate. And Yarden Talazac's strange insinuation that he might be an unknowing sympath—in fact, her very presence—had cluttered his life with odd, irreconcilable thoughts and emotions, questions without answers, mysteries without clues.

As before, he said nothing of Yarden's visit to him. And though he wondered what it meant—as he wondered about what their first midnight meeting meant—he did not let on to Pizzle that he knew anything about the passenger in the adjoining stateroom. This silence had its price, for Pizzle was about to stampede him around the bend with his continual badgering: "Let's try to sneak into the ventilator shaft," or "I'll watch tonight, you watch tomorrow night," or "We could rig up a camera with a motion detector to photograph the gangway at night."

Instead, Treet deflected Pizzle's obsession toward a subject of more consequence, at least in his own mind.

"You've read Belthausen," Treet said as they sat knee-to-knee over Pizzle's Empires console, the flat green grid glowing between them. "What do you think of his time distortion theory?"

Pizzle's rims flashed as he glanced up. "It's a sound theory; no question about it. But then he starts off in pretty safe territory. I mean, distort space and you distort time—that much is elementary."

"Fine, it's elementary. But doesn't it concern you just a little? We're blasting away into the unknown, and both you and Crocker act as if we're on a holiday excursion to Pismo Beach. Doesn't the prospect of time displacement frighten you at all?"

Pizzle shook his head slowly. "I can't say as it does." He shrugged. "It's all the same in the end, isn't it?"

"What's all the same?"

"This—space travel. It's always into the unknown, right? And as far as time displacement, what difference does it make?"

"Why, an enormous difference!" Treet exploded in exasperation. "A carking great pile of a difference!"

"How?" Pizzle blinked mildly back at him.

"What?"

"How? How does it make a difference? You can't tell me that whether I arrive today, tomorrow, or a week ago last Thursday is going to make a molecule of difference—not to me, not to the colonists, not to anybody else, including you." He jabbed a button on the console. "It's your move. Careful, I've got your coastal lowlands mined."

As much as he hated to admit it, there *was* a microgram of cockeyed logic in what Pizzle said. In essence, it wouldn't make much difference *when* they arrived since their arrival had no field of external objectification, to use Belthausen's unwieldy term—that is, no exact temporal frame of reference.

Their normal frame of reference, Earth's time, would have no bearing on Empyrion time, and no real meaning either, since the two were not contiguous. Any problems posed by a time differential were largely illusory—in the sense that any such problems were merely due to the perception of the individual observer.

Except in the area of communication with Earth. Passing

signals back and forth through a space-time displacement tube—another term for wormhole—did complicate matters somewhat, as Cynetics had already discovered. Once into the tube, the signals became subject to whatever quirky laws governed the thing. Time shifts could occur, and probably did, although there was also the distinct possibility signals could pass through virtually unaffected, like arrows through a wind tunnel.

"What about parallel time channels?" asked Treet, intent on pursuing the discussion as far as possible. "Your move."

"Boy, you *have* been reading that book, eh?" Pizzle lowered his head over the grid. "Just captured one of your frontier base camps. Your turn." He looked up again. "Okay, what about them?"

"Well, suppose we come out of the wormhole and there's no colony because we've entered a parallel time channel? A channel, let's say, where a colony ship never arrived. We can't reach them because they're on another channel, and there's no way to change channels. What do we do then?"

"First of all, parallel time channels are merely an obscure mathematical possibility at this point." Pizzle held up his hand as Treet started to object. "But let's say that by some incredible circumstance we *did* end up in a parallel time channel."

Treet nodded. "Let's say."

"I imagine Crocker would simply turn right around and we'd go back the way we came. What's so terrible about that?"

Treet hadn't thought of that. Of course—they could just go back. Whatever happened, they could just turn around and hightail it back to Earth. Here he had been upset about persistent time distortions—static futures, variable pasts, parallel time channels, and all the rest—and Pizzle's unshakeable common sense had cut through all that with the modest wisdom of a weekend traveler: if we don't like the hotel, we'll pack up and go home.

With something approaching admiration, Treet gazed at his partner across the green grid screen. That scruffy, over-large head had a brain in it, and a good one. What other talents did Pizzle possess?

"Your capitol is in flames, and your escape routes are cut off," Pizzle was saying. "Unless you have a secret escape plan, your only chance is surrender. That's the game!"

"Wait! What was that?"

"Your empire is ashes."

"No, I mean—listen!" Treet cocked his head to one side, and the sound came again. "What's that?"

"That's just an acceleration signal." Pizzle cleared the screen. "Want to play another game?"

"No." Treet got up. "I want to find out what that signal is."

"I told you—" Before Pizzle could finish, the chiming signal changed, becoming louder, more insistent.

"Come on," said Treet. He entered the gangway and turned toward the cockpit. By the time he reached the flight deck, the signal had become an alarm, a blaring, raucous buzz. Treet tumbled into the cockpit and Pizzle after him. "Is this it? Is it happening?"

Crocker sat frozen over the navigator's instrument panel, his long-billed cap lowered over an orange oval screen. Yellow numbers flashed on the screen, changing to red as he watched. Without looking up he said, "I . . . don't know yet . . ."

Treet glanced around at the instrument panel. Several buttons were flashing red, and at least two screens spelled out the word WARNING! in crimson letters across their faces. Fear tugged his muscles taut, but Treet forced himself to remain calm.

Pizzle, standing beside him, whispered, "Could be a meteor field the vipath beam's picked up."

This was meant, no doubt, as a reassurance, but Treet's mind flashed the image of a million moon-sized chunks of rock hurtling into their tiny fragile craft, smashing it into a smoking tangle of twisted space junk.

"Sweet Julius!" said Crocker, spinning around to face them. "This is it, boys. Event horizon."

"The wormhole?" said Pizzle. "So soon?"

"We're still six weeks away," added Treet lamely.

The pilot shook his head, spinning back to his instruments. "Evidently we're in its backyard, and it's coming to meet us."

"Coming to meet us?" Treet stepped behind the Captain's chair and peered over his shoulder. "What do you mean?"

"Two A.U. and closing fast," he shot back over his shoulder.

"How fast?"

"You'd better get strapped in."

"How fast?" Treet demanded, gripping the chair with both hands.

"At the rate of one hundred thousand myms per second. Get back to your compartment and get strapped in—now! Both of you. Get going."

Treet backed away, reluctant to turn his eyes from the flashing screens. He felt Pizzle's hand on his arm, pulling him away. "Let's go. I switched on the holoscreens—we won't miss a thing."

They dashed back to their rooms, their feet barely making contact with the deck. Pizzle ducked into his compartment, grinning. "See you on the other end!"

"I sincerely hope so," muttered Treet, throwing himself onto the couch. His hand smacked the console, and the couch angled into flight attitude. He drew the seatbelt over him, and safety harness too, for good measure. He lay back and closed his eyes, trying to compose himself for whatever would happen next, and thought—what about Yarden!

Unhooking the belt and harness, Treet leaped from the couch and dove for the gangway. He reached Yarden's door a split second later and pounded it with both fists. "Yarden! Can you hear me? Open up! It's happening! The wormhole—we're going in! Did you hear? Open up!"

There was no answer. Likely she could not hear him. He pounded harder on the padded surface. "Yarden, open up! It's Treet!"

"Treet!" The overhead speaker barked at him. "Get back in your harness! She'll be all right. Move it!"

"Crocker, she doesn't know!"

"She *knows!*"

"But—"

"Get back in your harness, Treet!"

With a backward glance at Yarden Talazac's sealed door, Treet hurried to his room and rebelted. He had just snapped the harness buckle closed when the holoscreen before him pulsed with a bright light. Then the cabin lights dimmed, and Treet found himself staring into the mouth of the wormhole.

ELEVEN

The wormhole, as viewed through the 3-D projection of the holovision, appeared as a quivery purple spot in the center of the screen, expanding rapidly, blotting out the light of stars around its spreading rim. It glowed, according to Belthausen, because of something called Cerenkov radiation, which Treet did not pretend to understand. It had to do with the rotation of the Schwarzchild discontinuity exceeding the speed of light, the mechanisms of which Treet also failed to grasp.

He watched with dread fascination as the thing drew swiftly closer. Swelling. Turning.

The wormhole filled the screen, the glowing singularity so violet that needles of pain pierced the retinas. We must be at the very edge of it, thought Treet. We're going in!

Crocker's voice shouted over the sound system. "Brace yourselves! We're . . . one . . . two . . . three . . . NOW!"

Nothing happened.

This is it? wondered Treet.

Treet closed his eyes, expecting to feel something—a shudder through the ship, a spinning sensation, violent rocking motion, the collapse of the known universe—anything.

He felt nothing.

Then the first gravity waves hit the *Zephyros*. Treet experienced a heavy tug in his gut; his eyesight dimmed as blood drained from his head. He was weightless an instant later, and then squashed into his flight couch by a monster sandbag flung onto his chest. A split-second later he was floating in zero-G, lighter than air; the very next instant his bones were changed to lead. Gravity rippled over him. His stomach wriggled; his heart lurched against his ribs.

The disturbing effect subsided gradually. He opened his eyes and looked at the holoscreen and still saw the sharp purple, but something else as well. In the center of the screen a bright white dot of light shone like a single sun, very far away. The light at the end of the tunnel, thought Treet. Not so bad after all.

The white spot of sun grew slightly larger, though it gave the appearance of moving in the same direction as the ship, so that apparently the end of the wormhole receded as they approached. Still, the fact that it was getting bigger, however slightly, meant that they were traveling at a faster rate and would overtake it eventually.

Treet lay motionless and watched the screen, wondering whether the gravity waves would commence again, or whether they had entered the theorized gravity-free core of the displacement tube. Aside from the queasy anticipation, he felt just the same as before. If anything, shooting the wormhole was a big anticlimax, about as exciting as—what was it Crocker had called it?—riding a trolley through a tunnel.

By slow degrees, the spot of light in the center of the screen blossomed and Treet saw that it was not a disk, but rather a ring, hollow in the center—a donut of light. The donut continued to grow larger as the ship came closer and eventually swallowed the craft as it entered the hole in the center.

Instantly upon entering the donut of light, the holovision flared white. When the screen cleared, Treet was peering into an endless tube of soft blue-white light. It was like flying through a fluorescing neon tube.

Occasionally streaks of light—red, violet, deep blue, and green—flashed by them, disappearing in a lazy spiral down the tube. As Treet watched the brightly-colored streaks, it dawned on him that the walls of the tunnel were moving. In fact, they were woven of trillions of microscopic light particles spiraling along the inner walls of the tunnel around them.

The significance of this stunned him when he finally realized what it meant. That they were overtaking the tiny streaks meant that the *Zephyros* must be moving at a rate faster than the speed of light! Or very nearly. The larger colored streaks shooting past them—like artillery tracer bullets burning through the night—must be ultrafast particles of some sort: tachyons or accelerated photon bundles, somehow sped up by the phenomenon of the wormhole.

Faster than light? Could it be? Belthausen's book had described the possibility of light beams being caught in the wormhole, being bent and distorted—though the significance of this now eluded Treet—but he recalled nothing specific about the possibility of a vehicle traveling beyond lightspeed. That was supposed to be plainly impossible for a number of very good scientific reasons. But then, so were giant wormholes.

Treet could not take his eyes off the screen; he watched it greedily, studying the image before him. The walls of the tunnel undulated slowly, he noticed, bending like a tube flexed by the wind. Yet, the ship stayed on a perfect course through the exact center of the wormhole.

He heard a sound emerge from the speakers overhead. It sounded like Crocker's voice, but something was wrong. The words were garbled—chopped up, mixed together, and overlaid so that what came out of the speakers had the sound patterns of a voice, but none of the recognizable features of speech.

Something's wrong with Crocker! thought Treet. I've got to get to him. He fumbled at the harness buckle and jumped up. Treet's brain squirmed inside his skull. He saw his hands moving to lift himself off the couch as his legs swung over the edge, but the movement seemed to take forever.

He watched in horror as his hands smeared before his eyes, elongating, stretching as if made of rubber. He turned his head and his room smeared too, the objects blurring together, fusing, becoming a solid mass of shifting color.

Treet held his head completely still, and presently the room snapped back to its original shape, as if nothing had happened. Sitting on the edge of the couch, he waved his hand in the air. Again it smeared and stretched before his eyes, but he stopped the motion and held his hand steady, keeping his eyes on it. Treet discovered that the smear was actually made up of an infinity of frozen images, like individual frames of movie film fanning before his eyes—movie frames with the sequence out of order so that some of the frames showed his hand already stopped while others showed it as not having moved, or some-where in between.

The effect made him nauseous. He closed his eyes and lay back. Above him the speaker buzzed again. He heard some urgency in the tone, but could not make out a single word; they were all clipped and jumbled and running over one another. The sequence was all confused. Something's wrong! he thought again. He's calling for help.

Treet struggled to his feet and the room shifted crazily, swerving and bending out of shape. He felt the couch behind his legs, closed his eyes, and staggered toward the open door and into the gangway. Holding his head very still, he glanced up the gangway, closed his eyes, and began walking toward the cockpit.

As long as I keep my eyes closed, I'm all right, he thought, feeling along the bulkhead as he went. He passed Pizzle's door and moved on, fumbling like a blind man. He reached the cockpit and entered, leaned against the padded doorframe for support, and allowed himself a quick look around. All was as before. Crocker sat in his command chair, strapped in, watching the screens, a look of immense satisfaction on his face. Sensing someone behind him, Crocker turned and Treet saw a most hideous sight—Crocker's head swerved in the air, his features losing solidity and blending together as if liquefied. Eyes ran together; hair and skin mingled; teeth, lips, and nostrils melted into one another. He appeared to Treet to be dissolving before his eyes.

The Captain spoke. His words tumbled out of his mouth helter-skelter, an unintelligible mish-mash of syllables.

Treet cringed back from the monstrous sight, and the movement caused the cockpit to spin and smudge crazily. The flight deck buckled beneath his feet and he fell back, unbalanced by the illusion of motion. In the same instant Treet felt the queasy, watery sensation of nausea wash through him. His stomach heaved, emptying its warm contents over the front of his singleton.

He slumped to the floor, eyes closed, stomach and brain quaking as darkness swam out of the bulkheads to engulf him.

"I told you to stay strapped in, Treet." The voice was Crocker's. "You okay?"

"Huh?" Treet turned toward the sound and raised his head. "What happened?"

"We reached wormhole terminus, and you fouled yourself."

Treet raised a hand to his chest and felt the sticky wetness there. The stench of vomit made his stomach roll again. He swallowed hard, tasting bile in his throat. "I thought you were in trouble."

"I was trying to tell you that terminus was coming up." Crocker knelt over him, a hand on his shoulder. "Okay now?"

"I think so. Motion sickness. I—how long have I been out?"

"Out?" Crocker lifted his hand. "You weren't out. Maybe just a second."

"It was terrible. I saw . . . you looked like a monster."

"You don't look so chipper yourself. Can you get up?"

"Sure." Treet placed his hands flat on the floor and pushed up on all fours.

"Woo! Who puked?" Pizzle came striding into the cockpit.

"Treet got a little seasick. He's okay now."

"Wow! Look at that! It's beautiful!" Pizzle dashed by him, and Treet lifted his head to see what had caused the outburst.

On the mainscreen before them the brilliant white ball of a sun blazed in the upper left, with several hundred other bright spots of stars salted in a sable field. In the center of the picture was the sight that had evoked Pizzle's ecstatic response: a brilliant green globe, wonderfully round and smooth, wrapped in a near-invisible veil of shimmering blue which thickened to a sparse dotting of puffy white clouds nearer the surface of the planet.

"Empyrion." The men's heads jerked around to see Yarden Talazac standing in the doorway behind them, her eyes too on the screen. "Realm of the gods."

"Miss Talazac!" exclaimed Pizzle in a hushed voice. "It was *you*—" He hesitated and faltered.

She glanced at Pizzle once quickly—as though to silence him—as she entered the room, and then turned her attention back to the screen. Pizzle appeared slightly embarrassed, then shrank away from her as she came to stand with them.

For a long time nobody spoke. They merely gazed at the slowly turning world before them on the screen, each wondering what they would find waiting for them down there. Finally a chime sounded on the instrument board, and Crocker moved to his chair.

"Well, we're twelve hours to orbit entry." Crocker spoke softly, almost reverently.

"How long to landing?" asked Treet.

"Depends on what the scanners find. We'll have to locate the colony before going down, but we'll start broadcasting on the spectrum right away. If they're listening—and they surely are—we'll get directions and landing instructions and go right on in. Maybe eighteen hours. No more than twenty-four."

"Great!" cried Pizzle, fairly dancing in place. "I can't wait! This is going to be ultrafantastic!"

"Let's just hope we're up to it," said Treet, and then wondered immediately why he had said it. Certainly he felt every bit as excited about what lay before them as Pizzle.

"My thoughts exactly, Mr. Treet," said Yarden, stepping up beside him. "You must have read my mind."

TWELVE

"This is the sixth pass, Captain, and still nothing on scan—what's the problem?" Treet stood beside Pizzle, who leaned against the Cyclops housing looking bored. Behind them a great green expanse filled the mainscreen as *Zephyros'* cameras scoured the landmasses beneath them, searching for the colony.

"The problem—for the tenth time—is that we can't raise them on the radio. We're having to do a visual which is like . . ."

"Like looking for a quark in a quagmire," offered Pizzle.

"Why don't they answer the transmission?"

"I don't know why. We'll just have to be sure to ask them, won't we?" said Crocker, impatience lending him sarcasm. The last twelve hours had produced nothing but headaches; fatigue slumped his shoulders. "Look, this is going to be a long wait. Why don't you two go and get some sleep while you can. I'll call you if—*when* I find something."

"Good idea," offered Pizzle. "Come on, Treet. Let's leave the Captain to fly his ship. We're just getting in the way."

"Okay, but you'll call us—"

"I'll *call* you!"

They filed out of the instrument-jammed cockpit and along the gangway, pausing at Pizzle's compartment. "He's right about getting some rest, you know. We may not get much of a chance later."

"What do you mean?" Treet heard something in the words and spun on his heel to face Pizzle.

The close-set eyes darted away quickly. "Oh, nothing—just that, you know, it's likely to be somewhat hectic down there. First visitors from home and all."

"That's not it!" Treet took a step closer, confronting Pizzle. "Tell me what you meant."

"That's all I meant. I swear." He turned to go into his room.

"You meant that something's the matter down there. Admit it."

"Nothing's the matter." Pizzle yawned and shuffled into his compartment. "You'll see; nothing's the matter."

"Then why don't they answer the signal?" Treet shouted at his disappearing figure. The door slid shut, cutting off Pizzle's reply.

Three meals, four games of Empires, sixteen hours, and nine revolutions later, Crocker called them all back to the bridge. Treet fairly flew down the gangway with Pizzle close on his heels. Yarden came behind them at a more stately pace. Crocker, haggard and showing two days stubble on his jaw, sat hunched over the Cyclops keypad, a pile of silver mylex printout tape curling around his chair.

"Well, boys and girls, I think I've found them." His tone was less than certain.

The others remained silent, waiting for the pilot to continue. When he saw that no one had anything to say, he went on. "Don't everyone jump up and down at once! I said we've located the colony."

"You didn't sound any too overjoyed yourself," replied Treet. "What's wrong?"

Crocker bent over the keypad again, tapped a key, and then slumped back in the chair, rubbing his face with his hands. "I don't know. There's something screwy down there, that's for sure. I wish I could figure it out." He reached down and grabbed a handful of the mylex printout. "Look at this! I've run every scan and probe in my very fat manual, and I can't figure it."

Pizzle took off his glasses and rubbed the lenses on his shirt. "You might as well go whole-hog," he said, "and tell us what you know."

"It's pretty complicated, but the long and short of it is that every time I get a steady fix on the colony, it shifts. Rather, I get two readings—first one place, then somewhere else again." Crocker's words met with blank stares. "Here's a map—" He tapped a key and a green-and-gold landmass appeared on one of Cyclops' three screens. There were two red dots marked on the map—one in the center, near what appeared to be a blue, winding thread of a river, and another red dot in the lower right quadrant, nearer a tawny gold coast.

"Not much to go on," remarked Treet.

"We're still too high for a more detailed picture, and we don't have a snooper pack, but it'll give you the general idea. Of the three major continental land areas on the planet, this is the largest." Stabbing a finger at the red spot in the center of the map, Crocker said, "I get a fairly strong reading here—in the neighborhood of point zero eight seven nine, which ought to indicate a settlement of considerable size. Trouble is, the methane signature isn't what it should be—hardly anything at all. Over here, though, I get a reading of point zero six six two, with a good healthy methane signature."

"What's that mean exactly?" asked Treet.

"Two colonies," said Yarden. Crocker looked at her and nodded slowly.

"Yeah, two colonies. See, it took me a long time to separate the two because I didn't want to accept the readings. But that's what it looks like—two colonies. One nearly as big as the other."

"How is that possible?" asked Pizzle. "That would mean the first colony would have had to double in size in less than five years. That can't be right."

"I don't see anything so odd about it at all," said Treet. "It's probably natives."

"I thought of that too, but the transcripts of the landing party don't say anything about an extensive native population. Besides, they wouldn't have chosen this planet in the first place if there had been sentient humanoids down there—that would violate the IASA charter."

"Maybe they're not humanoid," said Pizzle. "Maybe it's a mob of long-horned blue kangaroos."

"That would have to be a sizable mob," replied Crocker flatly. "It's a density of point ninety-nine per square meter. Herds and such tend to be less dense—I looked it up. Strong LFR, too—that's life force reading—above 85 percent. It's the same reading you get from a well-populated city." He looked at Yarden, who was staring at the mainscreen where Empyrion turned slowly on its axis as they flew over its smooth terrain. "She said it: two colonies."

Treet rubbed his neck with his hand. "So why don't we just fly on down for a closer look? I don't see the problem."

"I wish it were that easy," said Crocker. "No, we're going to have to choose a landing site and take our chances."

Treet's features convulsed in a furious frown. "Take our chances! What is this? A game? Is that what it is? Roll the dice and see what comes up?"

Crocker glared at him. "I wouldn't say that. The colony *is* down there."

"Is it? You're sure, are you?" Treet fumed, getting red in the face. "Then why don't they answer our signals?"

"Obviously radio failure of some kind." Pizzle darted a look from one to the other of the two men.

"Radio failure, he says! They could have as easily gotten eaten by that swarm of blue-horned kangaroos or whatever. Shall we go down and make it dessert?"

Crocker waved aside the comment. "You're overreacting."

"Tell me I'm overreacting when you're simmering in your own sauce on a bed of hot coals."

"I'm sure there's a rational explanation," offered Pizzle.

"I'd like to hear it!" Treet demanded.

"We have weapons, Treet," intoned Crocker.

"We do? Well, why didn't you say so before?"

"Last resort, dire emergency, and all that. But yes, we have weapons. Does that make you feel better?"

Treet hated to admit that it did. "Somewhat," he replied grudgingly.

"Good. At last. Well," Crocker stood slowly and stretched, "it's agreed then, right? We go down on the next flyover and head for the larger blip." He pointed to the glowing red dot in the center of the computer screen, then glanced at Yarden Talazac.

Treet saw the look and wondered at it.

Yarden nodded once sharply. "I agree, Captain." She turned back to the screen.

Treet watched her for a moment; he felt a queer, uneasy sensation at the thought that somehow *she* was controlling this decision. Maybe she was. "How soon?"

Crocker consulted an instrument. "We're coming up on the continental landmass in thirty minutes. We'll start our descent in about fifteen. Actual landing won't take but a few minutes."

"And then?"

Captain Crocker stared at Treet levelly. "And then, Mr. Treet, we shall see what we shall see."

• • • • • •

What they saw, streaking through the atmosphere like a meteor, was a turquoise world, blue-green with vegetation, water, and sky. As the *Zephyros* sped closer, its wings folded back into knife-thin stubs, the landscape rolled out before them, puckered like a rumpled tablecloth, and laced through with blue-white water. Their descent brought them over a rugged range of jagged mountains, a flat expanse of plains, and the sinuous waves of a desert of stark white dunes which faded into an earthy brown, then changed once more to pastel blue-green as they rocketed across the shallow valley of a wide silver river.

Treet, strapped to his flight couch, watched the holoscreen. Although the land seemed fair and inviting, it was empty. He did not see any signs of life: no animals or birds of any description—no sign that the planet supported anything but plants—and possibly insects; there were sure to be insects.

As the land rolled by beneath him, Treet realized that he was seeing a world no one had ever seen before—except the colonists, and perhaps not even them. Here was a virginal world, rich and ripe, ready for the hand of a husband, a world offering a fresh start for those who would make their homes upon her.

Such was the mood the alien landscape cast over Treet. His heart stirred to the sight of endless miles of verdure and fresh, clean water under sparkling blue skies. No dark cities with hanging shrouds of foul air; no yawning ore pits scarring the earth; no highways or fences tying it down; no stinking, festering hellholes filled with humanity's untouchables. No war. No disease. No famine. No want.

Here was a new beginning, a dream worth fighting for—perhaps even dying for.

Treet wondered at his response to this place. He had traveled far and wide, had seen grand vistas and beautiful landscapes many times before. Some had moved him, it was true, but none like this; none as much as Empyrion. Why? Landscape was just landscape, one hill or river pretty much like another in the final analysis. And yet . . . this place *was* different. He could feel the difference, though he could not name it.

Perhaps it was the absence of mankind here and all that represented: a free, unspoiled, perfect world. A paradise which had not cast out its keeper. An Eden where no serpent slithered.

A realm of beauty, yes, but of beauty which was as much promise as physical presence.

The overhead speaker clicked as Crocker opened a circuit. "What a place!" he said in awed tones. Then came a long pause, after which he added, "We're coming up on the colony now. ETA two minutes. I'm feathering in the drag engines."

At that moment Treet heard a hissing sound like sand blowing over glass. The straps tugged at his chest as the *Zephyros* responded to the increased drag by slowing. They were skimming over the landscape now, wings extended to offer maximum lift. The picture on the screen tilted slightly and then righted itself, and Treet saw a ridge rising up across a valley. The ship flashed over the valley, climbing slightly.

"And here it is, lady and gentlemen," said Crocker, all business again. He might have been a bus driver casually announcing the termination of his route.

"Where? I don't see it." The voice was Pizzle's, but it spoke Treet's thoughts as well.

"The lower center of your screen," returned Crocker. "You'll see it . . . now!"

Leaning forward as far as his restraining straps would allow, Treet saw a dull, metallic-looking mound growing in the center of the screen near the bottom. "We'll make a reconnaissance pass," said Crocker, and the picture tilted sharply. The grayish mound dipped from the screen, and Treet saw a sky of intense blue above a turquoise horizon.

"Sensors report no radio or electromagnetic activity below. I've got a strong LFR confirmed." Crocker read off his instruments. "We are shedding altitude. Our second pass will be closer."

Again the picture tilted, and the horizon slanted up. Treet glimpsed a bit of white sunlight through the tiny oval window above him. On the screen the landscape showed pastel green and barren rounded hills and flat places all around, with brown bluffs above a river in the far distance.

"I've got a visual," said Crocker. "The landing area is clear. I'm going to put her down."

Treet swallowed with a dry mouth; he heard a loud drumming sound and realized that his heart was thumping in his ears. His fingers dug into the fabric of the couch. This is it! he thought. We're landing!

The rumble and jolt of the engines suprised him, but he did not take his eyes from the screen for an instant. The picture shook momentarily, steadied, and then the horizon began flattening out as they came down vertically.

"Forty-two hundred," said Crocker. "Coming down nicely. Thirty-five. Very good." Another rumble rocked the ship. "A little more thrust; that's right. Good. Twenty-eight hundred. Slowing. Twenty-six . . ."

Where is it? wondered Treet, straining forward in his seat, eyes frozen on the screen. I don't see the colony! Where is it?

The holoscreen showed a panoramic view of a blue-green field of tall grasslike plants where wind sent waves rolling like breakers across the plain. The wind was exhaust from *Zephyros'* jets as the ship lowered itself from the sky. The picture spun and Treet got a glimpse of something rounded and glittering, rising up nearby—the mound he had seen moments before. The ship came around, and the object slid away.

With a soft, cushioned bounce like an elevator coming to a stop, the *Zephyros* touched down. "Happy landing, folks," announced Crocker. "Welcome to Empyrion."

THIRTEEN

"Is this really necessary?" asked Pizzle, grimacing with distaste. "I mean, really? We already know that the air is breathable—there's more oxygen in it than Earth's!"

"Just put it on, will you, and stop stalling," ordered Crocker. "It's by the book or not at all."

"But . . . the colonists breathe it, for crying out loud—"

"Shut up and do it, Pizzle. You're holding things up." Treet glared nastily at the balking Pizzle. "What are you afraid of?"

Grumbling, Pizzle lifted the massive helmet over his head and brought the neck seal down on the tabs. Crocker flipped the catches and checked to make sure it had sealed.

"Okay, we're all set. Everyone ready?" Crocker looked at each of the passengers in turn, waiting for a nod. "Let me hear you."

"All set," said Treet. His legs trembled with anticipation, and he thought, This is it! We're going out; we're really going out there! Mingled with this expectation was a distinct undercurrent of fear: the unkown. What lay on the other side of that hatch? Heaven? Hell?

"Ready," said Pizzle. He glanced nervously around at the others.

"I'm ready," said Yarden, her graceful form wrapped in a bulky, shapeless, red atmosphere suit like the others.

"Okay, I read you loud and clear. Let's go." The Captain reached out and tapped a code into the switchplate next to the outer hatch. There was a muffled whoosh and the hatch withdrew, swung outward, and slid away to the side. A stairstep ladder unfolded below the hatch, and Crocker stepped into the open hatchway. "One at a time. Follow me."

Crocker stepped over the threshold, turned, and backed down the steps, holding the handrail. Pizzle looked at Treet and gestured to the ladder.

"No, you go next," replied Treet. "I'll go after Miss Talazac."

Pizzle shifted his gaze to Yarden, nodded silently, and stepped into the hatchway. He disappeared, the top of his helmet sinking from sight as he went down.

"Your turn," said Treet, turning to Yarden.

"Thank you," she replied, turning crisply and descending without hesitation.

What is it with her? wondered Treet. He sighed and then stepped to the hatchway, turned, and lowered himself onto the first step, counting the steps as he went down.

When he reached the bottom he turned, expecting to see the others waiting for him. There was no one. A twinge of fear flitted over him. He spun around quickly, scanning the perimeter.

Then he saw them, at the rear of the ship behind one of the stilt legs. With instant relief Treet ducked beneath the heatcone of an engine and walked under the belly of the ship to join the others, who stood motionless, their back to him, apparently engrossed in something. Treet could not see what it was. The suit radios were silent; no one said a word.

Treet stepped from under the obscuring edge of an engine shield and came to stand beside Crocker. Only then did he see what the others were seeing: an enormous sparkling wall of glass shot through with veins of black swept up from the landing platform. Beyond this wall rose bank upon bulging bank of crystalline domes and cupolas, billowing one on top of another beyond counting.

Treet raised his eyes higher and higher still. The many-domed mound rose like a great multifaceted mountain of crystal. Here and there spars poked through the domes, trailing thick, dark cables which gave the appearance of lifting the mass like cathedral spires or the poles of a circus tent. Up and up like foothills climbing to the summit, the bright domes swelled—all sizes jumbled together, gleaming in the sunlight like wonderful, gigantic soap bubbles dropped from the sky—some big enough to cover a building or two, others, larger by many times, able to enclose a small city with room for a few suburbs.

The glistening mountain stretched away for kilometers on either hand, and wherever the eye rested, the glimmer of bright transparency winked back. Empyrion stood an enchanted crystal mountain whose top reached shimmering into the clear blue sky.

"Impossible!" said Treet, his voice hushed in awe. "I can't believe it."

"Incredible," agreed Pizzle. "It's unimaginable! How could they build this . . . this bubble city in so short a time? It isn't possible."

"Look at this," said Crocker. The three turned to look where he pointed. His gloved hand extended toward the ground. They saw the platform beneath their feet littered with small rocks and pebbles, bits of glass, warped fibersteel plates, and something that looked like crinkled pink moss growing in thickly scattered patches over the structure. "This landing field doesn't get much use, I'd say." He swiveled around and took in the broad expanse of the platform. "It looks like it's been abandoned for years . . . decades."

"The colony isn't that old," put in Pizzle.

"I know." Crocker turned back to the others. "I can't explain it."

"Maybe this isn't the colony," replied Treet simply, then shuddered to think what he had just said. Not the colony? Then who. . . ?

"It is the colony." Yarden spoke with such certainty that the men pivoted toward her. She stood stock-still with her arms pressed to her sides.

"What is it, Yarden?" asked Crocker. "What are you getting?"

Just then she stiffened and pointed at the wall directly before them about a kilometer away. "They are coming to meet us," she said, but the words were flat, no happiness or excitement in them, but rather something darker, almost sinister.

Treet saw a portion of the wall raise up and a dark shape emerge, followed by another and then a third. These came rapidly toward them on clouds of dust, filling the air with a ringing whine as they drew nearer.

Closer, the travelers could make out men standing in these strange vehicles—men dressed as they were, in atmosphere suits, dark and close fitting, however, and made of a material that shone with a faint luster. A helmet with black faceplate obscured their faces, making them appear monstrous and malevolent.

"I don't like this," said Treet. "They don't look too happy to see us. Where are the weapons?"

"We probably surprised them," suggested Pizzle. "No prior radio contact—they probably wonder who we are."

"Shh! They can probably hear you too," snapped Crocker. "Let me handle this." He stepped forward. "Yarden? Anything?"

The young woman was silent for a moment, then shrugged. "There is something there, but . . . it's blocked. I can't read it."

Now the first vehicle swept up, slowing only minimally as it approached. Men stood in the rear of the machine, darkened faceplates turned toward them. One man, a driver, stood ahead of the others, holding controls in both hands. Then the thing swung sideways, and Treet saw two wheels beneath its smooth belly throwing up dust. Another two-wheeler swung around to the other side and the third parked between them, somewhat closer than the other two.

The two groups watched each other. No one moved.

With a shock Treet recognized the snub-snouted barrels of weapons in the hands of the dark-suited colonists. "They're armed!" he whispered harshly.

"Shh!" Crocker hissed. "I'll do the talking."

With that, the pilot stepped forward slowly, raising his right hand in the classic greeting. "Brothers," he said, his voice confident, controlled, "we're glad to see you . . ." He hesitated as there was no answer, no sign of recognition from the other side. One hand went to his forearm panel to make an adjustment. "Wide-band broadcast," he said to himself, then continued boldly, "We've come from Earth." No response. "From Earth."

At this a harsh, guttural growl issued from one of the colonists—more a bark than a voice.

It was difficult to tell which one had shouted, but Treet saw a figure in the center two-wheeler jerk his hand upward and the men around him disembarked, stepping from the vehicle to advance cautiously toward them, weapons at the ready.

"Tell them we're friendly," Treet said urgently. "Tell them, Crocker!"

"We're *friends*. We've come from Earth," repeated the Captain, to no avail.

The line of men stopped just short of the travelers, and the man who had given the signal approached. He stepped closer and examined each of them carefully, his dark faceplate reflecting sunlight like the shell of a beetle.

"What is this?" Treet addressed the man. "What's going on? Why don't you speak to us?"

The man appeared not to have heard, but went on with his inspection, moving to Pizzle, Talazac, and Crocker in turn. The colonist stepped back a pace and looked at them, as if trying to decide what to do next. Clearly their presence here posed some kind of problem for the colonists. Treet sensed that a decision was being made and that the next few moments were critical. He had to break through to them, but how?

"We're from Cynetics," Treet said, speaking out suddenly. The colonist and his men jerked their attention to Treet. "Cynetics," he said again, repeating the word distinctly.

At the word, a garbled mutter broke out among the colonists. Treet heard it in his helmet as a gibber of voices talking over one another with subdued excitement, whereupon one voice cut through the others with a shout, and there was silence again.

The colonist raised his hand and pointed at Treet and said something, his low voice buzzing. Two men stepped forward quickly and grabbed Treet by the arms.

"Hey! Let me go!" cried Treet. "Hey!"

"Stop!" shouted Crocker, dashing up.

"Help!" Treet struggled in the grasp of the colonists, but they hauled him bodily along. "Shoot them!"

Behind him he heard the sounds of a scuffle: short breaths, grunts, and curses—presumably from Crocker and Pizzle; a gabble of thick, unintelligible syllables, from the colonists.

The fight sounds halted abruptly. In order to see behind him, Treet had to turn his whole upper torso around, which was difficult, pinioned as he was between the two who were dragging him toward the center two-wheeler. When they paused at the vehicle to shove him in, Treet managed to twist around. He saw two bodies lying on the platform, and the third—Yarden?—being dragged to one of the other two-wheelers.

"Crocker!" he screamed. "Pizzle! Talazac!"

There was no reply. He felt hands on him, hoisting him up into the two-wheeler, and he was tumbled in headfirst. Then they were speeding back to the wall and into the crystal mountain beyond.

FOURTEEN

"Where is this one going?" A Nilokerus guard stepped into the corridor, halting the suspension bed maneuvered by a second-order physician.

The physician stopped abruptly, turned stiffly toward the guard, and held up a packet with a violet Threl seal. "He's for the Saecaraz. Jamrog's initiative. He wants to keep an eye on this one personally."

The guard stepped close to the floating bed and peered curiously down into the face of the man lying there. "Is he the one that called on Cynetics?"

"No. I hear that one's to remain with the Supreme Director in Threl High Chambers. This is one of the others."

"Looks harmless enough." The guard shrugged and stepped aside, and the physician shoved the body-bearing bed away once more. They had traveled no more than ten paces when the guard turned his head to his shoulder and whispered, "The prisoner is on the way, Subdirector Fertig."

A click sounded in the folds of the guard's clothing as the circuit opened. "Acknowledged. Report to Fairweather level in Tanais sector for reassignment."

"At once." The shoulder mike clicked off, and the guard spun on his heel and hurried along the deserted terrace toward his new destination, muttering, "This is news! I'll get a round for this tonight. Maybe two!"

Orion Treet was awake, and his head felt stuffed with oatmeal. A small spot on his upper arm ached, as if he'd been burned with a lighted cigar just below the shoulder. Or branded.

Branded? The thought caused him to sit bolt upright on the suspension bed. He sprang up too quickly, the bed dipped, and Treet rolled onto the floor. Black spots of dizziness pinwheeled before his eyes. Presently the spots faded and, still sprawled on the floor, he looked cautiously at his right arm where he saw only a thin scratch and a tiny red bruise. He rubbed the spot for a moment as he studied his cell.

It was a small, pie-shaped room with a ceiling that curved upward, toward some apex beyond—a section of a dome. The ceiling was translucent and glowed light green, softly tinting the bare walls of the cell. The doorway, narrow, but with strangely rounded posts and a lancet arch, stood open. There was no door, and a further door glimpsed beyond a connecting room was open too. Either the colonists had no use for doors, or they had a more efficient way of sealing rooms.

Treet guessed the latter: a barrier field of some sort.

This inspection done, Treet turned his attention to the rest of the room. He saw a black-and-silver bundle on a shelf which jutted out from the wall. Since it was the only other object in the room besides the suspension bed—and since he was naked and beginning to feel foolish sitting on the floor—Treet decided to investigate.

Pushing himself up slowly—so as not to start the black spots dancing again—he moved toward the shelf, stealing a glance through the open doorway as he went. He was alone; no one appeared in either doorway, nor could he see anyone in the room beyond.

Taking the bundle from the shelf, Treet shook out the folds to reveal a lightweight robe of a material that looked and felt like silk. The robe—short, with a large V-shaped hole for his head—was black with silver diagonal stripes. A second garment fell out of the first—a pair of coarse, baggy black leotards with molded synthetic rubber soles sewn into the feet. There was no undergarment, but, not feeling at all choosy, he pulled on the leotard and drew it over his legs; the high waistband came all the way up to his solar plexus.

Next he slipped the flimsy, long-sleeved robe over his head. The garment reached midcalf, but once the two broad silver bands dangling from his waist were wrapped around and tied at his side, creating a sash, the hemline rose to just above his kneecaps.

The clothes were remarkably comfortable—more so than the singleton he always wore. The fine quality of the robe, and the silky sensation against his skin, made him feel like a Chinese emperor. He smoothed the folds beneath his hands and, with nothing else to do, sat down once again on the edge of the bed to wait, replaying in his mind all that he could remember of the scuffle on the landing field.

He had disembarked and was immediately met by three vehicles carrying colonists. An attempt at communication had been made, at which point he had been attacked. Treet remembered being buffeted around somewhat—a sore thigh and ribs told him he had taken a blow or two—and then dragged toward one of the vehicles. At some point after being hauled aboard, his memory went blank.

Then he had awakened in this cell. He could remember nothing else after that, and only isolated patches from before. He remembered his conversation with Varro and meeting Neviss; he remembered eating a fine meal, but not what he ate; remembered a satchel full of money, now gone; and before that being hauled from a public bath at Houston International at gunpoint. Only snatches—a jigsaw puzzle with lots of pieces missing, islands of clarity surrounded by seas of featureless confusion.

But there should be more, he told himself. What about the others?

Certainly there had been others—he could hardly have come here alone. There had to have been a transport, and *someone* would have had to fly it.

I did not come alone, he thought. There *were* others, *had* to be others. Why can't I remember them?

The room in which Yarden Talazac found herself was faintly reminiscent of her childhood home. There was no ceiling, but the soft, shifting light, filtering in from high above, sending faint ripples of dappled shadow across smooth white walls, reminded her of the seaside villa of her father. Her room had been adjacent to the inner courtyard and open to the sky. She had always loved the feeling of freedom the room inspired, and at twilight, when the plexidome was raised for the night above the courtyard, stars shone down upon her bed.

But this room was not in her father's house. Somewhere else then. Where? She could not say. She had the feeling, though, that she had come from very far away to this place. How she had come, and why, she did not know.

At the same time, she felt that she had always been here—in this room, sitting on the bed, watching the shadow shapes drift like clouds over the wall. That could not be, she knew. There must be a life outside this room, but . . .

Thinking about it made her tired. She yawned and lay back against the pillows she had piled in the middle of the bed. She closed her eyes and gave herself to the cozy warmth of sleep, feeling safe and secure: a child in her father's home once again.

The moment he opened his eyes, Pizzle reached out to release his safety harness. It was gone. He pulled back his hand and wondered what had made him do that. Even as he tried to think about it, the thought evaporated.

For a moment he had the impression that he would remember something very important, that if he only concentrated hard enough it would come to him. But concentration eluded him; random thoughts drifted in and out of his head, and he forgot why he was concentrating in the first place.

He yawned, slid out of bed, and stretched, pulling his arms over his head and bending at the waist. It felt good to stretch; he'd been sleeping too long.

Pizzle slipped his yos over his head and tightened the sash at his side, blousing up the folds properly so that the hem reached midthigh. He stopped and looked at his hands. Where had he learned to arrange a yos?

Hadn't he always known? Wasn't it a thing everyone knew?

For a moment he experienced a strange sense of reversed deja vu—of doing for the first time things he had been doing all his life.

Oh well, it was probably nothing. Nothing at all.

FIFTEEN

Sirin Rohee, Supreme Director of the Threl, stared around the ring at his grim companions. Worry stretched his normally pouty expression into a deep, oppressive frown. Everyone in the darkened, heavily-draped room felt the full weight of that frown; it was like gravity—pulling all attention toward itself.

At last he spoke. His voice warbled slightly, a clue to his advancing age; but his hands were steady as he clasped his ceremonial bhuj. "The threat, though very great, has been averted, Directors. We have managed to isolate the intruders, and amnesiants have been administered."

"There was no trouble?" Kavan asked, averting his eyes briefly. The Supreme Director waved the bhuj to his left; the polished blade flashed in the light.

"None," replied Hladik. "They were but a small force; our own Invisibles subdued them easily."

"Weapons?" Cejka spoke in a raw whisper.

Hladik regarded him frankly from beneath his heavy brows and answered, "We found no weapons."

"But," added Rohee quickly, "there is no doubt that the intent of their mission was to discredit our security. Therefore, you will describe weapons of undetermined origin. Our official statement will be that we have, owing to tireless vigilance, thwarted a plot by Fieri spies."

Tvrdy, the sly, practical Director of Tanais, leaned forward in his seat, cleared his throat, and said, "What of this vehicle of theirs? I understand the spies possessed a spacecraft."

Saecaraz Subdirector Jamrog answered without waiting for a nod from his superior. "Obviously the vehicle must have been a decoy."

"Oh?" said Tvrdy. "I had not heard this." He glanced at Cejka, and then continued. "What would be the use of a decoy?"

"Deception," said Jamrog. "The Fieri are deviously clever.

They hope to make us believe that they have achieved space travel. We know this is impossible."

"Should not this decoy craft be mentioned in our statement? The people are certain to hear about it."

"You will make no mention of the decoy craft. It does not exist."

"Where is it now?" asked Tvrdy. "I would like to have it studied. It may be that it hides some clues to Fieri magic."

"It has been removed," Jamrog replied tightly.

"Yes. So I would expect. And where is it being kept? I wish to send Tanais magicians to study it."

"You will be notified when that becomes possible," said Jamrog.

"I see. And what prevents me from seeing it now?"

"I say when—" began Jamrog angrily.

Hladik, Director of Nilokerus, raised a hand and cut him off. "You will see the vehicle in due time, Tvrdy. I realize both you and Jamrog will have keen interest in the craft—even though it is but an elaborate toy. However, the Supreme Director asked me to make absolutely certain the machine poses no security threat."

"Of course." Tvrdy smiled. "I was merely curious, you understand." He nodded toward Jamrog. "I am sorry if my request upset you."

Piipo, the long-faced, taciturn Director of Hyrgo Hage, twisted uncomfortably in his seat and spoke up. "Supreme Director, if I may return to other matters, you said the spies have been isolated. Am I to believe they are being held in the reorientation section?"

"Allow me, Supreme Director," said Hladik as the Threl leader glanced toward him. "The force was small—only four. Since their presence was certain to be discovered by the Dhogs if they were placed in adjustment cells, I thought it best that they be introduced unobtrusively into suitable Hages. Of course they will remain under close surveillance until the effect of the psi-lobe is rendered permanent."

"You don't think they would pose an even greater threat loose among the populace? They could conceivably make contact with Dhogs who are sure to recognize them."

"Of course," replied Hladik equably, "such a thing is possible. But in their present condition they would be in no position to help their comrades." The Nilokerus leader smiled broadly.

"Besides, as I have said, their movements will be monitored very closely. Any attempt to contact the Fieri underground within Empyrion would compromise their organization. We would strike instantly and crush them once and for all."

Supreme Director Rohee raised the bhuj and rapped the gold-plated staff sharply on the floor. "The session is at an end, Directors. You will assure your Hagemen that we have dealt our treacherous enemies a decisive blow; we are now very close to smashing their network and ridding Empyrion of their hated presence forever."

With that he stood slowly, supported by Jamrog who held his elbow, turned, and shuffled from the circular chamber. The seven remaining Threl watched him go in silence.

As the others filed past, led away by their waiting guides, Trvdy stepped from the procession and walked to the terrace rim. He put his hands on the smooth surface of the breastwork and looked out over the Hage. The undulating arcs of a thousand terrace rims, falling away in sweeping stairsteps on every side, descending to teeming tangles of warrens and cells below, met his gaze.

There was much that had not been said in session about this so-called invasion of spies. What were the spies doing *outside* the dome? Why were they not simply terminated upon capture—standard policy for Fieri agents and Dhogs? Why had their spacecraft been hidden? Why was there no preliminary report from Saecaraz magicians? Which Hages had been selected for hiding the alleged spies?

"You look but do not see," remarked a withered voice behind him. Tvrdy nodded and turned to meet Cejka.

"I see too much that I do not like. But you are a Rumon; you must see even more than I." Tvrdy leaned against the terrace rim once again, turning so that a lipreader would not be able to observe their speech. Cejka joined him, and both men gazed out over the man-made hills and valleys of the colony's interior.

"I see that Jamrog and his puppet Hladik have been busy obscuring the facts. But one thing is clear—there is much they are not telling about these alleged Fieri spies. Therefore, they are afraid."

"Where are they, do you think?"

"I don't know, but I will find out. Rumon rumor messengers are already at work, and our agents have been alerted; you can be sure we will find out very soon."

"And then?"

"And then we will talk. Kavan, you, and I—also Piipo, if he will come."

"You trust him?"

"Yes. We have had opportunity for much informal discussion of late. He may not join us, but he will not betray us. He can be trusted."

"What of Dey? Should we try him?"

Cejka groaned. "The Chryse are in bed with the Saecaraz. We have lost Dey, I am afraid. No matter. Hyrgo is more important anyway, and it's true they have no love for Jamrog. Eee!" Cejka shuddered. "The prospect of Jamrog as Supreme Director . . . it's abhorrent . . . unthinkable!"

Tvrdy nodded absently. "I wonder if it could be true . . . do you think? Could the intruders really be Travelers?"

Cejka's shoulders lifted in a shrug. "Who knows? Stranger things are possible, I suppose. Though I think we will find that the Fieri are perhaps becoming unusually bold—that is more likely."

"I have heard that one of them invoked the ancient name . . . Cynetics." Tvrdy glanced sharply at his friend.

"Yes, very puzzling. I don't know what to make of it. It is said the Dhogs still worship Cynetics." He shrugged. "Well, we will find out—a Rumon always finds out." Cejka looked around him; across the terrace several people were milling aimlessly. He leaned close to Tvrdy and said, "We had better leave now. We are beginning to attract attention. I think I recognize one of Hladik's so-called Invisibles over there."

"Yes. Well, contact me as soon as you find out the intruders' whereabouts. We must work quickly if we want to save the information; otherwise the psilobe will destroy it."

"Of course," said Cejka, moving off along the rim, signaling for his guides to lead him away. "I'll contact you as soon as we have found them."

Tvrdy remained gazing out over the colony's terraces for a time—until his own guides approached to lead him back to Tanais Hage.

SIXTEEN

"Where are you from, Hageman?" The man working beside him straightened, pushing back the brown hood to reveal a thin face twitching with curiosity.

"What?" Pizzle straightened too, feeling sharp stabs of pain in his lower back. They had been working for hours in the stinking muck, raking the thickened crust over to let the air get at the still-wet sludge beneath. "Ow!" He dropped his rake and rubbed his back.

"I've not seen you here before," the man said. "You're new to the Hage?"

Pizzle stared blankly at his co-worker. Other brown-hooded workers gathered around, staring and mumbling, eyes bright with questions. They waited for him to say something. He dragged a sleeve across his forehead, wondering what to say to them.

Fields of dun-colored sludge, arranged in rice-paddy style—in terraces, one above another—surrounded him on every side. Above, so high above as to form a sparkling, crystalline sky, the dome stretched its inconceivable canopoy over them, its dark-veined facets glinting as the sun struck their surface. How many times had he watched the glimmer of sunrays play across the planes of the dome?

All his life apparently.

"He makes no answer, Nendl. Why?" asked a worker, poking the man next to him. "Too proud to work the night soil?"

This caused a murmur among the others. Some nodded and others remained leaning on their wide rakes, staring at him, trying to make up their minds about him. Nendl shrugged and said, "It makes no difference. He wears the brown hood of the Jamuna. Wherever he comes from, he is one of us now. We will accept him and his pride." The thin-faced man took up his rake once more. "This field must be finished before allotment. I would not have the priests angry with us—my stomach suffers enough."

Pizzle watched this exchange and, strangely, understood what had taken place, though the words spoken were unfamiliar. Not a foreign language, exactly—the cadence and sound patterns he understood. But the words themselves were blurred, just slightly twisted so that clarity remained elusive.

He pondered this as the others turned away and went back to work, then stopped to retrieve his rake, pulling its handle from the mire and wiping his hands on his rump. He drew the tool over the crusted muck, thinking, trying to remember what had happened to him.

He had awakened after a sleep—long or short he could not tell—and had dressed himself. A red-hooded man had come for him then, and after a long journey through many winding tunnels he had been handed over to a man in a yos like his own, black with a brown hood and a wide brown stripe at the hem. He had been led out from the small, featureless room, through a low tunnel that curved as it went down. They had emerged from the tunnel onto tiers of fields. A rake had been pushed into his hand, and he had followed the other workers out into the field.

At first the acrid fumes rising from the fields of sludge had almost choked him. But he had gradually become numb to the stench, and as he watched the others he remembered what to do with the rake in his hands. Then he had fallen into the rhythm of raking, walking, raking, walking . . .

That was all he could remember. Had he always lived among the Jamuna? Where had that word come from? Oh yes, Nendl had said it. The Jamuna, yes.

Thinking about these things, the effort to remember, made his head hurt. Remembering is important, a voice deep inside told him. Yes, perhaps. Perhaps remembering was important, but it was hard work and it hurt. Forgetting was painless, and it was easier—easier to let the fuzziness that wrapped his mind in its gentle fog take away all memory.

The plaza was surrounded on three sides by brightly-colored stalls, and on the fourth by a low, ridgelike hump of grass. Beyond the plaza, stacked terraces rose up on every side, their broad, curving arcs stepping away into the distance to tower above the tall, finger-thin trees ringing the square.

Vendors hovered around the stalls, hawking their merchandise to anyone who wandered near. And although the plaza was filled with people—wandering aimlessly in groups of three or more, or sitting in clusters on the pavement—no one seemed interested in buying. All just looked politely and moved on.

Yarden, watching the thronging plaza from her place on the grassy ridge, wondered what the vendors sold in their stalls. Why did no one stop to buy? She turned to the young man sitting next to her, and asked, "Bela, will you take me down there?" She nodded toward the stalls.

Languid, long-limbed Bela, his hands clasped behind his head, raised himself up just enough to see where she meant. "Down there? Why?"

"I want to see what they sell. Take me please."

"Take you? You're free to go. You don't need my permission."

"Director Luks said—"

"*Sub*director Luks is an old mother. The Chryse go where they will and do what they please—that's how art is made. Luks and his kind will never understand." He cocked a round blue eye at her. "But you want to go?"

"Yes." Yarden bobbed her head.

"All right." Bela stood up and began ambling down toward the plaza. At the foot of the mound he paused and called back to the others, a group of fifteen or so, still gathered on the grass. "Give me a few minutes at the stalls and then come down. We'll do *Rain and Wind* for the crowds before allotment."

"Rain and wind?" Yarden asked as they walked across the saw-tooth-patterned bricks to the stalls. The speech of the people around her still sometimes confused her, but comprehension was fast returning. How could she ever have forgotten?

"It's a simple mime." He glanced at her puckered brow. "Don't worry. Just watch what we do and imitate. Nothing to it."

"Oh." Yarden accepted his reassurance and shifted her attention to the stalls. There were several of them directly ahead; tentlike structures all in different colors: red, blue, gold, violet and some in bold stripes and splotches. Each stall was open in the front and the merchandise arrayed on low shelves within.

The merchants stood wheedling before their stalls, trying to convince indifferent browsers to step inside for a closer look at their wares.

The first stall they came to offered bowls of various sizes, some ornamented and others plain. Yarden looked at the bowls quickly and then went on to the next stall, where she saw miniature tables covered with highly-polished disks arranged in formal designs. The objects seemed familiar, though she could not remember their use.

"Bela, what are they?" she whispered.

"Those? Tuebla pieces."

"A game?"

"Very good! You see?—it's all coming back. You'll be teaching *me* soon."

The vendor made a move to join them, waving his arms as if to pull them inside. Bela shook his head and pushed her along.

The next stall, blue with bright yellow splotches like sunspots, offered lengths of cloth in various colors and designs. A woman in a black yos with the sky-blue hood and single diagonal blue stripe of the Bolbe stepped up beside Yarden. "You like my cloth—I can tell. A Chryse knows good craft, seh? Here—" She lifted a length and handed it to Yarden. "Feel the quality of it. Much better than you get in allotment. You see?"

Yarden felt the cool, satiny smoothness as she ran her hands over the folds of scarlet cloth. "It's very nice," she agreed.

"Do you sew? Of course, you do—you're Chryse, after all. You could make a nice Hage robe. With your dark hair—beautiful! Or if you like . . ." The woman leaned close, whispered, "I know someone who would sew anything you wished. Very reasonable, too. Needs the work—she's trying to become a tailor."

Confusion swept over Yarden; the woman's voice became a buzz in her ears. She stared at the deep red cloth in her hands and at the vendor, feeling lost and unable to think clearly.

Bela, who had been watching the interaction closely, saw her distress and stepped in. "Can't you see that she's been in reorientation? Leave her alone!"

The woman's eyes darted from one to the other of them.

"Please," said Yarden, coming to herself again. "I—it's all right." She turned to the vendor. "I like the cloth. How much?"

Bela nodded to the woman, who withdrew a slender pen-shaped probe from the folds of her yos. "Normally fifty shares—" She glanced quickly at Bela, who shook his head, and then added, "But I think thirty would be enough."

"I'll take it," said Yarden.

The woman stepped close. "You've made a very good choice." She placed a hand on Yarden's arm and raised the probe.

Yarden saw the probe come close, its point glowing bright red. "No!" She jerked her arm from the woman's grasp and backed away.

"She just wants to read your poak, Yarden," explained Bela. "Remember? It won't hurt you."

The woman smiled. "Exactly right. I just need to see your poak for a moment. The stylus won't hurt you."

Muscles rigid, Yarden allowed the woman to raise the sleeve of her yos. The stylus came up, shining in the woman's hand, and the glowing point brushed the brown skin of Yarden's upper arm. The place where the instrument touched tingled for an instant, but that was all. She relaxed.

"You try to cheat me?" the vendor suddenly yelled, her voice becoming shrill. People strolling by the stalls turned to look.

"What's wrong?" asked Bela. "Be quiet!"

"She buys the cloth for thirty, but she has only ten shares in her poak!" She turned the blunt end of the stylus toward him so that he could read it. "What am I supposed to do for the rest?"

"Be quiet will you? A Chryse does not cheat Bolbe vendors. Here—" He held up his sleeve. "Take thirty from me. I'll buy it for her."

The woman wasted no time placing the probe against Bela's arm, saying, "It's very good cloth. It will look lovely on your Hagemate."

"Yes, yes," snapped Bela impatiently. "You remember your manners—it could be *you* who is taken for reorientation next time. I should report you to your priests for discourtesy."

"No, I'm sorry. I didn't mean anything." The cloth merchant whirled around and reached into a bundle and brought out a long, silver ribbon. "Here, a gift for you. For your beautiful hair."

Yarden accepted the gift silently. Bela took her arm and steered her from the stall to join the other members of the troupe who were now assembling in the center of the plaza. "A hair ribbon, seh? Very nice."

Yarden folded the bundle of scarlet cloth over her arm. "Thank you, Bela. I—"

He cut her off, saying, "Those phat-eating drones of Luks!—they release you with only ten shares. Their heads are full of night soil! How do they expect a person to live on only ten shares?"

"I will pay you back," Yarden offered.

"Forget it. I wanted to do it. Besides," he gave her a broad smile and an exaggerated wink, "maybe you will wear your new Hage robe for me when you finish it, seh?" He laughed. Yarden smiled too and realized that she was very deep in Bela's debt—just how deep she was only beginning to discover.

SEVENTEEN

He knew that he was being watched. Constantly. But in two—or was it three?—days of captivity, he had not seen a single guard, and none of the people he *had* seen impressed Orion Treet. All were drably dressed and mouse shy. They watched him warily when they came into his cell—the barrier field across the door erased any doubt that he was indeed a prisoner and not a guest—and left with relief visible on their silent faces. He spoke to them, but they did not answer, nor did they seem to understand what he said. Their eyes remained dull; the spark that ignited intelligence failed to catch.

His food, brought once a day and left in bowls, though satisfying enough, was bland—vegetables, mostly raw, without seasonings or spices: daikon, yucca, chayote, adzuki beans, nori, and a cheesy substance that looked like tofu. No meat of any kind.

The water, in a wide-mouthed jug, tasted flat and quite stale, with that metallic flavor water takes on when left standing overnight in an open container. Treet drank it anyway when he got thirsty enough.

Dull fare and stale water aside, the simple fact that he recognized most of the food he was offered gave him a tremendous psychological boost. At least his diet was not against him; here was a common bond, however tenuous, with Earth.

Between feedings he sat on the bed, walked around the pie-shaped room swinging his arms, did a few light exercises to keep the blood flowing, and sang rude songs at the top of his lungs. All this failed, however, to keep him at the peak of mental alertness. Treet was used to a more stimulating existence, and wondered whether he could last any length of time in solitary confinement without losing his mind altogether.

Therefore, he made the most of every opportunity to express his fundamental dissatisfaction with the terms of his confinement. Every time a visitor came into his cell—usually a food bearer, or the dingy little woman who brought clean bedding and fluffed up the rumpled bed every day—Treet did his best to strike up a conversation. Never did he get a word out of any of them.

Obviously, he thought, they had been instructed not to communicate with the foreign devil. That could well be—he sensed a certain fear when any of them entered his presence. He wondered what they had been told about him.

Treet was sitting on his bed, munching a crunchy slice of jicama root, when the incessant insect buzz of the door's barrier field cut out—a signal that someone was coming to see him. It was still too early for food service, and the maid had been in to change the sheets hours ago. This was something else then. Treet's pulse quickened.

Presently he heard footsteps in the adjoining room, and two men stepped into his cell. For a moment the two men merely looked at him, but from their long, unguarded glances Treet guessed that they were of a different order than the serving people he had met thus far. He returned their frank stares with one he hoped was equally frank, and remained sitting on the bed.

Both men were wearing the black kimonos they all wore, but these had white sleeves and red hoods. From the way they stood—hands loosely at their sides, feet wide apart—Treet guessed they were prepared for anything. No doubt they had weapons concealed in the folds of their clothing.

Treet had no thought of escape. Where would he run to? His only hope was that he might be allowed to make contact with someone in a position to help him. There had, he felt, been a monstrous misunderstanding at the landing field—to put it mildly. If he could only make someone understand that he was simply a traveler who had come in peace with greetings from their friends back on Earth, Treet was certain the difficulty could be cleared up straightaway.

What he did not care to admit—although it was a thought seldom long from his mind—was that something had obviously happened to the colony. Something very wrong.

The guard nearest him said something in an authoritarian tone of voice. Treet recognized some of the words, but they were changed subtly—as if the language had undergone a shift, though a shift toward or away from what, he couldn't say. The words were smudged and blurred, slurred and warped in unexpected ways, although still vaguely recognizable.

As Treet made no move to get up or answer, the man repeated himself, raising his voice. It came to Treet then what his visitor's speech was like: it was like listening to a foreigner trying to speak your mother tongue. A few words came out nearly right, others did not; the sounds were all stretched and puckered.

Treet addressed the men, keeping his tone flat and even, though his heart beat a tattoo in his throat. "I am Orion Treet. There has been a mistake. I mean no one any harm. Please believe that. I am unarmed, and I wish to talk to your superior."

The two men looked at each other. One shrugged—it was such a human gesture that Treet knew they shared some kind of common ancestry. But what had happened to these people?

"Come." The red-hood nearest him gestured toward the door.

Treet understood both word and gesture perfectly. He slid off the bed, stood, and walked toward the doorway. The second red-hood stopped him with a hand placed against his chest, waved a wand over him front and back—a weapons detector of some kind, guessed Treet—and then led the way through the narrow doorway and the connecting room beyond. Treet followed, and the other man came along a few paces behind.

Tanais Director Tvrdy reclined in a suspension bed which undulated in slow ripples to the soft music drifting into his sleep chamber. Though his eyes were closed and his hands lay folded over his chest, he was far from sleep. He was waiting and piecing together a plan by which he meant to visit the captive intruder being held somewhere in the stacked mazes of Saecaraz Hage.

This bit of information had come to him earlier in the day. It confirmed what he had already guessed—that Supreme Director Rohee had not, as he intimated in session, placed all of the intruders in Hage: one had been kept. And this one Tvrdy meant to interview personally.

The Rumon rumor messengers had done their work well. Thanks to Cejka's network of informants, he now knew the whereabouts of the other three intruders as well. One had been placed among the Jamuna, another with the Nilokerus, and the third with the Chryse. The Jamuna and Chryse captives had actually been spotted in public.

Jamrog was wasting no time in covering up the affair. But why cover it up at all? What was there about these intruders that demanded these unprecedented measures? Who were they? Why were they being hidden in Hage? Why run such a risk? Why not simply destroy the spies? Why announce their presence to the Threl and then refuse to allow anyone else to talk to them? Why? Why? Why?

Tvrdy meant to find out.

"Director . . ." Pradim, the Tanais Director's guide, stepped quietly into the sleep chamber, his fingers weaving the air.

"I am not asleep," replied Tvrdy, getting up. "What is it?"

"A message—" Pradim turned his empty eye-sockets upon his master.

"And is the messenger still here?"

"Yes. Shall I bring her?"

"No, have her wait in the quiet room. I wish to question her."

The guide departed silently as the Tanais leader drew on a shimmering green Hage robe, then stepped over to a terminal set in the wall. "Systems check," he said softly. "Quiet room."

The screen instantly flicked on, presenting a schematic of the quiet room's webwork of anti-eavesdropping sensors. All were working and none showed signs of tampering. A second later the screen went blank, and Tvrdy strode out of the room.

The messenger was sitting on a cushion in the quiet room's pit. She jumped up and gave a quick, stiff-armed bow. "Cejka sends his greetings," she said.

This was a code phrase which meant that Cejka wished a full report of the proceedings. "You may give my regards to your Director," replied Tvrdy. This meant that Tvrdy intended to contact Cejka personally. Tanais Director joined the messenger in the pit and lowered himself to a cushion. "You may sit."

"I am hearing many interesting things from Saecaraz section . . ." the woman began, glancing around quickly.

"This is a quiet room," offered Tvrdy. "We can speak freely." The woman relaxed; a hand went to her hood and drew it back. She was young and sharp-eyed. No doubt one of Cejka's best. "You have located the intruder within Saecaraz?"

"Yes. I have not seen him, but I talked with the old mother who changes the bedding. He is deep in Threl High Chambers—on a level called Greenways. This, I am told, is near the Supreme Director's personal quarters."

"So! Just as I suspected!" Tvrdy rubbed his hands together very slowly. "Now then, how is the prisoner held?"

"Unidor."

"No chemical restraints?"

"Possible, but unlikely. The prisoner has been observed walking about his cell; he talks to the food bearers—although they have all been instructed to refrain from speaking to him. He also—" She hesitated.

"Yes? Tell me."

"He *sings,* Director."

"Does he indeed?"

"Several of the Saecaraz have heard him when they bring his food. They all talk about it."

"And what have they been told of his identity?" Tvrdy leaned forward, listening intently. He was getting good information from this messenger.

"They have been told that he is a close relative of one of the Threl leader's Hagemates, and has rejected reorientation, thus suffering regrettable mental trauma."

"I see. And do they believe this?"

The messenger shrugged. "They ask no questions."

"Has the prisoner been moved?"

"No."

"Visited?"

"No, but he is under continuous remote surveillance."

"As I would expect." Director Tvrdy nodded to himself. "I have only one more question. In your opinion, would it be possible to steal the prisoner or meet with him?"

The young woman blinked, taken aback to have her opinion asked. But she answered without hesitation. "No, it is not possible to remove the prisoner from his cell without alerting the Nilokerus—there are two at all times in the room adjoining. It may be possible to visit him briefly, if disguise were used effectively and the guards distracted."

The Tanais leader stood abruptly. "Well done, Rumon! I will see to it that one hundred shares are added to your allotment from now on."

"It is not necessary—" The woman rose quickly, replacing the hood as she stood.

"We reward our people, messenger. You have performed a difficult and dangerous assignment. Accept a leader's gratitude."

"Thank you, Director."

In a moment the messenger was gone. Tvrdy sat deep in thought until his guide entered the room. "Does the Director wish anything?"

"Yes, Pradim, contact Cejka at once. I will meet him in Hage—designation seven-six." At once Tvrdy rose and stripped off his robe. He moved to a cabinet standing against a wall, pressed the lockplate with his thumb, removing a blue-hooded yos from the drawer as it slid out, and began donning his disguise.

EIGHTEEN

Treet stood before a flinty old man who watched him carefully with hooded eyes. He had a sharp beak of a nose, and the wattles beneath his chin wobbled when he moved his head. Across his lap the old man held a stubby, curved broadknife affixed to a long ornamented handle—obviously a symbol of some official function. Judging from the extreme deference paid him by the guards—who had retired to a far corner—Treet guessed the old geezer was a high mucky-muck of Empyrion leadership.

The room also betokened high status: a great, round cylinder with a ceiling that arched dramatically overhead. Dark, richly patterned hangings draped the walls all around, and the ceiling as well, so the effect was that of entering a sultan's tent.

The sultan himself had been waiting for him on his throne—a tall, high-backed chair mounted on a raised pedestal. Treet had been led to stand before this seat, in a circle embossed on the floor. The moment he had stepped into the circle, the faint telltale whizz of the barrier field told him he was a prisoner once more.

The old man spoke. "I am Sirin Rohee, Supreme Director of the Threl and all Empyrion." He paused and nodded toward Treet encouragingly. "Do you understand?"

Treet heard several words he thought he recognized; but with the old man's wavering voice coming through the faint distortion of the barrier field, he could not be certain. Still, he assumed he had been addressed in some kind of introduction, so offered one of his own, speaking up loudly. "I am Orion Treet. I am a traveler. I have come from Cynetics."

Treet pronounced the last word distinctly, hoping for some effect. The last time he'd uttered that word, it had caused a considerable sensation. This time, however, the consequence was more subdued than at the landing field; the old man—Rohee, was that a name he'd heard among the barely intelligible syllables?—merely nodded knowingly and pursed his lips as if he'd expected just that sort of response.

The guards—the two who had brought him and two others who were waiting in the chamber with the old leader—were slightly more demonstrative, murmuring loudly to themselves. Treet kept his attention on Rohee and tried to look both impressive and nonthreatening at the same time. The effort taxed his limited repertoire of facial expressions.

"Why have you come?" Rohee asked simply.

Treet blinked in mild surprises: he'd gotten all of that speech. By concentrating on the pattern of the speech rather than the words themselves, he could apparently understand simple sentences. He tried to couch his reply in simple words of single syllables. "I have been sent."

Rohee looked puzzled. He lifted the broad blade in his hands and gestured toward a guard. The man departed silently, returning only moments later with three others. These were dressed in silver-striped kimonos like Treet's, but each had a large silver medallion that looked like a two-pronged, wavy lightning bolt on a thick chain around his neck. They stared at Treet openly as they approached, then acknowledged their leader with a quick, stiff-armed bow. The three stopped at a point midway between the throne and the prisoner.

Interpreters? wondered Treet. The three looked more like judges. Or inquisitors.

Supreme Director Rohee flashed the curving blade at the foremost of the three. He turned toward Treet and asked in slow, deliberate tones, as one would address a child, "What do you know of the Fieri?"

The last word threw Treet. He shrugged and replied, "I do not understand."

The three looked at one another. "Fieri," the first one repeated. "Tell us."

"I can tell you nothing." Amazing! thought Treet. It wasn't so difficult to talk to these people once you caught the knack. Emboldened by success, he added, "I am a traveler. I have been sent here by Cynetics."

Again the word caused a slight sensation. The three inquisitors grew round-eyed and stared at one another. They put their heads together in conference and mumbled. Rohee looked on, a smile faintly spreading his lips. There was a quality in his expression Treet couldn't quite name—what was it?

While the inquisitors debated the implications of his last utterance, Treet studied the Empyrion leader in an attempt at unraveling that enigmatic smile. He was still trying to decipher it when he was addressed again.

"Speak to us of Cynetics," said the first inquisitor. No doubt he was the official spokesman of the group. Treet noticed that when the man spoke, he seemed to be consciously forming his mouth around the words.

Treet spread his hands—what could he tell them that they didn't already know? "What do you want—" He halted as the implications of the statement jolted him. They didn't know about Cynetics! At least, they didn't know it in the same way that he did, and they were testing him.

Trouble was, *he* didn't remember precisely either; it belonged to that hazy confusion on the other side of that mental fog blank. Wanting nothing more than to be left alone to ponder this bit of information, Treet frowned at the inquisitors, who were waiting for an answer. He sensed that to disappoint them would make things much more difficult for himself in the days to come.

"I can tell you," began Treet importantly, relying solely on bluff and instinct, "that Cynetics is very great, very powerful— more powerful than ordinary men can imagine." Treet did not know if they were getting all of this, but he continued, liking the way his speech sounded. "Cynetics commands whole nations and rules the lives of millions. There is no other as great as Cynetics."

There, thought Treet, let them puzzle over that. He had intentionally—instinctively?—invoked the storyteller's tone of high pomp and consequence. The dodge appeared to be working, for the three inquisitors stared awestricken.

He glanced quickly at Rohee—the man's enigmatic smile had increased; he was positively beaming. Instantly the riddle was solved: the old coot was proud of his prize! He is pleased that I have stumped the experts, thought Treet; he was hoping I'd astound them, and I did.

From that moment, Treet placed his hopes of survival on the old fossil. He smiled back at the Empyrion leader as much as to say, *See, we are alike, you and I; we should be friends.*

• • • • • •

Nendl waited patiently, resting on one of the many mush-room-shaped projections ringing the open-air booth. Pizzle sat next to him, dimly aware of what was going on, yet anxious because he could not remember more clearly. They waited as, one by one, their fellow workers—Hagemen, Nendl called them—approached the booth.

"It's allotment," Nendl explained. "You'll remember."

When all the others had gone forward and hurried off again, Nendl rose and went to the booth. Pizzle followed. The men in the booth wore brown-hooded yoses like his own, but each had a large bronze medal across his chest: a double-ended arrow bent into an ellipse. The medal hung from a heavy chain around their necks, and Pizzle understood upon seeing the symbol that these were Jamuna priests.

"Yes?" asked a priest, looking up. Before Nendl could answer a second priest said, "Allotment is over."

"This one is new to our Hage," explained Nendl.

The priests frowned. One of them bent over a terminal and asked, "Name?"

Nendl nudged Pizzle, who stared for a moment, terror rising in him. *My name! What's my name?*

"Well?" snapped the priest. "How do you expect to claim your shares if you don't give us your name?"

"He has recently undergone reorientation," explained Nendl. "He has not perhaps been issued a new name."

"I see," grumped the priest. He nodded to one of the others. "What do you have there?"

The second priest gazed into a glowing screen, tapped a few keys, and then answered, "There are no new reassignments in the records."

"Erased most likely," replied the first priest. "Come back next allotment and we will see."

"Please," said Nendl quietly, "he cannot wait until next allotment. How can he live without his shares? How can he work?"

The first priest frowned even more deeply. "All right, all right. Put him down as—"

"Pizzle!"

The priests looked at him. "What did you say?" asked the first.

"My name is Pizzle . . . I think."

"Pizol?" The priest stared into the screen and shook his head slowly. "Nothing under that name."

"Enter it," commanded the first priest, and the other did as he was told. "We'll give him standard shares for a first-order gleaner."

Pizzle thought this sounded fair enough. He nodded, but Nendl protested gently. "He's worked very hard—he's one of my order, not a wastehandler."

The priest glared. "You challenge our authority?"

"You know what is best, Hage priest. I merely point out that he is a good worker because I know that you are fair. It is well-known that the priests of Jamuna Hage reward hard work generously."

"True enough," agreed the priest. "I will make this a lesson to you," he said to Pizzle. "Your allotment is fifty shares."

"Thank you, Hage priest," said Nendl, nudging Pizzle with his elbow.

"Thank you," Pizzle repeated. The priest picked up a glowing stylus and took Pizzle by the arm, raising his sleeve. He rubbed the point of the stylus over the skin of his upper arm.

"There, tell your Hagemen of the generosity of Jamuna priests. We take care of our own."

"Of course, Hage priest," replied Nendl as they backed away quickly. The priests grunted and began closing up the booth.

Nendl led them back along the wide, brick-paved walkway. Odd, flat-topped trees lined this winding boulevard; here and there the mouths of tunnels opened, and stairs led down to the other levels. Once out of sight of the booth, Nendl said, "Not bad, Pizol. They gave you two days' shares. Don't think that will happen again, though. The Jamuna Hage priests are fair enough as priests go, but they are priests all the same, and not often given to extravagance—unless it is their own poak."

"Fifty shares," said Pizzle. "You must help me, Nendl."

The thin-faced man stopped and faced him, placing strong, callused hands on Pizzle's shoulders. "We are Hagemen, are we not? You ask my help, and I will give it. You have fifty shares, and I have twenty-five from today's work. If we put them together, we can eat well tonight. What do you say?"

"I am very hungry, Nendl."

"So am I. Then it is settled. We'll put our shares together

and eat like Directors! I have no Hagemate at present, so you can stay with me. My kraam is not so big, but there is room for you if you do not mind sharing a bed. Later, when you have been in Hage a year, you can petition the priests for a kraam of your own. If one becomes available before that—so much the better."

Off they went, Nendl leading the way, fatigue suddenly forgotten. He led Pizzle down one of the nearby tunnels, and they emerged on a lower level where tiny shops, amassed in tiers and joined by flying walkways, lined the broad, circuitous avenue. Crowds of people—almost all of them dressed in Jamuna brown—pushed along the avenue and swamped the walkways. The din of voices rang from the ribs of the roof far above: vendors haggling over prices, patrons whining and wheedling, people arguing—arguing and doing business nonetheless.

"Ah, the Jamuna markets. No Hage has a more lively marketplace, I'm told. Let's go collect our dole and then—" He smiled broadly, revealing crooked teeth. "Then we will begin!"

They hurried through moving knots of people toward a yellow-topped kiosk standing in the middle of the avenue. The waves of shoppers broke around it, passing on either side. "Here it is," said Nendl. "Good, we won't have to wait. Come on."

He pushed Pizzle up to the kiosk. "Dole," said Nendl.

"Name?" asked a fat, bored clerk in the green-and-yellow yos of the Hyrgo.

"Nendl," the Jamuna replied. "And Pizol."

The clerk consulted a screen. "I have you, but not him." He reached down and placed a parcel on the ledge of the kiosk.

Nendl took up the cloth-wrapped parcel and replied, "He's been in reorientation. Check with the priests if you don't believe me."

The clerk grunted and placed another package on the ledge. "There. I believe you."

Pizzle took the package, and Nendl pulled him away. "What's inside?" he asked.

"Some coffee, a little tofu, a bonaito or maybe a jicama, flatbread if we are lucky. That's all. But we can buy the rest. Here—a cheese shop!" Nendl elbowed his way into the press at the entrance to the cheese shop. "What kind today?" he asked.

A Jamuna next to him replied, "What difference? It all tastes the same."

"White and red," said someone close by. "And they are gouging as usual—three shares per kil."

"Could be worse," sighed Nendl. When his turn came, he ordered half a kil of each, stuffing them inside his yos. He pushed Pizol up to the vendor, who brushed his arm with a poak reader.

They moved on along the avenue, Pizzle's head swiveling as he went, trying to take it all in. Everywhere he looked, people crowded and hurried. "Is it always like this?" he wondered aloud.

"Only after allotment. We have come late, but it's just as well. The stocks are holding up, and the crowds aren't so bad." Nendl dived into another throng surrounding a meat shop. He came back holding two small, plump, birdlike carcasses. He handed one to Pizzle and tucked the other into his yos.

"What is it?" Pizzle looked at the naked pink flesh.

"Cheken. A delicacy, believe me."

"Chee-ken," repeated Pizzle, nodding. "I remember chee-ken."

"Good! It's coming back!" Nendl pulled him away again, and they continued on down the avenue. "Now to the bake stall. I think there is a second-order bake stall further down. They are said to supply the Directors' tables. We'll see."

Pizzle walked as one in a dream, marveling at all he saw, the strangeness of it, and yet the eerie familiarity. He had been here before, seen these things, walked this avenue . . . why couldn't he remember?

Sitting in Nendl's kraam before a small brazier filled with black fuel pellets, the disjointed carcasses of the two chekens sizzling on the glowing coals, Pizzle listened to his host describe his life.

"You would do well to listen to an old man," said Nendl. "I may not be a Hage magician, but I know much and have seen much more."

"You're not old, Nendl."

"Old enough! But listen, I don't know what you did to deserve your punishment—your reorientation—and you don't have to tell me. I don't care. Probably it was nothing anyway. The stinking Invisibles, called such because of their cunning and stealth, watch everyone; and what they can't see, they imagine. It's all the same to them—they're scum."

"Scum," Pizzle repeated. "But you're not. You're not scum, Nendl; you're my friend." Pizzle's head felt mushy from the sweet liquor he was drinking freely. He felt light and airy, like a cloud expanding from its center. He beamed at his host proudly. "You helped me."

"I helped you, yes. Do you know why?" He leaned close even though there was not another soul in the filthy, cramped dwelling.

Pizzle leaned toward him. "Why?"

"Because I *know* someone."

"Oh!" Pizzle nodded, much impressed. "You know someone."

"Someone important. He said I was to watch for you and help you if I could. He said you would be coming. So I watched for you, and when you came I helped you."

"Thank you, Nendl."

"Shh!" Nendl cautioned. "They can hear everything. They can see through walls." He too had been nursing from the souile flask liberally and felt like talking. "But I don't care. I know someone. I am protected. If I have any trouble, I have someplace to go. I will be safe."

Pizzle nodded, his head wobbling loosely. "The cheken smells good. I'm hungry."

"It's just about done." Nendl reached over and flipped a few pieces over. "Have some more cheese." He offered a chunk to Pizzle and bit off one for himself. He gazed at his guest thoughtfully and said, "You know what the rumor messengers are saying about you?"

"No." Pizzle put the cheese in his mouth and chewed.

"I have heard rumors of Fieri spies," said Nendl, winking.

"Spies."

"Do you know anything about them?"

Pizzle shook his head slowly.

Nendl reached into the brazier and gingerly handed him a piece of cheken. "Eat! It's good." He picked out a piece for himself and licked his fingers. "Directors don't eat any better than this!"

"It's good," echoed Pizzle happily. The sound of chewing and lip smacking overcame conversation for a few minutes.

When they had finished the first two pieces and were well

into a third, Nendl raised his head and looked at his guest thoughtfully. "If you were a Fieri, I know you wouldn't tell me—would you?"

Pizzle considered this and then shrugged. "I don't know. Am I a Fieri?"

Nendl went sly; his eyes narrowed. "You might be. Then again you might not. I don't expect you'd tell me if I didn't tell you something." He thought for a moment. "I will tell you something, Pizol. Would you like that? I'll tell you something, and then you tell me something. What do you say to that?"

Pizzle nodded readily. "I'd like that. You tell me something, and I'll tell you something."

"A secret," added Nendl.

"Yes, a secret."

The Jamuna recycler leaned close and lowered his voice to a whisper. "Nendl is my Hagename. I'll tell you my private name, but you must promise never to tell anyone else—especially a priest or magician. Swear it?"

"I swear."

"Trabant take your soul?"

Pizzle nodded, eyes growing wide.

With a quick sidewards glance, Nendl put his forehead close to Pizzle's. "My private name is Urkal." He smiled grimly and sat back.

"Urkal."

"Shh! Never repeat it! If a lipreader saw it, he would tell a priest—or worse, an Invisible—and they'd have power over me. If I didn't do what they told me, they'd curse me and I'd be without a guide through the Twin Houses; I would never become immortal." He looked eagerly at his guest. "Now it's your turn. Tell me your secret."

Pizzle's face scrunched up in thought. What secret could he tell his host? He didn't have any that he knew about. "Ahh," he said at last. "My name is . . . Asquith." How had that come to him?

Disappointment rearranged Nendl's features in a scowl. "Askwith," he replied flatly. That wasn't the secret he wanted to hear. "Is that a Fieri name?" he asked, thinking himself very smart.

"I don't know. Is it?"

"I have never heard it before—it must be. That means *you* are a Fieri," he deduced with satisfaction.

"If you say I am. Is that good?"

"Bad, more like. Fieri are hated here."

"Why?"

"I don't know. Some say they are trying to destroy us; others say other things. Who knows? The Directors know. Ahh, but I know someone too. Someone who will help me if trouble comes. I'm safe. You're safe too—as long as you stay with me." He took a long swig on the souile flask and passed it to Pizzle. "Drink! And eat—we have more cheken!" He took another piece from the brazier, licked his fingers, and smiled contentedly. "It's been a very good day, Hageman Pizol. A very good day."

NINETEEN

Yarden sat in a corner by herself, watching the others. They chattered to one another and laughed as they watched a holovision program calling out the names of the Hagemen they recognized. Bela's kraam, a flattened oval room with a low, gently rippled ceiling, lit with soft amber dish-shaped lights set in smooth, buff-colored walls, was warm and stuffy with so many people in it—ten others besides Bela and herself. But no one else seemed to mind. They lolled on overlarge silken cushions on the floor, bodies intertwined casually, dipping fruit from a large red bowl, and laughing.

"Among the Chryse, Bela's kraam is well-known," he had boasted to her with a wink as they walked along an arching aerial walkway far above terraced green fields and small, dome-shaped dwellings—one of Empyrion's preserves, Bela had told her, though what was preserved below she could not tell. "To-night will be all laughter. You'll see."

Laughter yes, but Yarden did not share in it. After she had been introduced, she had quietly edged away to her cushion in the corner where she was content just to observe the others, as they were content to ignore her. She suspected that her presence was perceived as an intrusion—at least by the other women. She was a stranger, and therefore a potential rival for the men's attention.

So she sat alone, schooling herself on the manners of her new friends, watching them for clues to custom and behavior, alert to the nuances of speech and action that revealed the inner person. Outwardly passive—all but immobile—inwardly her mind whirled with activity: searching, sorting, cataloging, storing each minute observation and detail of her surroundings. This felt right; it was something that belonged to her, that she recognized as her own. At the same time, this intense mental activity puzzled her. Where did I learn this? she wondered. Haven't I always lived here?

No doubt her feelings of vagueness, of forgetting, had to do with the *reorientation* Bela spoke of. Whatever that was, it stood like a barrier between her present and her past, blocking out all memory on the other side. Yet, at odd moments now and then, she caught glimpses of another life—intimations that there had been a life on the other side of the barrier much different than the one she now knew.

"You are lost, cherimoya," said a voice above her.

Yarden looked up to see Bela standing over her. "I am just a little tired," she replied. Yes, tired—so many new things to observe and comprehend exhausts one's soul.

"Come then. Bed with me," he said, offering his hand. He smiled. "I am tired too."

Yarden caught the implication of his words, but was not alarmed by it. "Where do you sleep?" The kraam, as far as she could see, was but a single large room.

Bela laughed. "Wherever I like; it makes no difference."

"Do you all sleep together?"

"Sometimes." He shrugged. "Tonight I want to sleep with you."

The directness of his approach confused her; perhaps she misunderstood. "For pleasure?"

"Yes." Bela sank down beside her, grinning. "What else?"

Yarden peered back at him, not quite sure what her response should be. Certainly Bela was an attractive man; she could see that he would likely be a sensitive lover. She felt herself drawn to him, yet repulsed at the same time. At any rate, she doubted whether she could make love in a room full of strangers.

She was saved from having to make an answer by a clamor which arose across the room. "Bela!" someone shouted. "Bela! Dera is here with the flash!"

Bela looked away. A tall, flame-haired woman with large dark eyes and a shimmering yos that matched the color of her hair stood in the doorway. "Dera, my delight!" Bela called, jumping up. "What have you brought for us?"

She came to him, stepping over the knot of people on the floor in front of the holoscreen. Yarden watched as the two exchanged a lingering kiss. The woman's long fingers played in Bela's dark curls.

When they separated, Dera reached into the folds of her yos and drew out a black bag. Bela took the bag and hefted it, then opened it and put his nose in. "Ohh!" He rolled his eyes. "For this you will be made immortal."

Others had gathered around, grabbing at the bag. "Share it, Bela. What are you waiting for?"

"Patience!" He lifted the bag away from them. "You will have yours. Dera has brought enough to soak a priest."

He turned to Yarden, knelt, and held out the bag. "You first. You have been longest without it."

Yarden reached into the bag and withdrew several flat, dark pellets the size of beans. They were highly polished and slightly oily to the touch. "What is it?"

"Flash," said a curly-headed man in a brilliant, flower-printed yos. They all watched Yarden, smiling encouragingly. "Go ahead, you'll soon remember." The others laughed, and the man snatched the bag away. Attention now turned to the flash-bag as it was passed quickly around.

Yarden gazed at the lozenges in her hand. They had a faint aroma, like roasted nuts. She glanced up to see Bela still watching her. "Flash?" she asked.

"It has other names," he said, taking one of the pellets. "Each Hage has its own. The Hyrgo call it bliss beans, and among the Bolbe it is known as third hand. Don't ask me why, but that's what they call it."

"What does it do?"

"Here, I'll show you." He placed the seed between his front teeth and, tilting his head back slightly, bit down hard. The seed cracked, and a thick syrup oozed out. He closed his eyes and sucked his lips shut, and in a moment his features softened. When he looked at Yarden again, his eyes were muzzy and unfocused.

"Try it," he said, then laughed with sudden giddiness, rolling on his back. Instantly Dera was on top of him, a seed between her teeth. She bit it and then kissed him, sharing the syrup between the two of them. They came up laughing moments later, and then rolled into another embrace.

Yarden looked around her. The man in the flower-print yos was giggling loudly as he twirled around, his arms outstretched. Someone put a seed in his mouth and he bit it, then fell full-length backwards onto two women who were caressing each other. They broke apart, laughing, and began pulling off his yos.

Others were cuddled together, working each other out of

their clothes, naked limbs writhing. Music had begun playing: a light, drifty sound like wind in the trees or water slipping over stone in a tide pool.

Yarden put a seed in her mouth and bit down hard. The syrup splashed onto her tongue, and she tasted smoked honey. With the taste came a rush of pure pleasure—a flash which burst over her and then ebbed away, taking all thought, all tension, all desire with it. Her first thought was, "More! I need more!"

She quickly popped another seed in her mouth, bit, and felt time coiling around her like a silken rope. Her mind reeled in the sheer joy of flowing forever through endless time, flowing like music, rich and many-toned and deep as an ocean.

A picture floated up into her mind of a vast, limitless sea of gold and green. She saw herself floating beneath gentle waves, sinking, drifting. The water was warm; the current tugged her along past long ribbons of undulating seaweed. Down and down and down.

Yarden began to cry; tears rolled over her lashes to splash down her cheeks. The picture, she knew, was from her other life—the life she could not remember anymore. She felt that other life slipping further away beyond her reach. The tears fell heavy with strong, sweet sorrow. She took another seed in her mouth and let the waves carry her away.

Director Hladik rode the lift down toward Cavern level, the lowest level of Nilokerus section. Slanting bands of light flickered over his face, each marking a terrace or kraam level. Four levels above Cavern, he slowed the liftplate's descent, dropping the last two levels at quarter-speed and braking hard as Cavern came up. It took quick reflexes and an utter disregard for safety, but Hladik enjoyed overriding the automatic controls.

Hladik felt the momentary tug of gravity in his stomach and stepped through the capsule door, striding out into a rock-cut chamber before the lift had come to a complete stop. "Fertig!" he shouted, his voice echoing back from the empty spaces.

He waited, then marched across the chamber to the entrance of a tunnel, switching off the unidor at the console pedestal before the tunnel entrance. Lights blinked on as he stepped in, faint green lights at foot level illuminating the tunnel floor. Along the sides, a red light above each one, cell doors yawned, their unidors opaqued.

At the end of the tunnel, the Nilokerus Director halted before a rock wall. He reached into the folds of his yos and produced a sonic key, pressed it, and waited. From behind the wall came the sound of muffled hydraulics, and the wall tilted up and away. He ducked under the receding wall and entered the hidden room.

A guard in the white and red of the Nilokerus snapped to attention, giving a quick, stiff-armed bow, eyes to the floor. "Where's Fertig?" Hladik demanded, barely acknowledging the salute with an impatient wave of his hand.

"Subdirector Fertig is with the prisoner," the guard replied.

"Have the physicians been summoned?"

"Yes, Hage Leader. They are with him as well."

Hladik nodded, and the guard stepped aside. He pressed his sonic key, and the portion of the wall behind the guard rolled outward. Stepping over a puddle of water, he slipped through the opening quickly.

"Director Hladik, I—" began Fertig, glancing up as his superior entered.

"Will he live?" Hladik asked, moving to the side of a suspension bed. He looked down at the gray-faced body in the bed.

"It is too early to tell," replied Fertig uneasily.

Hladik turned on him with a fierce scowl. The Subdirector swallowed hard and added, "We may have lost him, Hage Leader."

"Does Jamrog know?"

"No, he has not been notified." The Subdirector glanced uncertainly at his superior. "Do you wish it?"

"I do not!" Hladik snapped. "I will deal with this personally."

A physician, a heavy-shouldered woman with short, white hair and sharp blue eyes, mumbled something and Hladik glowered at her, saying, "Speak up, Ernina. I didn't hear you."

The woman frowned, her lips creased in wrinkles of sharp disapproval. "I merely wondered how long you will persist in killing your prisoners and then expecting us to revive the corpses?"

Few people dared speak to a Director so frankly, and ordinarily Hladik would have had the offender removed for reorientation without a second thought. But he just glared at the flinty physician across the bed; hers was a mind much too valuable to throw away lightly. Still, it didn't do to allow first- and second-order Hagemen to hear her address him like a wastehandler.

"You question my directives, physician?" he growled.

"Not at all, Hage Leader," she replied. Her tone mocked him. "I merely point out that if you wish us to save your sorry experiments, you must give us more to work with. This—" She gestured helplessly toward the body before her. "This wretch is almost beyond hope—even for me."

"But he can be saved?" asked Hladik. He glanced down at the body; the man's straw-colored hair was matted and tangled, his eyes and cheeks sunken, his jaw slack. If he still breathed, there was no outward indication.

Ernina, a sixth-order physician, the best of the Nilokerus, shrugged. "We will see. But I warn you, Haldik, one day soon you will go too far in this conditioning of yours and there will be nothing left to save."

Hladik accepted the warning; it was sincere. But for the benefit of the others looking on, he replied, "Perhaps reorientation is not so unpleasant as we might suppose. Would you care to find out for yourself, physician?"

She tossed off the warning with a shrug. "Hmph!" Then she turned to the other physicians gathered around her. "Have you taken root? Remove him. We can do nothing in this dank tomb. Get him started on the aura equalizer, and one of you go take an offering to the Hage priest for a healing benefice of ten clear days. Tell him we must have no astral interference for at least ten days. Make certain he understands. Tell him the directive comes from Hage Leader Hladik—that ought to get his attention."

Hladik nodded sourly as the physicians pushed the bed away. Ernina stood with her hands on her wide hips, her blue eyes snapping.

The Director grumbled, "Out with it. What else is bothering you?"

"When will you learn that you cannot carve human flesh to fit your ridiculous power schemes? The mind-body exists in a tenuous balance. Upset that balance and the entire astral entity is threatened." She gazed at Hladik unflinchingly. "I know you think me a prattling old mother, but mark me well, Hladik: Cynetics will be served. Your tinkering will weaken us all."

"Bah!" Nilokerus Director made a face and dismissed her with a quick gesture. "Just make certain this prisoner survives—that's all I care about. I want twice-a-day reports until he recovers. Understood?"

Ernina inclined her head stiffly. "Of course, Hage Leader. When have I ever disobeyed you?" She smiled in grim satisfaction and swept past him with a swish of her red-hooded yos.

Hladik watched her go. "One day, woman," he muttered, "you'll go too far."

TWENTY

In a kraam on the Sunwalk level in the Bolbe section of Empyrion, Tvrdy, Cejka, and Piipo—each dressed in the blue-hooded yoses of the Bolbe—debated the wisdom of trying to contact the Fieri spies. They had been talking for nearly two hours, but were now getting to the heart of the matter.

"You oppose the plan, Piipo," said Tvrdy, careful to keep his voice even. "Yet, you do not put forth a plan of your own."

"Don't judge me hastily," replied Piipo, his small, close-set eyes flashing across the table. "I have my own reasons for urging caution."

"We're all for caution," said Tvrdy, "but—"

Cejka cut in. "You have information?"

Piipo nodded slowly.

"What have you heard? Tell us."

The Hyrgo Hage Director's eyes flicked from one to the other of his co-conspirators. He hesitated, weighing, making up his mind.

"Tell us now!"

"Wait, Tvrdy," cautioned Cejka. "Give him time." To Piipo he added, "It isn't our way to pressure anyone, and we do not use threats, but time is short. If you have any information that can help us, then tell us. Whether or not you join the Cabal, we—"

Piipo held up his hand, palm outward. "I understand. If I hesitate, it is only because my reply will bind Hyrgo Hage to a course of action which could mean our ruin, not to mention the destruction of the work of six centuries."

Tvrdy nodded solemnly, "You remind us of the seriousness of our task. I thank you for that. And I hasten to assure you that we would not like to see another Purge. But our work is ruined if Jamrog gains Threl leadership."

"I agree," said Piipo, "or I would not have come."

"We respect your discretion," offered Cejka.

"Flattery is not necessary, Rumon. We know each other well enough, I think; we can dispense with formalities." Piipo took a deep breath. He had made up his mind. "I will join the Cabal. I have seen enough; it is time to act."

Tvrdy smiled broadly. Cejka slapped the table in approval. "I wish we had brought some souile to celebrate this moment," he said, grinning.

"We will save that for Jamrog's defeat." Piipo's eyes narrowed, and he leaned forward. "You said time was short. I'll tell you what I know. A Hyrgo administrator of the dole encountered one of the Fieri spies when he came for his food allotment."

"Where? Jamuna Hage?"

"You know this already?" Piipo looked at Tvrdy in surprise.

"Only that the spies have been located," replied Cejka. "We know that those placed with Jamuna and Chryse have been seen in public. The Chryse is a woman; therefore, it must have been the Jamuna your dole administrator encountered."

"I see. But I can supply a name, and it shouldn't be too difficult to discover where he can be found."

"Oh?" Tvrdy perked up.

Piipo smiled. "We have our methods, too. Actually, it was luck. He approached the dole kiosk in Jamuna Hage—Market level—in the company of a recycler. His name was given as Pizol. There was no record, of course, but his Hageman vouched for him."

"His Hageman's name?"

"Nendl, a third-order recycler."

Tvrdy and Cejka looked at each other. "This Nendl may be one of our agents," replied Cejka. "Jamuna is Covol's section; he will know."

"I will have a Tanais priest look up the kraam coordinates," suggested Tvrdy. "And then we'll go get him."

"Too risky. We must first discover whether this Nendl is under surveillance by Invisibles," said Cejka. "Better to have one of my rumor messengers make inquiries at the fields, follow them if necessary. We'll find out that way."

"That will take more time."

"It can't be helped," said Cejka. "We must make certain before we move."

Just then a Rumon guide disguised like his master in a

Bolbe yos stepped into the room. "Director, the occupant of the kraam is returning."

"Detain him until we're clear," ordered Cejka. He turned to the others. "Leave this to me. And don't worry—we will have the Jamuna captured and hidden before Jamrog discovers he's gone."

All three rose and placed their clenched fists over their hearts in a Cabalist's pledge of secrecy.

Treet had spent the day back in his cell. Whatever had happened at his inquisition—he thought he'd made a few points with the old leader, but apparently not enough—he was still a prisoner. So far nothing had changed.

Nevertheless, he hoped that Rohee—was that his name?— had been intrigued enough with him that he would want to keep him around a bit longer. Treet didn't trust the inquisitors; they looked suspicious and nasty—as if they suspected the worst of everything and everyone all the time. Perhaps they did. Treet had decided that everyone in Empyrion was suspicious; as a group, they were the most skeptical people he'd ever met.

This brought him back to the thought that had occupied him since he'd returned to the cell: what happened to these people? What made them like this?

Treet tried putting himself in their kimonos, and still came up short of a satisfactory explanation. Yes, visitors from outer space were prime candidates for careful scrutiny, at least until their motives were known. He agreed that arrest and confinement were prudent measures when strangers in spacecraft showed up on your doorstep. In fact, human nature being what it was, he allowed that he had gotten off lightly. They could easily have blasted him first and sorted out the details later.

But these weren't *aliens,* dammit! These were Earthmen like himelf who a little over fifty-three months ago had come to colonize this planet!

It didn't make sense. They should have been out on that landing platform waving handkerchiefs and throwing flowers. They should have called a holiday and given feasts in his honor. They should have begged him for news of Earth and showered him with gifts large and small.

Instead, they treated him like a criminal—and a dangerous criminal at that. It just didn't make sense.

Less than five years separated them from Earth. How could a society change so radically in so short a time? All he saw—their dress, their speech, their impossible city—everything about them pointed to a far older society.

There were two possible explanations. Either the colonists had encountered an alien civilization resulting in some unknown consequence, or . . . time distortion.

His scalp prickled, tingling with the sensation of closing in on the answer to a mystery. Yes, he was close. Very close. The mist that lay between him and the lost pieces of his scattered memory shifted and rolled as if driven by a fresh wind.

Concentrate! he told himself. Thinking made his head hurt. Ignore the pain and concentrate. This is important.

He squeezed his eyes shut and brought the full force of his attention to bear on lifting the veil that obscured his past. Think! You can almost see it. Concentrate! His temples began to throb. The pain surged in intensity. Treet cradled his head in his hands and forced himself to remember. Think! You can remember if you try!

The harder he tried, the more agonizing was his torment. But Treet gritted his teeth and kept at it. Sweat rolled in rivulets from his brow and down his neck. The pain was a red welt in his brain, a burning cancer that swelled and bloated, feeding on his effort.

But the effort paid off. He began to glimpse dimly familiar shapes lurking behind the thick, gauzy curtain. The fog thinned in spots and solid objects emerged, their outlines made sharp by the grinding in his head: a tall, slat-sided Texan with a pilot's cap . . . a smirking gnome in antique glasses . . . a dark-haired goddess, remote and mysterious.

Treet's head snapped up. Crocker . . . Pizzle . . . Talazac— the names tumbled into his consciousness. "I've done it!" he shouted. "I've seen them. I remember."

Now other names, details, and images emerged, one on top of another, thick and fast.

Belthausen . . . *Interstellar Travel Theory* . . . time distortion . . . wormholes . . . *Zephyros* . . . It all came flooding back at once. Oblivious to the drumming ache in his brain, he jumped up and began pacing his cell.

In another few minutes he had it all sorted out; and although a few of the details were still indistinct, he knew that his friends must be hidden somewhere within the colony, perhaps close by. He knew, too, beyond a doubt that in traveling through the wormhole they had undergone a serious time shift.

One or another of Belthausen's time distortion theories had been proved. But Treet felt none of the elation of the scientist riding the crest of a breakthrough discovery.

He shook his throbbing head; the effort at remembering sent fiery daggers stabbing into his cerebral cortex. He felt as if his brain were swelling inside his skull, threatening to burst its bony shell. Did it really matter *which* theory explained what had happened? Whether they had crossed over into a parallel time channel, or traveled through compressed time, or experienced some other bizarre phenomenon, functionally it was all the same.

The Empyrion they had discovered was not the Empyrion they had set out to find. That much was clear. Less clear was what, if anything, he could do about it. Here was a problem that would keep his poor palpitating brain occupied for some time to come.

TWENTY
ONE

On the Starwatch level of Nilokerus Hage, Empyrion physicians maintained a cluster of chambers beneath the heavy-corded webwork of the dome. In daylight, the sun shone through the translucent panes, warming the healing chambers with bright, white light. At night, the panes became transparent, and the stars shone through with crystal clarity. The physicians believed that light was a prime healing agent, sunlight being more intense and moonlight more subtle, but both essential in balancing a patient's aura.

Ernina, physician of the highest order—higher than any physician had ever obtained since records had been kept; high enough that if physicians had a Hage she would be a Director—held the status of a magician among her Hagemen. Her ways were certainly just as mysterious, and her knowledge of the healing arts just as far-reaching. Among the populace it was whispered that Ernina had come by her vast knowledge by communing with the oversouls of dead physicians from before the Purge.

But Ernina cared nothing about the orders or Hage stent. As she swept through the Starwatch complex, overseeing the care of patients, participating in the finer manipulations of body and aura when need arose, and teaching, always teaching her brood of eager followers, there was room in her mind for only one thought: healing. At night she worked alone in her large, many-roomed kraam—not communing with departed oversouls, but poring over ancient texts, searching into the wisdom of the old ones, probing ever further into the mysteries of healing.

Now, as dawn reached into the night sky, graying the black star canopy at the horizon, Ernina closed the book before her and rubbed her eyes. The cracked plastic binding creaked, reminding her of her own weary joints, which were beginning to declare their age. Black words on white pages still spooled before her eyes—old words, words whose meanings had been lost long ago.

Once again the sadness she sometimes felt upon rising from a night of reading came upon her. For one could not read very far into the ancients' books without understanding that a great change had taken place, a falling of almost unimaginable proportions. In these books were mysteries within mysteries. "What have we lost?" she murmured to herself. "What have we become?"

She rose, pressing a hand to the small of her back as she straightened, and went into the chamber adjoining her kraam. A single bed floated in the center of the room, the gleaming apparatus of an aura equalizer suspended above the sleeping patient. The acetic scent of ozone reached her nostrils. She sighed. *The equipment is getting so old, and we cannot repair it forever. The magicians are slow, and each time a piece comes back, it comes back changed. They will not admit it,* she thought, *but they are losing their craft. Empyrion is running down, falling apart—you can see it everywhere you look.*

Ernina reached up and flicked off the equalizer. Silence reclaimed the room, accented by the ticking of hot crystals inside the equalizer's housing. She shoved the machine back and stood over the patient, placing a hand on his forehead.

The man's skin was hot to the touch, but not, she thought, as hot as the day before. The sleep drug gave him some relief, though he must awaken soon and eat if he was to regain his strength. At least his aura had stabilized. The dangerous flares of red and yellow in his electromagnetic envelope had diminished considerably, and the blue and green had deepened and spread. He was out of danger now—for the moment, at least.

She smoothed his tangled hair back, allowing her hand to rest gently on the crown of his head. It was a womanly touch, as well as a healer's. Touch, she knew, was a healing agent, and in some could be made very powerful. But there was something about the man before her that made her want to cradle him, enfold him.

What did that imbecilic fool of a Director *do* to these people? The destruction caused by his *conditioning* was often permanent; many patients never recovered. And those were just the ones she saw, the ones Hladik wanted to save. What of those he did not bother to send to her? How many others died that she did not know of?

She shivered at the thought. "I don't know," she muttered. "I don't *want* to know."

A soft moaning whisper escaped the man's lips. Ernina let her hand slide to the base of his neck and felt the pulse there. It was not strong, but it was regular and even. She nodded to herself, thinking, Yes, at least this one will live.

His eyelids lifted, drawn up slowly, and he stared upward with cloudy eyes. Ernina bent over him, focusing the entire force of her healing energy upon him. "Who are you?" she asked. She waited a few moments for the question to sink in, and then asked again. "Who . . . are . . . you?"

The patient closed his eyes and sank back into unconsciousness. Ernina shook out the filmy body covering, and noticed for the first time since examining him a small round scar on his upper arm. It was an old scar, barely visible, just a faint white disk-shaped impression. She brushed the mark with her fingertips. Odd, she thought, I've never seen one of those before, and I've seen many scars.

She stepped to the opposite side of the bed and pulled back the cover. On the patient's right arm was a familiar mark—the narrow red scratch made by the insertion of the poak. That was one scar she had seen often enough. But what was it doing on a grown man? The poak was given to infants at the time of their Hage assignment, never to adults. There was no need.

On a hunch, Ernina went to a nearby equipment cabinet and took out a poak reader and placed it against the bruise. LED circuits flashed the number ten. Ten shares.

Just as I guessed, she thought. A very low number. This man had recently received a poak implant. Why? Unless he'd never received the poak as a child. How could that be? *Everyone* received the poak.

Her intuition screamed at her: He is not one of us!

An outsider then. But how?

There could only be one explanation: he was a Fieri.

Ernina stared at the man. If she could believe her eyes and her finely-tuned intuition, here before her lay a genuine, in-the-flesh Fieri—not a creature of myth, not a phantom of legend and speculation, but a skin, bones, blood, and sinew man! The Fieri were *real!*

The implications of her discovery collided with her awareness. She stepped slowly away from the bed, a dazed expression on her face.

Thoughts came spinning past her in dizzy flight—snatches of folklore from her childhood, shreds of rumor passed on among Hagemen. It was all true then—all the old myths of a separate race, once part of themselves, who had been cast out in times beyond remembering. A fair people, wise and strong, powerful magicians whose machine lore rivaled Cynetics. And there were those among them, the Dhogs—the shadow people, nonbeings who haunted the Old Section—who secretly revered their memory, handing down the old stories by word of mouth all these many hundreds of years—they knew the truth! Here was a discovery equal to any she had made in her lifetime.

And to think that the Threl mercilessly persecuted the Dhogs and killed them or consigned them to reorientation cells whenever they were discovered. Why? It made no sense, unless . . . unless the Threl knew, too, that the Fieri existed. Knew and feared the knowledge, feared it enough to destroy anyone who might share it—why else torture those who believed? The cold-blooded inhumanity of it astounded her.

I should have guessed long ago, Ernina thought. I have closed my eyes to this all my life. I have kept myself above the repulsive politics of the Directorate, and I have paid the price. I who prize knowledge so highly have wrapped myself in ignorance.

The man in the bed stirred. Ernina approached again and replaced the thin coverlet. "You must revive," she whispered to him. "We have much work to do, you and I."

Treet was awakened by a presence beside his bed. Pink-white light tinted the sky; the section of dome above him had not yet become translucent. He rolled over slowly and peeped an eye open. A young man stood a pace away, apparently waiting for him to wake up.

"What do you want?" Treet's sleep-clouded voice sounded suitably gruff.

The youth, dressed in the standard black-and-silver striped short kimono, opened his mouth, then closed it, as if he had forgotten what he had come to say.

"Get out then," said Treet. "I don't like people standing over me while I sleep." He rolled over again. "Come back when you remember what you came for."

"Supreme Director—" began the guide.

Treet's head whipped around, and he sat up. "He wants to

see me?" He threw his legs over the edge of the bed, smoothed a hand through his ruffled hair, and noticed for the first time that the youth was blind. Empty holes stared where his eyes should be. "Um . . . okay. Let's go."

The guide led him out of the room and through a long, sinuous tunnel-like corridor—red tiled ceilings, gray stone-flagged floors. Amber lights, shining from half-mood recepta-cles set flush in the wall near the floor, illuminated their passage as they wound further and further into the convoluted heart of Threl High Chambers. Broken tiles lay scattered over the floor; blank squares dotted the ceiling and walls; here and there a light had gone out. The place reeked of disuse, and made Treet think of a long-deserted subway station.

Treet padded after the guide, wondering how the blind youth managed to find his way so easily. Practice, he guessed. As they moved along, Treet began wishing he had not been quite so hasty. He should have spent a moment or two at the sanitary stall—he smelled like a buffalo, and his face itched from the healthy growth of beard taking over his face.

Did these people shave? wondered Treet as they walked along. Did they bathe? So far all of the men he'd met sported smooth, beardless faces. None of them smelled like he did, either. He guesed that he was being kept away from such things as razors and bathing paraphernalia—perhaps in the interest of safety for all concerned.

Still, his skin felt tight and dry—like wearing a parchment bodystocking. It had been too long since his last nutrient bath; the capsules aboard the *Zephyros* didn't count. I could use a good soak, thought Treet. I could use some red meat, too. Come to think of it, I could use a lot of things I probably won't get any time soon.

For the first time since arriving on Empyrion, Treet felt like himself. He enjoyed the feeling. The ache in his head had van-ished with sleep, taking with it the fog barrier that had blocked his thoughts. Now, aside from a few minor details—such as what had happened out there on the landing field—he remem-bered everything clearly and without pain. Furthermore, last night he had worked out a plan to ingratiate himself to the Supreme Director and win his confidence.

The guide entered a darkened, crumbling doorway and stopped. Treet remained standing in the corridor and realized that the guide had disappeared. He waited. In a moment the guide emerged and motioned Treet to follow him. Treet stepped into the darkness and felt himself turning—the floor was moving with him on it. Then the movement stopped, the light came up, and they were standing in a vestibule which opened onto a larger room.

Treet stepped into the room. It was, like all the rooms he'd seen so far, asymetrically round with a ceiling that sloped like a portion of the interior of a much larger tent. Sunlight, now a little stronger, had clouded the panes of the dome above, so soft white light shone over everything.

The room was formally arranged with many pieces of furniture of sleek, exacting design: clever cantilevered chairs, several elegant tables large and small, a free-standing cabinet with many shelves holding odd art objects, a strange, oblong chest or trunk made of a woven material, a mound of silken cushions in one corner, and something that looked for all the world like an ordinary holovision screen, surrounded by a ring of cushions, standing in the middle of the floor. The place could have used a good dusting.

"Do you like your new kraam?" The voice came from a cabinet in the center of the room.

As Treet watched, Supreme Director Rohee emerged from behind the cabinet. "My new . . . krawm?"

The Director waved a hand to indicate the room. "Kra-am," he repeated, accenting the syllables separately. "It is yours."

"It is?" Treet asked dumbly.

He had expected the audience to be much the same as their meeting of yesterday—conducted with official pomp from behind a barrier field, with guards and inquisitors in attendance. He had expected anything but to be offered his own plush apartment.

The old man smiled, his eyes disappearing into crinkled folds of skin, his jowls bulging. "We will sit." He led Treet to the cushions and pulled one from the mound, sinking down onto it with a sigh.

"Where are your guards?" Treet glanced back over his shoulder and sat down cross-legged.

"We will not need them anymore. I have made up my mind about you, Traveler." He smiled again, lips pressed firmly together. "You can be trusted."

Treet did not know what to say. This turnabout was blowing holes in his plan of ingratiation, but the effect was better than he could have hoped for.

"Can you understand what I am saying to you, Traveler?"

"I understand." Treet nodded. Yes, his facility for languages had served him well. He now caught nearly every word spoken to him—it was, after all, merely a mutated dialect of old reliable International English.

"Good! Good!" Rohee seemed very pleased with this information. "We can talk freely then."

"I hope so," replied Treet, taking the opportunity to launch into his prepared speech. "I mean no one any harm. I do not wish my presence here to cause anyone alarm. I have come to help you."

"Help me?" the Supreme Director asked. "How would you help me?"

"It appears to me that Cynetics is no longer remembered in Empyrion." Rohee's flinch told him his hunch was true. Treet continued boldly, "Cynetics is very powerful. Cynetics will help those who help me in my mission."

"What sort of mission, Traveler?" The old man cocked his head to one side. His fine white hair had been brushed until it shined. His quick eyes watched intently.

"To learn why your people have forgotten," he said, stretching the nature of his assignment slightly. Under the circumstances he didn't think Chairman Neviss would mind. He paused and then delivered his next revelation. "My friends will tell you—we all have similar missions."

Rohee gave away nothing by his expression. He merely peered back at Treet with a benign smile and remained silent.

Treet continued. "Yes, I remember my friends. I didn't at first, but I do now. In fact, I remember everything."

TWENTY
TWO

According to Bela, the Chryse were second only to the Saecaraz in Hage stent. This was important, he maintained; it meant that artists and sensitives could finally assume the exalted position they rightly deserved. It meant that the long years of austerity were over—as anyone could see by allotment. Now even musicians and storytellers, Chyrse of the lowest order, regularly received meat in the dole.

Yarden listened attentively as the troupe walked the teeming byways of Hyrgo Hage, with its multi-layered terraces all growing green, the smell of rich damp soil thick in the air. She liked hearing Bela talk; he had such a high opinion of himself and of all Chryse that it made her feel important. She suspected that Bela liked hearing himself talk too; he enjoyed the sound of his own modulated tones.

"The Nilokerus do not like this," he was saying, "since we've advanced over them. No one likes to lose stent." He shrugged, his lanky shoulders lifting under the ample yos. Today they were all dressed in the same sea colors of deep blue-green, head to toe, their hands and faces painted blue, their hair dyed or covered with close-fitting caps of the same color. Today they were playing *Ocean* for the Hyrgo and Saecaraz. "The Nilokerus should just be glad they're still above the rest; they value themselves overmuch."

Yarden nodded, not quite understanding this, but taking it in all the same. The effects of the flash still lingered. Her head felt soft and mushy, slightly detached from her body, which felt, not unpleasantly, lethargic, wrapped in a drowsy, cottony numbness that dulled physical sensation. She was happy just to walk and listen and not think—thinking had become such an exhausting chore lately she preferred letting her mind wander aimlessly. It was easier.

"It's pretty here," she observed. "It smells like . . ." Her voice trailed off. Strange, she had nothing to compare it with. "I like it here."

One of the other troupe members who had been walking close behind moved up beside them. "Wait until you taste their food! Everyone knows they save the best for themselves. Whenever we play the Hyrgo we eat like priests."

"True enough, Woiwik," replied Bela. To Yarden he said, "If we do well today, we'll be given gifts of food—it's a tradition with the Hyrgo. They are so proud of their abilities they always try to impress us."

"They impress *me!*" admitted Woiwik, rubbing his stomach and rolling his eyes.

"You're too easily impressed," Bela snorted. "The Hyrgo think that if they give away food they can improve their stent." He chuckled. "They don't know it doesn't work that way."

"And we'll never tell them," laughed Woiwik. "They're *growers!* Even their magicians—just growers all the same."

"Someone has to grow the food," said Yarden. "They work hard—harder than we do. I don't see what's so funny about that."

Both men looked at her askance. Woiwik opened his mouth to challenge her, but Bela warned him off with a glance and said, "It isn't the work. We all know they work hard. But their craft is not subtle; there is no art in it. Without art, life is . . . well, life is not life. Seh?"

"Maybe *she* was a Hyrgo," muttered Woiwik. "Before—"

"Hagemen!" Bela turned and shouted. "Let us play so well today that we will embarrass the Hyrgo if they don't send us away groaning with pleasure."

This exhortation brought a shout of acclaim from the troupe, which this day numbered forty because the nature of the play required that two troupes merge. They continued on to a place where the lower terraces met to form a wide quadrangle. The troupe stopped here to wait for their audience to assemble.

"How will they know to come?" asked Yarden.

"When they see that we are here, they will come," explained Bela. "Also, a Hyrgo always stops at midday to eat a meal, and they always eat together."

"That's why we always choose this time and this place to perform for the Hyrgo," Woiwik put in, looking pleased with himself. "We don't mind coming down here in deep Hage if it means better gifts."

Yarden nodded absently and raised her eyes skyward. The dome glittered faintly from far above—so high individual cords and panes could not be made out. It was a blank white shell, an enormous curving bowl above all, glowing with sunlight. The tallest of the narrow trees grew upward toward it, but did not begin to reach. Wide, flat terraces—fields with dwelling clusters interspersed—rose like stair-step mountains on all sides; the topmost layers formed plateaus crowned with orchards.

As she looked around her, Yarden saw figures moving in the landscape. As Bela had predicted, the Hyrgo had seen the troupe from afar and were coming down to meet them, calling to their Hagemen to leave their work and follow. In minutes the lower terrace rims began filling with Hyrgo Hagemen young and old, dangling their feet over the rimwall or squatting on their haunches below it. All were quiet and orderly, their faces radiating anticipation. Here and there a mud-stained smile welcomed the troupe, but for the most part the Hyrgo looked on in silent expectation.

When a sizable crowd had assembled, Bela motioned to some of the troupe members who, on hands and knees, linked themselves together to form a living platform. Climbing quickly to the top, he addressed the audience. "Welcome, all, to our performance," he said, his voice clear, deep, and fine. "We are happy to play for you. Today, as you can see by our costumes, is a special performance." A ripple of excitement fluttered through the audience. Bela drew out the moment, heightened the suspense. "Today we will perform *Ocean!*"

The Hyrgo loosed a roar of acclaim, chattering their approval. Bela allowed the outpouring to continue for a few moments and then cut it off just as it began to die away. He told them of the play's history, and briefly explained the various movements they would see. Yarden saw how expertly he manipulated the audience, working them into the proper mood for the performance. He ended by saying, "We do not wish to keep you from your midday meal, so please eat and enjoy the performance!"

With that the human stage broke and tumbled apart. Bela somersaulted once in the air and landed on his feet as the troupe scurried around him. In seconds the quadrangle was transformed into a blue-green sea where waves rolled over one another, rising, falling, rising, falling, breaking on the imaginary shore.

The players, arranged in staggered lines, each held the hem of the player in front, fluffing the garment in the air and letting it sink slowly down. Extra lengths of cloth had been sewn into each yos precisely for this purpose. As the billows filled and expired, the lines crouched and stood and stretched alternately, all the while murmuring in a low, throaty hum.

The blue and green of cloth and makeup became water, the voices water sounds. Yarden could hardly keep her mind on her part, so taken was she with the performance. She stole glances at the audience, seeing her own amazement mirrored in their eyes.

Presently the ocean's waves grew choppy, the water sound more discordant. Illusionary winds whipped the surface of the water, driving the waves onto the beach with increasing force. A storm was coming!

The players ducked their heads down and flailed their arms, snapping the cloth more frantically. The hum became a moan; rending sighs escaped as the waves towered and crashed, spilling over one another, pounding forward.

The crowd sat deathly still, totally absorbed in the clash of wind and sea.

Then, as the gale reached its crescendo, the sea waves gentled, the wind calmed. The storm passed.

Gasps of delight whispered through the audience. Yarden saw them transfixed, their eyes wide and staring. They were seeing the ocean, feeling it. The quadrangle itself had become a sea of faces, each one enthralled with the play unfolding. For the Hyrgo, the Chryse players *were* the ocean.

All day long Pizzle felt eyes watching him as he raked his way through the fields of muck. He would straighten and peer around quickly behind him, but would only see another Jamuna like himself, bent double, patiently turning over the drying crust. He would shrug, turn back to his work, and slog along a few rake lengths further before the feeling came on him again.

Finally, as the workday ended and the recyclers laid up their tools and began moving in from the fields, Pizzle saw two men standing on the rimwall of the field above. They were dressed like Jamuna Hagemen, but something about the way they stood—feet apart, arms held loosely at their sides—told him they had not been working the fields all day.

"They want you." Pizzle spun around to see Nendl coming

up beside him. He nodded toward the two men. "Go with them."

"Who are they?"

"They are friends. You won't be hurt."

"But—" Pizzle turned his face toward Nendl, trying to discover if there was cause for the alarm he felt. "I am afraid, Nendl."

"Go quickly. Don't wait. You must not be seen. They will take care of you."

"I want to stay with you," whined Pizzle.

Nendl took him by the arm and gripped it hard. "You must go with them. I've talked to them—it's all right."

"Then you come with me."

"I can't." Nendl darted a glance over his shoulder. As yet they had attracted no attention, but they could not stand talking together much longer. "You don't understand. I have to stay here. Go on!" He gave Pizzle a prod.

Pizzle took a few hesitant steps forward, then stopped and looked back. Nendl urged him on with a nod. "I will come later if I can. Now hurry!"

Other workers were walking along the rimwall toward the two men. Pizzle saw that he must make a decision. He lowered his head and moved off to meet them. When he reached the rimwall, he looked up to see that the men were now waiting for him at the entrance to the tunnel which led from the fields to the Hage warrens below. Jamuna Hagemen were passing by them into the tunnel; one of the men gave him a signal which meant he was to follow, and then stepped inside.

Pizzle followed, trying to catch the two men, but each time he looked up they were precisely as far away as before. They hurried through the Hage warrens, past dwelling blocks crowded with kraams, out onto open-air common areas, along boulevards lined with squat trees, across suspended walkways over terraced fields, and on. All he saw was new to him, and Pizzle realized there was no way back again, but also that the men had allowed him to draw nearer to them.

At last his mysterious guides disappeared into another tunnel which opened into the steep bank of a dwelling block overlooking a small lake fed by a splashing fountain in its center. Pizzle saw that the people at the lake's edge wore yoses he'd never seen before: gold striped with gold hoods. No one he saw wore the hood, however, unlike the Jamuna who wore them all the time except in Hage.

He stepped hesitantly into the darkened tunnel where the men had disappeared.

"Here, put this on. Quickly!" whispered someone directly in front of him. A bundle was thrust into his hands.

He stood for a moment, peering into the darkness. He opened his mouth to ask one of the many questions rising to his tongue, but felt hands on him, tugging at his clothes, before he could utter a syllable. There was a ripping of fabric, and his yos was stripped from him. "Put it on!" came the urgent whisper. Pizzle shook out the bundle and began feeling for the hem.

When he had pulled the yos over his head and tied the sash at his side, the guides took him, one at each elbow, and steered him back out onto the plaza where Pizzle saw that his new yos had gold vertical stripes like all the others he saw. They led him to the edge of the brickwork to where a wiry green lawn began its gentle slope down to the lake.

"Go on down there," said one of the guides.

"Wait at the water's edge. Someone will come for you," said the other.

With that, the two released him and stepped away. Pizzle turned back twice as he moved off toward the lakeshore. Each time he saw the two still standing where he'd left them, silently watching him.

He reached the shoreline and stood for a moment looking out across the lake to the fountain, gurgling and bouncing as it sent a thick column of water into the air. When he turned back, the two men had disappeared. Pizzle began strolling idly along the grassy shore, watching the others drifting, as he was, around the lake.

Short, round-topped trees, growing right at the water's edge, trailed vines into the water. Flowers with delicate white blooms floated up where the vines touched the surface. Pizzle stopped to examine the flowers, squatting down for a closer look. In among the stems and dangling water roots he saw the flash of a silver side and a swirl of fins. Also, reflected in the water's mirror, he saw two figures standing over him.

He stood and turned. One of the figures was a man, the other a woman. Both smiled at him and nodded. The woman stepped to his side and said, "I see you enjoy the lake." With the slightest tilt of her head, she turned him away from the water. "In that case we must come here again soon."

The man, still smiling, stepped behind Pizzle, and together the three moved up the slope once more to the plaza. They walked easily along, passing before tiers of dwellings, each with a large round window and balcony facing the lake. Occupants in colorful Hage robes carried trays of food or sat at tables eating. Pizzle's stomach growled, and he remembered he hadn't eaten since midday.

"Where am I?" he asked.

"Tanais section," replied his companion. "Would you like to eat something? We thought a meal might be welcome soon."

"I am hungry," Pizzle admitted.

"It's just a little farther. There are some people who want to meet you, Pizol."

He looked at her suspiciously. "How do you know my name?"

She laughed easily. "Didn't you know you had friends looking out for you?"

"Nendl is my friend."

"Oh, he's our friend too. A Hageman does not betray his friends."

Pizzle contemplated her last remark—had it been made for his benefit? A reminder of . . . what? Loyalty? Was she instructing him?

They walked on in silence, moving around the lake and above it, their feet soundless on the spiral-patterned bricks. At the far side of the lake, they approached an immense, multi-towered block of dwellings—so tall it commanded a clear view of the entire section. Aerial walkways arched between the slender towers, joining the upper levels to one another.

Overhead, the dome was now nearly transparent. A blue-gray dusk, deepening with the approach of night, triggered the miniature yellow lights hidden in the branches of trees and strung along the serpentine byways, and soon Tanais Hage basked in the golden wash of myriads of tiny lights.

"Here we are," said the woman as they stopped before the central tower. She ushered him in through a narrow slit of an opening three levels tall. Pizzle slipped in and found himself in an enormous, triangular hall. The hall was nearly empty. Only a few Hagemen, dwarfed by the proportions of the room, moved silently across the polished surface of the floor toward one of the three spire-shaped openings.

"This one is ours—" She pointed across the hall to the opening on the left, and led them quickly across the expanse. Upon reaching the entrance, she paused and explained, "It's a lift. We will leave you here, Hageman Pizol."

The man behind him reached inside the doorway, adjusted something, and then motioned Pizzle into the lift. He stepped in and heard a whizzing sound as the lift climbed swiftly away. Bands of light ringed the transparent compartment, dropping past so fast it seemed that the lights moved instead of the lift. Pizzle pressed his hands flat against the smooth sides and held on. Presently the falling rings slowed, and the lift stopped without a tremor. The static fizz of the unidor cut out, and Pizzle stepped out of the lift and into a kraam many times the size of Nendl's.

Wherever he looked, flat white surfaces met his gaze— ceiling, floors, walls—all soft white and smooth, uncluttered with objects or decoration of any kind, the floors covered with gray and white weavings. Before him stood a man, dark and imperious in a long, emerald green Hage robe.

"We have been waiting for you, Hageman Pizol," said the man, coming forward to take him by the arm. "You are safe here. And very soon, you will remember who you are."

TWENTY
THREE

Yawning, head pounding again, Treet sat hunched on a blue silk cushion, chin in hand, trying to keep his eyes focused. It had been a long day, filled with interminable questions and innumerable answers. Director Rohee had wanted to know everything about him and had questioned him endlessly. They had talked for several hours before the Supreme Director had gone, leaving him in the incredulous care of the inquisitors, who had also come heavily armed with questions.

All day long they had interrogated, and he had supplied answers—holding back only those aspects of his trip he thought best kept to himself: his time distortion theory, for one thing, and any direct references to Cynetics for another. Now he sat by himself, watching the three inquisitors discuss among themselves, trying to make up their minds about something. How best to proceed with the cross-examination, Treet thought. Whatever it was, he had lost interest long ago. They might have been planning to barbecue him and feed him to the blue kangaroos. Treet didn't care.

He hadn't done so much explaining since he had been caught crossing over from the New Frontier with a liter of Stolichnaya in his luggage. He just wanted to eat and go to sleep.

"Enough!" said Treet, standing up. He yawned and did a couple of toe touches by way of getting his circulation going again. "That's all. No more. I'm going to sleep."

The inquisitors looked at him. "We wish clarification on several points—" began the spokesman, a dry stick of a man named Creps.

"Come back next week. I'm through talking." Treet advanced toward them. "I'm hungry and tired, and you're becoming a pain."

"We will have food brought," offered Creps.

"You do that," said Treet, jabbing a finger at him. "And then clear out."

The three exchanged puzzled glances. "We do not understand," said Creps.

"Oh? Let me see if I can make it any clearer. Go away! Get out! Leave! Is that better!" Treet enjoyed the effect his words were having with the three stuffy inquisitors; expressions of horror bloomed on their officious faces. He continued, "You want to know something else? I'm tired of answering all your stupid questions. What about *my* questions? I'm not answering any more questions until I get some answers myself."

"We have been instructed to provide information," replied Creps. The other two nodded.

"Tell me this then: where are my friends? That'll do for starters."

After a quick consultation, one of the inquisitors turned and fled the room. Well, thought Treet, that got some results. I should have hollered sooner. Treet stood and glared at his two remaining guests until the third came back a few moments later.

"Food has been requested," Creps informed him. "Also, we have summoned the Supreme Director. He has asked to be informed of any unusual behavior."

"Fine," replied Treet. "Let's get the old boy back in here, and maybe we'll get somewhere." He plopped himself back on his cushion and sneezed as the dust swirled around his face. "And send someone up here to clean this dump!" he added.

A few minutes later, a guide—the one who had awakened him that morning—came in carrying a large tray, heavy with bowls of food: more raw vegetables, a thin, clear soup, and several small roast fowl. The guide placed the tray before Treet and backed away as Treet dove in. He seized one of the birds and tore off a leg.

Treet was licking his fingers and looking at the soup when Rohee entered the kraam. With a nod he dismissed the inquisitors, who looked relieved to escape. Treet smiled to himself; he hadn't realized it was that easy to intimidate these goons.

Rohee settled himself on a cushion and dipped his hand into a bowl of cherimoyas. He popped the fruit in his mouth and sucked the sweet juice, studying Treet, his eyes sharp and hard.

"Help yourself," said Treet, and went on eating.

"There will be no more questions," announced Rohee as he rolled another of the delicate fruits in his hand.

Treet swallowed. "Good." He took a tentative sip of the soup and added, "I thought you said you trusted me."

"Yes," replied Rohee thoughtfully. "But we are also curious."

"I'm curious, too. I want to know what happened to the people I came here with. You said you would tell me—I'm still waiting."

"They have not been harmed."

"So you say. But if they're all right, why can't I see them?"

The Supreme Director's wrinkles arranged an expression of extreme concern, but his eyes remained hard. "It is best that you be kept apart for the present. It is for your own well-being."

Treet's head snapped up. He swallowed. "What? Is that a threat?"

"It is a simple fact." Rohee gazed at him quietly. "I can explain."

"Go ahead." Treet wondered at the change in the old man. The first meeting had been stiff and formal, the second more friendly. And this—this was downright cozy. The Director was treating him like a confidant. Or, Treet reconsidered, a condemned man at his last meal.

Rohee tilted his head back and looked down his beak nose. "I am beset by enemies, Traveler," he began. "I am Supreme Director of the Threl, leader of all Empyrion. Naturally, my position attracts many who bow before my face, yet conspire for my power behind my back."

Treet wondered at this confession. Why was the old bird telling him this? "I understand. Are you telling me that my friends are in danger from your enemies?"

"Not precisely. If you have not guessed, Traveler, your arrival has put me in a very awkward position. My enemies would like nothing better than to get their hands on you and your friends. They believe that you could help them in their plots against me."

"I see. What do you think? We know nothing about any of this."

Rohee shrugged and reached for another cherimoya. "This is what they believe. I merely mention it because they are ruthless men whose schemes stop at nothing short of open opposition—which they dare not attempt." He lifted his shoulders again as if to say, I accept this; I live with it. "Therefore, I have

instructed my allies to take each of your friends into Hage.
They are hidden there, safe from my enemies. To move them
now would endanger them needlessly."

Treet nodded. "I see." He wiped his mouth with the back
of his hand and replaced the soup bowl. "Pardon me if I don't
believe you for one microsecond."

"You do not know Empyrion," Rohee stated firmly. He
returned Treet's gaze equably. "But when you have learned our
ways, you will be reunited with your friends, Traveler. I, Supreme Director, have so ordered it."

Treet remained silent for a moment, considering. He had
pushed the matter far enough for the moment; there was nothing to be gained by badgering Rohee about it. Best now to
change the subject. "What's going to happen to me?"

Rohee smiled, his eyes becoming slits. "I have been thinking about what you said this morning—about your mission."

"Yes?"

"I have decided that you will fulfill your mission, Traveler."

"Is that so?" Treet eyed his benefactor suspiciously. There
was a trade-off coming, he could feel it.

"It may be as you say—that it would prove beneficial to
everyone. We will never know unless you try."

"I'll need some help," suggested Treet, pouncing on this
unexpected opportunity. He wanted to see how much Rohee
was willing to give.

"I will assign a guide to you. He will be instructed to help
you in every way."

"Fair enough. But I want someone who knows his way
around and can get me the information I need—not one of
those three bozos—" He jerked his head toward the nonexis-
tent inquisitors. "I want someone smart."

The Supreme Director stared and then lightened. He
chuckled, "No, not one of those. They are Jamrog's security
advisors—chosen to prepare a report to the Threl about you.
Your arrival has naturally piqued the interest of our leaders."

"Why don't you let me meet them personally? I have nothing to hide."

"No. Not yet. In time, perhaps." Rohee shook his head,
drawing his sparse eyebrows into a knot. "It is better for you to
remain invisible for now."

"Enemies?"

"There are always enemies. You will be safer if no one knows who you are; you may pass more freely that way."

Treet accepted this. "Fine. Cynetics will be pleased. But soon I will need to see my friends again, of course."

"Yes. In time," said Rohee. He stood slowly, and Treet stood with him. "I open Empyrion to you, but no one may know what you are doing. Speak to no one else, do you understand? You will answer to me, Traveler."

Treet heard an unspoken threat in the leader's voice and felt the tension of balancing unknown factors, of coping with potentially lethal forces beyond reckoning. He then understood something of the risk involved in turning over the keys of the city to an alien. "You won't be sorry," he said, attempting reassurance.

Rohee only nodded, then rose stiffly and shuffled away. In a moment Treet was left alone again. He ate some more and lay back on the cushions, but soon discovered he was not the least bit tired anymore, so got up and walked around his new quarters, thinking, replaying all that had happened to him.

There were many questions left unanswered. But if he was very, very smart, he would find the answers. At least now he was being given the opportunity to dig them out for himself. Maybe that's what Rohee wants too, he thought. He wants me to find out for myself because . . . why?

That was something else to discover.

"He knows nothing," said Tvrdy in frank disgust, "and suspects less. In his present condition he is worthless."

Cejka nodded. "Patience. It will take a few days for the antidote to be absorbed into his tissues."

"Even then I'm not so sure we'll get anything. The damage is already done, I'm afraid."

"Where will you keep him?"

"Here with me. I have assigned guides to watch him so he doesn't wander."

"That could be very dangerous," the Rumon leader cautioned. "If he were seen, or if—"

Tvrdy brushed aside the warning. "No one will suspect he's here. I do not want him out of my sight."

"Have you notified Piipo and Kavan?"

"No, and they are not to know—not yet. Later, when he is ready to talk. For now, there is no need to tell them. There is nothing to tell."

"I agree." Cejka allowed himself a broad smile. "What a stoke of luck, seh? We've done it! Who could have dreamed it would be so easy?"

Tvrdy grinned, his lips curled in amusement. He placed a hand on Cejka's shoulder. "Jamrog will dig his heart out with his own hands when he learns what we intend." The grin faded suddenly. "But that is not for a long time yet. We must not become overconfident."

Still smiling, Cejka agreed. "Yes, yes, you're right. But it starts now—after all these years. So much patience, so much work . . . but worth the price, yes?"

"Did you ever doubt it?" Tvrdy smoothed the shimmering folds of his green Hage robe with his hands. "But we've yet to discuss taking the other spies."

"No," Cejka said. He pushed himself up from his chair and took up the orange Hage robe draped over a nearby table, pulling it over his head. "We've discussed enough for one night. I must get back to Rumon Hage before I am missed. Jamrog must not have cause to wonder about my movements. Besides, we must guard against overconfidence—yes? I think we should be satisfied with the one we have caught. We know where the others are; we can find ways to get them if that becomes necessary. Losing one will be enough of a shock to Jamrog." He smiled again. "I wonder what he'll do?"

"We'll find out. I wouldn't want to be in Hladik's yos when Jamrog explodes. That could be very messy." Tvrdy got up and moved to the lift with Cejka. "Do you want my guide?"

"I can find my way back. A guide might arouse suspicion. I'll be all right." He stepped into the lift and pulled the yos sash tight. "Send word when our friend is ready to talk."

"Of course. Good night, Cejka."

The unidor crackled on, and the lift dropped from sight. Tvrdy stood looking at the empty tube for a moment, chin in hand, thinking. Pradim came in silently and waited to be noticed by his master. "Nothing more tonight, Pradim," said Tvrdy when he stirred finally. "Just make sure our guest is comfortable before you go to sleep."

Pradim padded away quietly, his fingers waving in the air.

Tvrdy crossed the room and went out onto the balcony. Tanais Hage spread out before him, sparkling with the light of tiny yellow lights. The byways were empty and shadowbound; the intercrossed mazes of Empyrion wore night faces. The patter of the fountain echoed up from far below, and Tvrdy turned his eyes toward the dark outline of the lake. There, slipping among the trees winding along the shoreline path, a figure moved with quick stealth.

"Soon, Cejka," Tvrdy whispered to himself, "we will all walk in the daylight."

TWENTY
FOUR

Treet had been up for several hours and had taken his sweet time sampling the pleasures of his new sanitary stall. Warm water was a luxury, and the liquid soap he found in a crystal canister containing a pungent perfume with an astringent quality he found refreshing. He rubbed himself all over with thick, coarse-woven squares of fibrous grasscloth which, he assumed, served as both washcloth and towel.

I'd strangle a rhinoceros with my bare hands for a real bath, thought Treet. His skin cried out for a nutrient solution; he felt flaky and brittle all over and wondered how long it would be before his dry epidermis began peeling off in sheets. He sighed; at least it would be a passably clean hide.

He hummed as he laved the water over his face and neck, happy for the first time in a long time, having decided upon rising that he would play the Supreme Director's game—at least to all outward appearances. He would go along without a fuss and use his position to gather information, locate the others, and eventually reestablish contact with Cynetics.

There is no hurry, he told himself. The main thing is not to make anyone nervous or suspicious. I can wait; I've got time. My first task is to scope out the territory, get the lay of the land, and find out what these people are all about. What do I know about them really?

Not much. Only that they have changed. More to the point, *time* has changed. I'm seeing the colony at some point in its future, relative to Earth. Something happened in the colony's past to bring it to this state, and I have to find out what that something was.

The idea of a quest renewed in Treet a sense of adventure he thought he'd lost. Here he was, transplanted in a semi-advanced culture on an alien world—think of the possibilities! Who could tell what he might find, what secrets he might unlock?

The fire of adventure warmed Treet's blood. He was anxious to be off on discovery's road. He pulled his silver-striped kimono over his head and adjusted the sash, pulling the hem up to just above his knees, in the manner of the colonists. That was one thing he'd learned already.

He emerged from the stall ready to leap tall mountains and ravenous. He paused midway across the floor of his kraam, wondering how to summon breakfast. As he stood thinking about the problem, he heard a single chime and a moment later a young woman entered the kraam carrying a large oval tray.

"Breakfast!" said Treet. "Wonderful!"

The young woman looked at him curiously, ducked her head shyly, and proceeded to the nearest of Treet's tables where she set down the tray and began laying out the food. "I don't suppose there are any croissants on that tray—or coffee?" Treet muttered to himself.

"I do not understand, Traveler," replied the young woman in a clear, precise voice.

"So you *do* talk. Good." Treet sat down in a sleek chair of polished wood and began dipping into the various bowls. "Tell me then, when do I get this guide I'm supposed to have?"

The young woman regarded him closely. "I am to be your guide."

Treet sized her up: a slight but well-knit frame, shapeless under the flowing kimono; fine brown hair cut short over a high, spacious forehead; expressive hands with long, tapering fingers. Her quick dark eyes with a suggestion of epicanthic fold at the outer angle hinted at an oriental ancestry now far removed. With head erect atop a slender neck, she appeared intelligent and alert. "Great. Now then, you know your way around this dome of yours? You can get me into the places I want to go?"

"I have been instructed to help you in every way, Traveler."

"Okay." Treet nodded, chewing a feijoa. "First thing is cut out the traveler stuff. My name is Treet—Orion Treet. You can call me either. What do I call you? Friday?"

A puzzled expression played over the guide's young features. "I do not understand."

"What's your name?" Treet picked up a bowl of diced meat in a thick, white gravy and ladled some of it into his mouth with a paddlelike utensil from the tray.

She hesitated, as if deciding how to answer.

"My name is Calin," she said finally.

"Calin? Nothing else?"

"That is my name." She didn't sound any too convinced.

"Have you eaten this morning, Calin?"

The guide nodded, watching Treet carefully and still wearing the look of quiet wonder with which she'd entered the kraam.

"Well, drag up a chair and sit down here anyway. I don't like people hovering over me while I eat."

"You wish me to sit with you?" She acted as if she had never heard of sitting.

"Yes, I want you to sit with me. Look, unless I'm mistaken, we're going to be working very closely together for a while. I don't want anyone standing on ceremony around me. I have work to do, and I can't be tripping over formalities at every turn. See?"

Calin said nothing, but silently nodded her assent.

"Good," Treet continued. "Now why don't you tell me about yourself and we'll get acquainted."

Before the guide could speak, the chime sounded again and Treet looked up. "Company?"

Calin jumped up from the table as if her chair had suddenly become radioactive. "I have requested a shaver," she explained, running to the vestibule. She came back leading a humpbacked, bald-headed man in a white-sleeved kimono. The little barber carried a soft woven box and peered nervously at Treet, awe and fear mingled on his smooth-shaven face. "This one is a third-order Nilokerus. I requested the best."

"Good, Calin. You seem to have thought of everything. We're going to get along just dandy." He rubbed his prickly chin, turned his chair around and, tilting his head back, said to the barber, "You may begin."

With a tremble in his step, the Nilokerus shaver advanced, placed his box on the table, and went to work, rubbing sweet-smelling, clear lubricant on Treet's prickly face to prepare the beard. Treet closed his eyes and said, "The last guide I had was blind."

"Hage guides are blind."

"Why?"

"When they are assigned, their eyes are put out; otherwise the psi will not come to them. They are not magicians and have no other powers."

Such barbarism was not unheard of. Still, Treet winced. "But you're not blind," he pointed out. "How come?"

"I am a Saecaraz magician," she explained, pride creeping into her voice. "I was chosen by the Supreme Director because of my skill, and because I am a Reader. I have—"

"A magician did you say?" Treet opened his eyes and raised his head. The barber jumped back, razor in hand.

"Yes. Fourth-order."

"That's good, huh?" Treet put his head back down. "You'll have to explain that to me."

Calin shrugged. "There is nothing to explain. One serves one's function, and the priests reward one's achievement by advancing one through the orders. That's all."

"Well, we'll work on that a little more later. But I think I know what you're saying. Go on."

"There is nothing else to tell."

"Oh?" Treet cracked open an eye. "Are you single? Married? Do you live alone or with a whole bunch of other magicians? What does a magician do exactly? How big is this place anyway? How many people? Where does Empyrion gets its power? How do you grow your food? Why do you live under this dome? What's this business about Nilokerus and Saecaraz? What do you do for fun? How is the colony governed? Do you have laws? What's it like outside?" Treet paused for breath. "See? There's lots to tell."

"I am admonished," replied Calin, much taken aback with Treet's rapid-fire questioning.

"Don't worry about it. I just wanted to give you an idea of my interests. I'm interested in everything." Treet quit talking and allowed the barber to finish scraping his face clean of whiskers. When the barber took out his scissors, however, Treet waved him off, saying, "I'll skip the trim, if you don't mind. Next time." He rubbed his tingling face with pleasure. "Good job. Help yourself to a plantain or whatever those things are."

He turned to Calin, exitement bubbling through his veins. "I'm ready! Let's go!"

Calin smiled. She liked this unpredictable Traveler, and his enthusiasm swept over her like a rumor through the Hage. "Tell me where you wish to go. I will take you anywhere."

• • • • • •

They stood at the rimwall of the topmost terrace in Saecaraz Hage—the highest point in all Empyrion. The dome directly over their heads—a scant hundred meters away, Treet estimated—was not perfectly bowl-shaped. It was more like the inside of an old-fashioned circus tent, complete with poles.

He could clearly see individual panes large enough to cover whole city blocks back in Houston; the cords that bound them, like the strands of an enormous spiderweb, were as big as the trunks of California redwoods. The gigantic support poles which poked up through the dome were as big as hypertrain tubes.

"Some view," remarked Treet after a long moment of silence. The effect was like standing on an alpine mountain summit overlooking deep valleys with their huddled villages below. Only here, the mountain was a squat pyramid of plates stacked atop one another in descending circumferences, and the valleys were plazas and greenspace, although at least one river of size wound its way along the lowest level rimwall to disappear around a terrace curve far below.

Treet was no accurate judge of distance, but guessed that on Earth, on a good day, he could see perhaps twenty-five or thirty kilometers. The other side of the dome appeared to be at least that far, maybe farther—he couldn't tell because there was no haze to cloud distance and offer perspective.

"We are near the center of Empyrion. This is Saecaraz Hage. Threl High Chambers and the Supreme Director's kraam are below us. Over there," Calin pointed across space to another terraced hillside in the distance, "is Nilokerus hage. And there," she swiveled forty-five degrees, "is Chryse. Tanais is next to it, adjoining Saecaraz."

To Treet these landmarks were fairly meaningless since he couldn't tell where one place left off and another began. Like suburbs of a metropolis, one place simply merged with another. "Just what is a Hage?" asked Treet. "Is it a place or a social designation? You see to imply both."

"I don't understand social dez-ik-nation."

"It's . . . ah, like a class or a family." From the frown on Calin's face Treet knew he had explained nothing. "It's who you are."

Calin bent her head in thought, her forehead wrinkled. "It is a place," she said finally, "when one goes there. It is a social dez-ik-nation when one comes from there." She smiled, proud of her definition.

Now it was Treet's turn to frown. "I see. You live there you mean. It's home."

"Home?" Calin shook her head. The word meant nothing to her. "We live in Hage, yes."

"Everyone lives in a different Hage?"

"Yes, the Saecaraz live here, the Nilokerus there," she pointed across the distance again, "the Chryse there, and the Tanais, and the others," she indicated with a sweep of her hand, "each in his own Hage." Her tone implied that this was a most obvious and elementary fact.

Treet began to see the arrangement. Whatever else it was, a Hage was clearly some sort of social marker which aided internal organization. A caste system, apparently. "I'm beginning to get it, I think." They turned away from the wall and walked back to the lift entrance. "Take me to a Hage; I want to see one close up."

Calin cocked her head to one side. "We are in Hage. We are in Saecaraz."

"No; I mean I want to go to a different one. Nylokeerus—is that how you say it?—let's go to that one."

The guide hesitated. "Perhaps Bolbe. It's closer."

"Fine," replied Treet. "Tell me about it on the way."

They reached the lift and began their descent to what Calin called Gladwater level. "The Bolbe are a small Hage, and have little stent, but at least they are above the Jamuna—although some of their magicians are equal to the best Chryse players." This fact was illustrated with the graceful flip of an upraised palm, which Treet read to mean that things tended to even out, at least for some members of a Hage.

Calin continued, "The Bolbe are weavers mostly, and tailors. I will take you to their Hageworks where you can see what they do."

The lift stopped, and they stepped out into a dark, cavernous gallery hollowed from the stone crust of the planet. Dim lights set in the walls cast pale illumination into an oblong room whose slab-cut ceiling echoed with the ping of splashing water. A pathway described by tiny yellow lights led down to a waterfront where people had gathered. There were, Treet guessed, a hundred or so colonists—the most he'd seen so far—and they appeared to be waiting for something.

"What's going on here?" Treet asked. His guide pursed her lips—an expression which meant he had asked an incomprehensible question. He rephrased it. "I mean, what are these people doing?"

"They are waiting for a boat," Calin said. "We will go with them to Bolbe Hage."

"By boat?"

"Unless you are afraid of boats." She regarded him with concern. "Many people do not like boats. I myself like them very much. I ride whenever I can."

"Boats are fine. Wonderful. I like boats, too—only I never expected to ride one here, that's all."

They had come to the water's edge to stand waiting with the others gathered there. Treet could see kimonos in several different colors: gold-striped, red-striped, turquoise-hooded with silver-banded sleeves, green-sleeved with yellow hems. Those wearing identical robes stood together—well away from the ones wearing different colors. His guess was correct: the robes were uniforms. "These are the colors of the Hage?" He indicated the various clustered groups.

"All Hagemen wear the yos so that they may be recognized," Calin explained simply.

"Black and silver—that's Saecaraz?" Treet plucked at his own uniform.

"The silver bands are Saecaraz," Calin replied, "and the gold Tanais." She nodded to a group wearing yoses with vertical gold stripes. "The green and yellow is Hyrgo; the red is Rumon." She named the various ones around them.

"Saecaraz, Hyrgo, Rumon," Treet repeated. "How many are there altogether? How many Hages?"

The magician looked at him oddly. "Eight," she replied as if this should be self-evident.

"Eight? Why not six, or ten, or twenty?"

Calin shook her head slowly. "There are eight," she began solemnly, and then looked away as the crowd around them surged forward. "Look, the boat is coming."

Treet could not see the boat. The cave was not well lit, and the people pressed close to the rail at the water's edge. He saw a dark shape glide up, and heard the hollow scrape as the hull touched the wharf. Someone called out something in a loud voice which he did not understand. A murmur went through the passengers on the dock. In a moment the crowd began to move forward.

When they reached the rail to board the boat, Treet saw

three men in red-striped yoses and short, blunt wands in their hands, standing at the head of a wide gangplank. Passengers passed before these men, who pressed the glowing point of the wand against the exposed flesh of each person's upper right arm.

"What's this?" asked Treet.

"To ride the boat costs two shares," said Calin. "They read poak as you board." She raised the sleeve of her yos and presented her arm. The boatman pressed the glowing point against her arm as she stepped onto the gangplank.

Treet followed her example, watching closely. He felt a pleasant tingle where the wand touched his arm. The bored boatman waved him on, and Treet climbed down into the boat. It was a squarish, boxy carrier—more barge than boat—made for transporting cargo and passengers short distances: flat decks—three of them, one atop the other over three quarters of the boat, with the small third deck over the rear quarter—surrounded by a woven rope rail. There were benches along the sides and in the center; all the rest was deck space—filled with passengers and, here and there, mounds of stacked bales and bundles.

"I always ride there," said Calin, pointing to the topmost deck. She pushed through the other passengers toward the midsection of the boat where a stairway led up to the upper decks.

Treet followed her up to the third deck, gripping the handrail as the boat swung away from the stone pier. In the darkness there was not much to see, but Treet felt a sensation of motion and glimpsed the yellow lights of the waterfront sliding backward. They were off.

They journeyed in gloom, but Treet saw that they had entered a channel. Rock walls pressed inward, and the boat picked up speed as the river ran more swiftly through the narrowed course. After what seemed an interminable length of time, Treet saw the mottled gray stone lighten as it closed on them, and all at once they were out of the cave.

"It's fantastic!" cried Treet, blinking in the bright daylight. "I've never seen anything like it!"

TWENTY
FIVE

*I*f the view from above was impressive, the view from the river was spectacular. But, as Treet had noticed before, look more closely and you'd see that everything had a frayed and rundown appearance. The river—flat, broad, and blue-gray—crawled between undulating, step-sided mountains. Along the moss-covered lower rimwalls which formed the banks, short, knob-shaped trees trailed flowered vines into the water; fluffy, long-bladed grass of pale green fringed the water's edge.

The boat swept along with the water on its own unhurried way. Treet saw scores of people moving along the shoreline roads, some of them riding small, open-air vehicles, but most walking in tight little groups. The upper terraces were lined with curious, multiple-humped buildings, many four or more stories tall. Through the oblong windows he saw lights flash occasionally, which made him think of factories.

"What goes on up there?" he asked Calin.

She turned to where he looked. "One of the Saecaraz Hageworks," Calin explained. "That is where they repair the ems."

"Ems? What's an em?"

"Those—" She pointed to the movement along the terrace.

"Those little cars, you mean?"

"A kar is a veeckle, yes?" the young magician asked. Treet nodded, despite her mispronunciation of the word vehicle, so she continued. "As a Reader, I am allowed to examine certain old records. I have read of veekles such as kars."

"I see," said Treet. "Doesn't everyone read?"

Calin tilted her head to the side. "What would be the use? Only Readers read."

"Oh." Treet dropped the subject. He had decided that he would not offer the colonists observations about his world—even though he itched to point out the contrasts. In his travels, he had learned that such observations by foreigners were not only unwelcome, but most often had the effect of drying up the free flow of quality information—as if the host preferred not to toss his best pearls before the foreign swine. Who, after all, wants to risk himself, his country, or his customs to the ridicule of infidels?

A sponge I am; a sponge I will remain, thought Treet; and sponges do not make waves. He changed the subject. "Where does this river go?"

"It is called Kyan," explained Calin. She turned to view it, her eyes sweeping its curves. "It flows throughout Empyrion, through every Hage. There is a very old story about the river." She glanced at him tentatively.

"Go on, I'd like to hear it."

"The story says that long ago, before the cluster was closed, before there were Hages even, the old ones traveled on the water. An old one called Litol built a very big boat and took half the people with him to find a faraway place. While they were riding the water, the boat caught fire and sank, and Litol and all the rest were lost.

"Those left behind saw the red fire in the sky at night and knew that their friends would never return. They decided to make their own river, which they bent into a circle and filled with the tears from their eyes, for they wept over Litol and the lost. This is why the river flows as it does, so that whoever rides the water need never be afraid of getting lost since the river always comes back to its beginning."

Calin fell silent when she finished the story. To Treet's trained ear the story sounded familiar: just like scores of other folktales he'd heard. The story hid as much as it revealed, but it nevertheless countained elements of historic fact—grains of verity served up in a soup of mythic fancy.

"That's a nice story," remarked Treet.

Calin stirred, sighed. "It is a very old story. No one knows how old. There are others like it—I know them all."

"You must tell me more of them sometime. I like old stories." Yes, I do, thought Treet. Those old stories will help me piece together what happened here.

The river swept around the feet of the terraced mountains and now came to a place of sculptured hillsides which rolled gently down to the seamless rock wall of Kyan's banks. On a near hillside a dozen or so musicians, dressed in the turquoise and silver of Chryse, sat in a cluster playing for a small crowd of Saecaraz gathered below them. They were too far away to see or hear distinctly, but Treet caught a sense of the sound: light stringed instruments accompanied by dusky, low-voiced woodwinds.

Treet strained after the music, hearing it in wispy snatches. What he heard puzzled him, until he realized that it was the tonal equivalent of Calin's river story—pensive, possessed of a delicate melancholy. In fact, the music articulated the very atmosphere of the colony: brooding and old and tired, tottering to its fall.

Beyond the hills he glimpsed white towers, graceful spires linked with arches, rising above trees thin as tapers. The boat turned abruptly, taking the towers from view before he had a chance to ask about them. He turned and saw that Calin had moved to the other side of the deck. She held the rope rail and looked out toward the opposite bank. Treet joined her.

"You started to tell me about the Hages," said Treet. "I'd like to hear about them now. You said there are eight."

She nodded. "There are eight. The number corresponds to the Greater Requisites of the Sacred Directives. The Hages are Saecaraz, Chryse, Nilokerus, Rumon, Hyrgo, Tanais, Bolbe, and Jamuna. Each holds its place, and thus the eternal balance is maintained. This is also from the Directives."

"I see. And what are these Directives?"

Calin marveled at his ignorance. "You've never heard of the Sacred Directives? How do you live?"

Treet shrugged. "I manage. Perhaps I know them by another name."

"That could be," she allowed. "No one could live very long without them."

"Where did they come from?"

"Come from? The Directives have always been. Since the beginning. They were given—" She hesitated.

"Yes? Given how?" Treet pressed.

The magician's dark eyes darted right and left. She lowered her voice. "There are some things we don't speak of out of Hage."

"Oh? Why not?"

"I can't explain here," she whispered. "Later—I'll tell you later, when we're back in your kraam."

Here was a puzzle. What was there about these Sacred Directives that they could not be discussed in public? Presumably everyone knew about them—why the secrecy? Treet cast a glance to the others around them. No one seemed to be paying any attention to them. "All right, but don't forget. I want to know."

Presently the river widened and a boat traveling the opposite way passed by them. This boat was larger and sported three full decks, all of them crammed with passengers. It was brightly painted in carefree splashes of color—scarlet, yellow, and violet. Raucous music came across the water, along with the clatter of voices, laughter, and song. People mingled on the decks in colorful yoses, large jars in their hands, drinking, singing, laughing loudly.

"Some party," said Treet. The scene reminded him of a Mardi Gras celebration he'd witnessed once in Trinidad: flashy, forced, frenzied.

"It is a cruise," offered Calin.

"Oh, where are they going?"

"Going? They cruise—it is . . ." she paused, searching for a word Treet would understand. "A happy making," she said finally.

"They look happy all right." Treet watched the boisterous boatload pass. "What are they drinking?"

"Souile. Some call it shine. It is an intoxicant."

"So I see. Every last one of them is skunked!" As the party boat plied its way around the bend, several drunken passengers relieved themselves with obvious delight into the river from the aft decks. "They just ride around in circles on this boat and get waxed?"

"A very popular amusement. Once on board, the shine is free—also flash."

"Flash?"

"Pleasure seeds."

"I thought so. Free drinks and drugs! Welcome aboard! Some pleasure cruise."

"Look," said Calin, turning back toward the river bank, "we're coming into Bolbe Hage."

Treet followed her gaze and saw that on this side of the river, the hills had blossomed with color. Every meter of hillside was wrapped in fabric of the most dazzling color and design: shimmering reds and violets, swirls of emerald and chartreuse, glistening blues and deep vibrant browns, pearly whites. The hills were checkerboards with multicolored squares. Treet supposed that the display was a sort of advertisement for the Hage's handiwork.

A little further on, the hills gave way to a waterfront area—

a flat rectangular space ringed by banks of pale yellow mosque-shaped buildings. Two other boats were moored to posts beneath a long notch in the bank wall. Men in blue-hooded yoses were stacking bales on one of the boats, while men in green-and-yellow unloaded them from the other. The bales being unloaded were tumbled down an incline where they were picked up and trundled away on the bent backs of laborers. It was a scene typical of any waterfront on Earth—a thousand years ago.

The boat drifted closer to the wharf, nosing toward a post; ropes snaked out as the boat was snugged into its berth and the gangplank extended. As passengers streamed off, Treet and his magician guide joined the crush on the lower deck and eventually found themselves deposited on the wharf.

"This is where the Hyrgo bring the ipumn," Calin explained. "The Bolbe take it and begin making it into cloth."

"Ipumn is grown by the Hyrgo?" asked Treet. "They're the ones in the green and yellow yoses, right?"

"Yes, those are Hyrgo."

"And who are those in blue, over there—the ones with the medals around their necks?" He indicated a group of three Bolbe standing next to the growing mound of ipumn bales. One of the three held a flat clipboard object which he worked over with a glowing stylus. From a heavy chain swung a large blue-silver medallion which looked like the Greek letter pi with arms.

"Those are Bolbe priests," she said out of the side of her mouth. "They are recording the bring. All that comes and goes within the Hage, the priests record—as they record the dole." She steered him by the priests toward the nearest of the mosques.

"The dole? You mean handouts?"

"I don't understand han-douts," replied Calin. "The dole is given to all freely. It is the right of every Hageman to receive his tender."

"Food, clothing, shelter—that sort of thing?"

"Food and clothing, yes—these are given in the dole. The rest a Hageman must buy with his own shares, which are given by the priests at allotment."

Treet grasped the set-up. Very ingenious. Make certain nobody starved or went naked, meet the bare necessities, and then let them work for the rest, earn the currency with which they could buy the extras. A variation of the old-style socialism. "These shares," said Treet, "that's what the poak is all about?"

He touched his arm at the spot where he had been bruised. There was nothing to feel there now.

Calin nodded, smiling at him. "You learn quickly, Traveler Treet. The shares are given according to a Hageman's order and work record."

"The higher the order, the more shares you get. Slick. What's the highest order?"

"Six, I think, though I don't know if anyone has ever attained sixth order. I am fourth order—most Readers are."

"So you get more shares than a third-order magician, right?"

"Of course. But the allotment also depends on the stent of the Hage. Look there—" She pointed to several Bolbe before a low platform unwrapping the bales of stringy ocher ipumn. "They are perhaps third-order ipumn handlers. Those unloading the boats are first-order. These others," she gestured toward the Bolbe on the platform who were sifting the ipumn and sorting it into piles, "are ipumn graders—second- or third-order. They will receive more shares than the material handlers—as much as dyers, but less than weavers."

"I see," said Treet. "The only way to get more shares is to advance to a higher order or get a better job."

"Job is *function*, yes?"

"Yes. But how do you change functions? I mean, what keeps everyone from wanting to be a magician? If magicians get the most shares, I'd think everyone would want to be one."

"It is difficult to change functions, but it can be done. You must petition the priests. They decide."

"How do they decide?"

"I don't know. This is not for us to know. Although sometimes a Director will request a function change for a Hageman. Then the petition is always granted."

"The Directors run the show—isn't that always the way?"

"Please?"

"Never mind," said Treet. They wandered past the mosque-shaped buildings of the waterfront along a wide avenue bedecked with multicolored hangings and streamers and flags strung across the walkway on wires. At the end of the avenue, they entered a communal square where several work stations had been set up before flat-roofed sheds. Bolbe milled around the work stations, lugging bundles of ipumn. The air was filled with a fine ocher dust and the whine of high-speed machinery.

"This is where they begin breaking down the ipumn fibers. Over there," she gestured across the square, "they pull the fibers, there they separate them, and so on."

The air smelled of cinnamon—not unpleasant, but the dust was getting to Treet. He noticed that the workers wore no protective masks. "They breathe this stuff?"

Calin appeared unconcerned. She turned away, striking off along another path. They walked through Bolbe Hage following the ipumn through the various processes of becoming cloth. They saw spinners turning the raw fibers into hanks of glistening thread, fine as human hair; dryers with poles stirring long, loosely braided chains of ipumn in large pools of bubbling colored dye; dryers turning the braided chains on racks under lamps; weavers threading huge looms, and folding finished material onto square bolts. In all, Bolbe Hage fairly bustled with activity.

What impressed Treet most of all was the diligence and industry with which the Bolbe worked. Both men and women went about their tasks with quick precision; nowhere did he see any slackers or dawdlers. No one lingered over a job; no one sat with idle hands. "Everyone is so busy," he remarked to Calin when at last they headed back toward the boat. It was long past time to eat, and Treet was hungry. "It's remarkable. What keeps them at it?"

"The priests record transgressions against the Directives. Anyone who deviates from the Clear Way will be punished at allotment."

"His shares are cut, in other words?" Treet nodded to himself. Yes, very tidy. Keep them at it with incentives and threats. Reward the good workers, punish the bad. "The priests watch everyone all the time, I suppose? They know who's been naughty and nice."

Calin agreed solemnly. "The priests watch everyone."

They arrived at the waterfront in time to board for the return trip. As the boat pulled away, this time under the tug of a chattering engine, Treet turned for a last look at Bolbe Hage. "You know, we still didn't see where they make the really fine stuff." Treet gestured toward the glowing array of fabric spread on the hillside.

"That is Hage cloth, made in deep Hage. No one is allowed to go there."

"Never?"

Calin lifted a palm in that equivocal gesture which Treet understood to say, it all depends. She said, "The Bolbe guard deep Hage jealously. They allow no one from another Hage to enter. They don't want the secret of their craft revealed. It is the same with the Tanais and Rumon, but the Hyrgo and Jamuna allow anyone to come and go in deep Hage; they don't care. Of course, their craft has no art."

All the way back to Saecaraz and to his kraam Treet remained silent, digesting all he had seen and heard. Calin did not intrude on his reverie, and after seeing that food was brought for a late afternoon meal, she left saying, "I will come tomorrow the same as today, unless—"

Her listener glanced up distractedly. "Yes . . . come tomorrow, same time. Fine . . ."

Treet ate and lay back on his mount of cushions. Not bad for the first day, he thought. Innocent tourist—no surprises, no pointed questions, nothing to upset anyone. The Supreme Director will get a glowing report—he's probably getting it right now.

Treet knew that Rohee would be fully informed of his moods and movements, knew that he would be carefully monitored at all times. That was all right with him—let them watch until they got tired of watching. Then he'd make his move. Somewhere out there Pizzle, Crocker, and Talazac waited, and he meant to find them. One way or another he *would* find them.

The priest rubbed his long nose and gazed at Yarden doubtfully. Bela stood beside her, his hand around her waist. Coming to see the Hage priest had been his idea. He'd said that perhaps her memory would come back more quickly if she bought a benefice.

Together they'd walked through Chryse Hage, not to the temple, but to the Quarter—the place where the priests lived and held commerce with the populace. They waited in line for several hours as one by one the petitioners were admitted into a large mound-shaped structure built on a rise with steps leading up to a wide arched doorway.

"The priests will know what to do," he explained. "Very likely there is astral interference with your aura. If so, they will see it and recommend a suitable treatment."

Yarden thought about this, not understanding it completely. "Will I have to pay them?" she wondered, thinking that she did not have many shares in her poak.

"Of course."

"Is it . . . expensive?"

Bela had laughed. "Never more than you have. But don't worry. The priests understand. They will help if they can."

The room to which they were finally admitted was big and dark and sour smelling. Sweat, smoke, urine, and other unwholesome odors mingled together in a fetid perfume—as if whole generations of priests had lived and died in the room without ever cleaning or opening it to the light of day. The darkness and rank aroma were almost suffocating. Yarden gagged upon entering and would have turned back if Bela had not gripped her very tightly by the arm and urged her forward.

The priest, a bloated, rheumy fellow with drooping eyelids and a chin that rested on his swelling belly, sniffed loudly when they entered the room. He was sitting on a high-backed stool, his voluminous yos spread out around him so that he appeared to be floating in the air. A dirty medallion hung around his neck, shining dully in the light from two candletrees of smudgy candles.

"Step forward," he said tiredly. "Let me see you. What do you want?"

"Go on," Bela whispered as Yarden glanced at him. "Just tell him what you want."

"Well?" The priest cast a baleful eye at her, sniffed again, and sneezed into his hand.

"Tell him," Bela whispered. "Just say what I told you."

"If it please you, Hage Priest," she began in a tremulous voice, "I would like a benefice."

"A benefice," he had repeated flatly. "Of course. And what is the nature of this benefice?"

"My—my memory. I cannot remember things clearly. We—I thought a benefice . . ."

When the priest said nothing, Bela had stepped up, put his arm around Yarden, and explained, "She has been in reorientation, Hage Priest. Her memory is unfortunately—ah, displaced."

"Hmmph!" the priest snorted. He put a thumb in his nostril and blew. "Reorientation."

"Is there anything you can do?" Bela had inquired, thus plunging the priest into a period of deep contemplation during which he stared at Yarden as if she were the carrier of a dread disease.

Finally the priest shifted his bulk and yawned. "How much do you have?"

"Not much," Yarden replied shakily.

"How much?"

"Ten shares."

"It's not enough," he said dryly. "You may go."

"Wait," interposed Bela. "Perhaps you can think of something. Hage priests supervise the allotment, do they not?"

"You know well that we do."

"Then perhaps at the next allotment you could arrange to give her extra shares. She could pay you then." In essence Bela was inviting the priest to name his fee and pay himself.

"It would be expensive," the priest observed. He shook his head slowly, already calculating how much he could get away with.

"Of course." Bela gave Yarden a little squeeze.

"Reorientation." The priest's porcine eyes narrowed. "As much as a hundred shares. Maybe more."

"Maybe two hundred?" inquired Bela.

"Yes. Two hundred."

"You'll do a benefice for two hundred?"

"Very well." He withdrew a short, ball-tipped wand from his clothing and struck a bell hanging from a stand next to him. Another priest came forward with a tripod on which a brazier full of burning coals smouldered. He placed the brazier in front of his fellow priest, then retreated, only to reappear a moment later with a tray. On the tray were bowls of powder in various colors.

"Prepare a healing benefice," said the Hage priest, stifling another yawn.

"Mind or body?" asked his assistant.

"Mind. Make it twice strong. She has been in reorientation and has lost her memory."

The second priest lay down the tray and picked up an empty bowl. He began dipping into the various powders with his fingers. "I will add a sarcotic too, to be sure." He tossed powder into the bowl and stirred it with his fingers before handing it to Yarden.

She looked into the bowl, and the assistant priest smiled, revealing brown teeth. He inclined his head and pantomimed dumping the bowl into the brazier. Bela nodded in encouragement.

Yarden stepped up to the brazier and lifted the bowl, tipped it, and carefully emptied its contents onto the coals. There was a sputtering flash, and foul vaporous fumes arose from the coals. Resinous smoke rolled up into the darkness. Yarden stepped from the brazier, convulsed with coughing.

"*Benito, benitu, beniti,*" intoned the Hage Priest in a bored voice. He raised his hand in the air above Yarden's head. "In the name of Trabant, I cleanse the aura of all astral interference . . . and so forth. Let the Seraphic Spheres be content with the offering thus poured out. Restore—ah, what is your name, woman?"

"Yarden."

"Restore Yarden's memory to her in good time," continued the priest, "that she might serve her Hage and follow the Clear Way faithfully. Trabant Animus be praised."

They were dismissed then and left by a side door as the brazier was removed and the next petitioner ushered in quickly. On the way back to Bela's kraam, Yarden remained silent, reeling from the experience with the priest. She could not explain it, but felt dirty, as if she had wallowed in filth and now bore the stains on her face and hands. Waves of revulsion churned inside her. She gulped deep breaths and fought to keep from vomiting.

Bela watched her curiously, but said nothing until they were almost to the kraam. "Do you feel any different?" he asked.

Yarden shook her head, lips pressed tightly together.

"Oh well," said Bela sympathetically, "it often takes a little time. We may have to ask for another benefice if this one doesn't work."

"No!" Yarden turned horror-filled eyes on him. "No more."

Bela laughed. "All right. It doesn't matter. Let me know if you change your mind, though. I'd be glad to take you again."

Yarden turned away. I never want to go back there, she thought. Anger flared. This was Bela's doing. He insisted I go. He knew that would take place. But no, Bela is my friend; he stood by me the whole time. It wasn't his fault, and nothing bad happened.

Still, if nothing bad happened, then why do I feel so unclean?

TWENTY
SIX

The next day for Orion Treet, and the next, was much the same as the day before. In fact, for the next several days in a row he played the tourist, dutifully tagging along beside his guide, visiting each Hage in turn, viewing the life in each of Empyrion's spheres.

By day he was the sponge, soaking up all he could see and all he was told. By night he examined what he had absorbed. He paced the confines of his kraam, sifting facts and observations, trying to create, as with the tiny colored tiles of a mosaic, a single, sweeping picture of Empyrion.

The emerging portrait was that of a civilization in decline: old, decrepit, timeworn. The signs of advanced age were everywhere apparent—stone steps worn hollow by the tread of feet over the centuries; once-straight walls now sliding, tilting, wrapped in thick moss; towers whose shifting foundations bore the marks of decade upon decade of attempted repair; dwelling blocks in whose peeling facades one could trace the histories of whole generations of inhabitants, layer on layer; fetid catacombs where water-stained walls bore ancient graffiti. Empyrion wore a thick patina of time.

Treet sensed a primordial heaviness, the all-pervading lethargy of decay.

The untold years had witnessed the evolution of an extremely stratified society—not only distinct classes, each separate from the other, but classes within classes—and each stratum fiercely protective of its station and function while at the same time aggressively seeking to improve its position in relation to the others through a subtle ongoing competition, the rules of which Treet had not yet discovered, much less understand.

For the citizenry of Empyrion, the Hages were everything: home, family, country—all in one. A Hage was a political entity as well as a gear in a complex economic machine; it was both social matrix and utilitarian construct; it was a rigid caste system which created for its members a sense of place and purpose and belonging in return for work.

Each Hage was governed by a Director who, through his staff of Subdirectors, ruled his fief with despotic power, answering only to the Supreme Director, chief dictator among dictators. The power of the Director seeped downward through a bewildering hierarchy of priests and magicians. Hage priests supervised the allotment, paying out shares for work; they conducted the regular Astral Services and presided over the occasional feast day celebrations.

Calin had even taken him inside an Astral Temple. It was a big, black pyramid, empty but for rows of seats placed round a small stage. At a Service the priest read from the Sacred Directives—a body of writings that had come down from the earliest times—and exhorted their congregations to follow the Clear Way, a path of obedience leading to enlightenment.

The dome dwellers worshiped a god called Trabant Animus, Lord of the Astral Planes. It was Trabant who bestowed immortality on a soul and, if sufficient progress had been made during its lifetime, joined it with one of the many oversouls or spirits of the highly enlightened departed. Once joined to an oversoul, a soul journeyed through two realms or existences: Shikroth and Ekante. One, Shikroth, was called the House of Darkness; the other, Ekante, the House of Light. The journey through both was accomplished under the direction of sexless astral bodies known as Seraphic Spheres—entities of pure psychic energy.

The religion made no sense to Treet. Rather, it made about as much sense as any other religion he'd ever encountered. Treet had little use for religion, tending to see it merely as something to keep the dim, cold unknown from becoming too frightening. He wasn't easily frightened, so relegated religion to the dustbin of outmoded ideas.

Magicians, Treet learned, were just as mystical as priests in their own way, and just as bound up in an incomprehensible code of belief. Each Hage had at least six magicians assigned to it, and often many more. Their function was to maintain the electronic equipment and oversee the use of all machinery. They were technicians, but with a difference: in order to repair Empyrion's failing equipment, magicians had to steep themselves in technical knowledge—machine lore, Calin called it—which had been handed down from magician to magician for ages past remembering.

For this, some of them were schooled as Readers, as Calin had been, in order to scour old documents for references pertaining to the repair of machines. All were trained in psychic abilities, since most of the equipment was so old they often had to, as Calin put it, *merge* with a machine in order to repair it. The knowledge of how to manufacture the more complex machines had been lost in the second Purge. So magicians had their hands full just keeping up with simple maintenance and willing tired machines to go on functioning.

The rest of the tasks necessary for cohering a complex society fell to the workers. Everyone in the colony was assigned a job, and everyone worked. Children—and Treet saw very few children—were born into a Hage creche where, at the age of six months, they were assigned a function. Children were apprenticed in their crafts until the age of fourteen, when they were formally initiated into the Hage and took their places as adults beside the other workers.

Hage populations, therefore, were kept at fairly constant levels, adjusted as need arose. New workers replaced old. Treet had not learned yet what happened to those who were replaced. He presumed they stayed on in deep Hage, caring for children too young to work, since neither the very old nor the very young were visible in the places he'd visited.

This then was the emerging portrait of Empyrion. True, it bore little resemblance now to what its creators must have established. There was no trace of its original intent that he could see. Empyrion had evolved into a creature far different from any corporation colony Earth had ever seeded. The time shift, whatever its mechanisms, accounted for most of that, certainly. But there were other forces at work too, Treet knew.

He'd read of European miners in South America who, lost for years in the Brazilian jungle, had evolved a strange, cultic society with an entirely new language and culture. When they were discovered forty years later, none of the rescuers could understand a word they said, nor did the miners wish to return to civilization—they had their *own* civilization!

Something like that had happened to Empyrion. But what Treet saw around him had taken far longer than forty years to evolve. Just how much longer, he would have to discover. They must have a data bank, or some sort of official repository of information on the colony. And that, he thought, is the next place I want to go.

When Calin came for him the following morning, Treet hit her with his request. She did not react at first; she looked at him blankly, as if she had not heard. When Treet repeated himself, she became flustered. Her eyes slid away from his, and she twisted her features grotesquely.

"What's wrong?" asked Treet. "What did I say?"

"I—" She hesitated and started again. "We can't go there!" she managed to force out.

"What do you mean, we can't go there? Why not? And why are you whispering?"

"It is forbidden."

"Forbidden? The library is off-limits? I don't believe it." He laughed sharply. This seemed to agitate the magician even more.

"Don't talk so!" she rasped.

"I'll talk any way I please," sneered Treet. What had come over his guide this morning?

She reached out and plucked at his sleeve, inclining her head toward the door. Treet caught her meaning and nodded, and they both left the kraam without another word.

Once outside, Treet demanded, "All right, now suppose you explain what all that was about? Why the convulsions in there just now?"

Calin was pulling him along the corridor which led out to the Sweetair level terrace. "We could not talk in there," she said, glancing up at his face once and then turning her eyes forward once more. "Your kraam is . . . is—"

Treet supplied the word himself. "Wired? Is that what you're trying to say? Someone's listening in on me?"

Calin nodded solemnly. "They are listening."

"Who?"

"Invisibles." The word was a whisper.

"So what?" Treet shrugged. "I don't care if they listen. They can take pictures too, for all I care. I've got nothing to hide." Except my suspicions, he added to himself.

"It is not good to talk openly about such things," Calin said, returning somewhat to her normal demeanor.

"Not good for who—you or me?" Treet frowned and watched the dark-haired woman beside him. In the handful of days they'd spent together he had grown quite fond of her. She had loosened up around him to the extent that he felt he could ask almost any question that occurred to him. This little episode just now in his quarters served as a fresh reminder that he was not on a sightseer's holiday. These people were different from him in subtle yet fundamental ways; he would do well to remember that.

Treet stopped. Calin walked a couple of paces alone until she halted and faced him.

"Okay, spill it. What is the big secret around here?" he said. "I won't go another step until you tell me."

"I don't understand."

"You know what I'm talking about. You're all hiding something—what is it? What do you know that I don't know?"

Treet looked at her sharply. He hoped that his abrupt question would have the effect of shaking part of an answer out of her—if she knew anything. "Well? I'm waiting. Do we stand here all day?" Far down the corridor behind them came a group of Saecaraz Hagemen.

"I don't know what you mean," Calin pleaded. She glanced quickly at the approaching figures. "We must go." She turned, expecting Treet to follow. Instead he sat down.

Calin took a step and then turned back, her eyes growing wide with horror when she saw him squatting in the middle of the corridor. "Get up! You can't sit there like that!"

"Why not? I'm not hurting anything," Treet replied mildly. This was working better than he'd hoped.

"It is forbidden!" Calin stooped and tugged at his arm, trying to raise him. The Hagemen behind her came closer. They had stopped talking among themselves and were watching the scene before them. "Please, get up and let us hurry away from here."

"What happens if I don't?"

"The Threl will hear of it. The Supreme Director will punish me."

"Tell me what I want to know, and I'll get up."

The Hagemen were within earshot now, and were watching very carefully. Calin nodded, whispering desperately, "Yes, yes, I will tell you what I know."

"About the data repository, too?"

"Yes! Yes!"

The others were almost on top of them. Treet nodded and pushed himself up slowly, pressing his hands to his back. "I don't know what happened," he said loudly. "I must not have been looking where I was going. Nasty fall."

Calin had her hands on him, hauling him upright. She appeared properly concerned that he had not hurt himself. The Hagemen halted beside them, glancing at one another with puzzled expressions. "He is not hurt," she explained. They grunted and moved on, looking over their shoulders suspiciously.

"Easy, wasn't it?" said Treet. "Now, about those answers."

"We cannot talk here. But I know a place—the River-walk."

"Let's go."

The Riverwalk was a wide, ambling boulevard of square-cut stone which ran abreast of Kyan. Calin led Treet along the moss-grown rimwall which formed one bank for the river below. Hageman from various Hages—Saecaraz, Tanais, and Nilokerus mostly—moved along the tree-lined road, some in the small electric carts, ems, that looked like chariots without horses or visible wheels, and the rest on foot in isolated groups. Quite a few of the latter were pushing large hand-wagons of a type Treet had seen before in his travels: a sizable box slung over a U-shaped axle between two bicycle-type wheels with a third small swivel wheel in front. Each barrow was piled high with cargo, and those pushing strained to the task.

They had walked along in silence for some time. Treet could see that Calin was mulling the situation over in her head, trying to decide how and what to tell him. That was all right, but he didn't want to give her too much time; he'd get soft answers that way. "I think we've come far enough," he told her. "Let's talk."

"Many things are forbidden to us," she said simply. "We know this is for the best, so we do not question it. To question what does not concern you is unwise."

"Unhealthy, you mean?" He watched her closely; she walked with her head bent, eyes to the ground.

"Do not talk so loud," she warned, "and keep your mouth hidden. There may be lipreaders close by."

"Lipreaders—informants?"

Calin nodded. "The Invisibles use them."

"Okay, I'll be discreet. But tell me, why all the secrecy? What is everyone afraid of?"

"I have already told you," she said lightly. "It is for our good that certain things remain hidden. Only pain and death come from knowing."

"Ignorance is bliss, is that it? Keep the masses happy, give them bread and circuses, and trouble stays away from your door."

Calin peered at him strangely. Clearly, she did not comprehend sarcasm. "Your words bite, Traveler Treet. They veil your meaning."

"Never mind. So why can't we go to the library—or whatever you call it—where all the information about the colony's past is kept?"

She spoke into the folds of her yos, muffling her words. But her answer surprised him. "There are enemies among us who are trying to destroy our nation. They work in secret; so we use secrecy against them."

"I see. Who are they, and why do they want to destroy everything?"

"They are called the Fieri. I know very little about them, but I know that once, long ago, there was a great war in which the Fieri were overcome and cast out. They pledged eternal hatred toward us, and ever since have tried to destroy us. They have sown their evil among us and have won over some of the weaker of our people, twisting them with their hatred. That is why we must all be so careful. That is why we are watched and why we watch."

Treet knew enough about repressive regimes to understand that he'd just been fed the accepted party line. There seemed to be no reason to badger Calin about her explanation. Very likely she believed every word herself. He tried a different tack. "This war interests me. I would like to find out more about it."

"The Archives," she said softly. "The data bank you speak of."

His eyebrows went up. "Yes?"

"That is where you will find what you wish to know."

"I thought you said it was forbidden."

"It is. No one may go there—not magicians, not even Hage priests. No one but the Supreme Director himself."

"Or someone who had his permission perhaps?" Treet stopped in his tracks. "Take me to him now. I want to ask him."

Calin studied him for a moment, as if trying to read his thoughts from his face. "I will take you to him. But whatever answer he gives must be sufficient."

"Whatever he says goes. That's fine with me." They began walking the opposite direction, back toward Saecaraz deep Hage. "Do you think I have a chance?"

Calin smiled slightly. "I can't say. Perhaps. I know that he has given you special privileges for a purpose."

"What purpose I wonder?"

The magician shrugged. "He has not told me." Her tone became gravely serious. "It is said among us, however, that he who stands too near the Threl deserves his fate. You must be careful."

Treet gazed at the dark-haired magician. Her concern touched him; it was the first time she had given any hint of feeling for him. "I'll be careful," he told her. "Now, let's go see Rohee. I have a feeling he'll want me to see those Archives."

TWENTY
SEVEN

The Archives of Empyrion were like nothing Treet had ever imagined. The main room was a chamber half-a-kilometer on a side with a flat expanse of a roof a good fifty meters from the floor. In essence the enormous room was the colony's attic: a place where the flotsam and jetsam of an aging civilization was consigned to molder quietly into dust.

In entering the room, he and Calin had passed through a dark, steep downward passage protected first by sleepy Nilokerus guards and then by heavy metal doors at intervals of thirty meters, each with its own coded lock. The last door, twice a man's height and ten meters wide, had been sealed; it gave a whoosh of indrawn air when Treet, following Rohee's precise directions, pressed the code sequence into the pentagon of lighted tabs on the lock and twisted the opening mechanism. Dusky light filtered down from skylight wells overhead as they stepped down onto the floor of the chamber.

Treet had often fantasized about what it would be like to discover a lost Pompeii, or the forgotten tomb of an Egyptian Pharaoh in the Valley of the Kings. Upon setting foot in that silent room, his dream became reality. His heart palpitated; his throat tightened; his palms grew clammy and his knees spongy. Here was a vast treasure-trove of the unknown past, a mine of information about the colony's history. Its riches were his and his alone to discover.

Supreme Director Rohee had been cagey when approached about the Archives. He had not said no right away, neither had he agreed. Instead, with sly, hooded eyes, peering down his beak nose over steepled fingers, he listened to Treet's lengthy entreaty and then questioned Calin closely before making them wait six hours for his decision. The waiting had been maddening—all the time Treet suspecting he would be denied access to the Archives, and wanting it more by the minute. But his frustration melted at once when a Saecaraz Hage priest appeared at his kraam with the message that he was to come at once to Threl High Chambers. There Rohee had informed him that he and Calin would be allowed to examine the Archives in the company of the Hage priest who would keep watch so that the spirits of the place would not be disturbed.

The three of them had set off at once. It was still early evening and, since Treet intended to make his first visit a meaningful one, they had brought food and drink with them.

The Hage priest had not spoken a word since delivering his message. He remained a mute sentinel, hanging back as Treet tugged open the door, following warily, like a creature flushed from its natural surroundings. The priest's curious reluctance brought to Treet's mind a stock character in old 2-D movies: the cowering ethnic guide who is made to trespass on his fore-fathers' burial ground by gold-lusting fortune hunters.

"Jackpot!" Treet's voice rang hollow in the cavernous room as he stepped lightly down from the last of four steps which formed concentric ledges around the Archive's circumference. A fine gray film lay over everything—not dust, for the room was sealed. It looked like time itself, oxidized and deposited as silt to form a transparent shroud over Empyrion's past. Not a trace of a smudge anywhere, Treet duly noted; any intruders' foot-prints would be plainly visible on the floor. Therefore, he con-cluded that no one had entered the Archives in a very long time—years at least, perhaps centuries.

"I guess Rohee doesn't come down here much," said Treet, gazing around. The size of the room made his voice small. Directly before him lay a jumble of artifacts and machines and stacks and ranks of containers of various sizes and shapes, around and through which ran a maze of intertwined pathways. He fought down the impulse to dash forward along the first path at his feet and start prying into everything he saw. "We'll have to have a plan," he said, mostly to himself. "There's too much here to just run at it. We'd be here months before we even knew what we were looking at."

At that moment, the priest, above them on the steps where they'd left him, stretched out his arms and began chanting in a trembly sing-song. He held in each tight fist something that looked like a frayed black rope bound to the end of a stubby handle. As his voice rose and fell, echoing eerily back from the depths, he began flailing away with the ropes in loopy figure eights.

"What's got into him?" wondered Treet.

"He is clearing an astral zone for us to work in. There will be many spirits gathered here, clinging to the old things. He is reminding them that we, the living, are their masters. We should not have any trouble from them." Calin's dark eyes were wide with wonder as she spoke, her voice tinged with awe.

"Well, let's get started. There must be some sort of map for this place, or a floor plan or something. I would guess it might be near the entrance here. Let's look around for anything that might show us the layout."

Calin nodded, although she little understood all that Treet had said. Together they began searching the immediate area, stirring fine gray powder from everything they touched.

"Make a note: we'll need masks if we're going to be working in this stuff," said Treet after only a few moments. Clouds puffed up around his hands and feet; his clothes were already well decorated with powdery handprints. "We could use a vacuum cleaner, too. Hold on. What's this?"

Calin's head jerked around as she straightened up. "You have found something?" She came to where he stood bent over a pedestal set in the floor. It was covered with a cloth whose filth-encrusted folds had stiffened with age.

Slowly, so as not to dislodge an avalanche of "dust" onto whatever had been protected beneath, Treet lifted the covering. The pedestal was a free-standing data terminal, quite old—yet of a design Treet had recently seen on Earth.

A strange feeling of displacement stole over Treet. How odd, he thought, to find an object of the very latest modern design looking a thousand years old. Here was something that could not be more than five years in service at the more up-to-date corporate offices, yet bearing the marks of countless years of hard use. It was unsettling.

"Time travel," Treet whispered, letting the cloth drop at his feet. "I wonder if this thing still works." He regarded the terminal doubtfully. It was so *old*. And yet, silicon and platinum were hardly perishable substances. With a shrug he touched the sensor plate.

Nothing happened.

He tapped it and then punched it harder. Still nothing.

He turned to Calin. "You're a magician—do something."

The woman bent over the terminal and placed her hands against its sides. She closed her eyes, became motionless.

Treet stared at her in disbelief. His comment had been meant as a joke. But Calin apparently took him seriously, and acted on his suggestion. What could she be doing? he wondered. The colonists were afflicted with a weird regard for spirits and such, but did they believe they could communicate with machines too?

In a moment the dark-haired magician straightened and lifted her hands away from the terminal housing. She delicately placed a finger on the sensor plate and held it there. To Treet's amazement, the screen flickered to bright green life.

Magic?

"This one is very old. It needed coaxing," Calin explained.

"So I see." Treet scrutinized the young woman, seeing her in a strange new light. She appeared inexpressibly foreign to him just then: mystery wrapped. "No wonder they call you magicians," he said at last, then turned his attention to the terminal. "Let's see what we've got."

There were a half-dozen symbols embossed on the sensor plate and Treet recognized them as ordinary computer function designators. He brushed one with a fingertip, and a menu came up on the screen. "So far, so good. It's in the mother tongue at least."

At his shoulder, Calin squinted at the black letters. "This is the writing of the ancients," she said. "Very difficult to read."

"Oh, I don't know," remarked Treet, and rattled off a string of words from the menu.

Calin marveled at this achievement. "You know the writing of the old ones? But how?"

He decided on an evasive answer to save a lengthy explanation. "I learned it a long time ago." Treet scanned the menu and chose an entry called *General Reference,* made his selection, and watched as the screen cleared and another menu flashed up. He grinned at Calin. "Banzai! This is what we're looking for."

Among the entries on this second menu was a selection titled *Archival Orienting.* He chose it and watched as the screen drew a detailed floor plan of the enormous room, dividing it into multicolored sections. Lips pursed, chin in hand, Treet alternated his study of the screen with a survey of the room, fixing the layout in his mind.

Presently he looked up to find Calin sifting among a stack of sealed lightprint disks. "I found these over there," she said, inclining her head toward a formidable tower of barrel-shaped plastic containers whose base was littered with the disks. She held a handful out to him.

The magnetic ink on the yellowed plastic labels had faded almost beyond legibility, but Treet managed to decipher some of them. He read: *Maintenance: Fusion Core Ceramic Shields; Stress Factors in Spun Steel Suspension Systems; Integrated Circuitry and Biogenics; Crystal Patterning.*

"These are the instruction manuals," said Treet.

"Instruction manuals?"

"For the colony—all this." He waved his hand to embrace all of Empyrion. "Everything."

"Is this a *find?*" Calin asked.

"You pay attention, don't you? Yes, it's a find," Treet allowed. "But not exactly what I'm looking for." He turned back to the screen. "What we want is human documentation."

"Human doc—?"

"Records, files, disks, cartridges—but about people, not how to grow crystals," he said absently, studying the glowing screen before him.

There did not seem to be any particular place where documents were kept. What Treet hoped to find was a cache of diaries or logbooks of the colony's first years of operation. Surely such things existed. He had never heard of a colony that did not keep copious records on itself. Empyrion, being the first extra-system colony, would have monitored itself scrupulously and generated an ocean of data.

Treet heard a soft, grunting sound like an animal snoring, and looked back to the upper ledge where the Hage priest lay. He had spread his yos under him and now slept with his head on his arm. Strange bird, thought Treet. Doesn't he know what is here?

He punched up the menu again and spent the next hour trying its selections, but found nothing that promised immediate help. He sighed. This was going to be a long haul. Unless they stumbled over something accidentally, the information he sought would only be found through a methodical and painstaking search. The thought made him cringe—sectioning off a room this size with its jumble of articles . . . daunting, to say the least.

When Treet finally raised his head from the datascreen, he saw that the light had dwindled. Sinking into darkness, the shadows thickened in the room, fusing, deepening.

Where was the light switch for this place? he wondered. He

trotted back to the entrance, stepping over the body of the sleeping priest. He searched the area for a switchplate of any description, but found nothing. There must be lights somewhere, but where?

It was getting too dark to search, and without a clue to where the lights were, there was no hope of finding them in the dark. "Calin!" Treet called. "We'll have to come back tomorrow. It's getting too dark to see, and I can't find the lights. Calin?"

He listened. Nothing.

No sound came from the floor. She had been right there only moments before, standing next to him. Where could she have gone? He stared around him at a broken wall of dimming shapes, now pale and unreal in the twilight. In the silt of one of the many pathways through the mountains of discarded objects her footprints lay—but which one? It was now too dark to make out footprints anyway.

"Ca-a-l-l-i-n-n!" he called.

"Hageman, we want to talk to you."

Nendl, casting a quick glance over his shoulder, hesitated. Two Hagemen in Jamuna brown were coming up fast behind him. He hadn't known he was being followed. His kraam lay but a few meters ahead, so he put his head down and ran to it, slipped in, and snapped on the unidor. He lay panting against the wall.

They had seen where he went, he knew. But that could not be helped. At least he was safe in his kraam now, and it would be night soon; they would not wait for him all night. They would try to nab him in the morning on his way to the fields. But by then he would be safely hidden where they'd never find him.

He moved away from the wall and heard a heavy scraping sound, like someone boring through the stucco of his kraam. The wall began to vibrate. He put his hand out and withdrew it instantly—the surface was hot to the touch.

As he stood watching, the wall convulsed and a section collapsed inward, scattering dust and debris. The two men stood looking at him through the haze of dust. One of them had a flat, nozzle-shaped instrument in his hands; the other stepped into the kraam through the jagged hole.

"Hageman, you forget your manners," he said. His eyes were hard, his voice soft and silky. "Your name is Nendl."

"No," the Jamuna recycler replied. He swallowed hard, his heart beating in his throat.

The man smiled thinly. "Perhaps that is not your private name, but Nendl is your Hagename."

"Who are you? What do you want?"

"Only to talk to you."

"Go away. Come see me tomorrow."

"We will go away when you tell us what we want to know."

Nendl glared at the man, but clamped his mouth shut.

"Tell us where your Hagemate is."

"I have not had a Hagemate in several years."

The man smiled patiently. "The one who has been living here with you—where is he? Answer quickly—we grow tired of your impertinence."

"I don't know who you mean."

"Liar!" the man roared. Smiling unexpectedly, he moved closer. "Try again. Where is he?"

"I don't know." Fear made Nendl's voice quiver.

The man spun on his heel. Nendl did not see the leg swing up and the foot snap out. The kick caught him on the point of the chin and drove his jaw backward, breaking off the lower front teeth and dislocating his jaw. Nendl fell backwards, blood spurting from his mouth. The man stood over him, smiling, then lifted his foot and ground it into the recycler's genitals. Nendl screamed.

"You should have shown us some courtesy, Hageman," said the man softly, watching his victim writhe on the floor. He turned away abruptly and jerked this thumb over his shoulder at Nendl. "Bring him," he said to his companion, and strode out.

TWENTY
EIGHT

The message had been explicit; there was no mistake. Tvrdy had acted at once to arrange a meeting of the Cabal. Now he waited at the appointed place—a granary in Hyrgo deep Hage. He wore the green-sleeved yos of the Hyrgo and sat among bulging sacks of fresh-smelling grain. He waited patiently, knowing the others would join him soon, content to allow Piipo's personal bodyguard to keep watch over the meeting-place.

How long must we continue to practice our deceptions? he wondered. Not long, he guessed. One way or another there would be an end to their secret activity. The day was coming for open confrontation. He could feel the dread approach of that day in his bones. It would be a dark day. Yes, a dark, bloody day.

The quick flit of a shadowed figure hurrying along the aisle between the steep stacked bags of grain drew Tvrdy's attention away from his thoughts. He recognized the furtive step as that of Cejka's. He stood and welcomed his friend.

"No trouble tonight?" Tvrdy glanced past Cejka's shoulder—a reflex action born of years of exacting vigilance.

"I was not followed, nor was I seen. Don't worry."

"Did you see anyone else?"

"No one." Cejka studied him closely. "Should I have?"

"Piipo has several of his personals at watch. I thought it best to maintain extra security tonight."

"Your news is that important?"

A tight smile stretched the edges of Tvrdy's lips. "Do you think I would have pulled you from the arms of your Hagemate if it was not?"

"Listen!"

"That will be Piipo. He said he would come after us and seal the entrance. That way we will not fear discovery—at least while we are here."

There was a slight rustle of clothing close by, and Piipo

slipped into view from behind a small pyramid of grain sacks. He walked confidently toward them, his hood thrown back on his shoulders. "This is the best I could provide," he said, indicating their surroundings. "There was not much time." He regarded Tvrdy frankly.

"The information could no doubt have waited until tomorrow, but by then we might have lost an important opportunity to make contact with the intruder in Sirin's custody."

"Yes?" Piipo looked surprised.

"You were right to call us," said Cejka. "I wouldn't care to miss such an opportunity. How did you find out?"

Tvrdy settled back on his grain sack, and the others gathered close. "For several days I have been receiving reports of a stranger moving through the Hages in the company of a Saecaraz magician—a female called Calin. They have been careful not to go into deep Hage, but have moved freely enough among the populace. There does not seem to have been any attempt to disguise their visits."

"I have heard nothing of this," said Piipo.

"They came to Hyrgo two days ago," said Tvrdy dryly. "And to Rumon the day before that. It is not likely they would have been reported—the visits did not draw attention. They traveled on foot for the most part and were observed together at all times. There was nothing at all unusual about their visits."

"Then how do you know it *was* the intruder?" Piipo frowned, and Cejka glanced at him sharply. "I assure you I do not doubt your sources," Piipo hastily added. "But I don't see—"

"If Tvrdy says it was the intruder," Cejka cut him off decisively, "then stake your life on it."

Tvrdy raised his hands to quiet the two and continued. "Today, however, they stayed within Hage Saecaraz. In fact, they left the intruder's kraam three times only—yes, Sirin has given the intruder a kraam within the Supreme Director's chambers—and twice they went to see him in the audience room."

"A kraam for the spy?" wondered Piipo. "What does it mean?"

"And the third visit?" asked Cejka impatiently.

"To the Archives. They have not returned."

"The Archives!" Cejka gasped.

Piipo stared incredulously. "I don't understand. What does it mean?"

"It means," replied Cejka, recovering quickly, "that we may already be too late to learn much from the intruder. Either the psilobe has permanently altered his memory, or he has joined Rohee's reign."

"The Archives," Piipo muttered. "You put too much store by them. They cannot be that important."

"We have seen records—" began Cejka. Tvrdy warned him off with a stern glance. "You have no idea how important the Archives are. If we told you, you would not believe us."

"It is all old mother's prattle," Piipo scoffed.

"It doesn't matter," said Tvrdy. "All that matters now is whether we should risk trying to contact him. That is why I called you. I would not implicate you without your knowledge. If we tried and failed . . ."

Cejka nodded silently. Piipo looked from one to the other of his co-conspirators. Tvrdy's gaze was steady and patient. He had worked through the problem in his own mind, and wanted to allow the others a chance to reach the same conclusions for themselves.

"Well," Cejka said, breaking the silence which had grown heavy as the grain in the great vault of a room, "I see no other course but to try. We must be certain. And even if he has joined Rohee, we may discover a way to use him to help us gain entrance to the Archives."

"And you, Piipo?"

"I agree. In any case we have to know whether he has joined them or not. Yes, contact him as soon as possible."

"My thoughts exactly." Tvrdy beamed at them and began explaining his plan to make contact with the stranger. They discussed his plan from every angle and in the end agreed on how it should be carried out.

As they rose, stretched, and made to leave, Piipo asked, "Tell me—any news of our latest acquisition?"

Tvrdy shrugged. "Still too soon to tell. He was given a large dose—much larger than normal. They were taking no chances. But he is beginning to ask questions."

"That's a good sign," put in Cejka.

"Yes, there is some small hope. A partial recovery at least."

"What about the woman and the fourth intruder? Still no word?"

"The woman has been seen from a distance. Two attempts at contact have failed—the Chryse troupe she is with did not appear as scheduled. It could be that the troupe's leader has been instructed to keep her under close security." Tvrdy paused and added, "I wasn't going to tell you now—we've had enough bad news for one night . . ."

"Go on," urged Piipo, "we might as well hear it all. The night is too far gone for sleep anyway."

"The fourth intruder was taken to Starwatch level of Nilokerus several days ago. Condition uncertain, but he has been attended continuously by Ernina herself since his arrival."

"That's Jamrog's doing!" muttered Cejka.

"My source thinks not," replied Tvrdy. "There have been no official orders regarding his disposition upon recovery. I think Hladik is responsible and doesn't want anyone to know what has happened to the captive assigned to him."

"Conditioning?"

"That's my guess. I told you it was bad."

Piipo took a deep breath and squared his shoulders. "All the more reason to make contact with the remaining intruder as soon as possible. We are running out of alternatives." He smiled unexpectedly.

"Well? What is it, Piipo?" asked Cejka.

"Excuse me, I am still new to the ways of a cabal and I have difficulty believing in the need for such urgency. I am quickly learning, however, and I just had a thought. Why not take *all* the spies? We know where they are. It could be done. Isn't tomorrow a Holy Day?"

Tvrdy stared at Piipo, then broke into a wide grin. "Excellent! I like the way you think. I was afraid you were beginning to doubt your decision to join us."

"Never! It is the one thing I am pleased with in a very long time. I do not regret it. Once my word is given . . ."

Tvrdy clapped him on the shoulder. "It will soon get much worse, you know."

Piipo's smile broadened. "How else can it get better?"

The three sat down again and reformed the plan, each taking responsibility for securing one of the intruders. Another hour passed before they were satisfied and adjourned the Cabal. Piipo put his fist to his heart and then slipped away, dodging behind sacks of grain. Tvrdy and Cejka nodded silently, returned the salute, and then hurried off, leaving the way they had come.

· · · · · ·

Jamrog, forehead bulging menacingly, lips compressed into a tight line, twirled a bhuj between his quick hands. The spinning blade dashed light from its mirrored surface, flashing like the anger smouldering in the Director's eyes. Hladik sat to one side, frowning, dark brows pulled together into a ridge above his eyes, his jowls spreading over his collar.

Fertig, Nilokerus Subdirector, sweated into his yos and blurted out the rest of his news. ". . . but the usual procedures proved ineffectual. He lost consciousness when the second eye was burned out and died before we could administer revivants."

"What was he given before interrogation?" growled Hladik unhappily.

Fertig spread his hands in a show of innocence. "The usual pain enhancers. Nothing more. It was not known he had such a weak heart."

"Did you think to check his records?" Jamrog sneered.

"My men are better trained than that!" Hladik snapped. "Records are not kept on wastehandlers. Only the higher-order Jamuna have permanent files. This one was merely a recycler; the only record he possessed was his dole number. I looked into that myself."

Jamrog groaned and smashed the bhuj against the floor. A starburst pattern appeared in the cracked stone tile at his feet. "How is this possible?" he demanded. The Nilokerus at the ready behind Fertig stiffened.

"Calm down," Hladik soothed. With a wave he dismissed his aide, who, with the rest of the Nilokerus contingent, retreated gratefully without hesitation. "A third-order recycler's death—this Nendl, whoever he is—will not change anything. We'll get the spy back—where can he go? He has no friends; no one will help him. I would not be surprised if he were apprehended before the day was out."

"Are you really so stupid? Save your mindless chatter. I know better. We don't know how long Pizol has been missing. His absence was discovered this morning, but as far as we know he has not been seen for three days at least. Obviously he's been taken in somewhere. I suspect Tvrdy is behind this."

"What an accusation! Listen to yourself. Tvrdy is a Director, after all."

"A Director who will stop at nothing to worm his way into power over us. Don't be a fool. You know he is cunning. He's not a brainless lump like Dey or Bouc. Who can guess what he's thinking in that tight mind of his?" He glared at Hladik, defying him to contradict this.

"I know you and Tvrdy have your differences—"

"Differences? Hah! He'd kill me without a second's hesitation if I ever gave him the chance—and I would do the same. We are enemies, Haldik. Or are you talking this way because you are weakening?"

Hladik pulled a hurt face. So far his little exercise had accomplished his goal: averting Jamrog from further questioning him about their other prisoner—the one he had nearly killed through the conditioning. That had been his own idea, a little insurance. If Jamrog ever found out—better not to think it. That was inviting disaster. With any luck the spy would recover before Jamrog suspected anything was wrong. He made a mental note to pay the prisoner a personal visit.

Jamrog, still scowling, flung out his hand. "Stop playing the wounded innocent and tell me what we are to do now."

"As I said, Pizol will be found soon. In all probability he is still within Jamuna Hage. He will turn up. All dole kiosks have been alerted. It's only a matter of a few hours. Leave it with me."

"I wish I had your confidence, Hladik. All right, I will leave it with you."

Glad to change the subject, Hladik asked, "What have you learned about the Fieri spacecraft?"

"Very little. Their magic is of a different kind than ours. Completely different. Much of it is incomprehensible, although there are a few minor similarities, I am told."

"Is it genuine?"

"Yes, very much so. And that is the mystery of it. If the Fieri have regained flight, why did they send such a small force? It makes no sense."

"I begin to think we may have to interrogate the spy under Rohee's custody after all. I understand the Supreme Director has given him a kraam in the High Chambers. He's mad."

"Sirin is old but not insane. He has his reasons. We would do well to find out what they are before moving against the spy he has befriended." Jamrog fixed his eyes on a spot over Hladik's dark head. "I wonder—" He tapped the staff of the bhuj gently in his hand.

"Yes?"

"I wonder if we have not made a mistake in placing the intruders in Hage so quickly. You should have killed them."

Hladik's answer was direct. "The Supreme Director wished otherwise. We chose the best course open to us. If the Dhogs had found out about them, who knows what could have happened? This way we have kept them safely hidden from their own, and beyond the reach of Tvrdy's faction too."

"Ah, so now you admit that Tvrdy has a faction, do you?"

Hladik answered benignly, "Of course, was there ever any doubt?"

Jamrog's lips twitched in a thin, ruthless smile. "It seems to me he has shown less than a healthy interest in Threl unity of late. I think Tvrdy's kraam could bear additional watching."

"An excellent idea. I will see to it."

"Use Invisibles—this is no reflection on your security forces, but the fewer people who know about this the better. Agreed? I will see that Sirin sends his authorization at once."

Hladik nodded, pulling his chin thoughtfully. "If Tvrdy and his little enclave are up to something, we'll soon know it."

TWENTY
NINE

As Treet stood peering into the gathering gloom, wondering how and where to start searching for his lost guide, he saw what appeared to be a faint glimmer of light reflecting off the metallic surface of a large cylindrical object which rose up from behind the foremost rank of a series of stacked ventilator louver frames. He stared at the glow and it did not go away. So, tapping for the ledge's edge, he made his way toward the place, waving his hands in front of him like a blind man.

Ducking around a pile of motor housings, Treet lost sight of the light momentarily and spent a panicky few seconds trying to gain his bearings. When he found it again, the dull, yellow radiance was much closer than he had expected. He crept carefully around a pile of filthy hydroponic seeder tubes and stepped into a little circle of light cast by a yellow globe lamp on a stand. Beneath the lamp was what appeared to be an open, oval manhole in the floor.

Treet knelt down and hollered into the manhole. "Calin! Are you down there? Calin?"

He waited, received no answer, and cautiously placed his hand into the void while his mind constructed grisly pictures of Calin's broken body lying crumpled at the bottom far below. Dangling his arm just inside the hole, Treet found what he was looking for: the rungs of a metal ladder attached to the side of the hole just beneath the rim. He eased himself down into the hole, placing his feet gingerly on the unseen rungs.

If she had fallen in, wouldn't he have heard a scream or something? And who had turned on the globe? Maybe she hadn't fallen, he thought as he went down slowly, placing his feet securely on one rung after another. Perhaps she had climbed down—as he was doing—in order to check out what was hidden below. Then again, perhaps she was nowhere near the manhole in the first place.

He touched the floor and looked up to see the bright oval above him—a good five meters. He squatted on his haunches and touched the floor: dry, but not dusty. As far as he could tell, it was perfectly clean. There was no body huddled beneath the rungs, so he straightened and stretched out his arms. Fingertips brushing the walls on either side, he began to walk. The passage led down a fairly steady incline, and the walls were seamed at intervals, which made Treet think of pipe rather than a corridor. Perhaps this tube was part of a disused drainage system. If so, there was no real point in continuing the search—there was no telling where the pipeline led.

Just as Treet had made up his mind to turn around and go back, he came to a junction box. Two other large pipes converged to join into one enormous conduit, which showed a light a little further along. Treet entered the conduit and felt his way toward the light.

In a moment he stood blinking in the entrance to a large underground gallery lit with vapor tubes in long parallel lines above row upon row of metal shelving stacked with lightprint disks and holoreader cartridges. Amidst an untidy mound of disks sat Calin, her nose in a blue plastic-bound notebook.

"Comfortable?" Treet stepped into the room, gazing along the shelves and at the dark-haired magician engrossed with the book in her lap.

Calin smiled and looked up. "I have found a find," she said proudly, holding out the notebook to him.

Treet stooped to retrieve the book and closed its brittle cover to read the label: *Interpretive Chronicles—1270 to 1485.*

"Indeed you have, dear sorceress," said Treet softly. "You've found the granddaddy find."

"Banzai jackpot!" she shouted, beaming.

"Quadruple banzai jackpot!" He raised his eyes to look at the long rows of neatly arranged materials. It was all here—everything he needed, at his fingertips. "Do you have any idea what this means? It means that you have saved us both a carking fat lot of work, among other things."

He held the notebook in his hands and flipped it open at random. The pages were acid-free printout paper—thank the gods of small favors for that—written in a crisp hand, clear and readable in black ink. The margins were wide all around, allowing for the notes which had been added and initialed at a later date and in a different hand.

The dates caught Treet's attention. They were all wrong—unless, of course, the colony had simply begun its own reckoning. Even then, could they be right? He turned back to the title on the cover. 1485? Nearly fifteen hundred years?

He was convinced beyond the shadow of a doubt that the time displacement or compression or whatever involved probably several hundred years at least. But a millenium-and-a-half? Judging from the amount of material gathered on the long ranks of gray metal shelves, fifteen hundred years was just the beginning.

"Where did you get this notebook?" he asked, handing it back.

Calin pointed to a nearby shelf where a row of orange, blue, and green notebooks stood in an orderly row. "There are many more of these," she said.

"So I see." Treet stepped up to the shelf and scanned the dates on the spines of the notebooks. He called them out. "Foundation to 98, 110 to 543, 586 to 833, 860 to 1157 . . ." He ran his fingers along the row of notebooks as he moved to the end. "Incredible!" he cried as he came to the end. "It goes all the way to 2273!"

His head snapped around. "Calin, what year is this?" Why had he never asked her before?

The magician's face scrunched in thought. "It is the year 1481, I think. So say the priests."

That's why I never asked her before—they're dating from something other than the foundation of the colony. Think! There must be a key here somewhere. He scanned the orderly row of books. "If I go back 1,481 years—" He ran his finger along the spines of the notebooks, stopped, and frowned. "No, that's no good. I don't know how much time has elapsed since these books were placed here." His frown deepened.

At least he knew that the colony was 2,273 years old, and probably a whole lot older. The key to this mystery lay somewhere in these books, but finding it would take time.

Resisting the impulse to pull them all out at once, Treet went back to the beginning and gently tugged out the first notebook. The paper fluttered in his shaking hands as he read the first page. It was a personal note from the author, framed in the same steady, precise handwriting:

TO ALL WHO COME AFTER:
    These books are the work of one man's life. Treat them with respect. This record of Empyrion has been assembled from

many diverse sources, some of which were not completely reliable. It will be hard for anyone of a more enlightened age to understand the repression under which I have labored.

Where there are errors, know that they could not be avoided. I leave them for you to correct. But know, too, that what you hold in your hands is the truth—as far as can be told. I have told everything in the books.

Feodr Rumon
After Arrival 2273

Treet reread the short note and felt the uncanny sensation that the words had been written to him personally. He wondered how many others had read them. At least one other, judging from the margin notes he'd seen.

This was a find, all right. The one and only genuine original find of a lifetime. Trouble was, he was the only person in the whole wide universe who knew its significance. Not that certain others wouldn't be interested—Rohee for one, Chairman Neviss for another.

The Chairman's name triggered a chain reaction in his mind. Of course! It all fit. What a pinhead I've been, he thought. I should have guessed what was going on long ago. Of course Neviss knew what had happened—or had a Harvard-educated hunch—knew that the time distortion factor had royally screwed up the works. What was it that Neviss had said in their too-brief interview? Treet closed his eyes and remembered the words exactly: "The proposition I have in mind has to do with this colony. I want your help in solving a problem there."

So this was the "problem" Neviss had alluded to but never explained: a trifling matter of a few thousand lost years to be accounted for. Nothing to it. Send up a starving historian who'd sell his eldest daughter (if he had one) to the United Arab Emirates for a chance at the most significant historical discovery of the last several centuries and you could rest easy. Orion Tiberias Treet—bless his simple, hoodwinked heart—was on the job. He'd die kicking and screaming bloody murder before he'd let anyone deflect him from the trail once he got the scent.

And it had worked. Treet cursed the scheming Chairman and his smarmy assistant Varro and all of Cynetics' vast holdings and chattels. Yet, he admired the beauty of it. Despite himself, his historian's soul luxuriated in the golden glow of discovery. Although he had a good mind to call down the fates of economic failure upon Neviss and company, he also felt gratitude for being chosen to make the trip.

"That devious old scoundrel," murmured Treet, closing the notebook and placing it carefully back on the shelf, "trapped me with honey. He knew all along I wouldn't be able to help myself."

He turned to see Calin watching him closely. "Something is wrong?" she asked.

He grabbed her, gave her a big, sloppy kiss on the side of the mouth, and roared, "Nothing is right, my fine magician, but nothing is wrong." He released her and whirled back to the shelves. "Now then, let's see what other goodies are here, shall we?"

He scanned the ordered ranks of disks and cartridges, each and every one containing some piece to the Empyrion puzzle. Where to start, he wondered. At the beginning, like a good schoolboy? Or work back from the end, which might be quicker in some respects? Treet sighed. Why rush? He had nothing but time on his hands.

Starwatch level was nearly deserted as Hladik and his guide moved along the upper terraces and rimwalks. "Stay here and wait for me," he told the guide as he entered the physicians' cluster and walked among the beds there. Most were empty, but he wasted no time searching the others—he knew where to find the one he was looking for.

In a separate chamber two third-order physicians bent over the inert body in the suspension bed. As Hladik appeared, both straightened. "Good evening, Hage Leader," they said in unison, bowing at the waist. The physician nearest him added, "We were just about to—"

"Leave us. I wish to see the patient alone."

"Of course, Hage Leader." The physician took his instruments in his hands and nodded to his colleague; both backed from Director Hladik's presence.

Hladik approached the bed and peered down at the sleeping man. Although the slack features were pasty and deep blue circles swelled beneath the eyes, on the whole the patient's color had improved since the last time he'd seen him. Good, he was out of danger. "Kolari," Hladik whispered, using the postconditioning trigger name, "this is your Director. Do you hear me? Wake up."

The eyelids fluttered and opened, revealing dull, listless eyes beneath. "I am glad to see you are feeling better." He paused and glanced around. "Do you remember your theta key?"

The head bobbed once, then again. Excellent! The conditioning has succeeded, thought Hladik. "Good. I want to hear it. Repeat the theta key now."

Crocker spoke, his voice hollow, wasted. "The Fieri are our enemies. If they try to contact me, I go with them. I remain alert so that I may return and tell you where they hide. If anyone interferes . . ."

"Yes?"

"I kill them."

"Very good. Rest now. Close your eyes and sleep. You will forget that I was here. But you will remember your theta key."

THIRTY

Asquith Pizzle blinked his eyes and rolled out of bed. For the third night in a row he had been awakened by a feeling of suffocation. It started as a pressure in his chest which grew so great that his heart thumped wildly against his rib cage until his breathing stopped. In his sleep-sodden consciousness, it felt as though some dark malevolent being straddled him, pressing giant splayed thumbs against his windpipe, tighter and tighter, choking him until he awoke, panting and out of breath.

The feeling of immense oppression dwindled as Pizzle pulled on his yos, leaving only a quivery sensation through his midsection. Dressed, he sat on the edge of the bed, staring at the ceiling of the bare room, wondering for the nine billionth time in the last three days why he was here.

The man—Tvrdy, was his name—had helped him. He was sure of that. He could trust Tvrdy, even if he could not trust his own memory. And this was the mystery: where had he come from, why was he here, and where were the others who had come with him?

Each day he remembered more—as if the thick sheet of glacial ice which had frozen his memory melted a little more, uncovering a few more precious acres of once-hidden terrain.

He now remembered, imperfectly, faces of others whom he felt certain had come to this place with him. He remembered, too, that he had not always been in this room of Tvrdy's. He had been with someone else, had done something before coming here. But it was all fuzzy in his mind; he could have imagined it. Certainly most of what he remembered had an ethereal, dream-like quality.

But Tvrdy had helped him there too, providing what he called a guide to lead him back along forgotten pathways to retrieve important facts and events. Under Pradim's gentle prodding, he had made considerable progress, though he still had a long way to go.

As Pizzle sat on his bed thinking, his hand strayed up to his face. Something was wrong there. What was it? The beard that had begun to straggle over his unshaven chin? No, his ears . . . or eyes . . . *glasses.* The word came to him from out of nowhere, spinning into his consciousness like a windblown leaf.

I wear glasses, he thought. Or once did. What happened to them? What has happened to me? An inky jet of melancholy gushed up inside him, filling him with phantom grief for all he had lost—or imagined he had lost, for he really did not know precisely what his former life had been like. But the feeling was strong, a tide that swelled and flowed over and through him, tugging him along. A big tear formed in the corner of each eye. He bent his head.

When Pradim came in a few moments later, Pizzle had not moved. The guide came quietly around the suspension bed to stand in front of him. "Pizol, our Hageman has returned. He wants you. Come with me now."

Pizzle raised his face, wiped his eyes with the heels of his hands, and got up. "Your misery?" asked Tvrdy's guide.

"Yes, but I'm all right. I remembered that I used to wear glasses. It seemed important."

"Glasses?" Pradim looked at him strangely. "Are you sure?"

"I'm sure."

They went through two rooms to the small inner chamber, Tvrdy's quiet room. The Tanais Director was waiting for them when they came in. "Thank you, Pradim. Go now and do as I instructed you. Bring me back word straightaway when everything is ready. Traudl is waiting for the signal. And tell Amuneet to stay close by in case I need anything. She can bring in breakfast as soon as it's ready. I'm hungry, and there will be no more sleep tonight."

Pradim vanished and Pizzle entered the room, sitting opposite Tvrdy on a low, cushioned chair. He had come to enjoy these interviews with Tvrdy; they helped ease his mind.

"I'm glad you are awake, Pizol. I would have had to disturb you otherwise." Tvrdy spoke gently and easily, but Pizzle saw fatigue in the down-turned lines of the Director's face and the slump of his shoulders.

"I couldn't sleep."

"Neither could I." Tvrdy studied him a long moment, weighing him, gauging him for what would come next. Pizzle felt his interest quicken, and desperately hoped that he would measure up to whatever Tvrdy had to say so Tvrdy would tell him what was on his mind. Pizzle waited, feeling his nerves tighten with anticipation.

Finally Tvrdy spoke. "I have two things to tell you, Hageman Pizol." His voice was quiet, but his tone flat and hard, betraying an undercurrent of tension. "The first is this: there is trouble coming which I cannot prevent. You will be involved. You must get ready for it; I will help however I can, but it is up to you to equip yourself." He paused and when Pizzle did not say anything, nodded and continued. "The second thing I wanted to tell you is that I think it is time you knew about your friends."

"You know about the others?" Pizzle sat up. "I remember them—their faces. I *knew* I did not come alone."

"No, you did not. There were three others with you. We have found them, and so far they are safe—although they have been given psilobe too, and remember no more than you. They have been hidden within Hage, but we have seen them."

"Hidden? I—I don't understand. Why can't I see them?"

Tvrdy looked at him sadly, drew a hand over his face, and lay back against the cushions of his chair. "It is not easy to explain, but I will put it as simply as I can." He paused, his lips pouting in thought. At last he said, "There are some among us who thirst for power. Very soon they will force a confrontation which my friends and I cannot ignore."

"The trouble you spoke of just now?"

"That's right. If they win the struggle, there will be a Purge. In such event, the Threl Directorate would be overthrown, any who opposed them would be crushed, the Hages would be decimated. No one would be safe."

"And my friends are being held by these people?" Pizzle slumped in his chair. "You said you knew where they were."

"They have been seen, but not contacted. You are the only one we have been able to secure. And now that you have disappeared, the others will be much more difficult to reach. One is with the Chryse—a woman . . ."

"Long black hair, dark eyes. Slender with long limbs?"

Tvrdy smiled and nodded. "Good, you remember her. The other two are men—one, we recently discovered, is under care of the physicians."

"Is he all right? What happened to him?"

"We don't know. He was injured in some way, perhaps when you were brought in."

"And the other?"

"For some reason he was taken by the Supreme Director and has been given a kraam of his own in Threl High Chambers and freedom to move around. He is watched, of course, but we think Threl Leader is using him for some private purpose. We don't know what it is. It is possible he may have joined them."

"Light hair or dark?" Pizzle tried to think which of the two faces he remembered would have joined the opposition.

"He is a big man. Dark hair, heavy brows, and square head."

Pizzle nodded. Yes, that described one of the faces. "Treet!" The name spurted out and with it a dizzying string of associated images, as if another wedge had been removed in the logjam of memory, releasing its jumbled store. Pizzle sat stunned as the torrent of recollection tumbled through his mind.

"You remember something now," replied Tvrdy, gazing at Pizzle closely. He sensed what was happening behind the man's dazed eyes, and wondered if this was the time he had been waiting for—time to ask the question he most desperately wanted an answer to. He hesitated, then leaned forward, touched Pizzle on the arm with his hand, and asked, "Tell me, Hageman, are you a Fieri?"

Yarden followed the troupe along a low-lying rimwall through still-dark streets. Far above, the faceted planes of the dome pearled gray as new sunlight struck them. It was early morning, and they were on their way to what Bela had called an Astral Service.

"You'll see," he had said when she asked what it was. "Here, take this." He held out a pale, thin wafer. When she had hesitated, he added, "For your memory. I've explained that this will help you. You've taken them before, remember?"

She had taken the wafer and held it in her palm. Its center was discolored by a light purplish stain. She lifted it to her mouth.

"Bela, we should be going. The sanctuary will be filled before we get there, and we'll have to sit in the back," Dera had complained. She fixed Yarden with an icy stare and tugged Bela away.

"We're going now," he had said, sweeping Dera to him with his arm. "Come on, everyone! We will be late for the Service," he called as the troupe straggled together and led the way out of his crowded kraam.

Yarden had hurried after them. As much as she feared the Service, she did not want to be seen lagging behind. However, as soon as they reached the plaza outside the kraam block, she let herself fall to the rear of the party. As the troupe proceeded along walkways planted with ragged hedgerows, Yarden pulled her hand from the folds of her yos and, certain that no one was watching, dropped the wafer Bela had given her into the bushes. She then quickened her pace and overtook the last of the troupe.

At first Yarden had taken the wafers Bela gave her, believing that they were helping her remember. But the small white disks with the faint spot of purple in the center had the reverse effect—they increased the inertia of remembering and made her more forgetful, her memory more remote and ill-defined. This she noticed the third time she tasted the bland crust on her tongue.

Thereafter she had avoided taking them, successfully hiding the fact from Bela, whose insistence had made her suspicious. As a result, her memory improved dramatically. She now knew herself to be different from those around her, knew that she did not belong to the Chryse, knew that theirs was a world foreign to her. She also nursed an airy belief that she was separated from others of her own kind who could help her—a belief which, thanks to her intuitive distrust of Bela's drug-laced wafers, was hardening into a fair certainty.

Be patient, she told herself, it will come to you. Use your mind; fight the laziness. *Think!* Concentrate on the past. Try to remember. It will come back.

That was how she spent her every waking moment, fending off the lethargy which had been cast like a pall over her mental functions, peeling back that deadening numbness to free whatever lay trapped beneath. She was careful not to mention to anyone what she was doing, lest Bela find out. Careful, too, to keep up the dazed and perpetually confused demeanor which had first characterized her.

After palming the wafer for the second time—they were

given to her at two-day intervals—she knew that Bela was not her friend and that he meant to stop her from remembering. Why this should be, she couldn't say. However, since the encounter with the hideous Hage Priest she felt it as strongly as she felt the importance of restoring as much as she possibly could of her memory. And with each passing day the potency of the drug diminished, unlocking more of her memory.

Yarden kept her eyes open as she followed the Chryse band out of deep Hage toward the river she had been told ran through the center of Empyrion. In an hour or so they came to a wide, tree-lined plaza. Across the square, through the thin, gnarled, leaf-shy trees, the Kyan flowed dull behind its low-walled bank.

In the center of the plaza stood a great squatty black pyramid with ramps leading up from all sides. People streamed across the square, moved up the ramps, and disappeared inside the pyramid through pillared entrances. At the sight of the pyramid, the troupe surged forward and hastened across the white, stone-flagged square to the pyramid. Yarden unwillingly joined the crush of people forming at the foot of the incline and moved slowly up.

As the low arch closed over her head, Yarden experienced a sudden and overwhelming sensation of suffocation. She staggered, gasped, and clutched the sleeve of the Chryse nearest her, another young woman named Mina. The player took Yarden's arm and guided her into the sanctuary.

Inside the Astral Temple, the sensation of oppression swelled. It was as though a heavy object lay on her chest and constricted her breathing passages. Try as she might, she could not draw sufficient air into her lungs. She grew dizzy and her vision narrowed, becoming a pinched, black-bounded, unfocused field. Shapes swirled around her: indistinct and chaotic movement accompanied with bursts of raking sound. The voices around her were magnified into terrible shrieks, piercing her ears and penetrating her skull like hot knives.

Powerless to stop or turn or flee, Yarden was pushed deeper into the sanctuary by the press of bodies flowing into the pyramid temple. She reeled forward and was eventually pushed into a seat at the end of a long row. The influx surged past her; she became separated from her troupe in the moil of bodies.

Shaken, she sat down to await a thinning in the stream of worshipers, her only thought to get far away from the dreadful temple as soon as possible.

She watched and, when the human traffic abated, struggled to her feet, hands gripping the back of the seat. But as she stepped into the aisle, the light changed. She looked back toward the entrance where priests labored to slide enormous door panels into place, sealing the entrances. In moments the interior of the temple was plunged into stifling darkness.

Yarden collapsed back into her seat, a scream rising in her throat. Trapped! she thought, fighting to keep herself under control. *I am trapped!*

THIRTY ONE

Treet raised burning eyes and closed the book in his lap. His brain buzzed with information. He felt as if his skull had been opened up and the contents of a very large data bank dumped in and then stirred with a stick for good measure. How do I make sense of all this? he wondered, looking at the blue notebook in his hands. It—it's like nothing I've ever read.

Correction—it is exactly like something I've read: one of those ancient historical works penned by quasiliterate scribes in the dark ages.

However, knowing that it came to him from three thousand years in the future, in a manner of speaking, made the reading of it eerie and unsettling. Why unsettling? He looked again at the blue notebook, and the answer came to him: that manuscript, lettered so neatly by hand on computer printout paper . . . the subtle juxtaposition was strangely symbolic. Here was an artifact of a far-flung future, reeking of the long-gone past.

Or vice versa. Treet couldn't decide which. He still had trouble thinking of himself as having arrived in the colony three thousand years in its future, but that's the way the numbers added up. It made his mind flip-flop to think that he stood looking at a civilization that old when, strictly speaking, back on Earth none of the things described in the notebook had happened yet.

It was true. If he were strolling the Piazza D'fortuna in Fiorenze, Italy, right now and stopped to gawk up at the stars, chancing to glimpse that small spark of light called Epsilon Eridani, Empyrion's first colonists would still be poring over their initial environment probes of a virgin world. Yet, in this place and time those probes had happened so long ago they were not even remembered.

How is this possible? wondered Treet. Old Belthausen and

his *Interstellar Travel Theory* didn't know the half of it. Nothing he'd read in that book, with its incomprehensible charts, dizzy diagrams, and endless dry calculations, had prepared him for this.

He returned the blue notebook to its place in the center of the row of colored notebooks. It was the one Calin had pulled out at random; he had intended to begin at the beginning like a good and diligent scholar, but in flipping through the book he had become so absorbed in it he'd read it straight through. It had raised more questions than it answered, unfortunately. But at least he had glimpsed something of the scope his inquiry would have to take. And he knew a great deal about what had happened between the years 1270 and 1485—eventful years for the Empyrion colony.

During that time the enormous work of sealing Empyrion under the fabulous crystal domes had been completed, enclosing the eight separate cities of the Cluster. A deadly second Purge had shaken Empyrion to its core when the death of the first Supreme Director touched off a string of Directorate assassinations, ending in a citizen's revolt and the ultimate establishment of the Threl.

It was this last event, he had discovered, that the colony now dated from. The year 1485 added to the current year 1481 equalled 2,966—slightly less than three thousand years. Unbelievable, but true. He had arrived 2,966 years into Empyrion colony's future and stood looking down a long corridor of years at monumental and life-changing events.

Interspersed with these major events were smaller happenings, faithfully recorded by the patron saint of Rumon Hage: the yearly fluctuations in productivity, the rise and fall of birthrates and deathrates among the populace, the institution of assigned marriage, the abolition of assigned marriage, the slow succession of Directors, the dredging of Kyan, the advent of the poak, and much more. There was little doubt in Treet's mind that were he to read each and every volume, as he indeed intended, he would find them all equally exacting and painstakingly precise as the one he'd just finished.

Here in this orderly row of long-hidden notebooks were the answers to all his questions—including the primary one: what had gone wrong? He still didn't know the answer to that, nor to the other ten thousand that occurred to him, such as, who were the Fieri and why were they so hated in the first place? What had caused the first Purge? How had the colony been governed before the Directorate? Why had the Cluster been closed? And on and on. But the answers were here within his grasp—thanks to Feodr Rumon, who, nearly seven hundred years ago, had hidden his books in the unused sewer below the Archives.

Treet unfolded himself from his squatting position on the floor and stretched stiff muscles. How long had he been sitting there? Four hours? Eight? It seemed only minutes, but his back assured him it had been much longer. Next time he'd have to make sure to bring a chair—he looked around to see Calin sound asleep, stretched out on the floor behind him—and a bed wouldn't be a bad idea either.

"Rise and shine, Calin," said Treet, still pressing his knuckles into the small of his back, trying to loosen the kinks. "I've had enough for one night. It's time to go back." He stooped and shook her shoulder gently, lingering over the feel of her warmth through the silken smoothness of the yos.

She moved, and Treet withdrew his hand. She came fully awake and glanced around, remembered where they were, and relaxed again. "Yes, we're still down in the cellar, but it's time to go." Treet extended a hand to her and lifted her up. For a moment they stood close, then Calin lowered her eyes and stepped away.

"You wish to go back to your kraam now?" she asked.

"I'm exhausted. We'll sleep, get something to eat, and then come back here." He let his gaze travel the length of the room, sweeping the shelves and well-ordered rows. "There's a lot to do, and I want to get at it."

Calin nodded and then led them back into the pipeline. Treet walked beside her. "Tell me," he said, as they felt their way along in the darkness, "how did you know the secret room was down there?"

"I used my psi," she answered simply. "I knew it was there when I found it."

Treet thought about this. "Of course. But if you didn't know it was there until you found it, how did you know where to look for it?"

"My psi showed me."

"Your psi."

"You wanted to find records and disks, you said—about people. I asked my psi to show me. He led me to the place."

"*He* led you? Your psi is a *he?*" For a second it seemed like she was talking about some kind of psychic ability or magic. Now she implied that her psi was a person. "Explain him."

"Each magician receives energy from his psi—one of the higher entities who are part of the Universal Oversoul. The psi energy bodies give magicians their powers."

"Universal Oversoul? That sounds noo-noo na-na to me, Calin. I don't believe in any such thing."

Calin seemed not to mind his agnosticism. She continued, "I asked Nho—that's the name of my psi entity—where to find the records you sought. He led me."

"Yeah. Well, whatever." Obviously the trick worked, however it was accomplished. Who was he to argue with success?

They came to the junction box, took the left branch, followed the pipe to the metal ladder, and climbed it to the oval manhole above. The skylight wells cut into the ceiling of the Archives showed daylight once again. They'd spent the entire night in the hidden room. "Was this just open like this?" Treet indicated the oval hole in the floor.

"No, I uncovered it." Calin pointed to a massive cylinder.

In the faint daylight Treet saw a wide ring around the manhole. The circumference of the ring corresponded precisely to the circumference of the standing cylinder.

Calin touched the nearby lamp, and the globe went dark. She removed it and walked to the cylinder, placed her hands flat on its sides, closed her eyes, and grew very still—just as she had done with the computer terminal. A few seconds of silence ticked by, and Treet saw the huge metal vessel move. He stared as the cylinder trembled and raised from the floor the merest fraction of a centimeter and hovered toward the hole. The slender magician, palms still flat against the sides, not guiding so much as merely maintaining contact, did not appear under any stress at all. If the enormous object—it must easily have weighed several tons—caused her any strain, she did not show it. Her face remained as calm and expressionless as it had in sleep.

Treet gaped as the cylinder settled into exactly the same spot as before. "That's what I call impressive," he said softly.

Calin stepped from the cylinder and turned to face Treet. "Nho's energy is strong. It flows from the Universal Oversoul; I am merely a channel."

They threaded their way back to the entrance where the

Saecaraz Hage priest still slept. They climbed back up the wide steps to stand over the priest. Treet nudged him with a toe. "Should we just leave him here?"

"He must make a report to Rohee."

"How can he do that? He's been asleep the whole time." Treet kicked him gently and raised his voice. "Come on, Sleeping Beauty! On your feet—it's your turn to dance."

"Mff-ugh," the priest snorted. He climbed clumsily to his feet and shook out his yos; the creases were sharp and probably permanent. With a suspicious glare at Treet, he snatched up his black-handled ropes and retreated back through the Archives entrance.

Treet pressed his full weight against the door. It boomed shut, and he resealed the entrance before joining Calin, who was waiting a little way up the passage. The priest was nowhere in sight.

"He didn't waste any time, did he?" said Treet.

"Today is a Service day. All Hages celebrate the Service, and all priests officiate."

"A high Holy Day, is that it? Well, sorry I'll have to miss it. I've got more important things to do—like sleep." He yawned and they started off, back toward the first of many sets of metal doors fifty meters away.

Ernina sat over a bowl of spiced chayote broth, dipping a rusk to soften it. She pondered the night's reading: a book about genetic factors in blood and circulatory system diseases. As always, she was left awed and a little depressed by the ancients' skill and knowledge. Their words spoke to her across a chasm of years; they, long dead and forgotten, knew secrets she could hardly grasp—even when she read them for herself. Such knowledge, such power they had possessed.

Where had it all gone? Cynetics gives, and Cynetics takes away, she sighed. Even that name, once holy and spoken only with greatest reverence, had lost its significance. No one believed in Cynetics anymore. In fact, most of the lower-order Hagemen did not believe the ancients had ever existed. Even the priests had long ago stopped reciting the Credo in worship.

She sighed again, raised the soggy rusk to her mouth, and chewed thoughtfully. These last few days a pensive, almost wistful longing had filled her waking moments. She found herself returning again and again in her mind to thoughts of the elder times. This, she knew, was due to the presence of the Fieri in the room beyond her own.

His body of bones and flesh and blood was a living link between the here and now and those far-distant days, the First Days. His existence was proof of the Credo of Cynetics; and instead of bowing at his feet in all humility and honor, ignorant men like Hladik and Jamrog and all the rest did their best to extinguish memory of the old ones by hounding any who still revered them, reorienting believers or killing them outright.

It was madness—madness born of hate. Ernina had seen enough of it in her life to know that hate was the twisted child of fear. Why did they hate so? What did they fear that they had to destroy even the memory of a race long deceased?

But they were *not* all deceased. The Fieri in the next room attested to that. Somewhere, somehow they still existed. And this, no doubt, was what the small-minded men feared.

Ernina sipped the last of her broth and placed her bowl on its tray. She rose, went to her inner room, and closed the book she had been reading, then put it safely away.

Today perhaps her special patient would feel like talking. He was recovering rapidly. Soon he would be able to walk. And then what? He would go back to Hladik.

No; not if she could help it. The Dhogs knew and protected one another. The Dhogs, Hageless nonbeings, lived out a shadowy existence in the no-man's-land of the ruined Old Section, it was believed. She had never seen one, or known anyone who had. But if the rumors held any truth at all, they must have leaders and there must be a way to reach them.

In that moment Ernina made up her mind. She would risk all to contact the Dhogs. What does it matter if I am caught? she thought. What can they do to me they have not already done to many others? They can kill me but once. I will see this Fieri safely hidden among the Dhogs. At least they will know how to help him.

She heard a movement in the patient's quarters, and dashed back through her rooms. It was too early; he mustn't try to walk yet, even if he did feel stronger. He needed rest.

Ernina entered the room and froze. The bed was empty, her patient gone.

THIRTY
TWO

In the darkness of the sanctuary Yarden huddled in her seat, knuckles pressed against teeth. She waited. The mass of bodies around her waited too, hushed and expectant. The air within the temple vibrated with the pulse of three thousand bodies, all straining for the moment of release and transcendence. All except Yarden who waited only for release from the stifling temple.

From the rear of the sanctuary a low, thrumming sound began, and a purple light shone down on the celebrants from above. Presently a line of priests carrying thick, smoking tapers appeared, moving slowly down the wide aisles from the four corners of the pyramid. They walked backward, chanting. M-M-M-Ah-Ah-O-O-O! M-M-M-Ah-Ah-O-O-O! The sound rose on the first syllable and fell on the second. M-M-M-Ah-Ah-O-O-O!

The congregation picked up the chant, and soon the entire temple hummed with the deep, resonant sound: M-M-M-Ah-Ah-O-O-O! M-M-M-Ah-Ah-O-O-O! M-M-M-Ah-Ah-O-O-O!

The chant grew in volume. M-M-M-Ah-Ah-O-O-O! M-M-M-Ah-Ah-O-O-O! Pulsing. Throbbing. M-M-M-Ah-Ah-O-O-O! M-M-M-Ah-Ah-O-O-O! The sound vibrated eardrums and diaphragm. It bored into the skull; the brain quivered with it. M-M-M-Ah-Ah-O-O-O! M-M-M-Ah-Ah-O-O-O! The blood pulsed with the rising sound. M-M-M-Ah-Ah-O-O-O! M-M-M-Ah-Ah-O-O-O!

The tempo quickened. M-M-Ah-O-O! M-M-Ah-O-O! The priests came closer. M-M-Ah-O-O! M-M-Ah-O-O! The candles stank of burning hair and fat. The priests moved backward down the aisles, holding their flickering lights high. M-M-Ah-O-O! M-M-Ah-O-O!

They reached the front of the sanctuary, came together, and placed their foul lights on stands, then raised their hands high above their heads. M-M-Ah-O-O! M-M-Ah-O-O! On each raised palm was the painted symbol of an eye, glowing faintly in the purplish light. M-M-Ah-O-O! M-M-Ah-O-O!

The entire temple rocked with the chant, now louder and more insistent. M-Ah-O! M-Ah-O! It rumbled from five thousand throats. Swelling. Booming. Rolling. M-Ah-O! M-Ah-O!

The sound was deafening. Yarden pressed her hands to her ears to keep it out, but the horrid noise beat through her palms and into her brain. She squeezed her eyes shut tight and held her head. M-Ah-O! M-Ah-O! M-Ah-O! M-Ah-O-O-M-M-M-M-M-m-m-m. . . .

The chant died away to a whisper.

The sanctuary shimmered in sparkling silence. Yarden looked at the faces of those around her. Bathed in the soft violet light, each was a mask of intense animal expectation—relaxed and ready, features slack, eyes alert, but vacant and inhuman. Yarden turned away from the sight of those blank faces and cringed back in her seat.

She forced her eyes back to the front of the sanctuary where a smaller pyramid, radiating a pinkish light from within, rose slowly up behind the row of priests. When the radiant pyramid came to a stop, suspended in the air above the priests, a seam opened in its side and it split into two halves, scattering rays of rosy light through the smoke-drenched air of the temple.

A faint, wispy music accompanied the opening of the pyramid—less music than the sound of air rushing over the mouthpiece of a flute, or wind sounding the open mouths of empty jars. From within the luminous pyramid came a voice, deep and sonorous. It spoke as from the depths of some dark recess, echoing through the sanctuary:

"Hear your god and remember!"

The celebrants responded in one resounding voice: "Trabant be praised!"

"I am Lord of the Astral Planes. The Shikroth and Ekante belong to me."

"Trabant be praised!"

"The Houses of Light and Darkness belong to me. The Seraphic Spheres hear my voice."

"Trabant be praised!"

Although the words meant nothing to her, as Yarden listened, the words entered her. The voice took control of her mind and pulled her consciousness along with it.

She saw a picture in her head: bright, transparent orbs of

light, swirling with color over luminous clouds. One of the spheres hovered in the center of the others, grew larger and larger until it blotted out all the others, and then shrank away, becoming the pupil of a gigantic eye. The eye in turn divided, becoming two eyes; below the eyes, lips formed a mouth. The mouth uttered the incomprehensible words of the voice from the pyramid.

"From Everlasting the Golim have sought me. The over-souls of the departed stand naked before me."

"Trabant be praised!"

"You who live and breathe are mine. Your hands are my hands, your feet my feet, your voices my voice. I am in you as you are in me."

"Trabant be praised!"

Yarden looked and could not keep herself from looking. The voice altered, took on a slightly higher pitch, became female. At the same instant the eyes and mouth became a female face attached to a female form. The body wore a glistening, filmy raiment and floated just above the iridescent clouds. The sky behind the figure convulsed with vibrant color, melding from red to blue to green to orange and back again almost simultaneously. The woman spread her lithe arms wide and said, "Come to me. Bring me the gift of your minds. Make your wills a fragrant sacrifice. Feed me with your desires. Put your flesh on the bones of my perfect way."

"Trabant be praised!"

"Your praises are the liquor of sweet communion. Your bodies are the mansions of my pleasure. Come to me that you may know me as I know you. Taste the life that death steals so quickly."

"Trabant be praised! Trabant be praised! Trabant be praised!" The voices of the celebrants rumbled in unison, escalating in volume as their features quickened. Many were standing now, reaching out their hands toward the floating pyramid. "Trabant be praised!"

Yarden felt herself rising toward the figure, her arms stretching out to the opened pyramid and its vibrating light, pangs of longing overwhelming her. In her mind the Trabant Woman looked at her with half-closed eyes, a sensual smile on her full lips.

"Come to me," she said breathlessly. "Consummate our love on the altar of pleasure and delight. Come to me."

The Trabant parted her lips with the tip of her tongue. Her head tilted back as her hands spread the shimmering garment and held it open, revealing full breasts, a firm, flat stomach, and shapely thighs. "Come to me." Trabant's voice was a whispered seduction. "Come . . . to . . . me!"

Yarden felt an ache in her loins, and her hips began moving rhythmically as around her the entire congregation swayed together. Her hands played over her body and then other hands joined hers. Yarden opened her eyes and saw that a man stood before her, stripped to the waist, his skin glistening in the rosy light of the pyramid.

She moaned. The man's hands were under her yos, roaming over her body, and she felt her flesh alive under his touch. She pressed herself against him, and he embraced her. Their mouths met hungrily and Yarden yielded to the kiss, clutching at her unknown lover.

The voice of the Trabant, now husky with passion, spoke inside her head. "I am your master. Feel me inside you. I will never let you go!"

An image of unspeakable horror flashed in Yarden's mind. She saw a vast host of corpses rising from a putrid swamp, writhing as decaying flesh fell from their long bones. The corpses mingled and began to caress one another, lipless teeth against shiny bone.

Bile churned up into Yarden's throat as a staggering wave of revulsion swept through her. The man before her, now naked in her arms, grasped her and pulled her to him. A dread as powerful and black as any she had ever known descended upon her, and she thrust the man away. He pulled at her, clawed her, his face contorted with lust.

"Give me your body!" demanded the Trabant. "Give me your soul!"

"Don't give in!" Yarden recognized the voice as her own, even though she did not know herself to have spoken. "I won't give in!" she said louder.

The Trabant became even more insistent. "Worship me and I will fill your life with pleasure. Come to me—let me satisfy all your longings."

Never! Yarden struck at the man before her with all her might. She caught him off balance as he pressed toward her, and he went down on his backside. Yarden whirled and pushed into the aisle, now swarming with the sprawling, convulsing bodies of men and women mingled in grotesque couplings. Stumbling over the conjoined pairs, she fought her way up the aisle to the doors where she crouched unseen and tried to push from her mind the awful ceremony being consummated around her.

Hold out, she told herself. They can't touch you as long as you don't give in to them. Hold out!

The last of the metal doors slammed shut behind them as Treet and Calin emerged from the debris-littered passageway that led to the Archives. Two Nilokerus sentries stood at their posts, looking bored and indifferent. Neither of the men gave them so much as a cursory glance, staring ahead, faces nearly covered by their crimson hoods. As Treet and his guide moved abreast of them, however, one of the guards stepped forward. He had a hand on Treet's arm before Treet knew what was happening.

"You will come with me, please," said the man, pulling Treet close. "Quickly! There is not much time."

Treet jerked back, but the man hung on. "What's going on? Let me go!"

Calin froze. "These are not Nilokerus!" she said.

The other guard stepped up, taking Calin by the shoulder. "No, we are not Nilokerus. Come with us, please. We only want to talk to you."

"We can talk here," said Treet, prying the first sentry's hand loose from his arm. "Start talking—and it better be good and interesting."

The first guard signaled the other one, who released his hold on Calin. He slipped the hood back from his face. "We have information for you about your friends."

Treet's head snapped up. "What about them? Talk!"

"We are instructed to tell you—but only if you come with us," answered the second sentry, still within clutching distance of Calin.

"No, you have it backwards. First you tell us, then we go . . . maybe." Treet put all the authority into his voice that he could muster.

"The change of guard is expected any moment. If they find us here—" began the first.

"Then quit wasting time and talk. So far you're not saying anything interesting."

A glance passed between the two false guards, and the first one made up his mind. "Your friends are being held by enemies. We know where they are."

"Where are they?"

"If you come with us, we will tell you."

"What enemies?"

"Your enemies."

"I don't have any enemies," replied Treet. But that wasn't exactly true. *Everyone* here was a potential enemy. "Calin, what's he talking about?"

Calin stared at the sentry. "You are . . . *Dhogs*." She said the word as if it were lethal.

Treet worked his mouth to speak. The first guard cut him off. "Listen!"

Footsteps echoed in the corridor beyond. "The Nilokerus are coming. You must come with us now. We can tell you no more."

Treet still hesitated. "No. Tell me where my friends are."

"We will take you to them."

"You said they were being held by enemies. How can you take me to them?"

"No time to explain," said the second guard hurriedly. He gestured to the corridor. "Come with us now!"

The footsteps sounded closer. Treet had to make up his mind. He was disinclined to go with the two men, but if it was true that they knew something about his friends—as apparently they did—if they could put him in touch with them—that was perhaps worth the gamble. "You will help me reach them?"

"Yes," replied the first sentry without hesitation.

Treet glanced at Calin; she had overcome her initial shock. Whoever they were, the Dhogs did not frighten her. "Okay, we'll go with you," said Treet at last.

Just then two figures appeared in the vestibule and advanced toward them. The false sentry nearest Calin put his hand under his yos and started to withdraw it. His companion telegraphed a quick warning with his eyes, and the man concealed the hand once more.

The new guards came ahead slowly.

"Go and wait for us at the end of the corridor," whispered the first sentry. "Now!"

Treet nodded to Calin and stepped forward. The two new guards looked at each other and then stopped them. "Is all in order here?" one of them asked.

"They have the Supreme Director's authorization, Hageman," replied the first false guard. "We have checked."

"Then be on your way," said the Nilokerus guard to Treet.

Treet and Calin continued on. As they reached the place where the vestibule joined the main corridor, they heard a voice utter a surprised exclamation. A sharp snap, like the crack of a whip, cut the air. A second snap sounded—an instantaneous echo of the first. Treet looked back in time to see one of the Nilokerus stagger and go down, his face smouldering. His companion, weapon in hand, was gazing in disbelief at a smoking hole in his stomach. The man toppled backward, his head cracking on the stone floor. The body rippled once and lay still.

The false guards came flying toward Treet. He stared at the two bodies and at the sooty smoke still rising from their wounds. One of the men grabbed him and spun him away. "Hurry!" he shouted and Treet was yanked along the blue-tiled corridor, his mind reeling with the horror of the violence he had just witnessed. He felt his stomach squirm and heave; he swallowed hard and allowed himself to be propelled from the scene.

THIRTY
THREE

Yarden felt hands reach out to take her arms, felt herself being guided through the milling crush of bodies leaving the temple. Her eyes, soft and unfocused, stared dazedly ahead. She let herself be pulled along, unresisting, uncaring, her mind numb from the assault practiced upon it in the temple. She felt as if she had been raped.

It had taken every last grain of strength to resist the insidious presence of the Trabant. She had escaped—barely—but was exhausted, unable to fight anymore. She would return with Bela and the others to the Hage, or they would go somewhere and perform. It didn't matter. The Service—an orgy so hideous and unthinkable that her spirit recoiled from it as from the kiss of a corpse—was over and she had escaped. That's all she cared about.

They moved slowly down the long ramp, Yarden on wooden, unfeeling legs. Celebrants, sated and spent from their grotesque revelry, pressed in around her, but the hands still guided her. She turned to see who held her. "Bela?"

"Shhh, say nothing," instructed the woman beside her. She wore the turquoise and silver of the Chryse, but Yarden did not recognize her as belonging to their troupe.

They reached the foot of the ramp, and two guides pulled her quickly away, dodging among the retreating celebrants as they hurried across the white square to the shelter of a standing row of trees. Something in their movements—so quick and furtive and sure—assured Yarden that these were not members of her troupe. They were strangers, and they were leading her away from her Hagemen.

Let them take me where they will, she thought. It doesn't matter. Nothing matters anymore. I am lost.

They came to a place along the path out of sight from those following. They stopped. "Will you come with us?" asked the foremost guide, still clutching her arm.

"I don't know you," said Yarden, peering into their faces. What was that she saw there? Concern? These people cared about her. Why?

"No, you don't know us, but we are friends. We have been following you."

"You were. . . ," she hesitated, "in there?" She looked back. The temple was out of sight behind the sword-leafed trees.

"No; we saw you go in and waited for you to come out. There are people who want to see you. They are your friends, too. They asked us to bring you. It isn't far."

What would Bela say? she wondered. But at the thought she realized Bela did not care for her. When had she ever seen concern in *his* eyes? She remembered the wafer he had given her that morning. Had she taken it, she would have been incapable of resistance; she would have given in, become one of them.

"Will you go with us now?"

Yarden nodded. She had nothing to fear from these people. She could trust them far more than she could trust Bela. "Yes, I will go with you."

Then they were hurrying along secluded walkways, heading toward the winding river and away from Chryse deep Hage. Yarden kept pace willingly, though she had no idea where she was being taken. Whatever their destination, it would be safer then remaining with Bela and the others. Friends . . . safety—the words lifted the edges of the darkness that lay upon her soul. She felt her heart quicken with hope as she hurried on.

Through the labyrinth of Saecaraz deep Hage, up and up through the levels, out across terraces, past Hageworks and many-windowed kraam blocks, over connecting skywalks and through deserted market squares the fugitives ran toward snaking Kyan. Their flight was fast but measured, their progress sure. There was a purpose to the apparent aimlessness of their trail, which Treet decided was to confuse any pursuit.

When they reached the rimwalk at the river's edge, they paused at a clump of tall bushes with long, feathery yellow branches which arched up gracefully to twice a man's height. From a hiding place within the cluster of brown stalks, one of the guides tugged out a concealed bundle, opened it, and passed out black-and-gold yoses. He stripped off the Nilokerus garment and slipped on the new one.

"Tanais," said Calin. "I cannot wear this."

"Wear it," said the first guide flatly. "A Tanais boat will come by here in a few moments carrying only Tanais. It will pick up three *or* four Hagemen—you decide."

"Hold on! Are you threatening her?" Treet turned on the man, his head half in the yos. He pulled it down and glared defiantly. "I won't have it."

The man returned Treet's glare icily. The other guide spoke up. "He is merely saying what must be. It is a Tanais boat and will carry only Tanais. If she will not come—" His glance flicked to his comrade's hand beneath the yos.

"You'd kill her? Like you killed those other two back there?"

"We'd have no choice. She has seen—she knows!"

Treet saw how it was. Their escape route was set up to handle few variables and no surprises. "Well?" asked the guide. "The boat is coming."

"For crying out loud, Calin, get that thing on!" said Treet, snatching the yos from the man's hands and shoving it at the magician. When she hesitated, he took it and yanked it down over her head. She did not resist. "There. It just isn't worth getting killed over, okay?"

Calin gave him a dark look, but remained silent.

"All right, we're ready," said Treet. "What next?"

"This way," replied the second guide, shoving the Nilokerus yoses into the bushes.

They continued on along the rimwalk, with the gray river to the right, the long elegant steps of terraces to the left. Soon they came to a place where the rimwalk dipped down close to the water as the river crawled around a sharp bend. "Over here," said the first guide, scrambling over the stone breastwork.

Treet dropped over the edge and landed on his feet. The boat, a square-nosed barge of medium size riding low in the water, rounded the bend and came directly toward them. Four Tanais Hagemen stood idly on deck. But as the boat neared the shore, the four sprang forward and produced a short gangway which they pushed out over the nose. As soon as it was close enough, the first guide leaped onto the plank. Calin scurried aboard, the second guide close behind her. Treet followed, and no sooner did the boat touch the bank than the engines reversed, and it pulled away again. As the boat drew away from the shore, the four who had been standing idly on deck ran out onto the gangway and jumped to the bank, the last one barely clearing the water's edge.

A complete exchange, thought Treet. Very tidy. And all in less than ten seconds.

He looked around and noticed that this bend was fairly well hidden from the rest of the river. Also, a boat disappearing around the bend would be out of sight from the opposite shore until it emerged again on the other side. No doubt the place had been carefully chosen for that very reason. Every detail had been thought of—right down to the passenger exchange. These people were definitely not taking any chances.

Treet remembered the two dead bodies and grimly reminded himself that the stakes were very high. How many more people would die before this was over? Just what had he gotten himself into? He crossed his arms over his chest and watched the scenery slide by as the boat pulled itself back out into deep water and continued on around the bend.

They traveled against the current for a few kilometers, Treet guessed, before they entered a different Hage. He knew at once when they entered it by the change in architecture. He recognized the shapes of the buildings—tall, spire-shaped edifices with flying buttress arches—but couldn't remember its name.

"Calin," he said to the magician beside him. She had not said a word since setting foot on the boat. "Where are we?"

"Tanais Hage."

Was that resignation or despair making her voice so hollow? Treet turned and regarded her more closely. "What's wrong?"

"I am dead."

Her response startled him, and he laughed. "You're what? *Dead?* What are you talking about? There's not a scratch on you." The mirth went out of his voice when he saw the bleak futility in her dark eyes. "You're serious."

She did not answer, but stoically gazed out across the water.

"Calin, I know there's an awful lot I don't understand. But you're going to have to explain this to me. Are you afraid you can't go back?"

Tears misted over her voice. "I can never go back. When the Saecaraz discover what I have done, I will be erased. And the Tanais will not allow me to stay—I am a Saecaraz magician!"

She sounded so forlorn that Treet put his arm around her shoulders and held her to him. "Look, nobody is going to erase you." He realized how silly that sounded, but he was sincere. "I really don't think we have anything to worry about."

Actually, there was plenty to worry about, as Treet well knew. The deaths of the two Nilokerus and his own disappearance would not, in all likelihood, establish him further in the Supreme Director's good graces. Calin had a point: they *couldn't* go back.

Without his knowing it, he had booked them on a one-way flight. No return. Treet thought about this for a moment as he stood with his arms around the frightened magician. Then, as there was nothing he could do about any of it, he shrugged and held Calin out at arm's length. "I won't let anything happen to you, okay?" She pulled away and went to stand by the rail.

She was still standing there when the boat entered the Tanais marina. It was a semicircular jetty extending into a cove which had been carved out alongside the river. At least thirty other boats, large and small, were docked, and several more were at that moment entering the cove with them. Both the wide, curving dock and the waterfront area beyond were crowded with people milling about.

Treet saw the plan at once: pull in with three or four other boats—each, he noticed, with four passengers visible on deck—and lose yourself in the crowd. Anyone following or watching would be pressed in the extreme to catch their trail. Obviously some careful thought and planning had gone into this operation. Yes, the stakes *were* high—maybe higher than he realized.

The boat slid into an empty berth alongside another craft of the same design. A third boat nosed in beside them on the other side, and twelve passengers disembarked at once to meld with the idle confusion on the dock. Single-file, they threaded their way through the ambling crowds on the waterfront. At the far side of the wharf they paused and allowed a group of four to move ahead of them and disappear down a shadowed walkway leading to deep Hage.

When the first group had gone, they moved on again, and after a few level changes, the entering and leaving of many dwelling blocks, and a long wait in a dark tunnel while one of their guides went ahead to make sure the way was clear, they arrived at a generous plaza bordered on one side by a small lake with a fountain bubbling up in its center. Gently-sloped green lawns ringed the lake on every side, and around it grew lollipop trees which cast nets of white-flowered vine into the water.

Mirrored in the lake was an imposing structure made up of several independent sections clustered around a tall central tower and joined together at the upper levels with airborne walkways. The plaza and lakeside, like the dock and waterfront, swarmed with people wandering in groups of three or four. The guides struck off along a path that wound around the lake, eventually arriving at the plaza to lose themselves once more in the human maze.

Once across the square they wasted no time in entering the central tower, where they ran through an enormous hall over a highly polished floor to dive into a lift. The four crammed into the lift—clearly designed for one or two passengers—and up they went.

Treet lost count of the levels, but guessed that when the lift slowed, they were somewhere near the top. The barrier field withdrew, and Treet stepped out into a spare but spacious kraam. Standing in the center of the room were two figures, one of which he recognized.

"Well, well, Pizzle! Long time no see."

THIRTY
FOUR

"Treet? Orion Treet, is that you?" Pizzle bleated uncertainly.

At first Treet thought Pizzle had suffered brain damage, judging by the way he squirmed and squinted, but then realized the bookworm was not wearing Z. Z. Papoon's glasses. Treet stepped forward. "Yours truly, at your service. You okay?"

"I lost my glasses," said Pizzle, smiling broadly. "But it's not so bad. I'm getting used to it."

"So I see." Treet returned the smile and added a handshake and a slap on the back for good measure. He never in a trillion years would have dreamed he'd be so glad to see that homely, gnome-faced grin. He stood beaming and patting Pizzle's back as if he'd contracted a mild case of idiocy, and then noticed the man standing behind Pizzle. "Who's your friend?"

The man came forward, lips pursed, hands folded with fingers interlocked. He nodded to the two guides, who climbed back into the lift and vanished. "I am Tanais Director Tvrdy," announced the man. "We have been waiting for you."

Pizzle saw the look of cool appraisal Treet gave the Director and piped up, "You can trust him, Treet. He saved me. They were giving me psilobe—a kind of mind drug—and he got me off it. He wants to help us. Honest."

Treet glanced back at Calin, who still lingered near the lift. She looked like a small, defenseless animal that had been cornered by a much larger animal and now had given up, resigning itself to more powerful jaws. He decided to dismiss the polite formalities and get directly to the point. "They said you'd tell me about my friends. Here's Pizzle. Where are the other two?"

"The woman, Talazac, is on her way here now. I expect her to arrive within the hour. Crocker has been hurt and cannot yet travel. He has been removed to a place of safety. You can go to him if you like, but I would advise against it. You might be caught."

Treet appreciated the straight answer. He relaxed. "What's going to happen to us?"

Tvrdy appeared to consider the question carefully, looking at each one of them in turn. Finally he said, "I do not know. Much depends on your willingness to help us."

"Help you do what?"

"Help us save Empyrion," he said simply.

Jamrog and Hladik reclined together over a tiny round table in Jamrog's kraam, sipping the fiery souile from small round ceramic cups gripped between thumb and forefinger. Jamrog's Hagemate, a supple young woman in a filmy Hagerobe of radiant saffron, knelt between them with a ceramic jar over a warming flame, pouring more hot souile whenever their cups became empty.

Hladik let his eyes wander over the luxurious interior, coveting all he saw: vibrant Bolbe hangings and floorcoverings of intricate design, fine antique artifacts from Empyrion's Second Age, sleek furnishings of rare wood, exquisite Chryse metal carvings—two of them erotic pieces executed nearly lifesize. His envious gaze came to rest on the comely form of the young woman kneeling beside him. He smiled, his lips a straight line bending at the corners. "You live well, Jamrog. I commend you also on your good taste in companions."

Jamrog lifted a caressing hand to his Hagemate's flawless cheek. "If you find her to your liking, Hladik, take her," he said absently. The woman lowered her eyes.

"Be careful. I might accept your offer." Hladik made his tone light, but glanced greedily at the woman's curves beneath the transparent Hagerobe.

Jamrog let his hand fall away. His angular face hardened in a fierce smile. "I would be insulted if you refused, Hageman. Take her—I give her to you."

Hladik placed a hand on her folded knee, stroked it. "You are in a very generous mood today, Jamrog. Tell me, would this have anything to do with—" He halted. A peeping tone sounded from his clothing. He touched his shoulder and bent his head to one side. "Yes?"

"Fertig," came the answer. "Security protocol has been violated. I require instructions."

"Where?"

"Horizon level. Archives checkpoint."

"Do nothing. I am coming down." Hladik jumped up, swaying slightly as the souile rose to his head. "You will excuse me, Hageman."

"I am coming with you," said Jamrog.

"Until more details are known—"

Jamrog rose abruptly. "You waste time." He strode toward the door. Hladik cast one last glance back at the lovely woman still seated beside the low table, hands resting on her knees, then followed Jamrog out.

They rode Hladik's em through the secret connecting tube between Saecaraz and Nilokerus Hages. The tube had been installed in the early days of Saecaraz supremacy and was now forgotten, except by the few authorized to use it. Within minutes, thanks to the speed of Hladik's vehicle, the two Directors were standing in Hladik's private council chamber within the security section of Nilokerus Hage.

A very pale Subdirector stood before them. "The situation has worsened," he explained. "We have had two more reports."

"What is the damage?" asked Hladik. Jamrog stood to one side with arms crossed and head lowered, frowning.

Fertig gulped air and saw that he could not cushion the blow, so rushed ahead. "The Fieri woman has disappeared. Bela informs us that his troupe attended Service in Chryse Hage, and she was not with them when they came out."

"The fools! They should have been watching her more closely. I will have them all in for reorientation!"

Jamrog's eyes narrowed. "The other report?"

"Treet and the magician guide have not returned to the kraam. We have discovered that Rohee granted them permission to visit the Archives. They were admitted sixth watch yesterday and did not emerge until first watch this morning." He took a deep breath and continued. "There was a Saecaraz priest with them, but he has not been identified. Second-watch guards were found dead at their station."

"What of the first watch?"

"When they did not check in, a messenger was sent to the checkpoint. That was when the bodies were discovered. The first-watch guards have not been found."

"This is Tvrdy's doing!" howled Hladik. "I know it. He has stolen the spies right from under our noses."

"Aided by your incompetence," fumed Jamrog. Hladik puffed up in protest, but Jamrog's eyes flared in deadly warning. "Yes, it's *your* fault," he said icily. "I'm holding you responsible. You should have doubled the security on the others when the Jamuna spy disappeared."

"How could I have known that—"

"That is your trouble, Director. You have consistently underestimated Tvrdy's cunning and resources. He should have been dealt with."

"Under whose authority? Yours, Jamrog? Need I remind you that you are not Supreme Director yet? We cannot move openly against another Hage Leader."

"Rohee has issued his own death demand with this. He's mad—letting a Fieri into the Archives! I should never have left him alone with the spy."

"We can get them back," Hladik offered. "If we strike quickly, our Invisibles can recapture them."

"No, it has gone too far. The spies must be killed. They should have been killed upon capture. If they were to make contact with the Dhogs, it would strengthen the resistance. How could this happen now—when we are so close to ridding ourselves of them forever!"

"We've made mistakes," said Hladik, "but nothing is lost. We will kill the spies and put an end to this. We will also deal Tvrdy a blow from which he'll never recover. That should warn anyone else who might be thinking of joining him."

"All right, do it. Use Mors Ultima and strike at once. I will take care of Rohee personally. He will die quietly in his bed this evening. By tomorrow morning my power will be consolidated and," he paused, a rapacious leer spreading over his features, "by tomorrow evening the Threl will have a new leader and Empyrion a new Supreme Director."

Fertig stood mute with terror, wishing he had not heard this conversation. It would be his death, he knew, if their plan did not succeed, or even if it did. Already he could feel the cold flame of poison licking his limbs, seeping through his blood. I have heard too much, he thought. When this is over, they will not let me live.

Hladik turned on him. "Well, what are you waiting for? Assemble the Invisibles. I will meet with the squad leader Mrukk in the ready room in four minutes to plan operational strategy."

"By your command, Hage Leader." Fertig vanished gratefully, leaving the two to their schemes. He entered the security command post and placed the watch commanders on alert, then summoned the Mors Ultima squad of Invisibles. His tasks completed for the moment, he returned to his monitor station to await further orders.

I must find some protection, he thought desperately. There must be a way—there *must* be a way. He sat rigid in his chair, staring at the eternally revolving monitor screens. All at once he leapt to his feet. Yes! There was a way—perhaps the only way to save himself. But he'd have to act fast. He spun in his chair and tapped out a coded message on a blank disk with a light stylus.

He leaped to his feet and took the disk to dispatch. It would be dangerous sending the message from here; it could be traced. But there was no time to take it elsewhere, and the secure lines connecting the Directors' kraams were the quickest. Fertig handed the disk to the dispatcher and said, "Tanais Director. First priority. Destroy upon transmission."

THIRTY
FIVE

"**H**elp save Empyrion?" Treet cocked his head to one side thoughtfully. "And just how would we do that?" Tvrdy's answer surprised him. "Do you know of the Fieri?"

"I am familiar with the word."

"For most of our people, the Fieri, if they are remembered at all, live only in children's stories of long ago. But there are those among us who believe they still exist."

"You, for example?"

"And certain others."

"This is interesting, but I really don't see a problem of survival here."

Tvrdy nodded and led them to cushions where they all sat down together. Calin did not join them, but stayed where she was—crouched next to the wall beneath a large, shapeless hanging. "Your coming has released an enormous amount of astral energy into our world. That energy must be dissipated or used."

"We've polarized their psychic plane," explained Pizzle. "We've upset the astral balance around here prodigiously."

Treet looked at him. "That's not all that's been upset apparently." He turned back to Tvrdy. "Exactly what are you trying to tell me?"

"Your presence among us is a catalyst for action. The energy you bring with you is strong—too strong to be resisted. It will be used; one way or another it will be used."

"Go on, what are you getting at?"

"For six hundred years the Saecaraz have ruled Empyrion—Subdirector succeeding Director."

"The line of succession runs through Hage Saecaraz. The Saecaraz Director always gets to be Supreme Director, is that it?"

"Precisely. Even though he is but a Subdirector, Jamrog sits with the Threl; his stent is equal to that of a Director. But when he becomes a Director—"

"Trouble with a capital T," put in Pizzle.

Tvrdy continued his recitation. "Sirin Rohee is old. Jamrog will not hesitate to remove him when he has outlived his usefulness. At present, the Threl is divided on what to do with you. Jamrog would use you as an excuse to seize power. My friends want to see Jamrog deposed and leadership of the Threl returned to the Directors."

"Ah, politics I understand," remarked Treet.

"Jamrog already suspects treason among certain members of the Threl. Should he come to power, there will be a Purge and Empyrion will be cast into chaos. Thousands—tens of thousands will die needlessly. Kyan will run red with the blood of our Hagemen, and we are powerless to prevent it."

"That sounds serious enough, but what's it got to do with this Fieri business?"

"They think *we* are Fieri!" Pizzle explained. "That seems to carry a lot of weight around here."

"I still don't see what everyone's so excited about," said Treet.

Tvrdy continued. "Fieri are stronger than we are, their numbers greater, their magic far more powerful."

Treet shook his head, "Fine, but we're not Fieri."

"I know that now. You are Travelers."

"How does that help you?"

"You could go the Fieri, explain what is happening here, and seek their aid. With the Fieri's help, we could overthrow Jamrog's regime."

Treet clucked his tongue. "Let me see if I've got this straight. You want us to contact the Fieri for you and see if they'll help you stop the opposition from tap-dancing on your heads. Right? Only relations have not been exactly cordial between you Dome Dwellers and the Outsiders for roughly two thousand years, give or take a few centuries. Just what makes you think they'll greet this proposal of yours with the proper degree of enthusiasm? Hmm?"

Tvrdy's eyes narrowed. "You have a quick mind, Orion Treet. You understand why we cannot go to the Fieri. That is why I ask you. You are Travelers. They will listen to you."

"Maybe. Then again, they might just assume we're spies and donate our bodies to the cause of Universal Misunderstanding. It seems to me others have done that around here."

Tvrdy said nothing. Pizzle, looking uncomfortable, tried to

smoothe things over. "It wasn't like that, Treet. They didn't know. It was a mistake."

"No mistake, Pizzy old boy."

"He's right," Tvrdy agreed. "It was no mistake. The things that were done to you were done intentionally. But I hope you believe that not everyone agrees with those tactics." He paused, features softening. "My friends and I have risked everything to save you. It would have been much easier to let Jamrog keep you."

"Oh, I'm not ungrateful," said Treet. "I just wanted *you* to know that I *know* what's going on around here."

Just then the lift arrived from below, and three more people tumbled into the Director's kraam. Treet only saw one of them. "Yarden!"

He jumped up and went to her, and would have taken her in his arms if not for the dazed expression on her face and the emptiness in her eyes. She looked directly at him without a flicker of recognition. "Yarden? Are you okay? Yarden, you're safe. It's Treet. Remember me? Orion Treet."

She stared around at her surroundings, and big tears formed in her eyes. She turned back to Treet and reached a quivering hand to his face. "I remember you," she whispered. The tears overflowed her lashes and streamed down her cheeks. She closed her eyes, swayed on her feet. "I remember . . . everything!"

Yarden collapsed into him, and he put his arms around her to hold her up. Long sobs shook her, and she buried her face against his chest and let go. Treet held her close, saying, "There now, you're safe. It's over. You're safe now."

After a while she stopped crying. At Tvrdy's suggestion Treet led her into the next room and made her comfortable on the suspension bed. She closed her eyes the moment her head touched the cushion; she was deeply asleep as Treet crept from the room.

"I think she'll be all right," he said as he rejoined the others.

"Sure," agreed Pizzle. He regarded Treet owlishly. "It's rough at first—takes some time to get yourself oriented. Once she's past it, she'll be fine."

Pradim, the Tanais Director's eyeless guide, entered the room. All turned to him and Treet saw from the man's pinched expression that something terrible had happened, or was about to.

Tvrdy moved to him, and the two men spoke softly to one another head to head. Tvrdy turned away, and Pradim hurried from the room. The Director's features were calm, but his voice was tight. "An unprecedented development has taken place. I have received secret communication from the Nilokerus Subdirector informing me of an attack."

"The target?" Treet asked, already guessing the answer.

"Us. Invisibles are moving against us now. We have approximately six minutes to make our escape."

"Six minutes!" cried Pizzle. "That's not much time; we've got to get out of here!"

"Stay calm," advised Treet much more calmly than he actually felt. He went to the adjoining room where Yarden slept, took her shoulder, and jiggled it. "Sorry to wake you so soon, Yarden, but we're leaving."

Her eyes opened at once. "Oh, it wasn't a dream! You *are* here!" She sat up and looked at her clothes and the room and Treet sitting next to her.

"No dream. I wish it was," he said, standing. "We can talk about it later. Right now we have some disappearing to do."

They reentered the main chamber to find Pradim handing out yoses. "Put these on," instructed Tvrdy.

"This won't stop them," scoffed Pizzle.

"No," agreed Tvrdy as he slipped on the red and white of the Nilokerus, "but it may give us a split second. Sometimes that is enough. Ready? Follow me. I've had an escape route planned for years against this day."

"Somehow that doesn't surprise me," said Treet as they headed to the lift.

They squeezed in, and Tvrdy set the controls for a fast plummet. As the capsule raced down through the levels, Treet inquired, "By the way, how'd they know we were at your place? I thought this whole operation was ultra-ultra."

"Jamrog does not know. I am merely his most convenient first target. They hope to gain knowledge of your whereabouts through me. Naturally, finding you in my kraam would have made their task much simpler."

"No need to do that."

The lift slowed and bounced to a halt. Tvrdy cut off the

unidor, and Treet stepped out and into a man in the colors of the Tanais, holding an oblong instrument with a barbed prong at the end of it. Two more men with identical weapons were running toward them across the entrance hall.

"Wrong floor!" shouted Treet, flinging himself back into the lift. Tvrdy's finger was still on the controls, and the barrier field was back in place as the Invisible's weapon discharged. By then the capsule was already dropping once more.

He drew a shaky breath. "Split seconds, you were saying."

"How'd they get here so fast? It hasn't been six minutes," observed Pizzle.

"Obviously the advance force was already here."

"Some of your own men?"

"Invisibles disguised as Tanais."

"What now?"

"We will lose ourselves in deep Hage, make contact with my friends, and wait."

"And hope the Invisibles don't find us before help comes?"

"It should be safe enough," said Tvrdy. "It will take them many days to search us out."

"I have a better idea," said Treet. "Suppose we decide to opt for your Plan A. How long would it take to outfit us? When could we leave?"

THIRTY SIX

Treet, Pizzle, and Tvrdy stood together at a datascreen set in the wall of a kraam located deep in the catacombed lower levels of Hage Tanais near the Isedon Zone, the ring of ruined Hageblocks that formed the boundary of Empyrion's Old Section. The kraam had been provisioned for just this sort of emergency. Every cubic inch of space was stacked with supplies. There was enough food, water, and weaponry to sustain a medium-sized insurrection indefinitely. Calin sat forlornly beneath a tower of transparent plastic water barrels. Yarden slept nearby, stretched out on a pallet of vantium shield sheeting.

The datascreen showed a map of a section of Empyrion. Tvrdy pointed to the lower left-hand corner and tapped the screen. "This is the Archive area," he said. "It is in Hage Saecaraz, as you know, so we will have to find a way to get you there."

"Can't we leave from somewhere closer?" asked Treet, peering at the map doubtfully. The route was so convoluted and confused he despaired of reaching the Archives without running into a party of Invisibles. "I don't see why we need to go to the Archives again anyway."

"You haven't been paying attention," said Pizzle. "Tvrdy already explained all that."

"Excuse me!" roared Treet. "I've got a few things on my mind at the moment. I missed it okay?"

Tvrdy gave both men a look of long-suffering exasperation and intoned, "You will need land vehicles if you are ever to reach the Fieri. If such are to be found anywhere in all Empyrion, they will be found in the Archives."

Treet nodded. Yes, that seemed reasonable enough. But he was still bothered by Tvrdy's lack of certainty. "You don't know whether there are land vehicles there or not, or if there are, whether they are still operable, do you?"

"You would be in a better position to answer that yourself. I have never been to the Archives. No one has."

"Well, you're right. And from what I saw, I'd say it would be a chancy enterprise. We couldn't count on finding anything useful."

Tvrdy shrugged. "We will go there in any case."

"Why not take us to our transport? We know that works." He saw Tvrdy shake his head slowly. "That is, it used to. What happened?"

"Jamrog will have disabled it. Saecaraz magicians have been studying it. Besides that, I have not been able to find out where it has been hidden." He glanced at Calin. "Ask her."

"Calin?" Treet turned imploringly toward the magician.

She rose and shuffled forward. "I do not know where the flight craft is."

"What about your psi spirit or whatever? Couldn't he tell you?"

The magician shrugged. "Nho is prevented from telling me. But I overheard talk in Hage. Your machine contained many wonders, they said, much strange magic."

"They took it apart?" whined Treet. "This is insane!"

"It's not that crazy," offered Pizzle. "You have to look at it from their point of view."

"Oh, do I? I'm tired of looking at everything from their point of view. I think it's time somebody looked at something from *my* point of view!"

Tvrdy continued equably, "Once inside the Archives, we can seal the entrance. There are doors here," he pointed to a further side of the bulge in the map, "which open to the outside beneath the landing platform. You will escape from there."

"What about Crocker? What happens to him?"

"He will stay here. Rumon Director Cejka is bringing him here tonight. You will see him before we leave."

Treet put a hand to his face and rubbed the stubble lengthening there. He looked at Pizzle. "Okay with you?" The jug-eared head bobbed readily. "I've got nothing better to offer. When Yarden wakes up, we'll put it to her. If she agrees, we go."

"Tonight will be eventful for all of us. Therefore, I suggest we all rest while we can." Tvrdy switched off the datascreen and sent them off to a light, skitterish sleep.

• • • • • •

Treet awoke groggy and confused. An evil-tasting film filled his mouth, and his eyes felt as if cinders had been strewn beneath his eyelids. His sinuses were stuffed, and his head felt blocky. Great, he thought, I'm coming down with the plague—just when I'm leaving on vacation. Isn't that always the way?

He heard a rustle next to him and put out a hand. "Piz? You awake?"

A face, moonlike in the darkness of the kraam, rose over him. "I want to go with you," whispered a tentative voice.

"Calin, I don't know. I don't thi—"

"Please. You must take me with you. I will die here."

"Tvrdy won't let anything happen to you. I'll tell him. You can stay here with Crocker."

"No. Tanais owes me no protection. I will not ask for it."

Treet paused, thinking. He tried a different tack. "It'll be a hard trip. We don't even know where we're going exactly."

"I have been thinking you will need a guide."

She had a point. A guide would be helpful. "You can guide us? Outside the dome, I mean? You know your way around outside?"

"Nho can guide us. I will ask him."

It dawned on Treet then that the guides did not know any more about getting around Empyrion than anybody else. They were *psychic guides*. The thought of an astral entity leading them on a chase around a virtually unexplored alien planet made no sense at all, but at least it made no less sense than any of the rest. "Oh," he said. "I see. Well, I still don't know abou—"

"*Please!*" whispered Calin desperately.

"What's this about traveling?" A second female voice spoke up, and Treet felt Yarden slide in close to him. "Have I missed something?" Though he couldn't see her features distinctly, her voice sounded normal.

"You've been a little out of it," said Treet. "The long and short of it is we think it would be best to leave the colony for awhile. You have a vote."

"Go to the Fieri," she said softly.

Treet raised up on his elbows. "How do you know about the Fieri?"

"I am a sympath," she acknowledged simply. "I felt your thoughts."

Yarden a brain dipper? That explained something, thought Treet—that remote, mysterious quality he'd always noticed about her. Maybe that was it. "You read my mind," said Treet.

"That's what everybody believes," replied Yarden. "But receiving another's thoughts isn't like reading a newspaper. Ours is a highly developed sensitivity to certain individuals whose psychomotive scan patterns closely match our own."

"Like me, for instance."

"Like you."

"How long have you been able to tap my brain?"

"Since the first moment I saw you. But we do not *tap,* as you say. Brain dipper," she said harshly, "is a vulgar term. What I do is much more subtle, much more sensitive than that. Besides, we can only receive from a person who is willing to send. You must be open to sharing your thought before I can receive its impression."

"I see." Treet squirmed in the dark. The uncomfortable feeling he always had in her presence returned in force. Only now he knew why he felt weird around her. And knowing made it worse. "Well, about the Fieri—as I was telling Calin, it will be a difficult trip. We don't know what we might find out there. Crocker will be staying here. You could stay with him, as I've advised Calin to do."

"Which would be dangerous too," said Calin.

"Yes. Unfortunately we don't have a lot of wonderful choices just now. Circumstances have kind of degenerated around here."

"I'm going with you," Calin said, her voice a challenge.

"I'm going," Yarden declared firmly.

Treet said nothing for a moment, then decided it didn't matter what he thought about the situation. He couldn't very well dictate what anybody else should or should not do. Still, the implication was that he was somehow the leader of this little expedition. How had that happened? "Look, if you're both waiting for my blessing, forget it. What you do is up to you."

"Then we can go?" asked Yarden.

"No one is going to stop you."

Just then a light came up in the kraam, dim and hazy. Tvrdy entered softly and come to stand over them. "It is time."

"Crocker isn't here yet," said Treet, getting to his feet. "You said we'd get to see him before we left."

"Cejka must have been detained elsewhere and could not get word to us. We cannot wait any longer."

There was nothing to do but agree. "All right. Give us a second to pull ourselves together. Pizzle isn't awake yet."

"Yes he is," said Pizzle, climbing to his feet. "I am now."

They ate a few clumps of a sweet, gummy daikon bread and drank some water Tvrdy had brought for them. They washed themselves and stretched muscles that had tightened while they slept. As they moved toward the entrance to the kraam, Tvrdy handed each one a long, black outer cloak and a tubular pouch which was worn slung over one shoulder and across the chest. "Inside are emergency provisions," he explained.

Tvrdy unsealed the door and darted out into the passageway. The others followed like quick shadows and moved off down a long, twisting corridor, then followed it until it became a wide, disheveled gallery joined by several other disused corridors radiating out like the spokes of a wheel. At the entrance to one of them, blind Pradim stood waiting. He greeted the Director and without a word led them off at a near run.

Once they cleared the corridor, Pradim eased the pace somewhat, but kept them moving smartly. "There is transportation waiting," he explained. "But we must hurry."

After what seemed like hours of chasing through endless tunnels, corridors, galleries and passages, they at last came to a wide portal and stepped through it and out into the night. Three small ems were lined up at the entrance. Tvrdy jumped into the driver's seat of the first one, Pradim took the second one, and Treet the third. The others climbed in on the passenger side, one to each em, and they were off.

Treet had never driven one of the little cars before, but found it quite easy: press on the pedal and the electric vehicle spurted forward, ease up and it braked automatically. All he had to do was steer, which was simple enough. More difficult was following Tvrdy, since they drove without lights through winding terrace roads along the snaky Kyan. Once in Saecaraz, they abandoned the ems and struck off on foot again, avoiding well-used byways.

At first Treet feared discovery beyond every turn and around every corner. But then he guessed that their route had been cleared for them. At regular intervals along the way and at blind intersections, sightless Pradim slowed and searched along the path, sometimes stooping to trail his fingers along the walkway. He always found whatever it was he sought—a sign or mark of some sort that told him the way ahead was safe.

Treet's guess was confirmed when they reached the Saecaraz central lift where Pradim paused, hunched over, and pressed his fingers into a crack in the lower wall, then straightened and spoke to Tvrdy. "This mark is old—several hours. Something is wrong."

Treet was close enough to overhear, and said, "Meaning we don't know what's waiting for us on the lower level."

Tvrdy frowned, his face taut. "We cannot wait here. Anyone may come by at any moment. We have to go on."

"And the second we climb out of the lift—BLAMMO! You can talk about us in past tense."

"If we wait here any longer, discovery is certain."

Treet whirled to Calin. "Listen, we've got a little snag here. See if Nho could help us out. Is there anyone waiting for us down there?"

Calin appeared about to protest, but nodded once and grew very still. Her eyes glazed over slightly as she entered that other dimension where she and Nho rendezvoused. Just as quickly, she was out of it. She drew a breath and the spell snapped. The trance lasted only seconds.

"Well?" asked Treet, genuinely fascinated.

"Nho does not see death for us," she said.

"What does he see? Grievous bodily harm? Imprisonment? Torture?"

"I can't say more."

"It is enough," snapped Tvrdy with finality. "We go now."

Treet nodded, and they gathered themselves and dashed across the open chamber toward the nearest lift. Other corridors joined the chamber and as the lift came up, withdrawing its barrier field, footsteps sounded loud in one of the adjacent passages. "Hurry!" whispered Treet. "Someone's coming!"

The others were pushing into the lift when a guide clothed in Saecaraz colors came flying out of the passage. He stopped instantly, a look of horror washing over his eyeless face, made a desperate signal to Treet, and then fled back into the corridor.

Treet made to duck into the lift. There was a shout and the sound of a small explosion. Out of the corner of his eye, Treet saw an object flying toward him. He looked and saw the guide shoot out of the passage, skimming through the air. The man screamed and clutched his chest, flames and blood sprouting from a ghastly hole. The body fell hard, skidded into the center of the chamber, and lay sprawled in an inert heap. Smoke rose from the corpse's clothes, while blood pooled on the stones beneath it. Another shout. Closer. Treet dove into the waiting lift, the barrier field snapped on behind him, and the capsule dropped.

"What was it?" Tvrdy eyed him with concern as he climbed back to his feet.

Grim-faced, Treet answered, "I think your man just took a hole in the chest to save us."

Tvrdy nodded. No one else spoke. Finally Pradim broke the silence. "We'll get off three levels above Horizon and take another way to the Archives. They will know where we're going otherwise."

"They probably already guess," said Treet gloomily. The vision of the mangled body still filled his eyes.

"If we can make it to the doors, they cannot reach us without decoding the locks."

"Or blowing them off their hinges," Pizzle piped up.

"You *are* a cheery fellow, aren't you, Pizzle?"

"Just thinking out loud," he said.

"The doors are shielded," offered Pradim. "We will have some time once we are inside."

"*If* we can get inside," said Treet. "What if I can't remember the entry code?"

"Start remembering now," said Tvrdy as the capsule slowed and slid to an abrupt halt. "Or there is no point in going further."

THIRTY
SEVEN

The lift's barrier field snapped off with a pop. Since Treet was nearest the door, he stepped out first, tentatively, ready to dive back in. But the long, arched passageway was empty. At a distance of thirty or forty meters, the tunnel divided, the left-hand side bending away and down, and the right fork continuing straight until losing itself in darkness.

Pradim pushed past Treet and flew to the fork, motioning those behind to hurry, then ran into the downward-bending tunnel. Treet pushed everyone ahead of him and followed, allowing Tvrdy to bring up the rear. After many branchings and turns, Pradim stopped to listen. There were no sounds of the chase; no one was behind them.

They pressed on and in a few minutes came to a rectangular room with a round railing in the center. In the floor below the railing was a hatch. From the debris on the floor and the cobwebs hanging in filthy sheets from the pipes in the ceiling, it appeared that no one had entered the room for decades. Pradim opened the hatch and dropped through the hole. One by one the fugitives followed. A steel ladder joined the two levels, the lower one of which appeared to be a water conduit of some size, though dry and apparently unused.

Large grated drains opened in the sides and bottom of the conduit at regular intervals of twenty-five meters. Pradim counted them as they passed each one and stopped at the twelfth. He reached up and tugged on the grate, and surprisingly the heavy steel cover came off without effort. Pradim tossed it aside, and it bounced soundlessly. Plastic, thought Treet. He wondered how many other such doctored escape routes existed throughout Empyrion's endless tangle of byways.

Blind Pradim hoisted himself up into the oval opening and turned to lift down his hands to Calin and Yarden in turn; Pizzle came next and then Treet and Tvrdy. They crawled on hands and knees in near total darkness for an eternity. Treet's kneecaps and the heels of his hands grew tender and then sore and then painful before the conduit angled upward slightly and then entered a brightly-lit room containing a row of enormous valves—all peeling paint and rusting.

Directly above the valves was a circular opening with a steel ladder leading to a hatch like the one they had dropped through earlier. Pradim, wasting no time, grabbed the first rung, pulled himself up, and disappeared through the hatch. When Treet joined the others, he emerged to find himself in a closet just off a main corridor. Pradim was missing.

"Have you remembered the code?" asked Tvrdy in a tense whisper.

"I think so. We'll soon find out."

Pradim came soundlessly back and motioned for them to follow him. They entered a blue-tiled corridor, and Treet recognized at once that they were near the Archives guard station. In a moment they turned a corner. Two Nilokerus sat leaning against the wall, their legs out stiff in front of them, weapons clutched in their hands. Although their eyes looked straight ahead, they did not see the fugitives hurry past.

"Dead?" wondered Treet aloud.

"No. Sonic immobilizer," explained Tvrdy. "They will tell those after us that we did not pass this way. Still, we must hurry; they'll only be restrained a few seconds."

Treet turned his attention to the first set of doors, walked to the lock plate, and studied the pentagon of lighted tabs. "Here goes nothing." He raised his index finger.

"Wait!" Yarden pushed up beside him. "I can help you remember correctly."

"How?"

"Shh! Close your eyes and concentrate on the tabs."

Treet closed his eyes and tried to think of how he had pressed the code tabs before. All he remembered was walking through a succession of doors, dreaming of what might be locked away on the other side of the last one. He distinctly did not remember pressing the buttons. "Sorry," he said.

"Concentrate! You pressed them correctly once. Your mind remembers. Picture yourself pressing them in sequence. Feel the tabs."

Treet closed his eyes once more, but now all he was aware of was the nearness of Yarden Talazac and the warmth of her breath on his neck. "It's not go—" he began, then felt her cool fingertips on his closed eyelids.

"Picture it exactly as it happened," she said softly.

Treet saw himself approach the big doors, saw his hand reach out for the first tab, was aware of Calin beside him and the ridiculous priest behind, watching nervously—he had not noticed that before—and felt again the surge of excitement at what lay ahead. He saw the first tab as his finger moved toward it.

The sound of pounding feet echoed in the corridor behind them. "They're coming!" said Pizzle.

"Got it!" said Treet and pressed the first lighted tab. The light went out.

"Go on," said Yarden calmly. "You will remember."

Treet closed his eyes and again felt her fingertips on his eyes. "Okay!" He pressed a second tab and the light went off. "Two down, three more to go."

"Get on with it!" squeeked Pizzle. Their pursuers sounded closer.

Treet raised his finger, and the third tab blinked off.

"They're almost on us!" cried Pizzle.

"I'm doing the best I can!" replied Treet through gritted teeth.

"They're here!" shouted Pradim as a squad of Invisibles rushed into the guard station behind them. He pulled a cone-shaped device from the folds of his yos, moved to the doorway, and aimed.

A fizzling crack split the air, and the cone device exploded in a shower of sparks in the guide's hand. Pradim turned toward the others and raised an empty sleeve. Where his hand had been, only two nub ends of clean white bone remained. His face went grey, and he lurched forward. Calin grabbed him and pulled him away from the open doorway as a second shot sent chunks of the door frame ricocheting around them.

"We're going to be killed!" screamed Pizzle.

Treet stabbed at the fourth tab, and it went off. "I remembered!" he hollered as he smacked the last button. The locking mechanism clicked open. Treet and Tvrdy attacked the door and heaved it open a crack.

Firebolts streaked the air. Scorching metal and stinging hot debris pelted into them. Somehow they all shoved through the slim opening at once and threw themselves at the door to close it as sparks and cinders rained in upon them.

Treet remembered the next code easily—it was a simple

variation on the first. He stabbed the tabs, the lock clicked open, and they all pressed through and shouldered the door closed behind them.

"That was a little too close," said Pizzle, his body shaking as much as his voice.

Yarden and Calin stood with Pradim, wrapping improvised bandages on his raw stump. But there was little blood—the weapon had cauterized the wound. The guide's face had gone dead white, and his body trembled oddly; he seemed not to know where he was.

"The doors will slow them down," said Tvrdy. "Until they find the code."

"How long?"

"Who can say? Rohee is the only one who knows it—besides you."

"Would he give it to them?"

Pradim moaned. The pain was beginning to hit him. Calin sat him down and took his head in her hands. She spoke to him in low, whispered tones, and he slumped forward. "He will sleep for a time," she said.

Tvrdy nodded gravely and said, "I am certain Rohee knows nothing of what is taking place this night. He would not move against another Director like this. At least he would observe Directorate Conventions. But Jamrog might dare to use other means to gain entrance."

"Such as?"

"They could put a code-breaker on the lock," offered Pizzle. "With only five code digits it would take a good computer just a matter of minutes to click through all the permutations."

Treet turned on him. "Whose side are you on?"

"We ought to know all the possibilities," Pizzle replied, unrebuffed. "Don't you think?"

Tvrdy agreed. "Such devices exist."

"Then we have only a few minutes. We'd better get moving."

Tvrdy lifted Pradim onto his shoulders, and the fugitives fled through the succession of doors as quickly as possible and at last entered the Archives. Tvrdy stepped across the threshold and lay the unconscious guide down, covering him with his outer cloak. Then he turned to stand in quiet amazement, gazing at everything around him. "It is like looking into the past," he said in hushed tones.

"Sure," said Treet. "Take the tour later. Right now why don't we try to find these vehicles you say we can't live without, and we'll be going."

Tvrdy stepped lightly down the concentric ring of ledges onto the floor of the Archives, found a pathway, and disappeared into the welter of junk piled with haphazard care throughout the vast expanse.

"Okay, everybody," called Treet, "spread out and make a noise if you see anything that looks like it might put some distance between us and those goons out there."

"Look at all this stuff!" shouted Pizzle as he dove into it. "Just like the old Smithsonian!"

Yarden chose a pathway and moved off quickly. Calin knelt over Pradim, lay her hands on his head once more, and then joined Treet. "Nho helped us once," said Treet. "Would he do it again?" Calin nodded and grew still.

"This way," she replied, striking off toward the middle of the room.

Fifteen minutes, and two mystical consultations later, Calin stopped and pointed to a row of shroud-covered humps next to the great doors that opened beneath the landing platform. "Hey!" cried Treet. "Everybody! Over here!"

Pizzle stumbled up. Tvrdy and Yarden, who had also heard Treet's cry, arrived moments later. Pizzle went to the first hump and yanked off the shrouds, stirring a veritable fog of the fine, gray powder. When the fog subsided he was leaning against the hood of a strange machine, grinning. "Nice, don't you think?" He sounded like an antique car dealer showing off his latest acquisition.

"What is it?" Treet peered doubtfully at the elongated red-orange machine before him and at its two blue-and-black companions standing a little way off.

"Transportaion," said Pizzle grandly, adding, "I'm almost sure of it."

Tvrdy squatted to peer at the underside. "What do you think?" asked Treet.

"Excellent!" cried Tvrdy. "You have found them. I had forgotten about the blades."

"The blades?" Treet stared at the vehicle. On either side of a narrow, open-aired passenger compartment, two long, thin runners swept down from the pointed nose to flare like curved sabers along the full length of the vehicle. The contraption looked more like a skinny, old-fashioned sleigh with its runners flattened and turned on edge than anything else Treet could think of.

There were three humps in the floor of the passenger compartment which corresponded to three, ball-shaped flexible wheels, which were made of overlapping metallic bands. The ungainly craft balanced precariously on these wheels, tilting back and forth on the runner-blades.

"Yes, you will need these," Tvrdy was saying as he pointed to two other vehicles exactly like the first. All three showed signs of wear and tear—places where the paint was worn to the metal, scratches and dents, torn seat cushions. Obviously the machines had seen heavy use in their day—whenever that had been. "I had also forgotten the sand."

"Sand?"

Calin spoke up. "There is a legend about a great sand sea between Empyrion and Fierra."

"A desert. Of course. Just what we need."

Calin, eyes turned inward, began reciting:

"On blades that race the sea is cut,
And scattered by the skimmer's wake.
On and on, the dune sea rolls
White gold in endless waves."

She came out of her trance and explained, "Nho says it is from an old song."

"Great," Treet frumped. "Well, do we wait for those lovely lads out there to figure out a way to get in here, or do we make a graceful exit?"

In the skimmers they found an assortment of blue, red, and green singletons much like the ones they had been wearing when they arrived on Empyrion. Treet was the first to start stripping off his yos. Pizzle found one near his size and squirmed out of his yos too. "Come on, ladies. No time to be shy," remarked Treet, stuffing a leg into the garment. "Get some real clothes on." He flipped two of the smaller-sized jumpsuits to Calin and Yarden.

When they hesitated, he explained, "Look, I'm not much of an explorer, but I've been on a few excursions, and we don't know what kind of conditions we're likely to find out there. But whatever it is, we're better off dressed for the occasion. Okay?"

Yarden nodded and ducked behind a large louver panel. Calin shrugged and began pulling off her yos. Treet turned his back discreetly and met Tvrdy as he returned from making his check of the vehicles, carrying bubble helmets and atmosphere canisters under his arms.

"Aw, do we need those?" whined Pizzle.

"It is advisable." Tvrdy handed helmets around. "We would not think to move outside the dome without a breather pack."

"How long are these packs good for?" asked Treet. The helmets looked brand new and never used. Strange to think they were likely several thousand years old.

"Five hundred hours. I have put replacement canisters for each of you in the skimmer compartments."

"That gives us—" Treet began calculating.

"Twenty days per canister," said Pizzle.

"We ought to be able to find the lost tribes in forty days, eh?" It certainly seemed like a long enough time to be wandering around in the wilderness. He turned to Tvrdy. "What do we do when we come back? How do we get in touch with you?"

"Come back here to this entrance." Tvrdy indicated the massive fibersteel doors before them. "There is a code lock on the outside. Press it and I will come to meet you or send someone."

"Fine, but I don't know the code and neither do you."

"It doesn't matter. All locks are monitored in Tanais Hage. When someone attempts an inappropriate code, a warning signal is tripped. We will know you are here."

Treet looked at Tvrdy for a long time and then said, "You sure you wouldn't rather come with us? You might live longer."

Tvrdy smiled grimly. "I'll survive. Once he knows that you have escaped, Jamrog will not persist on this course. I will bring charges against him before the other Directors, and he will deny them, and that will be that—for a while."

"Whatever you say. We'll be back as soon as possible. I can't promise anything, but we'll do all we can to bring help."

"We will await your return, Hageman Treet. Tanais priests will offer benefices to the outland spirits for your safety." Tvrdy seemed about to say something else, but turned quickly away, donned a bubble helmet, and moved to a pedestal near the great curving door. He pulled off the cloth covering the pedestal and studied the mechanism.

"Everybody ready?" said Treet. Pizzle, Calin, and Yarden stood lined up behind him. All were wearing singletons and had their helmets under their arms with breather packs attached. "Okay, let's get 'em on."

Helmets in place, Treet gave Tvrdy a signal, and the Director punched a button on the console. Nothing happened. He tapped it again, but the door did not budge. Without a word, Calin went to the pedestal and placed her hands on it. A moment later the doors ground into motion on huge, complaining rollers, sliding apart slowly, ponderously.

Treet went to the nearest vehicle and climbed on, settling himself in the driver's seat. There was a joystick affair for steering and two pedals on the floor which could not be reached with his feet unless he stood. He puzzled over this arrangement for a moment before realizing that passengers were intended to straddle the central humps and ride the skimmers like camel jockeys. Portions of the long cushioned seat flipped up for backrests. With joystick in hand, the driver pressed the pedals with his knees— though what the pedals did, Treet had yet to discover.

Pizzle stood close and pointed to the panel under the stubby windscreen. "They're electric," he said. "With solid-fuel assist generators."

"I can read," Treet pointed out. "Get ready. You and Yarden take that one; Calin and I will take this one." He indicated the sleek blue-and-black skimmer nearby. "And you better let Yarden drive." Pizzle flapped his arms in protest, but Treet cut him short, saying, "You don't have your glasses, remember?" Pizzle snorted, but climbed on the vehicle behind Yarden.

Pale, watery light spilled in from the widening crack as the doors inched apart. Treet pressed the ignition plate, and the machine trembled to life beneath him with a sound like the whine of a ramjet turbine. Calin scrambled up behind Treet and pulled a strap across her hips, raising two handgrips into position near her arms. Treet nodded and gave a thumbs-up signal to Yarden, who acknowledged it with a wave.

The doors slid slowly open and as Treet eased back on the joystick, inching the skimmer forward, he glanced up just in time to see black shapes boiling in through the gap. He saw Tvrdy rush forward. Someone shouted.

Treet jerked the joystick back and the skimmer lurched forward, stuttered, and died.

The black shapes swarmed around them, cutting off their only escape. Treet cursed and hit the ignition plate. Nothing. A hand snaked out and grabbed him by the wrist before he could hit it again.

THIRTY
EIGHT

Treet wrenched his arm away, but it was held fast. With his heart thumping triple time, he yelled for help, cutting his cry short in mid-yelp, for he witnessed a strange thing: Tvrdy running forward and embracing one of the attackers. Traitor! thought Treet. He has sold us out!

But no, they turned and came toward him together, Tvrdy slapping the side of his helmet. Treet found the radio switch on the neck and tapped it. A squawk of static burst in his ears, and out of the noise Tvrdy's voice emerged saying, "Cejka could not reach us. He and his men have been waiting for us outside."

Relief washed over Treet as the meaning of Tvrdy's words broke upon him.

"Crocker!" Pizzle leaped from his skimmer and ran to where Rumon Hagemen escorted a lanky figure through the door.

The pilot leaned heavily on those supporting him as he shuffled into the Archives. "Crocker, can you hear me?" asked Treet, throwing himself from the skimmer and rushing forward. "You okay?"

Crocker's voice sounded thin and wheezy in Treet's helmet. "I've been better." The Captain laughed, and the laugh lapsed into a dry cough. "I was afraid you were thinking of taking off without me."

"Wouldn't dream of it," replied Treet. "But are you sure? I mean—"

"You're *not* leaving me behind. I can make it." Treet heard desperation in the Captain's voice.

Treet glanced at Pizzle, who only stared noncommittally into space, and back to Crocker. "You're sure?"

Crocker nodded. "Please, I'll be fine."

"You may not thank me for this," said Treet. "But all right—if that's what you want, I won't stop you."

"It may be for the best." Tvrdy spoke up. "If Jamrog discovered he remained behind, his life would be in danger."

Cejka agreed. "It would be safer for everyone."

"You mean the chase will be off once we've disappeared." Treet nodded. "Okay, we'll take the other skimmer too. Calin, you're going to have to drive. Can you handle it?"

The magician nodded inside her helmet. "It won't be difficult."

"Good. Let's get going. As soon as we're out of here, we'll all feel a whole lot better." Cjeka's men helped Crocker to Calin's skimmer, made him comfortable, and strapped him in. Treet climbed up into the driver's seat once again and pressed the ignition plate, heard the muffled whine of the engine, felt the throb of mechanical life. When everyone was ready, he eased back the joystick and the skimmer scraped forward slowly, bumped over the outer doorseal, and pulled itself along under the superstructure of the landing platform—a dark forest of fibersteel pylons and beams.

The blade-runners carved through the bare earth beneath the platform, knifing a twin track in the dirt. Treet pulled the joystick back further and speed increased, stabilizing the tipsy craft somewhat. The wheels, flattened with the weight of the skimmer and its passengers, bit into the soil and churned them forward.

Now Treet cleared the edge of the platform and plunged into long grass, which dragged at the skimmer, swishing and hissing as the vehicle sliced through. He drove toward the rise of a low hill directly in front of him and glanced back to see how the others were navigating. "Everybody getting the hang of it?"

His question went unanswered. Just as he turned to look back, an explosion ripped the earth not five meters in front of him. "Look out!" screamed Pizzle, his voice sharp inside the helmet. Another explosion rocked the skimmer as a crater blossomed in the grass nearby. Chunks of smoking dirt rattled on the cowling of the skimmer as Treet hunched over the joystick, urging the machine faster.

"They're on the platform!" cried Treet, stealing a glance behind him as the vehicle plunged forward. Both Calin and Yarden had cleared the platform and were racing out over the grass. "Spread out! You're too close together."

Treet gained the top of the hill and slowed to look back. Calin had split off to one side, and Yarden had fallen behind somewhat. A brilliant flash leaped from the platform, and a sheet of flame engulfed the trailing skimmer.

"Yarden!" screamed Treet. His breath caught in his throat, and he threw the joystick forward.

"Keep moving!" cried Crocker. "Don't stop!"

Treet spun around and saw Yarden's skimmer come shooting out of a wall of boiling smoke and dust, the nose of her vehicle scorched black. "I—I'm okay. . . I think," she said into her helmet mike.

Three more fireballs exploded around them, but the skimmers reached the crest of the hill, plowed over the top, and were cut off from the direct line of fire of those on the platform. Treet leaned to the side, and the skimmer carved a graceful arc along the slope. "Hey, it's easy!" he said. "Like steering a sled—just lean into it."

The others followed his lead and they swept down the hillside, keeping themselves out of sight of the Invisibles on the platform. At the bottom of the hill, Treet turned to glide into a shallow valley between two hills. The valley flattened out after only two hundred meters, and once again they came into view from the platform. A volley of thundervolts strafed the ground, throwing charred landscape into steaming spires. The skimmers sped forward, sliding through the grass.

Desperate to get more speed out of the machine, Treet yanked the joystick all the way back. The action threw him momentarily off balance, raising his knees off the pedals. Instantly the skimmer streaked ahead—an arrow released from the bowstring—as the blades raised up.

Treet understood at once what had happened and informed the other drivers of his discovery. "On turf the blades drag; they're used only for steering. Raise up on the pedals and decrease the drag," he explained, and immediately the three were rocketing over the hills, rapidly outdistancing the hostile fire.

"Whee! This is fantastic!" chirped Pizzle. "Next best thing to flying."

Crocker spoke up. "If I remember the scan we took before landing, there was a minus eight dry land reading off to the southeast of the colony."

"Minus eight dry land. That would be a desert?"

"Think Sahara—that's minus eight."

"I caught a glimpse of it on one of our passes," said Pizzle. "I saw a river too."

Treet vaguely remembered seeing a river as the *Zehpyros*

streaked by, but so much had happened since they'd landed, that day and its events seemed impossibly remote.

Ahead, a rising slope flattened to a promontory. "Let's stop up ahead to reconnoiter," said Treet. "We'll get oriented, and then we can travel."

"Good idea," replied Pizzle. "But let's not delay too long. I wouldn't mind putting a few thousand kilometers between me and those Invisibles back there before lunch. They might decide to get serious about all this and come after us."

They stopped their machines on the little plateau and checked for damage. Other than a few more dents, and some fire-blistered paint on Yarden's skimmer, they all had come through unscathed. Treet craned his neck around and saw the magnificent silvery bubble cluster of Empyrion glittering like a jewel as the sun's first rays bathed it in early morning light. Far behind them, smoke spread and flattened on the breeze. There was no more shooting; the Invisibles had given up without a chase, or so it seemed.

Treet turned his eyes to the west. Pale green hills the color of turquoise stretched away to the horizon beneath a sky-bowl of pale, bird's egg blue. The country was wide and broad and astonishingly open. A rush of pure liberation whipped through him, and he realized just how cramped and confining the colony had been, how constricted and limiting.

"I was sure I'd never see the sky again," said Yarden softly. Treet turned, and she was beside him. He looked through the faceplate of her helmet and saw tears trickling down her cheeks.

"It's really something," said Treet. "I forgot what freedom was like. I don't think I'll forget again."

After consulting a very subdued Calin about direction, they started off, riding the green crests and valleys in search of the legendary lost Fieri.

Jamrog's eyes narrowed as he took in Hladik's information. When he finally spoke, his voice was ice and venom. "So Tvrdy had succeeded! Very well, let him believe he has won—it will make his fall the sweeter." He fell silent then, gazing into space while his fingers tapped restlessly on the side of the chair. Momentarily he came to himself again and regarded the Nilokerus leader sharply. "Well, tell me why I shouldn't have you thrown into your own reorientation cells."

Hladik had prepared for just this eventuality. He said simply, "Only that I may have delivered the Fieri into our hands."

"If this is a lie, Hageman, it is most ambitious. Tell me, how did you accomplish this remarkable feat?"

"One of the spies was placed in Nilokerus Hage . . ."

"Don't insult me, Hladik; I well remember. You said he had disappeared with the others."

"He did, but not before I had him conditioned."

Jamrog's smile was hard. "Your famous conditioning, yes. However, your subjects usually die, do they not?"

"Some do. This one survived. He is conditioned to return to me when he finds the Fieri."

"I see." Jamrog's expression became even more fierce. "Then let us hope for your sake that he finds them, Hageman. In the meantime we have Tvrdy and his cohorts to deal with. They must not be allowed to strengthen their position through this episode."

"I have some ideas about that, Director," offered Hladik hopefully. His face shone with a faint sheen of sweat. He knew how close he had been to invoking Jamrog's wrath against him. But now he could relax; the worst was over. "I suggest we discuss them over souile."

"Your tastes have become expensive, Hladik. I'm not sure I approve."

"It's no more than the Threl can afford, Hageman," he chuckled, keeping his eyes on Jamrog.

"Oh, in that case we'll drink to Rohee's health, shall we?"

"Yes—may it desert him in a most timely fashion!"

Jamrog laughed and took Hladik by the arm, and they went out together into Empyrion's twisted pathways.

THIRTY
NINE

"As I see it," said Treet, "our problems are only beginning."

The day had grown comfortably warm. Epsilon Eridani shone bright, a white disk directly overhead, smaller in the heavens than Earth's yellow Sol. Empyrion's sky fairly shimmered a fine, transparent blue—the color of flame. The company had stopped to rest and eat and, more importantly, plan their strategy for surviving in the alien wilderness.

Treet continued, "We have no food, no water—only the emergency rations in our packs, and at the rate they're going, those won't last long. In short, we're in it up to our furry eyebrows, friends."

Pizzle got up and wandered over to where the skimmers were parked.

"Am I boring you with this, Pizzle?" asked Treet, his voice crackling over the helmet speaker.

"No, I'm as concerned as you are. I just had an idea, that's all."

"We've got to rig up some kind of shelter," added Crocker. "We don't really know what the climate is like. It could freeze every night, or rain."

"We can at least make a fire at night," said Yarden. "Can't we?"

The group looked at one another glumly. No one wanted to add to the bad news by pointing out that they had no fire-making equipment and no fuel either. The treeless hills stretched out in every direction, an endless rolling sea of pale green, the color of turquoise or blue jade, without feature all the way to the horizon. Even if they managed somehow to make a fire, there was absolutely nothing to burn.

"Fire takes fuel, which we don't have. And speaking of fuel," said Treet, regretting his dismal inventory, "there's the matter of go-juice for the skimmers."

"They're electric," called Pizzle, bending over the side of the nearest skimmer.

"Gosh, thanks!" remarked Treet. "That helps ever so much. We already *know* they're electric, Whiz Kid. But their cells are recharged by generators which run on solid fuel."

"Yeah, and solar," replied Pizzle. "See?" He straightened and unfolded a winglike panel from the rear of the vehicle. "Solar cells. We can run on solar and, unless I'm mistaken, recharge the batteries at the same time. We'll save the fuel for emergencies."

Treet was impressed, but hardly felt in a congratulatory mood. "That helps a little," he admitted. "But it's going to take more than a few solar cells to pull us through. What else do you have there?"

"Give me a minute." Pizzle walked around to the other side of the skimmer and studied it, poking here and there around the machine, his putty face pursed in a scowl of concentration.

"Weapons," Crocker said. "We should have some weapons—even primitive clubs would be better than bare hands. There could well be carnivorous animal life around here."

"We haven't seen anything," said Yarden. "Wouldn't we have seen signs of any animals?"

"Not necessarily. They might be nocturnal." Crocker saw the face Treet made and continued, "Okay, maybe I'm wrong. My point is that we don't know this world at all and that until we get acquainted we better be on our toes."

"You're right, of course." Treet turned his attention to Calin, who had been strangely quiet all morning. "What about it, Calin? Any night-stalking meat-eaters we ought to be on the lookout for?"

Calin returned to awareness and looked blankly at Treet. "Animals?" She mouthed the word oddly. "I know of no animals. I have never been . . . outside . . . the dome . . ." Her voice trailed off, and she returned to her reverie.

"There's another thing I wasn't going to bring up—about the helmets," began Crocker.

"You might as well bring it up; we're on a roll. What about the helmets? We have enough air for forty days apiece."

"It isn't that. The thing is we can't take them off—which means we can't eat or drink."

Treet stared. It was true—there was no way to eat or drink without taking off the helmet. "We need some kind of airtight shelter. Fast!" He had a picture of them all slowly starving to death inside the oversized mushroom-shaped globes.

Pizzle's nasal yammer sounded in his ear. "I don't know if this will work or not," he said.

"If what will work?"

"This tent idea. Look here—" Pizzle came ambling back with a long, orange bag that bounced as he walked. He dumped it in front of them and set about emptying it. Slender fibersteel poles came sliding out, along with knitted nylon-type roping, thin and strong, and a flat packet of cloth that looked like crinkled orange silk.

Pizzled picked up the bright orange packet and shook it out, unfolding it into an ultrathin membrane with narrow pockets. They watched as he slid the poles into the pockets, stretching the material taut as the fibersteel bent into half circles. Within three minutes the tent was erected: a longish, ribbed tunnel affair with a mivex seal for a door. It looked like a culvert that had been flattened on the bottom and pinched down at one end. Clearly, occupancy was limited to no more than two people.

"*Voila!*" said Pizzle proudly, admiring his handiwork.

"Any more where that came from?"

"I should think so. There's a long, skinny compartment on the floor of the left-hand side of the skimmer. It was underneath the reserve air canisters. There should be one in each vehicle, and my guess is they're waterproof as well as airtight. You don't put a mivex seal on something unless you want to keep something in or out." Pizzle glanced around, lips wrapped around his imp grin. "You know this is just like *Escape from Nurakka*—I mean, they used airboats, but it's the same idea."

Crocker, pale and unsteady, leaned his hands on his knees and studied the tent. "We'd have to figure some way to bleed out the air inside and fill it again so we could breathe in there."

"We could use the spare canisters—valve off just enough to get a good mix," explained Pizzle. "We know that the air is not downright poisonous, so that shouldn't be any problem."

"Wouldn't we use up our oxygen faster?" wondered Yarden.

"Maybe. Not much though," replied Crocker. "We wouldn't be wearing our helmets inside the tent, so breathing time would even out somewhat. You'd lose a little every time you opened the seal, of course. Once inside the tent, we'd have to stay in."

Treet frowned inside his helmet. The whole enterprise seemed so half-baked in the clear light of day. "Then we eat only once a day," he grumped. "Fantastic."

"Twice," replied Crocker, straightening painfully. "When we put up the tents for the night and again just before we take them down in the morning. That won't be too bad."

"What about water? I can't go all day long without a drink."

"Maybe I could rig up some kind of straw gizmo and run it up through the neck seal of the helmet."

"We've got to *find* water first," Yarden pointed out.

"The river Pizzle mentioned is to the east. If we keep heading this direction, we'll hit it before long," said Crocker.

"What about the desert?" wondered Treet.

"Look," snapped the Captain, "one problem at a time. We'll solve 'em as they come, okay? You people are going to have to give up some of your ideas about creature comforts. This isn't a nature hike we're on. This is survival."

"Speaking of which," Pizzle chimed in, "I think we ought to be moving along. The further from that place back there," he jerked a thumb over his shoulder, "the better I'll feel. Since we can't eat or anything until we get the tents up, let's travel as far as we can."

The sun was aglow in the western sky, burnishing each hilltop a brassy green-gold and throwing each valley into deep blue shadow, when the company decided to stop for the night. Although the sun remained above the smooth horizon, away in the east faint flickers of starlight already glimmered. The sky seemed fragile and transparent, the sheerest of materials, lending the light an intense and vibrant quality—almost alive.

For the last two hours no one had broken radio silence. All were tired and preoccupied, steeling themselves for the rigors ahead. Treet had convinced himself that he would survive; one way or another he would make it. He would do all he could to help the others, but their survival, he reasoned, depended upon themselves. He was not responsible for getting them into this, nor was he responsible for getting them out—that was a problem they all shared equally. In Treet's opinion they were *all* victims.

This was the way his thoughts were bending. So it was with a shock that he heard his own voice cracking in his eardrums: "I think we'd better find a place to make camp. Since we haven't done this before, we don't want to be fumbling around in the dark."

Why did I do that? he wondered. Why couldn't I let Crocker take command? If anyone should lead, *he* should.

Crocker ratified his suggestion. "You're right. We're losing the light. Let's stop at the next flat hilltop you see."

The next flat hilltop was two hilltops away. Treet slowed the skimmer as it crested the hill and parked it so the solar panel could pick up the last of the sun's rays. He slowly unfolded himself from the driver's position and stretched out the kinks. According to the odometer on the skimmer's control panel they had covered slightly over two hundred and eighty kilometers since their last stop, which worked out to around five hundred and sixty for the day. Not too bad for the first day.

Treet did a few quick toe touches and torso twists as the other climbed down from their vehicles. "I feel like one of those old-time cowboys," said Pizzle. "You know, like Roy Rogers. I believe I'm getting saddle sores."

"You look a little bowlegged," said Treet, flipping open the storage compartment of the skimmer and pulling out the long tent envelope. He carried the tent to a level spot and dumped it out. The others chose spots nearby and began setting up their tents.

"Let's keep them fairly close together," said Crocker, "so we can talk to each other."

"Who's going to be talking?" said Treet. "Once I crawl inside, I'm sound asleep."

"It's eat first and then sleep for me," said Yarden. "I'm starved."

Crocker warned, "We'd better make our food last. It might be a while before we find anything edible out here." When no one responded, he went on more insistently, "I mean it! No more than a few mouthfuls—eat just what you need to keep yourself going. And drink only a swallow."

"Aye, aye, Captain Bligh," grouched Treet. "We get the picture. Let's don't dwell on it."

"Look, Treet. Maybe you'd prefer leading this expedition yourself. It's not in my contract that I have to be Bwana, you know."

"I didn't mean that you—I mean, I—" stuttered Treet. "Oh, forget it. We're exhausted, and we're all stressed out. Let's just get the tents up and go to sleep."

The sun had nearly dropped below the fading hill line when they climbed into the tents: Treet and Calin into one—the magician would not go with anyone else—and Crocker and Pizzle in another, since Yarden did not express an interest in sharing quarters with either of them and the men were hesitant to suggest otherwise.

Treet backed into the half-hoop structure, pulling two spare air canisters in after him. He sealed the mivex entrance and then opened the connector valves of both flat canisters, allowed air to bleed off while he counted seconds, and then said into his mike, "I've had both valves wide open for ninety seconds. Now what?"

"Take your helmet off," said Pizzle.

"You take *your* helmet off!"

"It'll work, don't worry," Pizzle coaxed. "Trust me."

"I don't know why I'm the guinea pig, but here goes." He took a deep breath and placed his hands on either side of the helmet, gave a three-quarter twist, and lifted it off, holding it above his head for quick replacement. He let his breath out and paused, then sniffed experimentally. Okay, so far. He drew more air in and held it—nothing unusual. Calin sat cross-legged at the far end of the tent, watching him with wide eyes. Then he gulped a deep breath and announced, "It works! Hey, it works!"

He breathed deeply, in and out again a few times. Besides a faint metallic tang on the back of his tongue, the air seemed perfect. "It feels great to get out of that plastic bubble!" He heard a faint voice, like the voice of his conscience buzzing at him. He picked up his helmet again.

"You forget something?" It was Crocker.

"Are you all right?" inquired Yarden with some concern.

"Yeah, sorry. It works perfect. You can take your helmets off now." He waited a few seconds and then hollered, "Isn't that better?"

"Marvelous!" came Yarden's answer through the tent membrane.

"Sweet relief!" called Pizzle.

Treet took Calin's helmet off as she made no move to do it herself. She looked at him oddly and then curled up in a ball where she sat. He opened their emergency pouches and brought out some food for them—dry wafers with the texture and taste of dog biscuits. He gave a couple to Calin and crunched down two himself, then rinsed his mouth with a few sparing sips of water.

He placed one of the flat air canisters under his head for a pillow and stretched out. Calin remained curled at one end of the tent. Rather than try to move her, Treet lay diagonally across the floor so that he would not have to keep his knees flexed all night. "Nighty night," Treet called as he settled himself to sleep.

He heard some mumbling from Pizzle and Crocker's tent, but closed his eyes and was asleep at once.

FORTY

The dog biscuits tasted no better just before dawn the next morning, but by then he was hungry enough to eat rocks. At least the single sip of water he allowed himself was refreshing. Calin awoke at Treet's merest touch and rose without speaking. They donned their helmets and climbed out of the tent. Treet walked down one side of the hill, Calin the other as the sky turned pink low in the east. Treet stood looking at the dawn-dulled sky, noting a line of gray clouds with rosy feathered edges chugging westward far to the south. Otherwise, the heavens were uniformly void.

When he retraced his steps up the hill, he met Pizzle coming down. "Sleep okay?" he asked.

"Fair. Crocker muttered all night; I think he's still hurting."

"Crocker can hear you, you know." The voice was Crocker's, loud in their helmet speakers. "I'll be all right. Don't you worry about me. I won't slow anybody up."

"Sorry," Pizzle said quickly. "I wasn't implying anything."

Treet turned to see Crocker stumbling down the hill toward them. "Is it true, Crocker? Are you in pain?"

"No!" the Captain denied, a little too forcefully. "Just worry about yourselves."

"We could stay put for a day or two and let you get some rest . . ."

Crocker jabbed a finger at Treet's chest. "Nobody is doing any such thing on my account. We'd waste food and water which we might well need later on."

"I didn't mean anything," said Pizzle sullenly.

"Yes, we know you didn't mean anything," snapped Treet. "Forget it. Let's get the tents down and head out."

The sun's pearl-white disk was peeping above the eastern hill line by the time everyone was ready. The skimmer's whine, muffled by the helmet, climbed into the upper registers, and Treet eased back the joystick for another day's journey.

"Keep the sun to your back and spread out. We can't afford any accidents," he said as his skimmer slid out over the grass, gliding down the hill into the shadowed valley.

Treet again took the lead, Calin maintaining a steady speed a little ways back on his left hand, Yarden nearly even on the right. The three vehicles churned their way across the rippled landscape, passing from sunlight into shadow as the turquoise hills rose and fell in even waves.

The next two days were perfect copies of the first. They ate, slept, woke, and traveled the wide, hill-bound country, which showed no variation and gave no indication of ever changing at all. A more monotonous land Treet could not imagine.

This, Treet reminded himself, could be considered a blessing, for it meant that their travel was unimpeded by the more diverting variations of scenery and weather. If there was nothing much to look at, at least no obstacles hindered them.

About midday the fourth day out, they halted to stretch and take another directional reading—as much as possible. Treet sat on the ground, tucked his knees up to his chest, and rolled on his back, working the kinks out of his lower spine. While the others were walking and limbering up, he approached Calin, who was sitting by herself on the ground next to the skimmer.

Her eyes were focused on something far away in the distance when he came up. He squatted down beside her and tapped her helmet. When she failed to acknowledge his presence, he reached out and touched her radio switch. "Calin, I haven't heard a squeak out of you since yesterday. Are you feeling okay?"

Calin did not move when he addressed her, but remained immobile, arms encircling updrawn knees, vision fixed on the unvarying horizon.

"Did you hear me?" Treet leaned toward her. "Calin?"

"Can I help?" Yarden dropped down beside him on her knees.

"I don't know what's wrong with her. She hasn't said a word all day."

As Treet spoke, the magician's body began to shiver,

though the sun was warm and the breeze fair. "Calin? Listen to me. Calin?"

The tremors became more pronounced. She raised her head, and Treet saw in her eyes a vacant, mindless stare—the look of a wild creature shivering with fright. He placed a hand on her shoulder and felt her muscles rigid and cold beneath his touch. "She's stiff as stone!"

Her head began thrashing inside her helmet. Her mouth worked silently behind closed lips, and a keening moan sounded in the helmet speakers. Her eyelids fluttered as her eyeballs rolled up into their sockets. Blood trickled from her mouth. "Her tongue—she's chewing her tongue!" cried Treet. "We've got to do something!"

Yarden bent close, putting her arms around the trembling woman. "Calin, this is Yarden." She spoke softly, calmly. "I'm going to take your helmet off."

"You can't do that!" shouted Treet. "It could kill her!"

Yarden moved behind the magician and cradled her trembling body. "She'll die anyway—she's swallowed her tongue. She's choking!"

It was true. Calin's face was now tinted a ghastly shade of purple; her lips were blue.

Yarden put her hands on either side of the helmet and gave a sharp twist. She pulled it off and forced Calin's jaws open with one hand, reaching deftly in with her long fingers and flipping the magician's curled tongue forward.

Calin gulped air and instantly her eyes bulged out in terror. "Aaiiee!" She screamed a ragged, throat-tearing scream which, even through the sound-dampening properties of their helmets, sounded like a death rattle. Her hands clawed at the air.

"For God's sake, get her helmet back on!" boomed Crocker, running up.

Pizzle stood frozen a little way off, staring at the writhing woman on the ground before him. Yarden still knelt beside her, holding her head. Calin inhaled and screamed again, this time her voice faint and far away. "Aaiiee! It bur-r-n-n-s!"

Treet snatched up her helmet and thrust it forward.

"No!" said Yarden.

"You're killing her!" cried Treet. He moved to put the helmet over Calin's head, but Yarden shoved it aside.

"No, wait!"

"Talazac!" roared Crocker. "Get that helmet back on her right now. What do you think you're doing?"

Treet stooped with the helmet in his hands. Yarden resisted once more. "Please stop. It'll be all right. Just wait a moment."

"What's gotten into you?" said Treet. He hesitated, his hands thrust out with the helmet between them. "Do you want her to die?"

"Wait, she's right," said Pizzle. "Look."

Calin lay still now, her color improving and her breathing, though still ragged and shallow, developing a more regular rhythm. She whimpered and moaned, but her limbs had stopped trembling and her head no longer thrashed. "It _burns_," she rasped.

"Well, I never—" observed Crocker. "She seems to be coming out of it."

"Get her some water," ordered Yarden. Pizzle returned seconds later with one of the pouches. He held up the collapsible plastic canteen to Calin's lips and she swallowed, her features convulsing with pain. "Her throat's a little sore I imagine," said Yarden, putting her hands to her own helmet.

"Wait! You're not thinking of taking off _your_ helmet." Treet stared incredulously at Yarden. "Have you lost your mind?"

"She needs me," replied Yarden simply. "I have to talk to her." She gave the helmet a quick twist and pulled it off. She paused, eyes closed, laying the helmet aside. Then she inhaled.

The pain twisted her features monstrously. She gulped air and shuddered, collapsing against the side of the skimmer. Her hands went to her throat, which she grasped as if she were trying to strangle herself. Tears streamed from her eyes. "Ahh! Ah-hh-hh . . ."

"Yarden! Put your helmet back on!" shouted Treet. He leaped forward, took up the headgear, and lowered it over Yarden's head. Her eyes flew open, and she knocked it away. "Help me, you two!" Treet shouted to Pizzle and Crocker, who stood motionless behind him. "Yarden, you're suffocating."

"She can't hear you anymore," said Crocker.

Treet raised the helmet once more, but Yarden reached out, gripped his arm, and dug her nails in. "She doesn't want it," said Pizzle. "She's over it."

Yarden's eyes opened slowly. She smiled weakly, painfully, then bent over the quivering magician and spoke to her. Treet saw her mouth move, but could not hear the words. Then Yarden straightened and turned to Treet, put her hands on his helmet, and nodded.

Treet shook his head furiously and grabbed her wrists. She smiled and mouthed the words, *Trust me.* He hesitated, then took a deep breath, and nodded. The helmet twisted and came off. Treet sat back on his heels, still holding his breath.

"Let it out slow and breathe in slow," said Yarden in a grating whisper. "It will sting like fury, but you'll be okay."

Sting wasn't the word for it. As Treet inhaled, it felt as if all his soft tissues had suddenly burst into flame—as if his nasal passages, throat, and windpipe had ignited. His lungs convulsed with the shock. Angry red flares erupted in his brain. It seemed as if he breathed pure fire.

The scream he loosed was far from pretty. It bubbled in his throat and tore up through his vocal cords in an explosive burst only to trail off into an agonized, choking wheeze. Tears blinded his eyes and he squirmed convulsively on the ground, thrashing from side to side.

"Don't fight it," Yarden soothed. He felt her hands on his chest. "Breathe in slowly. Stay on top and ride it out."

Treet fought the pain, pushing it down with an effort. He opened his eyes and saw Yarden bending over him, her eyes bright, coaxing him with encouragement. "You're almost through the worst," she said in a voice frayed and ragged.

He drew another shallow, shaky breath and felt his scorched tissues wilt. The pain seared through his lungs; it felt as though they had been turned inside out and singed with acid. He coughed and moaned.

His next breath was better, and the next better still. The pain subsided to a sharp tingle. He raised himself slowly, wiping the tears from the side of his neck. Calin sat looking at him, panting lightly as if she'd run a sprint to reach him. Yarden smiled. "Not so bad," she said hoarsely.

"Not if you're used to eating fire," replied Treet, his throat raw as frazzled wire.

Yarden motioned to Pizzle and Crocker to remove their helmets, but the two refused, backing away cautiously. Treet did not blame them in the least; in fact, he marveled at himself for acquiescing so readily to Yarden's request. Why had he done that?

"Let them keep them on if they want," rasped Treet. He

drew a tentative deep breath and though it still stung fiercely, the pain was not what it had been moments before. He could bear it. "Why did you do that, Yarden?"

She looked perplexed. "I don't know. I had a feeling about it—a strong feeling that we should do it. Calin had to have help in any case. I had to get to her."

"What do you mean we *should* do it? How could you know that?"

"I don't think I can explain it to you. It just seemed right, that's all. Besides, I couldn't bear the thought of being trapped in that thing for the rest of my life."

"Come on—the rest of your life?"

"I'm never going back to the colony." Yarden said this with utmost self-assurance, as if stating the most evident fact.

Before Treet could ask her about her declaration, Crocker tapped him on the shoulder. Treet glanced up into the faceplate and saw the Captain's mouth forming broad, muted words which he couldn't read. Treet shook his head. "You're going to have to spell it out! I can't hear you," he shouted.

"He says we should put our helmets back on. It's dangerous without them," offered Yarden.

Treet straightened and slipped his helmet on briefly. "I really don't think it's dangerous," he said into the mike. "I think you should take yours off—both of you."

"Funny, you don't *look* crazy," quipped Pizzle.

"Suit yourselves. I don't care what you do. But I think Yarden is right—this way is better."

Pizzle and Crocker swiveled to look at one another. They shook their heads, and Pizzle spoke for both of them. "No way. We saw you jerking around on the ground."

"No pain, no gain," said Treet, removing the headpiece once more.

He turned to the women. "You gave us a scare, Calin. Do you feel any better now?"

The slender magician nodded slightly. "I was afraid."

"I'll say. But what were you afraid of?"

She looked at him blankly and made no answer.

"Well, I guess it doesn't matter. We can talk about it later. Right now we need for you to get in touch with Nho and ask him about direction."

Calin went still and her eyes lost their focus. Yarden looked at her and said, "You shouldn't make her do that."

"She does it. I don't make her," Treet replied. "You act as if all this is my fault somehow. Let me tell you—it's not my fault!"

Calin came to herself again. "Nho says we are going the right way."

"That's all? Would he care to elaborate?"

"There is nothing else to say now."

They each took a sip of water, Pizzle and Crocker looking on thirstily, then remounted the skimmers again to slide even further into the hill-rumpled waste.

FORTY
ONE

That night Yarden sat alone on the hillside just below the hoop-shaped tents. Pizzle and Crocker were sealed in their tent, and Calin, who had earlier decided to join Yarden, was asleep in hers while Treet walked the tightness out of his legs and shoulders, striding up and down the nearby hills, swinging his arms. His lungs still ached—as if he'd run a very fast ten thousand meters—but the sharp burning sensation was gone. He came upon Yarden and flopped down beside her. Neither spoke for a long time.

"It's amazing, isn't it," he said at last. "The quiet. It's so . . . profound."

The air was still and deathly silent. He had never heard such an absolute absence of sound in the outdoors: no piping birdcalls, no burring insects, no rustling leaves or ticking branches. Nothing.

This is what it's like to be deaf, thought Treet.

"Not deaf," said Yarden. "More like immune."

Treet thought about asking her what she meant, then thought that she already knew he was thinking about asking her and decided not to. Instead, he leaned back and gazed upward at the stars beginning to glow in the deepening twilight. Empyrion had no moon, so the stars shone especially bright in the darkening heavens. "Do you realize we're looking at constellations we have no names for?"

"Mmm," said Yarden, "stars should have names. We could make some up."

"It wouldn't be official."

"Why not! Ours would be as good as anybody else's."

"Okay, see that wobbly string of stars just above the horizon, with that bright one at the head? We'll call that one Ophidia—the snake."

"How about that one with the brightest star directly overhead? It looks like a bird—there's the head, and those stars sweeping down on either side are the wings. A pretty bird—a nightingale, I think."

"Make that one Luscinia, then."

"Ophidia and Luscinia," said Yarden softly. "I like those. You're good with words."

"I'm a writer—or used to be."

"Used to be? What are you now?" she asked lightly. Treet could feel her eyes on him, but kept looking at the sky.

"I don't know what I am. Right now I seem to be an explorer."

"Yes, I see what you mean. None of us are exactly playing our usual roles." She lay back on an elbow. "I know I never will again."

"Fatalism?"

"No, I don't think so. More like realism. It's a feeling."

"Like the feeling you had about taking off our helmets?" Treet turned to look at her, noting her reaction.

"Something like that. Why did you do it? Pizzle and Crocker wouldn't, I knew that."

"I guess I'm easily influenced."

Yarden laughed, her voice still hoarse. "You are many things, Orion Treet. Easily influenced isn't one of them. I'm serious—why did you do it? Crocker is right; it could have been dangerous."

"Maybe I just wanted to be free of that blasted bubble."

"Your freedom is important to you."

"It is, now that you mention it. I guess that also explains why we're out here scooting across these God-forsaken hills." Treet pushed himself up on one elbow to face her. "I answered your question, but you still haven't answered mine."

"Which question was that?"

"The one I asked earlier: why you think you're not going back to the colony."

"You never asked me that," she said, giving his arm a push. It was the first truly spontaneous gesture Treet had ever seen her make.

"I thought about it—which is the same thing with you, isn't it?"

"I told you it doesn't work like that—I can't read minds. I just get thought impressions, that's all."

"You're evading the question."

She looked at him intently, eyes luminous in the dying

light, and said, "Empyrion is an evil place. I won't go back there."

Her answer surprised him. He replied, "I'll grant it could be better, but evil? It's not *that* bad." The look she gave him told him the subject was not open for debate, so he tried a different tack. "You were pretty shook up when they brought you to Tvrdy's kraam. What happened?" When she did not answer, he added, "You don't have to tell me if you don't want."

"It isn't that. I'm afraid you won't understand—I'm not sure I understand it all myself."

"I know that feeling, at least."

"Yes. Well, for me it was like this," she said, and began relating all that she remembered of her captivity among the Chryse. She told of the plays they'd performed and of the flash orgy and finally of the Astral Service. When she described the Service, Treet noted her voice growing smaller, fainter.

"If this hurts, we don't have to talk about it. Forget I said anything," offered Treet.

"I don't *want* to forget. I want to remember how close I came to giving in. I don't ever want to get that close again."

"Giving in?"

"To the evil of Empyrion." Her tone became intense, insistent. "I felt it in that Service, as I have never felt it in my life until that time—an overwhelming presence of inestimable hate, a force of pure, unremitting malevolence. Trabant, they call it—the name chills me! And this thing, this being is the essence of evil. It wanted me—*demanded* me. I resisted. If the Service had lasted any longer, I would not have been able to hold out."

"But you did hold out."

"Yes, and I never want to be tested like that again."

Treet looked at her a long time, considering her words. "You saved Calin's life this morning. I still can't figure out what happened with her."

"The same thing that happened to me."

"You lost me there."

"Fear."

"She said she was scared. I thought she meant scared of what we were doing."

"Put yourself in her situation. They have lived for untold generations under that dome of theirs. They never leave it for any reason—they view the outside world as an enemy. How would you feel if you lived your whole life believing that and were suddenly thrust out? The land is so big, so empty. It must have terrified her, and that terror worked on her mind until finally she just snapped."

"The same thing might have happened to you in the Service."

"Exactly."

They fell silent after that and just lay quietly in each other's company until Yarden got up and started toward her tent. Treet watched her go, called "Good night" after her, but received no reply. He glanced heavenward and saw that Ophidia had risen higher in the night sky, then got up and went to his tent and fell asleep pondering all Yarden had told him.

Early the next morning the company came in sight of the river. Yarden, with Calin riding behind her, was the first to spot it. She sped up and pulled the skimmer to a halt on the crest of a hill, allowing the others to catch up.

"Do you see it?" she asked.

"See what?" asked Treet. Pizzle and Crocker pulled up and sat staring from inside their helmets, looking at the others.

"The river. See? Down there beyond those hills. You can just see a little sliver of it shining through there." She pointed, and Treet followed her elegant finger to see a glittering spangle threading through the hills.

"Jackpot!" said Calin with a smile. She seemed wholly recovered from her ordeal of the day before—almost a completely different person. Yarden had apparently had a most beneficial effect on her.

"Yes, jackpot." Treet turned to Pizzle and Crocker, shouted at the top of his lungs, and pointed out the river. They looked and responded by nodding vigorously and giving him the A-OK sign. He squinted his eyes and estimated that the river lay at least four kilometers away. "We can be there in five minutes. Let's go. It'll be time for a rest stop when we get there."

They pushed off again and rode the hill swells to the river's edge. There they stopped and looked out over a broad expanse of flowing water, silver blue in the sunlight, its gentle, gurgling music a welcome relief from the skimmers' scream.

They dismounted and walked down to the water's edge. Treet squatted, stretched out his hands, and plunged them in.

The water was cool and clear, the bottom fine-grained sand. He cupped his hands and raised a mouthful to his lips, sipped cautiously, tasted, and then swallowed. The water had a slight astringent quality, but tasted as fresh and clean as its sparkling clarity promised.

"I say it's okay," said Treet over his shoulder to the others watching him. "See what you think." He dipped his hands and drank again and again and was immediately joined by Calin and Yarden. When he had drunk his fill, Treet rose, wiped his mouth on his sleeve, and beckoned to Pizzle and Crocker, who stood looking on like poor relations at a posh family picnic.

He pantomimed taking off a helmet and pointed at them. They stared doubtfully back at him, but made no move to remove the bubbles. Treet shrugged and turned back toward the water. The river stretched a good sixty meters across, flowing southward in unhurried ease, shimmering like quicksilver beneath a blue-white canopy. Although the channel appeared to deepen quite gradually, Treet estimated from its width that at midstream the water would be well beyond a skimmer's ability to navigate—even if the heavy machines had not already foundered in the soft river bottom.

Getting their transportation across would be a trick, no doubt about that. Just how it might be accomplished he could not imagine—until his gaze fell upon Calin, kneeling at the water's edge, drinking.

"We've got a problem, ladies," began Treet, settling beside them. "We have to find a way to get our vehicles across. I don't think they're made for underwater. Got any ideas?"

"A bridge?" began Yarden, then waved aside the idea at once. "Forget I said that." She looked at the desolate hills across the water. "That side is just as barren as this. We'll just have to look for a fording place."

"I guess so—unless Nho can help us out." He looked at Calin directly. "What about it?"

"Treet, no." Yarden put a restraining hand on his arm.

"Calin? Can your psi do anything?"

She considered this for a moment and then nodded. "It would be possible to carry them across perhaps. But I cannot—what is the word?"

"Swim?"

The magician nodded again quickly. "Yes. Swim."

THE SEARCH FOR FIERRA/269

"That is a problem," agreed Treet.

"You can't make her do it," said Yarden. "Do you have any idea what using psi power does to a person?"

"Not really," admitted Treet. "But we've come to a dead end, Yarden. I'm open to suggestions, but unless you know of a good ferry anywhere around, I don't know what else we're going to do."

"Couldn't we at least look for a place to ford? We might find one, which would make crossing a whole lot easier and simpler."

"True. Okay, we look. Here's what we'll do. You and Calin go south and I'll go north—say, for twenty kilometers."

"Thirty."

"All right, thirty. We'll meet back here and share what we've found. How's that?"

Both women agreed, so Treet pushed himself up and went to his skimmer, then donned a helmet briefly to speak to Pizzle and Crocker. "Look, you guys are going to have to get out of those hats. You're missing all the fun."

"What's going on?" asked Crocker.

"Well, we're trying to find a way to get across. Any ideas?"

Crocker glanced at the skimmers. "They're much too heavy to lift that's for sure. A ford, I'd say."

"That's what we decided. Yarden and I are going to split up and take a quick look both ways along the shore. You and Pizzle stay here with the other machine. We'll meet back here in an hour."

"Sounds good," said Pizzle.

"In the meantime, why don't you two work up your nerve and take off your helmets? As you can see, the air is fine. We're thriving. In fact, I think the oxygen content of the atmosphere is higher than Earth's. There's only a momentary discomfort, but that doesn't last."

"Momentary discomfort? Is that what you call rolling around on the ground screaming your heads off? No thanks," said Pizzle.

"Suit yourself. You're going to have to take them off sooner or later. Stay put. We'll be back soon."

Treet, Yarden, and Calin left, driving along the bank, following the slow curves of the river. It wound easily through the hills, and Treet noticed that the river valley was a narrow band on either side, which meant that the water course was relatively recent, geologically speaking. The river had not had time to cut away and flatten the hills along its sides.

Staying close to the bank, he steered the skimmer northward and noticed a ridge ahead which advertised a clear view of the waterway below. Treet left the bank and made for the ridgetop. The promontory did indeed offer a good survey of a fair stretch of river, and nowhere did he see any variation in its width which might indicate shallows. It rolled on placidly beneath the white sun and eventually disappeared beyond a ruffled row of hills away to the north. Though the skimmer's odometer read only fifteen kilometers, Treet decided to turn back, knowing that were he to proceed further he would find only more of the same.

Yarden and Calin were waiting for him when he returned. "There's a shallow place about twenty kilometers from here. It's real rocky and the river spreads out pretty wide, but it doesn't look like it gets more than knee deep," Yarden said, her face glowing with the excitement of discovery. "Did you see anything?"

"Nope. Let's go."

It was as Yarden had said. The river widened and flattened as it ran over a rocky shelf which it could not cut through as easily as the soft, earthy hills. As the others looked on, Treet waded out a few meters into water that came to just over his knees and announced that it appeared not to get much deeper. He sloshed his way back and stood before Calin.

"Well, shall we give it a try?"

Yarden spoke up. "There are a lot of rocks around; maybe we could—"

"What? Build a bridge? Yarden, for crying out loud, we'd be here for months. Be reasonable."

Calin stopped any further discussion. "I will do it." She pressed Yarden's hand, and Treet noted the gesture. An understanding of some sort, a sisterhood, had bloomed overnight between the two women—which was only natural, he supposed. They were, after all, the only females on this expedition, and they were entitled to their own company. But there was something besides the sisterly concern—a harmony between them. Perhaps the gifts they possessed drew them together in a unique way.

"I think it would be best for two of us to go with you. I could go on one side and Pizzle on the other—to steady you in case you slipped or something."

Calin nodded once. She had, Treet noticed, already begun retreating back into herself. Her dark, almond-shaped eyes dulled as her consciousness shifted to that other place where her power lay. She stared straight ahead for a moment, her body very still. Then she moved stiffly to the nearest skimmer, bent to place her hands lightly on its side just above the runner, and straightened. The vehicle floated into the air and hovered.

Pizzle and Crocker stood with mouths agape, and Treet chuckled to himself. He hadn't warned them about what they intended doing; the spectacle no doubt astounded them down to their toenails.

Treet stepped to Calin's side and gestured for Pizzle to do likewise. Pizzle only stared in uncomprehending amazement, so Yarden said, "I'll go with you." She put her hand on the magician's shoulder, and together they walked out into the water.

The river had worn the rock shelf smooth, but it was not slippery. Still, they carefully placed each step, moving slowly out into deeper water to midstream. Even at its deepest point, the water was clear enough to see the bottom, allowing Treet to steer them around the few holes he saw. Soon the water grew shallower again, and they were climbing back out on the other side.

Treet guided them to a flat place near the shore, and Calin put the skimmer down. She straightened, her eyes still dull, her face expressionless. "Do you want to rest or anything?" asked Treet. Calin shook her head, so he said, "Okay, only two more to go. Let's take it slow and easy; we're doing great."

The second crossing went as easily as the first, but when Calin released the machine, it slammed down heavily, bouncing on its suspension. Yarden's wrinkled brow showed concern; she threw a quick, imploring look to Treet which said, *Do something!*

"I think we should rest for a second, Calin," he said. "There's no hurry. We're almost finished."

But the magician turned and started back across the river once more. Yarden's worried expression accused Treet. "I tried to stop her," he said weakly.

The third crossing began like the first two, and proceeded

without incident until they reached midstream. Treet noticed trouble when the skimmer began to waver in the air. Calin stopped abruptly.

"Cal—" began Treet. The skimmer dipped dangerously toward the water.

"Shh! Don't disturb her," whispered Yarden harshly.

Calin became a portrait of exertion: eyes closed tight, sweat beading on forehead, features darkening with strain, knotted veins standing out on her neck. The skimmer bobbled, its bulk rocking wildly as if slipping through her grasp. One runner touched the water.

"Concentrate," cooed Treet. "You can do it. Go slow. Just a little farther; we're almost there."

They took one more step.

"Ahh!" Calin cried, falling back. The skimmer twisted in the air and plunged into the river with a tremendous splash.

FORTY
TWO

Water showered over them as the machine crashed down. The resulting wave knocked them backwards off their feet to flounder helplessly in the backwash. Treet, aware that Calin had fallen, blindly reached out for her, snagged her collar, and held on.

Though the current was not swift, it was strong and Treet was pulled downstream. He flailed his arms and kicked his legs as he fought for a foothold. Finally he managed to get his feet under him and stood, staggered as the water pressed against him, but stayed up. He felt hands on him and cried, "I'm okay! Help me get her out!"

Dashing water from his eyes, Treet saw Calin's limp form slung between Pizzle and Crocker as they sloshed toward the near bank. Yarden stood behind him, hair plastered to her skull and hanging in long sopping ropes. The fright in her expression was replaced with malice as Treet began to laugh.

"Just what's so funny, mister?" she sputtered belligerently, shoving dripping sable locks over her shoulder.

"You look like a wet cat," he laughed. "You okay?"

"As if you cared." She turned and stomped toward the shore.

Treet followed, watching her shapely form moving beneath the clinging wet singleton. Desire spread through him in an instant, shocking Treet with the force of its presence. Yes, he admitted, Yarden Talazac was a very desirable woman. Perhaps he'd wanted her since the beginning, or perhaps now she seemed more of a warm-blooded woman to him and less the cold, ethereal mystic.

He joined her on the shore and said, "I'm sorry I laughed. I just—"

"You just have no sense of compassion!" she snapped. Her light copper skin glowed with anger; a magenta blotch tinted the base of her throat.

"You're really mad." Treet's tone was quiet astonishment.

Yarden quivered—whether with rage or chill, Treet could not tell. Her voice, however, was stiletto sharp. "Of course I'm mad. You could have gotten us all killed with your stupid insistence. I tried to tell you, but you wouldn't listen."

"Wait a min—"

"You can't absolve your guilt in this one! It's your fault."

"My fault! How is it my fault?" Desire was dwindling rapidly as indignation piqued. "Just how do you figure that?"

"You made her use psi. I told you it was dangerous, but you insisted it was the only way. It is *never* the only way."

"Maybe not, but it was the best way."

"No, not even the best way."

"Suppose you tell me what would have been better?" Treet glared, and Yarden glared right back, the magenta blotch deepening and spreading up her throat.

"Oh sure, pretend ignorance. It won't work. You're not shifting blame, Orion Treet," she huffed. "Think about it." Yarden spun away, leaving him with a stinging reply on his tongue and no one to say it to. He watched her march over to where Pizzle and Crocker bent over Calin, trying to revive her by rubbing her hands. Except for the glassy helmets and breathing packs, it was a scene out of a Victorian melodrama where the ineffectual male drones cluster around a fainted female offering smelling salts and encouragement.

Treet snorted and splashed back into the river. The skimmer had landed on its side and was half in the water, one blade gleaming in the sun. Eddies in the current formed whirlpools around the machine, making little sucking noises along its underside. Treet tried to rock it back onto its runners, but even with the push of the current to help him, the vehicle was too heavy to budge. He gave up and joined the others on the bank.

Calin's eyes were open, and she blinked at those bending over her as she came to. She moved to get up, but Yarden said, "Rest a moment. You're safe now. Nothing happened."

She lay back again and her eyes went to Treet. "I—am sorry. I have disappointed you," she said.

"Disappointed me!" He knelt down beside her. "You haven't disappointed me. It was an accident. I'm just glad you weren't hurt, that's all."

Calin looked at him strangely, as if she were distrustful of anyone expressing concern for her. She glanced at the others around her and sat up, looking at the marooned skimmer. "I failed."

"That's all right," said Treet. "We'll find a way to get it out. Don't worry about it right now."

Treet donned a helmet from a nearby skimmer and put it on. "Is Calin okay?" asked Pizzle.

"She seems to be. We should try to get that skimmer out," Treet said into the mike.

"There's probably no hope. Water tends to ruin electric circuits something fierce." Pizzle shook his head dismally inside his helmet.

"We should try in any case," remarked Crocker. "It could be that the circuits and motor casings are sealed. We won't know until we fish it out."

"I suppose you don't want to take off your helmets for this little salvage operation. It would make things easier."

"How would it make things easier," inquired Pizzle, "to have us writhing and crying and coughing our lungs out?"

"It only lasts a second," said Treet.

"Later maybe," said Crocker. "Give us time to work into the idea."

"You've had enough time already." Treet clamped the helmet's neck seal down and felt it grab at the tabs on his singleton. The air inside the helmet smelled stale and unwholesome—like the air of a tomb—after breathing the stringent, light-drenched atmosphere of Empyrion. "I'm not going to argue with you about it. Let's get that skimmer out."

Together they waded into the stream and put their backs into rolling the skimmer onto its runners. They succeeded in getting it rocking and eventually managed to tip it right-side-up once more. Water washed over the sleek nose of the machine and flooded up through the floor to pool around the seats.

"Now what?"

Crocker peered at the craft dubiously. "You think your little magician could take another crack at it?"

"Maybe. But not for a while. She's pretty shaken up," said Treet. "After a good night's rest, who knows?"

"Sixteen hours in the water won't do this machine any good," Pizzle pointed out.

"You said the harm was already done. If that's true, sixteen hours won't matter one way or another."

"Right. So, what are you suggesting?"

"We stay here for the night, let Calin rest, and try it again in the morning if she's willing."

"What do we do while we're waiting?" wondered Crocker.

"I for one could use a bath. It's not a nutrient solution, but this water feels pretty good on this old skin. We don't know when we'll see water again; I'm suggesting that we make the most of it. Take a bath, do the wash, drink a few liters."

"We should also rig up some way to carry water. If we're heading into minus eight desert, we're going to need every drop we can take with us." Pizzle smiled, pleased with himself.

"Okay, Einstein, hop to it."

Treet explained the program to Yarden and Calin and then hiked downstream a few hundred meters and around a bend so he would be out of sight of the rest of the company. He stripped off his singleton and, after thrashing it furiously in the water for a minute or two, spread it out to dry on the bank. He slipped back into the water and lay down in the sun-warmed shallows, letting the water lap over him, feeling its tingle on his skin.

No, it wasn't a nutrient bath—that most blessed of modern conventions—but it was wet and took the parched, crackly quality out of his hide. He turned his face to the sun, enjoying the warmth on his flesh and the solitude. His thoughts turned immediately to Yarden.

What a tight bundle of contradictions she was. Last night she had shown him a side of herself that she rarely revealed. Probably only a handful of others in her entire life had ever seen the warm, caring, sensitive, romantic?—yes, romantic—woman he had seen. They had talked easily together, comfortable in one another's company. And she had seemed relaxed; that transparent barrier field she maintained between herself and everyone and everything else had faltered for a time, and she had shown herself an amiable companion.

Whatever he had seen last night, there was none of it left this morning, however. Her barrier field was back up; she behaved toward him as if the evening had never happened—as indeed, nothing of consequence *had* taken place between them.

Maybe I'm just moonstruck, thought Treet. Maybe I'm inventing something that was never there in the first place. I've been wrong about these things before—like that time in Lucerne with the Contessa Ghiardelli. Women, even under the best of circumstances, were impossible to read precisely. And this insane trek was far from the best setting for deciphering the mercurial movements of romance. If Yarden was behaving slightly schizoid toward him, who could blame her?

His head heavy with these thoughts, Treet closed his eyes and dozed, listening to the water sounds as the river swept by.

He awoke only moments later, seemingly, but the sun had slipped further down in the sky, and when he looked he discovered his singleton had dried on the bank. Treet got out of the water and stood on the bank with his arms outspread, letting the easy southerly breeze dry him before climbing back into his jumpsuit. His skin felt pliant and supple for the first time in a long time.

What was it Crocker had said about this planet? *By all accounts a paradise* . . . Paradise, thought Treet. Yes, there was a little of that here: balmy temperatures, soft warm breezes, and the like. But the landscape was peculiarly barren—too desolate, really, to be considered much of an Eden from any biological point of view. Where were the animals? The trees and larger plants? Where were the birds and insects? Even if nothing else could exist in this place, there should be insects.

Yet, there was only the grass—thin-bladed, wiry stuff that spread over the contours of the interminable hills like a shag carpet gone berserk, seamless and unvarying in its limitless turquoise expanse.

Some paradise. No palm trees; not even a parrot. Yet the atmosphere was congenial—once a person got used to it. The first few breaths of Empyrion "air" were undiluted agony—like breathing fire. Most likely the effect was due to the high concentration of oxygen in the atmosphere in combination with other gases which were either not present or were mixed in different proportions on Earth. Whatever caused it, the result was amazingly painful for those first few seconds.

Empyrion, thought Treet, realm of pure elemental fire, home of the gods . . . I wonder. Someone had shown a strange sense of humor in naming the place.

He sighed and rubbed droplets from the hair of his legs and chest, then pulled his singleton on. He would have preferred underwear, truth be told; wearing a jumpsuit without shorts felt slightly decadent. At least he was out of that foolish, flizzy yos, which was an improvement.

Treet strolled back to where he'd left the others and found only Pizzle, sitting on the ground with a helmet between his knees, working on it with some odd-shaped tool that looked like a cross between a hammer and a dinner fork. Treet tapped him on the helmet. Pizzle glanced up and mouthed a few words which Treet didn't catch.

"What are you doing?" asked Treet after he slipped on a helmet. "Where'd you get that tool thing? And where is everybody?"

"Curious thing, aren't you?" replied Pizzle. "Everybody else wandered away like you to take baths, I guess. I found this 'tool thing' in the skimmer kit. These neck seals are expandable, and I'm trying to see if I can't get them to seal all the way shut so we can carry water in the helmets."

"Good idea. Do you just come up with this stuff, or do you have to think all the time?"

"A little of both," replied Pizzle smugly. "Thinking wouldn't hurt any of the rest of you, you know."

"Let's just say none of us are in any immediate danger of overdosing on it. The way we act, you'd think we were on a tour of Versailles: 'Which way to the palace, my good man?' " He paused and watched Pizzle fiddling with the pliable neck seal, working it back and forth, open and closed. "They won't carry much water," Treet observed.

"About five or six liters, I figure. Maybe more. I intend taking out all the innards."

"Do you intend taking off *your* helmet too?" Treet jibed.

"I've been thinking about that. We really should have somebody inside a helmet so in case we come up against anything really unexpected, at least one of us could still function. I don't mind wearing it, so I volunteer."

"You don't mind wearing it!" Treet brayed. "Pizzy, my friend, you were the biggest baby of all when it came time to put them on. I distinctly remember you wimping about it. Crocker had to order you into it as I recall."

"I've gotten used to it," sniffed Pizzle.

"You'd get used to breathing this air too, if you'd give it a try."

"There could be wind-borne viruses or bacteria lethal to human beings. Something could eat away at our respiratory systems, and we'd never know it until we awaken one morning hacking up blood clots big as your fist."

"Yeah, and giant flesh-eating turtles could swoop down from the sky on leather wings with snapping jaws to gobble us up for hors d'oeuvres, too. In the meantime, I'll take my chances. Sometimes you just have to risk it or you're not really alive."

"You think what we're doing isn't risky enough?" Pizzle whined. "Life is plenty risky the way it is; I don't feel the slightest impulse toward increasing the stakes." He got to his feet and took up the helmet. "Now let's see if it works."

Treet watched his slope-shouldered companion waddle into the river, take the helmet, and carefully sink it into the water. He brought it out a few seconds later, made some kind of adjustment with his funny tool, and tipped it over. The water stayed in for the most part, although it dripped in a steady stream from the gathered seal.

"I think with a few more adjustments we'll be okay." He grinned at his own cleverness. "The main thing is it works."

"I still don't think it's enough water."

"Let's hear your idea, smart guy," huffed Pizzle.

"How about one of the tents? They're airtight, which means they're probably watertight, too, doesn't it? One of those would hold a lot of water."

"We'd take turns carrying it on our backs, I suppose. Do you have any idea how much a tent full of water would weigh?"

"No. Who cares? We could use one of the skimmers to haul it—have our own personal movable waterhole."

"Impossible," snorted Pizzle, striding toward the bank.

"Why—because *I* thought of it first?"

"No. The weight of a tank that size would—Hey!" Pizzle dropped the helmet and flung out his arms as he sank into the river. He disappeared with a plunk.

FORTY THREE

Treet sprang forward. "Pizzle!"

Pizzle's helmet broke the surface before Treet reached the water's edge. Pizzle's arms thrashed the water into a froth as he screamed into his helmet mike. "Help! It's got me! Something's got me!" He bucked and whirled as if fending off invisible sharks.

Treet waded in, looking for signs of whatever it was that had Pizzle in its grasp. Pizzle screamed and disappeared under the water once more.

"Pizzle, I'll get you out," shouted Treet, sloshing toward the spot where his friend had gone down. There were dark circles indicating holes in the river bottom all around the area and Treet stepped carefully around them. Just as he reached the place where he'd last seen Pizzle's helmet, the water erupted in a jet and Pizzle came flying up with a silver something attached to his chest. His hands clutched at it as he tried to tear it off.

Treet grabbed Pizzle by the arm and jerked him forward, his only thought being to get back on dry land. The thing in Pizzle's arms wriggled and flapped ferociously as Treet propelled them all to shore. Once there, he heaved Pizzle out and fell on the thing that had attacked him.

"Wait! No, wait!" hollered Pizzle, throwing up his hands. "Don't hurt it!"

"What!" Treet stopped.

"Wait," repeated Pizzle, throwing the thing off and rolling over. "Let's see what it is."

"I thought you were being killed."

"I was—at first. But I caught it," said Pizzle. "Look!"

Before them lay a long, floppy eel-like creature with a flat, shovel-shaped head which ended in a wide, fringed mouth. Two bulbous pink eyes on top of the head stared at them as the fish writhed on the bank. It was, for all practical purposes, transparent. Its small brain, veins, muscle tissue, and internal organs could be seen all too clearly beneath its smooth, silvery skin. Its

shape was reminiscent of an overfed torpedo. Two sets of fin-
gery protrusions flexed on either side of its loathsome head, and
it emitted a greasy grunt—*reet, reet, reet*—as it jerked its finless
body around in the grass.

"It's ugly!" said Treet. "Did it bite you?"

"I don't think so." Pizzle leaned forward on his hands and
knees to study the creature more closely. "Just think—our first
alien lifeform."

"And it had to be an eel." Treet grimaced. "Careful, don't
get too close. It might take another nip at you."

"Look at that soft mouth—it can't have any serious teeth."

"Serious teeth or not, I wouldn't get too close. Maybe it
squirts hydrochloric acid."

"This reminds me of *Six Trillion Tomorrows,* where these
guys find this octopus thing in a crater on this asteroid flying
around this binary star."

"What did they do?"

"Who?"

"The guys in the book with this octopus."

"They ate it."

"Ate it?" Treet looked at the pulpy thing quivering at his
feet—it seemed to be expiring. "Are you actually suggesting we
eat this . . . this ghastly little monster?"

"I wasn't, but it's not a bad idea. We're going to be running
out of food soon. So far I haven't seen anything else around here
that looks like proteins."

"Gack! I'd rather eat the tent poles."

"Relax. Let's skin it and cook it and see how it tastes. It
might be a rare delicacy."

"And it might send us screaming into the night."

"I thought you were a gourmet."

"You don't get to be a gourmet by eating whatever slithers
out from under just any old rock."

"How about snails?"

"Escargot? That's different."

Pizzle shrugged and picked up the fish by its pudgy tail. It
gave a weak flip and hung still. It was about seventy centimeters
long and weighed, by Pizzle's estimation, between four and six
kilograms. "We could make a fire using some of the solid fuel
from the skimmers."

"What's all the excitement?" Crocker's voice boomed in
the helmet speakers. "I was taking a nap, so I turned off the

radio. When I turned it back on, I heard the fight." Crocker, his singleton still damp from its washing, came striding up. He took one look at the eel-fish in Pizzle's hand and whistled into the mike. "Sweet Mother McCree! The catch of the day. Where did you get that . . . that repulsive reptile?"

"In a hole in the river," said Pizzle, and explained the events leading up to the capture of the specimen.

Crocker looked properly impressed, and Treet guessed he would be a good man to have along on a fishing trip. He took the eel from Pizzle, hefted it, and looked at it more closely. "It won't win any beauty prizes, but I wonder how it tastes?"

"You too?" hooted Treet. "I don't believe you guys."

Crocker shrugged. "You get hungry enough and you'll eat just about anything. I must confess, however, those survival wafers are starting to taste like billiard balls. I, for one, welcome a change." He held the eel up triumphantly. "Dinner!"

Pizzle had heaped a small mound of skimmer fuel in a circle of round rocks gathered from the river bank. He had disconnected two wires from the generator of the skimmer and held them poised over the powdery yellow fuel. It had taken him the rest of the afternoon to get the experiment set up, and it was now almost dark. The sun had set in a silvery haze nearly an hour ago, and night was sweeping in from the east.

"I'm almost ready. Everybody get back; I'm not sure what's going to happen here."

"Any day, Pizzle. It's getting past my bedtime."

"Whose fault is that, Treet? We could have been eating hours ago if you hadn't inflicted your dumb obsession on me." Pizzle's voice was hoarse and ragged.

"He *is* something of a monomaniac," cracked Crocker.

"Okay, okay—you win. Put your helmets back on if you want to. I thought you'd thank me for getting you out of those plastic prisons."

"Oh, no." Crocker wagged a finger at him. "You don't weasel out of it that easily. We've lived up to our part of the deal. Now it's your turn."

"Will you guys stop sniping at each other? Let's get on with it. We're starving!" Yarden sat sideways on the seat of a nearby skimmer, Calin next to her with chin on knees.

Shortly after Pizzle and Crocker had begun discussing how best to cook the prize catch, Treet struck a bargain with them: he would brave the first taste of alien eel if Pizzle and Crocker would take off their breather packs.

"What is it with you and these helmets?" Pizzle had demanded.

"He's one of those people who can't be happy unless everyone is exactly like him," said Crocker. "He can't stand it that we're different—it threatens his security to be disagreed with."

"Sure, that's it. I admit it. You're ever so right. So don't take them off—we'll communicate in sign language for the rest of this trip because I find it a pain to go hunting up a helmet every time I want a word with either of you. Your adolescent obstinacy is making it difficult for us to cohere as a single working unit."

"Lay it back at our feet," said Pizzle.

"He's right, you two," replied Yarden, who had returned shortly after the discussion started and had donned a helmet in order to get in on it. "We all need to work together. How can we when two of us are isolated from the others?"

In the end, with much protest and breast beating, Pizzle and Crocker gave in and the deal was struck. The next hour was spent coaxing them out of their bubbles and holding their hands while they underwent the trauma of taking their first breaths of Empyrion's astringent atmosphere.

Pizzle held his breath until, red-faced, eyes bulging, he had to inhale. His screams almost made Treet wish he hadn't made such a major production out of removing the breathers. Pizzle then rolled on the ground for an hour afterwards whimpering and cursing between clenched teeth.

For his part, Crocker faced the ordeal stoically, with an air of doomful regret—like a deposed monarch going to the gallows. He removed his own helmet, closed his eyes and inhaled deeply, clutched his throat, and doubled over while the tears streamed from his eyes. He moaned but did not cry out. When the worst was over, he perked up considerably.

It was a long time before either one of them would speak to Treet.

"Hit it!" croaked Pizzle now, and Crocker punched the ignition on the skimmer and engaged the generator. As the skimmer's powerplant revved, Pizzle brought the two bare ends of wire together over the pile of fuel.

A fizzly shower of sparks streaked out and the fuel erupted with a whoosh, sending up a ball of brilliant blue flame that knocked Pizzle on his rump and singed his eyebrows.

"You did it!" cried Yarden.

"Nice work," said Crocker.

"How long will this thing burn?" wondered Treet, watching the flames dubiously. Unlike a fire on Earth, the flames of Empyrion were pale blue, like the thin, almost transparent flames of burning alcohol.

"Long enough to cook dinner," squeaked Pizzle. "Here, you can do the honors." He handed Treet a makeshift spit—a tent pole on which chunks of the gutted eel had been speared.

"Here goes nothing." Treet grasped the tent pole at midpoint and lowered the eel to the flames. In moments the meat was sizzling merrily, and Treet's expectations took an unexpected upturn. Maybe it wouldn't be so bad after all.

He turned the spit continually, careful not to let any portion get too done. The others crept closer to the fire and commented on his cooking technique, wondering aloud what the fish would taste like. When at last Treet announced that it was done, they all leaned forward expectantly, their eyes shining in the light.

Treet raised the cooked eel to his nose and gave a studied sniff. "Slightly musky aroma," he announced.

"Get on with it," the others replied.

"Please, you asked my opinion, you're going to get your money's worth." He picked at a piece of flesh. It came off in a long, fibrous strand. "Composition stringy, but not objectionable."

"Taste it!" they cried.

"I'm getting to that." With a mild grimace Treet brought the strand to his mouth, took it in, chewed thoughtfully, then picked off another piece, chewed that, and swallowed, all the while his expression deadpan.

"Well?" asked Yarden. "What do those well-schooled tastebuds of yours have to say for themselves?"

Treet looked imperiously at the ring of faces around the fire. "Smoked olives," he said.

"Smoked olives! What kind of answer is that?" complained Pizzle.

"No," said Treet chewing again, "it isn't oily enough. More

like mountain oysters, only saltier. Or tongue marinated in a weak Marsala. Or maybe . . ."

"Treet!" Crocker interrupted the expert commentary. "Stop playing food analyst and tell us if it's edible."

"Okay. Since I'm not falling on the ground in a coma or retching uncontrollably, yes, it's edible, I think." He handed the wobbly skewer across to the pilot. "See what you think."

They solemnly passed the eel around, each taking a portion and putting it in their mouths. They chewed and swallowed and peered at one another timidly.

"Verdict?" Treet inquired.

"Sort of a cross between chicken and lobster, I'd say," offered Pizzle.

"Wrong," said Crocker. "It's veal, definitely veal."

"I don't know," said Yarden. "It has more a poultry flavor—like duck or goose."

They all turned to Calin, the only one who had not offered an opinion. She glanced around at the company and said, "I can't say what it tastes like; I've never eaten much meat. But I'd like some more."

The eel was divided up and distributed in roughly equal portions. They ate in silence, listening to the smack of lips, the flutter of the ghostly fire and, further off, the riffle of water around the drowned skimmer.

They really were an unlikely party of explorers, thought Treet: a bunged-up transport jockey, a wily executive mind-reader, an otherworldly magician frightened of all outdoors, a bookwormish Trend and Impact Analyst Boy Scout, and a knockabout history hack with delusions of grandeur. They were ill-equipped, ill-provisioned, and ill-guided, and right in the middle of an ill-fated mission.

So much for reality.

Treet licked his fingers and flicked the last curved rib bone into the fire. "Not bad, but it positively begs for garlic and herb salt. Now, if we don't die of some hideous toxic reaction in our sleep, we ought to be on our way tomorrow morning first light." He stood, brushing bones from his lap. "Good night."

FORTY
FOUR

"**H**old it! Not so fast," said Crocker with a voice that sounded like he'd swallowed live sparrows. "Sit down, Treet. I want to propose a change in our evening activities."

Treet sat. Crocker, having caught everyone's attention, went on to explain quickly. "I had an idea while we were all sitting here that this is a cozy little group. We've been through a lot together. And, Yarden, I admit you were right about the breather packs—it is better without them. Now then, since we can all talk to one another like human beings once again—"

Treet opened his mouth, but Pizzle cut him off before he could speak. "No wisecracks. Let's listen to what he has to say."

"Thanks," continued Crocker, "the same goes for you. Anyway, it occurred to me that all of us had different experiences while captive in the colony—we've each seen a slightly different view of things there. I thought it might be interesting to compare notes, you know, share impressions. Since I spent most of my time flat on my back in a floater, I'd especially like to know what went on with the rest of you." He looked across the fire. "Okay, Treet, you wanted to say something?"

"Only that I think it's a good idea. It would help pass the time."

"More than that, we may get a few clues to what we're up against here. Our survival could depend on it."

"I agree," remarked Pizzle. "And I think Treet should start."

"Me?" Treet raised his eyebrows.

"Sure. Apparently you were the only one free to roam around. The rest of us were drugged most of the time. So, with the exception of Calin here, you know the most about it."

"Maybe we should have Calin tell us all she knows," said Treet.

Yarden protested quickly. "No. She should speak last— after we're all through. Otherwise, what she said would color our own perceptions. She's lived in the colony all her life, and we would begin to see our own experiences through her eyes. I think we need to be as subjective as possible."

"Don't you mean *objective?*" asked Pizzle.

"*Subjective.* Look, we've all had different experiences, and we interpreted them in different ways. But it's the interpretation that matters—the gut-level feelings we got, the conclusions we arrived at, what the events meant to us."

"We certainly don't want our perceptions blunted by reality," scoffed Pizzle lightly.

"She has a good point," replied Treet. "Who can say what the reality of Empyrion is? It's too big, and we know too little of it and its past to speak with total objectivity. All we know for certain is what we experienced and what those experiences meant to us at the time. Let's get those out, share them around, and then we can begin to construct the big picture."

Yarden nodded at Treet over the campfire. Treet noticed that the fire made blue shadows in her hair and eyes. Her smile puzzled him. What did I do to earn that? he wondered.

"Agreed?" asked Crocker. "Okay, Treet, the floor is yours."

Treet held up his hands. "One more thing I'd like to suggest—that we postpone the start of our campfire stories until tomorrow night."

"Aww!" complained Pizzle.

"No, I mean it. I'd like each of us to spend tonight and tomorrow thinking about what happened and how we want to tell it. That could be important, I think."

"Fair enough," said Crocker. "Everybody agreed? Fine. Tomorrow night we begin."

The sun was already up when Treet emerged from his tent. He'd stayed awake a long time after retiring, thinking about how he wanted to tell his story the next night. He had finally fallen asleep undecided—there was so much to tell, he didn't know the best place to begin.

Pizzle and Crocker were already up and were standing by the shore, looking at the waterlogged skimmer out in the middle of the river. "Any hope?" asked Treet as he joined them.

Pizzle wagged his head dismally. "Not a chance in a zillion. I say it's ruined."

"We've got to find out one way or the other, which means we fish it out in any case."

"Maybe we could pull it out with one of the others."

"No rope or chain or cable or anything to tie 'em together. I already thought of that."

"Oh."

"The way I see it, Calin is our best bet."

"You saw what happened yesterday. I think Yarden would have something to say about her using her psi like that again."

"We need that vehicle," Crocker reminded them. "There's a desert out there somewhere and if we're going to get across it, we've got to have every available resource."

"So we ask her," said Treet.

"*You* ask her. Yes, you. She trusts you."

"Why do I get the feeling there's something distasteful about this?"

"Survival is distasteful to you?"

"That's not what I mean, and you know it."

"Just get her to do it. We'll all thank you later," said Pizzle.

When Calin and Yarden joined them a little later, Treet took Calin aside and explained the situation to her. He ended by asking, "Will you do it? Crocker's right; it could make the difference between life and death later on."

Calin's expression was one of pained reluctance. "I—I can't do it."

"What do you mean? You did it yesterday; we all saw you."

"I can't use my psi. Yarden told me that it's not good for me. It's dangerous. She made me promise never to use it again."

"She did what?"

"She told me many things I didn't know about it, and I promised her never to turn to it—to use it is weakness."

"Well, maybe just this one more time."

"Yarden said there will always be one more time, and then one more. I have to stop and never go back."

Treet stomped back to where Pizzle and Crocker waited. "It's no go. She won't do it."

"You're joking. Why not?" Crocker demanded.

"Yarden has given her some story about how using psi is dangerous and unhealthy. She made Calin promise never to use it again."

"Oh, great," sighed Pizzle. "Well, you can kiss one skimmer good-bye and maybe one or two of us as well."

"Stop being melodramatic." Treet frowned at Pizzle.

"Right. I forgot you volunteered to *walk* across the burning waste. We have one skimmer to carry the water, and we need the other two for passengers."

"You laughed at my idea for hauling water."

"I changed my mind."

"We're not getting anywhere this way," grumped Crocker.

"Have you tried driving it out?" The men turned to see Yarden watching them, arms crossed, chin thrust out, daring them to laugh at her. Calin stood quietly behind her.

"Well, no, we haven't," replied Crocker diplomatically. "There didn't seem to be much point."

"Why not?" Yarden came to stand with them as they stared out across the water to the skimmer—an island all its own in the slow-moving current.

"Why not? Uh, tell her why not, Pizzle," said Crocker.

Pizzle shot a venomous glance at Crocker. "It's my belief that the water has damaged the circuitry, or at least shorted it out. There's no point in trying to drive it out of there because it will never in a million years start while it's sitting in water."

"Do you know this for fact?" Yarden turned her eyes on him and bored into him. Treet enjoyed the show.

"Well, no. But, I—"

"Why not try it and see? It seems to me that any vehicle made to traverse the desert can probably take a little water."

"Yeah," echoed Treet, "why not try it and see?"

Pizzle rolled his eyes and harumphed, but Crocker said, "What have we got to lose? Give it a try."

Without a word Pizzle walked into the water and out to the skimmer, climbed onto the seat, and pressed the ignition. He nearly fell off when the machine started up at a touch.

"Pizzle, you're a genius!" hooted Treet. "Only trouble is, Yarden is a bigger genius."

She smiled acerbically and looked at the men with a smugly superior expression on her face. She and Calin walked upstream, leaving the men alone.

Pizzle drove the vehicle slowly out of the river, grinding the runners over the rocks. When it finally reached dry land, it gave a sputtering jolt and died. "Okay, so the motors and circuits are sealed. How was I supposed to know that? It would still be a good idea to let it dry out before running it again—just in case."

Treet raised his eyes to the sky. The sun was climbing

rapidly, spilling light over the hilltops and into the valleys. Another perfect day—like one more perfect pearl added to the string. "Shame to waste the day," he said. "What shall we do while we wait for that buggy to dry out?"

Crocker spun toward him. "I was just thinking the same thing. You know what? I think we should go fishing."

"Fishing!"

"I'm serious. That eel last night tasted pretty good, considering. And since none of us expired during the night from any unknown toxic effects, and since there are bound to be more where that one came from, I say we go after them."

Pizzle brightened, and Treet saw the computer chips that Pizzle used for a brain light up. "We could catch a million to take with us into the desert! I should have thought of that yesterday."

"How are we going to take a load of putrefying eels into the desert? They'll rot before we get two days from here."

Pizzle rolled his eyes in exasperation. "We *dry* them. On rocks. In the sun. It's easy. And we'll have food all across the desert. Water, too."

"This is just one big jamboree to you, isn't it, Pizzle?" sniped Treet.

"Starving appeals to you?" Crocker mocked. "Let's get started."

They discussed several techniques for catching the eels, including making rods and line from the tent poles and braided thread, and rigging up makeshift harpoons. Neither possibility, nor any of the others they considered and discarded just as quickly, suggested success. So they sat stymied until Treet said, "Actually Pizzle didn't catch that eel as much as that eel caught Pizzle."

"What do you mean? I caught it."

"If I remember correctly, you fell into the hole and it grabbed you. When you came rocketing out of the water, I saw that thing attatched to your chest. You were flapping your arms around trying to get rid of it."

"Oh, yeah?" Crocker turned an appraising eye on Pizzle.

"Hold it! What are you guys thinking? You can't be serious. I'm not—hey, wait a minute . . ."

"Food all the way across the desert, Pizzy," said Treet.

"You're crazy!"

"It's easy," said Crocker. "We used to do it all the time

when we were little kids—slip down along the river bank and find a hole and reach inside. A good grappler could catch some pretty big old catfish."

"You're *both* crazy!" Pizzle edged away. "I won't do it."

"It's the only way. Besides, it was your idea. You should get the glory."

"It's only right," agreed Treet. "We could tie something around you to hold on to so you wouldn't drown or anything; you have nothing to worry about. We'll be there right beside you."

Within ten minutes, Pizzle's protests notwithstanding, they were wading out into the river together, Treet and Crocker holding opposite ends of a piece of tent cording which had been secured around Pizzle's waist. "Look, there's nothing to worry about," offered Treet. "They don't have teeth. From what you said, they just sort of suck onto you and there you go. We'll pull you up if you get into trouble—so don't get yourself in a nervous tizzy."

"You'll be fine," assured Crocker. "In fact, after the second or third time, you'll start to enjoy yourself."

"If I live through this," muttered Pizzle darkly, "I'm going to get a good lawyer and sue both of you into debtor's prison. There must be laws against using a person for fish bait."

"You won't sue us," predicted Crocker, "you'll thank us."

They found the hole Pizzle had dropped into the day before, and several more near it, one of which was big enough to admit a man. With murder in his close-set eyes, Pizzle took a deep breath and dropped in. Treet and Crocker held the ends of the cord and counted, figuring they would give Pizzle twenty seconds to accomplish his task.

He was back in ten. The hole was empty. And so was the next. After several more attempts, they moved on a little further downstream and came to a place where more holes dotted the river bottom. Here their luck changed. The second hole Pizzle tried contained an eel about the size of the one he'd caught the day before. This one attached itself to his back and when they pulled Pizzle up, Treet grabbed it and flipped it onto the bank.

The rest of the holes in the area were empty. "We won't find any more eels here," said Treet after the fourth try. "These critters have territories. I think all the holes in a given area belong to one eel. If we want to catch another one we'll have to go further downstream."

"The water gets deeper," observed Crocker.

"We'll stick to the shore." Treet looked at the eel expiring on the bank. "This is going to take a lot longer than we thought. I think we ought to streamline this process. You two could catch them, and I'll gut them and get them drying out."

"Good idea. We'll get a regular little production line going." Crocker and Pizzle headed off downstream, and Treet—using a tool from the skimmer kit—made quick work of the eel and carried it back to camp. The two women were waiting when he got back. He gave them the eel, explained their plan, and repeated what Pizzle had told him about how to dry the meat on rocks in the sun. "We'll be back later on this afternoon," he told them.

By the time Treet reached the place where Pizzle and Crocker had been, he found another eel on the bank—this one half again as big as the other two they'd caught. The two "fishermen" were already working their way further downstream; he could see their torsos swaying above the water as they searched for holes in the riverbed.

The day stretched out into a rhythm of walking and working and waiting and walking again—a rhythm Treet found enjoyable. The eerie silence of the place was modified by the plap and gurgle of the river as it moved quietly along. With the sun on his back and the company of his thoughts, Treet went about his task happily, enjoying the solitude and serenity of the day.

By late afternoon they had worked far downstream. The sun dipped near the horizon, signaling the end of a good day's work. Treet lost count of the number of eels they had caught. He decided, however, that it was enough for one day and was gutting the last eel before hurrying ahead to call Crocker and Pizzle back when he heard the whine of a skimmer behind him.

Yarden, her dark hair streaming, piloted the skimmer expertly over the ruffled river bank toward him. He stood and waited for her. "Call it a day," she said. "Talazac taxi service has come to fetch you home."

"Thanks. Pizzle and Crocker are somewhere up ahead. Why don't you go get them and I'll finish up here. We can pick up our catch on the way back."

"You've caught enough to last three months. I counted twenty-eight, and I may have missed a few." She gave him a smile and a wave and glided away. Within minutes she was back with two tired fishermen in damp clothes. She had found them a little way downriver lying on the bank drying out before heading back. Treet squeezed onto the crowded vehicle and they worked their way homeward, stopping at intervals to pick up their catch.

They arrived back in camp as the sun faded behind the hills, washing the westward sky a pale eggshell white as the east darkened to indigo. Calin had a fire going and an eel on the spit as they climbed down and unloaded the toppling stack of flayed eels. Treet noticed that the tents had been moved and that beneath each one was a thick bed of bunched grass. "We've been busy all day, too," said Yarden proudly. "We made grass mattresses."

"My dear lady," said Crocker, "each and every one of my brittle, aching bones thanks you. If I weren't so hungry, I'd crawl in right now and go to sleep."

As they ate around the fire, Treet noticed that everyone's spirits were markedly improved. They all talked and joked and smiled at one another. Even Calin joined in shyly from time to time. Something important had happened to them that day; a milestone of some sort had been passed. Treet worked it over in his head and decided that the buoyant feeling was due to the fact that today was the first time they had worked together as a group toward a common goal of survival. Today they had become a team.

When all had eaten, they lay back as the blue flames flickered. "Well," said Treet, "I guess I'm the entertainment for this evening. Are you sure you all want to hear a story?"

FORTY
FIVE

Treet began like this:

"After the scuffle on the landing platform, I woke up by myself in a room—fuzzy-headed, naked, and sore. I put on the clothes I found in my cell and waited. I was brought food, which I ate, and I slept. Two or three days went by and I was taken to meet the Supreme Director of Empyrion, a cagey old cuss named Sirin Rohee.

"Three of his advisers showed up and asked me questions. I answered. We talked a little, and he sent me back. It was a day or two later, I think, when I remembered who I was, where I was, and who had come with me. The drug wore off, I guess— or maybe they didn't give me such a heavy dose. When Rohee sent for me again, we met alone. I told him I remembered, and told him *what* I remembered. For some reason—I still don't know why—he took pity on me and gave me quarters of my own. He provided Calin to be my guide and allowed me the run of the place, although I'm fairly certain I was watched constantly nevertheless.

"I toured each Hage of Empyrion—at least those areas open to inspection. There are places within Hage where outsiders are not allowed, and we of course stayed out.

"After about a week of this touring, I asked Rohee if I could see the Archives. He debated about it for the better part of a day and decided to allow me. I think he had some private plan in mind for me, or hoped I would discover something useful for him, or maybe he was just curious—I don't know.

"Calin and I, along with the obligatory priest, went to the Archives and looked around. The place was full of old machines, parts, and junk, and it was my impression at the time that the place had not been visited in many years, generations perhaps. Anyway, we didn't find what we were looking for—at least not at first. Then, as I was getting ready to leave, I noticed Calin had disappeared and went looking for her. I found her in a hidden room under the Archives—a room full of historical data on the colony which had been hidden and sealed about seven hundred years ago. That's an educated guess.

"On leaving the Archives, we were contacted—waylaid, actually—by some people who said they had information about my friends. These turned out to be Tvrdy's people, and they reunited us all. Things heated up, and we moved to the Archives to make good our escape. We fled the colony and have been making our way across some of the most desolate country I've ever seen.

"And," Treet summed up, "here we are."

Into the silence that followed Treet's account, Pizzle bleated, "That's it? That's what we've been waiting breathless all day to hear?"

Crocker made a move to join the protest, but Treet raised his hand for silence. "Not so fast. Those are just the bare facts. I wanted to construct the skeleton first; now I'll hang some observations on the bones."

He paused, gathered his thoughts, then said, "Empyrion is not the colony Cynetics established. Rather, it *was,* but is no longer. It has changed, evolved. As near as I can figure, we are seeing the colony nearly three thousand years after its foundation . . ."

"Three thousand years!" gasped Crocker. "Impossible."

"I knew it was old," said Pizzle, "but I never dreamed—"

"According to Belthausen's theories, it's possible," said Treet. "Someone who knows a whole lot more about these things than I do is going to have to figure it out, but . . . Well, let's just say we're dealing with a culture which has had a good long term of isolated development. Empyrion has evolved into an extremely stratified, regimented, organized, and highly repressive society.

"There are eight Hages, each with its own societal function. They're organized around necessities: food, that's Hyrgo; Bolbe, clothing; Saecaraz handles energy; Nilokerus takes care of security, health care, social services; Tanais is structural engineering, construction, housing, that sort of thing; Rumon is communication and what you might call production, traffic, and quality control—anything that has to do with movement of goods and services through the colony; Chryse is fine arts and entertainment; Jamuna is waste recycling."

"Don't I know it," remarked Pizzle.

"A Hage is more than a vocational guild, although it is that. It's also home, family, city, and state."

"It's a caste system," said Yarden.

"Yes," agreed Treet. "There are strong elements of caste in the mix. It isn't hard to guess how this caste system came about: survival. A colony arrives with all the basic components necessary for establishing a viable society. If something happened to cut the colony off from its source of supply, it would quickly organize itself into skill areas vital to survival.

"Whenever you have rigid occupational stratification—some jobs are essential, waste recycling for instance, though hardly the most prestigious or attractive, so these low-status tasks must be assigned—an enforced hierarchy soon develops. In order to preserve its place in the hierarchy, occupational protectionism takes over. If I am a genetics technician, which is near the top of Hyrgo Hage, and I want to stay secure in my position, I guard my professional knowledge and expertise jealously. Over time, it becomes nearly impossible for anyone not born into the caste to develop the knowledge and skills.

"Just as there is a hierarchy within Hages, there is a hierarchy of Hages within the colony as well, with intense competition for control of leadership. The top man of each Hage is the Director, who serves on a sort of Board of Directors called the Threl, with the Supreme Director acting as Chairman of the Board."

"They retained the old corporation structure," observed Pizzle.

"Yes, but how these people come to power, I don't know. They're not elected, that's for sure. I suspect the reins of power are handed down in much the same way as early trading companies or political parties handed down power: through hand-picked successors chosen by dint of their loyalty and adherence to the party line, then groomed for the job. Factors such as birth or qualification would have little to do with the choice. Once in power, it would be nearly impossible to get someone out of leadership since the whole structure of the system is designed to maintain the status quo.

"As time passes, the whole society slowly becomes ever more firmly entrenched in preserving the caste code that allowed its development. Any person or group threatening the code is seen as an enemy of the state. In the early years, malcontents would have jeopardized survival and would have been dealt with harshly. All energies had to be channeled into supporting the common good, and any deviation could have been disastrous.

"By the time survival became less of an issue, the system was firmly established and functioning autonomously. It became self-protecting. Physical survival was transmuted into ideological survival."

"I'm not sure I follow," Crocker broke in.

"Think of it like this: the system was set up to reach only one goal—the physical survival of the colony. It reached that goal. Then what?

"Apparently the leaders of Empyrion colony failed to appreciate their position, and instead of redirecting the colony on to higher, more universally fulfilling goals, they merely abstracted the old goal. Physical survival became political survival. Instead of threats from the outside, they became concerned about threats from the inside. The system equated opposition with danger, ideological purity with safety, loyalty with consensus agreement. In essence, the system emerged as an entity in its own right and claimed primacy over the interests of individual citizens. The leadership saw to it that the system continued serving itself, devoting as much energy to its own survival as it had previously devoted to the survival of its citizens."

"Those evil people," said Yarden softly.

"Evil? I don't know," replied Treet. "It was probably easier to go with the flow than dismantle the entire apparatus of colony government and redirect the energy of the citizenry to higher ideals."

"It could have been done. Societies have always done it," Yarden pointed out. "What monstrous selfishness."

"I suppose it could have been done, but remember they were cut off, isolated. The wormhole closed or shifted or whatever wormholes do. And anyway, the leadership had effectively silenced any opposition, so there was no real challenge to their authority or values."

"What about the Fieri?" asked Pizzle. "I thought they were the hated opposition."

"I was getting to that," said Treet. "The documents I've seen indicate that long ago—a few hundred years after foundation—something catastrophic happened. I have not read the specific documents to find out what it was, but it was a severe shock to the colony—maybe a natural disaster of some sort.

They came through the crisis, but in the following years there were disputes over how to reorganize and rehabilitate the colony.

"At one point, I believe, the colony actually split into three factions. There was a Purge, and the smaller faction was eliminated or consolidated. Sometime later one of the factions, the Fieri, left the colony or was forced out.

"You would have thought that would be the end of it, but their leaving signaled the beginning of about three hundred years of political upheaval. The power structure of the colony was gutted by the pullout of the Fieri; there were bloody coups and countercoups and eventually a revolt by the citizens, followed by a second Purge, which ended in the establishment of the Threl."

"When did all this happen?" asked Pizzle. He leaned forward, chin in hands, listening with rapt attention.

"About fifteen hundred years ago, by my reckoning. The Second Purge began what colony historians call the Third Age— a period characterized by continual, fanatical harassment of the Fieri."

"But why?" asked Yarden. "I thought the Fieri left. What reason could the colony have for persecuting them?"

"I don't know the details. My guess is that at first the Fieri were simply a convenient target—a scapegoat. The colony was in trouble. Among other things, it was rapidly losing its technology; things were beginning to run down and nobody knew how to fix them. The Threl chose to point to the Fieri as the source of all their ills. Persecuting them diverted attention away from the colony's real problems, which the Threl were no doubt struggling to contain.

"But even after that, when the Fieri were no longer a threat—if they really ever were—the Threl did not give up. Over the years the hatred, so useful before, became an obsession. Fanaticism grew up. They simply could not let it go. I think the Threl were jealous of the Fieri for having the courage to leave, to follow their own destiny. Since there was no other way to punish the Fieri, the Threl plotted to hound them into oblivion."

"And succeeded," said Yarden.

"That's what I thought, too—at first. But the Fieri still exist, though it's been a long time, a thousand years at least, since anyone in the colony has actually seen one. They thought *we* were Fieri, remember. And I doubt Tvrdy and his cohorts would have sent us out if they didn't believe we had a chance of finding them. They're desperate for help, so it wouldn't make sense to send us knowing there was no help to be found.

"That's it in a nutshell. I had planned, of course, to go back and study Empyrion history in detail, but—well, that's as far as I got. Things got too hot, and here we are." Treet finished and everyone sat silent for a long time, staring into the faint blue flames, watching the ghostly flicker, conjuring up visions of times long past in the Third Age of Empyrion. Without a word Yarden got up and went to her tent; Calin followed immediately.

Crocker yawned and rose. "You sure talk pretty, Treet," he said and shuffled off. Pizzle and Treet sat together for a time, staring into the dying fire, listening to the sizzle of the solid fuel as it burned away. When the last flame died, Pizzle crept away, leaving Treet alone with his thoughts and the star-dazzled night.

They stayed another day on the banks of the river to allow the eels caught the day before to continue drying in the sun. They swam a little and napped, resting up for the next leg of their journey. Pizzle fiddled with various ways of securing a water-filled tent to one of the skimmers and toward the end of the day came up with a solution that offered at least the barest possibility of success.

"There's no way to know if it will work until we try it," he said regarding his handiwork.

"Elegant it ain't," offered Treet, "but it ought to do the trick." He studied the limp tent encased in a latticework of cloth strips and cording and strung over the vehicle like a deflated balloon. Pizzle had removed the passenger's seat, creating a trough for the water bag to rest in. "You've done a fine job. By the way, where did you get the cloth?"

"I tore up a spare singleton. The thing is, we won't be able to fill it up as much as I'd hoped, which means we'll run out faster. We won't be able to travel as far. That worries me a little—we don't know how big this desert is."

"No way to know. We'll just have to do the best we can."

Pizzle nodded, but the frown that creased his brow did not go away. He fussed and mumbled for several more hours until Crocker came by and ordered him to go swimming and get his mind off the problem for a while.

By evening, everyone was rested and in good spirits, eager

to be traveling once more. They ate and discussed the rigors of the desert. Then, after a pause in the talk, Yarden said, "I want to tell my story."

She described her life with the Chryse in fine detail—their forays into various Hages to perform the plays and mimes, the flash orgies, rehearsing new plays, lolling around the market-places on allotment days, and other things she had experienced and observed.

"It sounds like you had it pretty good," remarked Pizzle. "How did you get your memory back?"

"I became suspicious of Bela, the troupe leader. At first he was kind to me, wanted to make love to me—tried on several occasions. When I cut him off, he changed toward me. He was still solicitous, but I saw an ugliness beneath his bonhomie, a duplicity that I distrusted. I came to feel he was using me in some way.

"In fact, he became quite brazen about giving me the mind drug. I think at first it must have been administered secretly in my food or drink, but later he offered it to me in the form of a little wafer and made me take it myself. I did the first time, but palmed the wafers and threw them away after that.

"I soon discovered that without the drug my memory start-ed coming back. The drug blocked memory somehow, but if the doses were not kept up, the fog barrier thinned. It took some effort, but I was finally able to break through. It got easier after that.

"Unfortunately, I did not have time to regain my memory completely. On the last day I was taken to an Astral Service." Yarden's voice quavered, and her shoulders shivered with an imaginary chill. "It is still so vivid in my mind . . . the most horrible experience of my life." She paused, looked into the campfire.

Treet watched the light shifting over her handsome fea-tures. He'd heard the story before—she'd told him a few nights ago when they were alone on the hillside. As Yarden talked, Treet remembered that night, and wondered if they'd ever again be as close as they were those few moments. Strangely, he began to feel sorry for himself, and resentful of the fact that she was telling her story to the others just the way she'd told him.

Their time together that night had been an intimate mo-ment, and now she was letting everyone else in on their shared secrets. It was like kissing and telling. He told himself it was silly to feel that way, but the argument lacked conviction and he succeeded only in stirring up a little guilt to go along with the self-pity. He retreated further into himself, reliving the intimacy of those moments.

"Don't be angry with me."

"Huh?" Treet raised his head. Yarden looked at him across the dying fire. The others were moving off toward the tents. He'd not heard the party break up. "I didn't— I'm not angry."

Yarden cocked her head to one side. "No, maybe not—not yet. I had to tell them, you know. We agreed."

"Sure."

"But I didn't want you to feel like I was betraying you."

"Why would I think that?"

"Not think, Orion. *Feel.* I sensed you were upset. Emotions have a logic of their own." She rose and came around the ring of stones to him, bent over him, touched his chin, and raised his face to hers. She kissed him lightly on the lips.

"What was that for?" asked Treet, his voice thick and unsteady. He was genuinely bewildered by the kiss, but trying valiantly to cover it.

"That's for us. It's something I won't share with anyone else."

She was gone then, leaving Treet to his befuddlement, still reeling from the kiss. When at last he took himself off to bed, he was no closer to an answer to the riddle of Yarden Talazac.

FORTY
SIX

The better part of the morning was spent filling the tent with water. After striking it for the last time, Pizzle arranged it loosely under the network of straps and they began hauling water from the river in their helmets. Pizzle oversaw the operation, keeping a tally of the number of helmetfuls that went into the tent. By his calculation one helmet full of water equaled one day's water supply for the group. When they had seventy-five helmetfuls he sealed the tent.

"But we can carry a lot more," said Treet. "The tent isn't even half full."

"That would be dangerous. Fill it any more, and we won't be able to steer the skimmer. Besides, the weight would snap the straps and the tent would roll off. This way it acts as ballast and lies relatively flat."

"He's right," said Crocker. "Let's leave well enough alone."

They snugged down the rigging, packing the dried eels under the straps all over the surface of the orange bag. "It looks like something out of *The Gypsy Pirates of R'Enno*," said Pizzle. "I hope it works."

"We'll soon find out." Crocker looked back at the river. "I suggest everybody take a good long drink of water. It could be the last fresh one we'll get until who knows when."

They drank their fill from the crystalline river and somewhat reluctantly mounted the skimmers. Treet and Crocker rode one, Yarden and Calin another. Pizzle, despite his myopia, piloted the skimmer with the water bag, claiming he was the only one who understood the physics of it. They started up and slid away. At the top of the first hill, Treet looked back over his shoulder to the river valley below. We forgot to name it, he thought. Then the hump of the hill took it from view as the skimmer began its glide over the downward slope.

The land changed almost immediately. Once away from the river, the grass grew shorter, more sparse. At a distance of forty kilometers, the hillscape flattened, and the hills became less rounded and further apart, separated by long, ramplike inclines.

By midday the carpet of pastel grass was worn thin and patchy. Treet noticed that the soil showing through the sparse covering was lighter, drier, sandier. When they stopped late in the afternoon to erect the two remaining tents for the night, the sandhills had become small bluffs whose soft soil was cut away by blowouts on the windward side. The blowouts showed white-blue in the fading daylight.

"The desert can't be much farther," remarked Crocker, scanning the barren countryside. "What a wasteland. It's so empty it scares me."

"What do you suppose could cause it?" wondered Treet aloud. He peered into the distance, noting how the violet shadows deepened and slid up from the lowlands to swallow the heights.

"Cause it? What do you mean, *cause* it? It's a natural landform. Lack of water is what causes it. Didn't you ever learn any physical geography?"

"I'm a purist." Treet shrugged. "It just seemed very *un*natural to me. Too empty. It's a total void. I've seen a few deserts, but nothing this completely—"

"Annihilated," put in Pizzle, finishing his thought. "Even deserts have life, but this place is antilife."

"You think this is something, wait till we reach minus eight," Crocker snorted. "That'll make this look like a rain forest!"

Crocker's prophecy came true two days later. The travelers climbed to the top of a long rise and stopped to stare upon a vista of white dunes. Like the endless swells of a milk-white sea, the humpbacked dunes swarmed to the horizon and beyond.

Speechless, the company viewed the spectacle in a silence broken only by the sound of their own breathing. The sun, behind them on its downward arc into the west, painted each dune a dazzling white.

After a while Treet turned his eyes back the way they had come. The barren hills showed light turquoise that smudged to powder blue in the distance. By comparison, the desolation they had passed through now appeared almost shockingly verdant, luxurious in its rampant fertility.

What a strange, wounded land, thought Treet, then wondered why the word *wounded* had come to him.

Minutes later, still without having spoken a word, the company began its descent to the desert floor. As the machines touched the sand, the blades sank deep. For an instant Treet feared they might founder. The sand buried the runners, making the craft grind ahead sluggishly. But Treet, remembering that the skimmers were designed specifically for desert travel, pulled back the joystick and leaned forward on the knee pedals, lowering the runner blades still further. The skimmer leaped ahead.

Amazed at the machine's response, Treet held the joystick back and allowed the skimmer to gather speed. Gradually the machine rose on its blades until it fairly sliced through the sand with all the effort of a skater flying over ice. Nothing they had experienced of the vehicles' capabilities had even hinted at the breathtaking velocity they could achieve.

Exhilaration flooded over him in an instantaneous gush— as if he had taken a plunge into a rushing cataract. His heart quickened; his blood raced as adrenalin pumped into his veins. He gulped for air and gripped the joystick tightly with both hands, then heard a long, high, wailing sound over the scream and whizz of the skimmer and realized Crocker was howling in pure delight as they dipped and glided over the undulating dunes. The still desert air snapped their clothing into sharp creases that rippled over their limbs.

Out of the corner of his eye he glimpsed a shape gaining on him. He glanced over to see Yarden leaning forward over the joystick, her knees pressed to the pedals, crouched like a jockey in the saddle of a thoroughbred racehorse, features compressed into an expression mingling ferocious intensity with rapture. Her long black hair gleamed in the sunlight as it streamed out horizontally behind her.

She streaked past, her skimmer's wake a high, white plume as the tiny scoop-shaped depressions of the metallic wheels jetted the fine dry sand into the air. Treet leaned forward to cut wind resistance, clenched the joystick, and urged his machine to chase, willing it to go faster. When he looked at the speedometer it read 400 kilometers per hour. He gulped, astounded by the speed.

He made a good race of it, cutting back and forth behind Yarden as they swerved along, threading the bases of the dunes, back and forth like a waterskier zipping in and out of a speed-

boat's wake. Gradually Yarden pulled away from him; he
watched as the plume dwindled, eventually shrinking to a mere
white puff which disappeared behind a dune far ahead. There
was no catching her.

"I've never felt anything so absolutely, ecstatically thrilling
in all my life!" shouted Yarden when they finally found her
again. She had stopped to wait for the others. Her face flushed
and ruddy from the excitement, eyes luminous with pleasure,
she raised her hands to her windblown hair and smoothed it.
"It's like a dream—like flying in a dream." She fairly hugged
herself with ecstasy. "Isn't it wonderful?"

They all agreed it was indeed wonderful—Pizzle a little less
enthusiastically than the others, feeling martyred by the necessi-
ty of having to drive the water bag at a snail's crawl while
everyone else flew like eagles.

Treet was fascinated by Yarden's response. The flight of the
skimmer seemed to have ignited an inner fire that burned from
her eyes and made her whole body glow. He thought if he were
to touch her skin it would sizzle. The sight was enchanting; he
would have been embarrassed to stare so brazenly if not for the
fact that Yarden was oblivious in her bliss.

"It reminds me of the first time I took a trainer up," said
Crocker reverently. "Suborbital jumpjet—little more than a
rocket engine with a seatbelt. I never wanted to come down."

With difficulty Treet tore his eyes away from Yarden, but
not before she noticed his look and returned it with a smouldering glance of her own. He noticed Calin standing off to the side,
watching them. She, too, radiated live heat, but her expression
was impossible to read—composed of too many emotions, or of
one that Treet had never encountered before. Her almond eyes
sparked strange fire in their depths.

"Well, what say we make camp here for the night?" he
asked.

"There's still a lot of daylight left," observed Pizzle.

"Oh, let's do go on," Yarden said a little breathlessly. "One
more ride—I want just one more before we stop."

"This time *I* get to pilot," Crocker stated firmly.

"Fine," said Treet.

They rode for another hour or so. Epsilon Eridani bulged
just above the horizon, a white incandescence that turned the
sky and sand white gold.

Crocker was following Yarden's skimmer furrow in the

sand. Treet sat in the passenger's position behind Crocker, clutching the handgrips and hoping Yarden would have sense enough to stop soon, when he saw the blue mist. At first he thought it a cloud of insects—it had that swarmy, diaphanous quality—but it was much too big. It looked like the rain edge of a thunderstorm viewed from a distance as it sweeps across the landscape, though closer and not as dense or dark.

It hovered directly in front of them, an immense curtain several hundred meters in the air and perhaps ten or fifteen kilometers wide. It was hard to tell exactly because the curtain lost itself in the dunes at the edges and faded into the air high above. Before Crocker could pull up, they were through it, proving that the misty curtain was much closer than it appeared.

Treet felt a splash of coolness on his exposed skin, as if he had been sprayed with rubbing alcohol from an atomizer. Then they were through, the veil of mist behind them, shimmering pale silver in the sunset.

Moments later they rounded the foot of a low-humped dune and came upon Yarden and Calin. The women had dismounted and were waiting for them on the shadow side of the dune. Circling once, Crocker brought the skimmer in. A few minutes later they heard the whine of Pizzle's machine as it came sliding around the dune to park beside them.

"Anybody notice that fog?" asked Pizzle as he climbed down from his vehicle.

"Yes," said Yarden, "we noticed it. Rain do you think?"

"Not rain. At least not any kind of rain I ever saw," offered Crocker. "No clouds."

"It was wet like rain," put in Treet. "Like mist. Maybe Pizzle's right—maybe it was a fog of some kind."

"Fog in the desert?" Crocker scoffed lightly. "In bright daylight? That's a first."

Treet lifted his shoulders. True, there had been no change in temperature as they went through the curtain, which would argue against any kind of fog. Yet, he felt an unmistakable dampness as they flashed through. His forehead and the skin on the backs of his hands still tingled faintly. He rubbed his forehead, but it was now dry. Whatever had been there had likely evaporated.

The company went about setting up camp, pitching the two remaining tents on the flat sand between dunes. Night came on quickly, the stars intense in the desert dome. They made a small fire in a depression in the sand, then gathered around to talk quietly, their voices drifting in the silent air. They sipped water and ate some of the dried eel, which, to their surprise, tasted just as good dried as fresh, though chewy in the extreme.

After eating, Treet got up to stretch and walk before turning in. He climbed to the top of a dune, his boots sinking and sliding in the fine, loose sand. He did some torso twists, toe touches, deep knee bends, and side bends, then stood with his hands on his hips gazing up at the velvety sky.

Here in the desert the sky appeared darker, the stars brighter, their light sharper, more intense. He was still watching them when a voice behind him said, "Ophidia is well up already, I see."

Treet turned slowly. "Yarden, I didn't hear you come up."

"Am I disturbing you?" She came to stand beside him, and Treet felt a flutter in the air, as if an electric current vibrated the molecules between them.

"No, you're not disturbing me." He glanced skyward once more. "I was just thinking."

"Tell me."

"It was nothing."

"I'd like to hear it anyway."

"Well, I was thinking that this world, Empyrion, is far more different than it appears at first. It takes time to discover the differences; they're subtle."

"Hmmm," agreed Yarden, "I see what you mean. Some people are like that, too."

There was something in her tone he had not heard before. He turned to look at her face, but could not read her expression in the starlight. Is she talking about me, he wondered, or herself?

Before he could wonder further, she said, "You're very different than I first thought. There's a lot to you, but you don't make much of it. Most men, I've found, have an erroneously high opinion of themselves and don't mind sharing it at every opportunity. But not you. That's just one way you're different."

"There are others?"

"Oh, yes, Orion Treet. There are lots of others. I have not discovered them all yet. But give me time . . ."

She paused. Treet saw the liquid glint of her eyes as she gazed at him. He reached out and touched her arm, soft and pliant and warm. He pulled her to him.

"No," she whispered, tensing.

He put his lips to hers. She did not return the kiss, but pushed against him.

He held her in a tighter embrace. She struggled in his arms. "Stop!"

"It's all right—" he persisted.

"Let me go!"

She stiffened and pushed him away as he let go. Off balance, he fell backward onto the sand. She stood over him, her eyes flashing in the starlight. "You're no different!" she said harshly. He felt the bristling heat of her anger.

"Yarden, I—" he began, but she was already gone, confusion hanging in the air where she had been.

Treet picked himself up and slip-walked despondently down the dune to his tent.

FORTY
SEVEN

Yarden's wild screech brought Treet out of a deep sleep. He was on his feet outside the tent, Crocker and Pizzle stumbling out behind him, before he knew what it was that had summoned him. The sky was light, but the sun was not yet up. A second later he heard a strange whimpering sound coming from the women's tent. He went to it and said, "It's Treet. What's wrong?"

Calin answered, "Don't come in here!"

The three men looked at each other uneasily. Crocker responded, "We won't come in, but you're going to have to tell us what's wrong."

"My—it's my . . . Ooohh!" Yarden moaned.

The men waited. Presently the tent flap opened and Calin stepped out, then stooped to help Yarden, who came out slowly, doubled over. She straighened, and Treet's heart dropped a beat. Pizzle sucked his breath in sharply.

"Good Lord, girl!" gasped Crocker.

Treet took a step closer.

"Don't touch me!" warned Yarden. "I might be contagious. Please, stay away."

"We need to see—how else can we help you?"

"I'll show you," she said, "but just don't touch me, whatever you do."

She raised her face and stretched forth her hands. Angry red blisters pimpled every square millimeter of skin, including eyelids and fingertips. The only places where the blisters were not in evidence were the crevices between fingers, the triangular expanse of skin under her chin, and the crescent folds behind her ears.

The blisters were raised bumps with translucent, fluid-filled caps, elongated rather than round, red at the base, but yellow at the top. They looked as if the slightest touch would burst them and disperse the fluid.

"What are your symptoms?" asked Pizzle. "Fever? Itch?"

"No fever." Yarden shook her head. "No itch. They don't hurt, although my skin tingles like crazy. I didn't feel anything or notice anything until I woke up like this. Oohh!" She raised her hands to her eyes. "What am I going to do?"

Treet could see that she was close to hysteria. He desperately tried to think of something comforting to say. "It isn't so bad," was the best he could come up with.

"Not so bad!" she wailed.

"That fog!" cried Pizzle. "Look, the blisters only cover the exposed places—wherever the mist touched. Everywhere else is normal—I mean, I assume it's normal?"

Yarden nodded. "Nothing so far. Only where the mist touched me."

"Then how come none of the rest of us have any blisters?" asked Treet.

Pizzle shrugged. "Different genetic makeup, different body chemistry—who knows? Maybe Yarden was allergic to whatever was in the mist and the rest of us aren't."

"I'm not allergic to anything," replied Yarden petulantly.

"That you know of," said Pizzle.

"It doesn't look like any kind of allergic reaction I ever heard of," observed Treet. "More like a disease."

"Thanks," muttered Yarden, chin quivering.

"Are you suggesting we quarantine her?" Crocker appraised her with narrowed eyes. "It might not be a bad idea."

"What good would it do?" objected Treet. "We all rode through the mist. It's just a matter of time until the rest of us come down with it."

"Oh, great!" Pizzle frumped. "Let's look on the bright side."

"Well, what do we do now?" wondered Crocker.

"Yarden, do you feel well enough to travel?" asked Treet. "One of us could drive for you."

Yarden nodded silently.

She's more shook up than she lets on, thought Treet. Why did this have to happen to her? All that flawless, porcelain skin now blotched and swollen and . . . ugly!

They struck camp and skimmed over a gray land into a hard pewter sunrise. The blades cut grooves in the fine sand as they rode the lift and fall of the round dunes like the swell of an ocean. They stopped once midmorning for a drink of water and a survival wafer. Yarden showed no change in her condition. She said she still felt okay, though worried.

When they stopped a few hours later to take a direction check, Pizzle's rubbery face showed distinct discoloration—clumps of spots on his cheeks and across the bridge of his nose. Crocker mentioned that his throat felt dry. Calin seemed okay, but said little. Treet noticed that his skin was tender where the mist had made contact. He knew it was just a matter of time.

Next morning three bloated and blistered faces peered at one another fearfully in the orange halflight of their tent. After a moment's examination of hands and a tentative exploration of facial features, Treet sighed. "It looks like we're in the game, gentlemen. What's our move?"

Crocker thought for a minute and said, "I say we keep going—as long as we can. We don't know the course of this . . . this condition, but if we could reach the Fieri we'd be better off."

"Keep going till we drop, eh?" cracked Pizzle.

"It's our best chance," snapped Crocker. "What do you suggest—that we just lay down and scoop the sand over our heads?"

"Stop it, you two. We've got to think about this. I agree with Crocker—we don't know anything about this malady, so we might as well keep going. Maybe it will go away in a day or two."

"Then again, maybe not."

"Yes, Pizzle. Maybe not. But laying around here won't get us anywhere. And as long as we don't *feel* sick, there's no reason to sit around wallowing in self-pity."

All day long the company monitored themselves for minute changes in their conditions. Calin, too, had fallen victim to the malady; but other than tingly, tender, blistered skin and dry throats, no one had anything new to report. By nightfall, however, Yarden had developed new blisters on her arms and chest. The condition, whatever it was, was spreading.

Then the itching started.

At first it was merely an upgraded version of the tingle they had become used to, but by morning the intensified tingle was a fire on the blistered hide, impossible to ignore or satisfy. Scratching didn't help—made it worse, in fact. The pustules burst at the slightest touch, oozing their syrupy contents onto the surface of the tortured epidermis, spreading the contagion.

"Don't scratch!" Treet shouted through clenched teeth. "You'll only make it worse." They were sitting in the shade of a dune near the tents, each with a helmetful of water within reach.

"Thank you, Doctor Feelgood," grumbled Pizzle. "Ooo! I'll go insane if this doesn't stop." He squirmed and writhed like a worm in hot ashes in an attempt to refrain from scratching his sores.

"I say we get on the skimmers and ride," offered Crocker. "It will help take our minds off the itch."

"Go kill yourself!"

No one else felt like traveling either; each nursed his agony in his own way. Yarden and Calin slept fitfully. Pizzle flailed and cursed, and at one point attempted to burrow into a dune headfirst. Crocker paced and moaned, clenching and unclenching his fists. Treet walked, swinging his arms and striding long strides, counting each step, willing himself not to scratch.

But scratching was inevitable. The blisters burst, and a yellowish purple crust formed on the pitted skin. The crust hardened and cracked, fluid oozed between the cracks, and the itching increased. They took off their clothes so the material would not stick to the skin and pull it off.

All night long Pizzle howled and thrashed. Treet and Crocker whimpered in their own misery and kept an eye on him so he didn't injure himself with his maniacal gyrations. The sound of weeping emanated from the women's tent—the soft, blubbery sobbing of utter despair.

By morning the blisters were so numerous over the rest of their bodies that no one got up. They all lay flat on their backs, sniveling, scratching until fingernails bloodied and pus ran red.

Treet slept—a nightmare-ridden, fevered torpor that gave no rest or relief. He dreamt of preying birds picking flesh from his bones, of steam springing from superheated rocks to scald him, of sitting up suddenly in bed and leaving his skin behind, stuck to blood-caked sheets.

When he woke he could not open his eyes, the crust was so thick. His throat felt shredded, as if he had been gargling hot razor blades. Breathing through his nostrils was difficult; the air wheezed in his lungs. In his groggy, partially coherent state he feared that the pustules were now forming in the soft mucous tissue of his breathing passages. He tired to speak, to cry out, but his voice would not come.

Then he noticed that the itching had stopped.

With quivering fingertips he explored his ravaged face. The crust was a lumpy shell, seamed over where, through some movement, he had cracked it and the fluid had bubbled out and dried. He could no longer feel the pressure of his fingers on his skin. Either the crust was thick enough to insulate feeling, or the delicate nerve endings were numbed . . . or destroyed.

From the nape of his neck to the balls of his feet, his whole body was now covered with the suppurating crust. Treet was literally encased in a cocoon several millimeters thick. Every movement cracked the cocoon and made the fluid run into the crevices. Underneath the crust the skin was dead, but at least that was better than the maddening itch.

The day passed—maybe two or three days, for time melted together to become a solid, ill-defined mass. Treet vaguely remembered rolling himself up with a tremendous effort, grappling with his empty helmet, and stumbling outside to get a drink, cracking his cocoon in a million places, making the foul yellowish fluid drip from him like poison rain. When he came to again, he was back in the tent as before; maybe it had been a dream after all.

He faded in and out of consciousness. Once he awoke to a bone-parching fever and imagined he was wrapped in foil and lying on red-hot coals. Another time the sound of his heart drumming double-time wakened him, and he was certain his heart had burst through his papery skin and was beating outside his body. He lay like a mummy. Inert. Unmoving. More dead than alive. Waiting for his vital functions to falter and stop. The sound of his heartbeat eventually dwindled away, and he knew he was dead.

Waking or sleeping, the terrible, fever-induced hallucinations continued. But as Treet sank further into unconsciousness, the nightmare images and sensations dwindled to dull discomfort. The fever raged, but Treet was beyond its reach.

Some time later the fever broke, and the weltering heat gave way to cool relief. He felt as if his withered body had been dipped in thick, cooling menthol balm. For the first time since the blisters appeared, he relaxed and slept peacefully.

The coolness persisted, and when Treet came to awareness once more he realized that the worst was over. This he knew instinctively. He listened for his heartbeat and heard a regular, strong thump-a-lump rhythm. He was hungry and achingly thirsty, but clearheaded and calm. The cobwebs and cloudiness had vanished from his brain, and along with them the gnawing fear. He still could not open his eyes, and breathing was difficult. He felt weaker than he ever had in his life, but he was, despite these modifications, himself again.

He must have slept again, without knowing it, for when he woke he could open his eyes—or at least open them inside the cocoon. Weird purplish light filtered through the crust, which seemed to have ballooned like an expanding foam. He felt a sudden urge to move, to break out of the cocoon.

Starting with his right hand, he wiggled the fingers and found that after a moment the interior of the casing loosened and he could move his fingers. With a little more effort he could twist his hand. Balling his fist, he succeeded in cracking the casing a little, then punched through it.

The cocoon came away in chunks after that—first the right arm and then the left. Then, hands pounding at the dense, pebbled surface, he cracked the area over his chest and peeled it away upward toward his throat and head until he was able to pull it from his face in one masklike section. With an Atlaslike shrug, his shoulders broke free and he sat up and looked around, blinking in the early morning light.

He was outside the tent on the sand next to one of the skimmers. The bottom half of his body was still trapped in a grotesque purple-black and marbled yellow casing that looked disturbingly like charred flesh—puffed up like a marshmallow held too close to the flame. The cocoon was at least three centimeters thick over his entire body. The shapes of his legs could barely be discerned as individual objects; they were joined from hip to knee. His feet were lumpy mounds.

Treet beat on the shell and broke it apart with his hands, freeing hips, thighs, and knees before kicking his feet out. He stood slowly, unsteadily and leaned against the skimmer.

It was then that he realized his skin was completely healed. Holding his hands before his eyes, he marveled that the skin was smooth and supple, slightly moist. His body hair curled in ringlets, holding tiny beads of moisture like pearls. There was not a trace of a blister or scab anywhere. The skin of his arms, legs, and torso was also uniformly without blemish. As far as he could see, there was not a mark on him. He had emerged whole and unspotted from the ordeal.

He snatched up a helmet from the seat of the skimmer and held its faceplate in front of his face to see himself in its smoky reflection. His bearded features appeared not only unharmed, but youthful. From what he could tell, there was not a line or wrinkle showing on his face.

As the awareness of this miracle broke over him, he was overwhelmed with giddiness—an intense, nonsensical desire to dance and sing, to prance and cavort and abandon himself to sweet, reckless joy.

He threw back his head and laughed, thinking, How wonderful to be alive! I am reborn!

FORTY EIGHT

Not a sound came from the tents. Treet didn't think the others were dead, but the possibility crossed his mind. The day was new, the sun not yet beyond the first quadrant. A partial breeze stirred the tent flap and lifted the hair on his rejuvenated skin, and Treet remembered he was naked.

He went to his tent and peered cautiously inside. Crocker's and Pizzle's grotesquely bloated shapes were stretched out like obscene vegetables, swollen and discolored, or like the ghastly larvae of some gross, monstrous insect. With more difficulty than he would have imagined, he dragged the unwieldy sarcophagi from the tent and into the open air. Then, after a moment's consideration, he did the same with the bodies of the two women.

Next, he fished his soiled jumpsuit from the heap outside the tent where they'd discarded them. It stank with a powerful, nose-shriveling stench and was so besmirched with urine, blood, and ooze that the cloth was stiff as cardboard. There would be no wearing that singleton again—best just to bury it, or better still, burn it. Burn them all.

He remembered Pizzle saying something about spare jumpsuits in the carry compartment of one of the skimmers. He tried the nearest one and, underneath some hastily folded yoses, came up with a new red singleton nearly his size. He climbed into it and then turned his attention to the bodies arranged before him. They looked like effigies sculpted in plastic foam and then baked in a fire pit, the scoring of the flames still evident on the tough shell.

Of the two women's shapeless forms, he thought he could tell which was Yarden and decided to free her first. He knelt down and lifted his fist to smack the shell, then hesitated—what if she was not ready? What if freeing her too soon would somehow interfere with the healing process? It was best, he decided, to wait until he detected some stirring from within. Then he could help and know it would be all right.

He had just settled himself to wait when he heard faint scratchings from one of the cocoons. He bent over the nearest one—Calin's, he thought. There was movement inside. With the palm of his hand he pounded firmly on the shell high up on the chest just below the base of the throat, cracked it, and then worked across and down the left arm.

In moments a soft, bronzed-skinned limb came forth, its hand scrabbling and grasping. Treet caught hold of the hand and squeezed it. "Calin, can you hear me? Don't worry. I'll have you out of there in a second."

He fell to the task with restrained fervor, smacking the hard carapace carefully so as not to injure the body trapped within. He heard a muffled yelp when he pressed too hard in removing the headpiece. But when he lifted it away, Yarden blinked and smiled faintly up at him.

"Don't look at me," were her first words. "I must be a horror."

Treet swallowed and whispered, "You are beautiful." He touched one flawless cheek with a finger and let it trail down along her throat. It was true—Yarden was even more beautiful than before, if that was possible. Her fine skin had lost none of its silkiness, and the tiny laugh lines at her eyes and the corners of her mouth had been erased. She appeared years younger.

She blushed under his gaze, a rosy tint spreading from throat to cheeks. He pulled away the cracked encrustment over her torso, allowing her to sit up. She shrugged her right arm free and brought it over to cover her breasts demurely. Now it was Treet's turn to blush. No stranger to female anatomy, he nevertheless turned away and handed her a yos to put on, keeping his eyes averted.

"How long have you been up and around?" she asked. "You can turn around again. It's incredible we're still alive."

"Not more than a minute or two." Treet bent to finish freeing her from her crumbling prison. She kicked her legs, the cocoon shattered, and she stood up.

She looked at her hands, legs, and arms with wonder. Treet followed her gaze, drinking in the glowing freshness of her body. She had never appeared more lovely, more desirable than at that moment. He felt a pressure in his chest, and his throat constricted. He couldn't speak.

"Ahhh!" yelped Yarden amiably. "Oh-h-h, it feels so *good* to move, to be alive!" She burst out laughing just as he had done, then shook out her hair, brushing away the clinging pieces of crust. Treet watched her with utter fascination.

No woman has ever had this effect on me, he thought. It's like I've never seen a woman before. I feel like an awkward kid.

"What's wrong?" asked Yarden, her eyebrows arching gracefully. "You're looking at me funny."

"I—I am?" Treet blustered. He turned away. "I feel a little funny."

"Come on, let's get the others out of those horrible body casts!"

Together they worked at pulling Pizzle, Crocker, and Calin from their loathsome cocoons and finding the newly-released captives something to put on. When all were presentable, they stood around gazing at one another, beaming foolishly, grateful and happy to have survived, and full of the wonder of the transformation each had undergone. Even Pizzle's looks had improved; he appeared less jug-eared, his features less haphazard than before. His straggle of beard had thickened out, and the little bald spot on the top of his head grew new hair.

"There's no explaining it," said Treet. "We can't even begin to know what happened to us. Even if we could explain it, I'm not sure I would believe it anyway—it still seems far too incredible. By all rights we should be moldering corpses. Instead, we're all standing around fresh as baby's breath, looking fifty years younger."

"An exotic virus or bacterial infection—" put in Pizzle.

"I don't care," said Crocker. "I'm just glad we survived. Did any of you others have dreams?"

"Did I!" Yarden said. "They were terrible. I've never had such bad dreams."

"I know—maybe an enzyme of some kind," continued Pizzle, shuffling away deep in thought.

"How long do you figure we were out?" wondered Crocker.

"Your guess is as good as mine," Treet answered. "I have no idea. The last thing I remember is getting up to get a drink. That was maybe two days ago. At first I thought it was a dream, but I woke up out here on the sand, so maybe not."

"You got a drink?" Something in Pizzle's tone made them stop and turn toward him. He was staring at the skimmer with the water supply.

"Yeah, I think so. Why? What's wrong?" Treet exchanged a quick glance with Crocker.

"Then this is *your* fault . . ." Pizzle turned to the others, his face grim, the light dying in his eyes.

"What's my fault?" Treet moved toward him, then froze. The waterbag was limp, deflated. "No!"

Pizzle spoke softly, but his words boomed in their brains. "It's all over now. We've had it. We're out of water."

"We can't be!" shouted Crocker, dashing forward. He stopped in his tracks when he saw the tent, now flaccid, its mooring straps hanging loosely, the whole thing collapsed. The inner flap that had sealed in the water gaped, having been carelessly ripped open and not closed properly. The seal had dropped below the waterline, allowing the water to leak away. The sand beneath the skimmer was a shade darker, still damp from the water it had absorbed.

Long seconds passed before anyone spoke. Treet stared in disbelief at the empty tent, his face ashen. Pizzle and Crocker turned on him as one. "You did this!" they accused. "Because of you we're all going to die!"

"I—I'm sorry . . . I didn't know . . ." Treet mumbled, stunned.

"It's all your fault," said Pizzle darkly. "This whole expedition is your fault—it was your idea in the first place. We're going to die out here because of you. We can't last even three days without water."

Treet bristled at this. "What choice did we have? You tell me that."

"We could have stayed in the colony. We could have hidden somewhere and been safe," snapped Pizzle.

"That's crazy!" Treet turned imploring eyes on Crocker. "Tell him it's crazy, Crocker. We had no choice."

Crocker scowled darkly. "What's crazy is being out in the middle of this wasteland without water. He's right, it's your fault."

"Stop it, you two!" Yarden charged into the middle of them. "It is *not* his fault. How dare you blame him? He was out of his head with fever—as we all were. He didn't know what he was doing. Besides, we don't really know what happened at all. It could have been any one of us. Maybe *you* didn't close the seal properly, Pizzle!" She thrust a finger in his face.

"Me!" Pizzle flapped his arms in exasperation. "He's the one that got us into this mess. Why are you defending him?"

"No one got us into this predicament. We all went willingly. Only Treet had the courage to follow his instincts. Let's forget about laying blame and figure out a way to survive."

Pizzle crossed his arms and stalked away.

Crocker fumed for a while, but eventually came to his senses. "We just got a little panicked, that's all. It's a bad shock." He looked at Treet with raised eyebrows. "No hard feelings?"

Treet nodded, accepting the apology. "Pizzle's right though," he said glumly. "We won't last three days without water. What are we going to do?"

FORTY NINE

"Maybe Nho can help us," suggested Crocker. He glanced around quickly. "Hey, by the way where is Calin?"

"She was here just a second ago," said Treet. "Check the tent."

They searched the tent and the immediate vicinity. Treet turned up some footprints leading away from camp. He found Calin sitting hunched up in the sand at the foot of a dune, head down, her arms drawn around her knees. He sat down beside her.

"We've been looking for you, Calin," he said gently.

She made no answer.

"If it's the water you're worried about—"

"It's not the water," she said, her voice trembling.

He waited, but she did not continue. "What then?"

"It's Nho . . . I can't—he's . . ." She raised a round, tear-stained face, lips quivering. "He's gone!"

Treet sat looking at her for a moment, then put his arm around her shoulders. "Hold on now," he soothed. "What do you mean he's gone? Where could he go?"

Calin shook her head in dismay. "I don't know, but it happens sometimes. I've heard of it before. The psi gets angry and leaves, and the powers vanish. There is no way to get it back. I've been trying to contact him, but . . ." Her voice quivered, and the tears started again. "I'm not a magician anymore!"

Treet pulled her close, feeling a little foolish. How do you comfort someone whose psychic entity has disappeared into astral never-never land? "There, there," he said. "Maybe he will come back. Maybe you just need a little time to recharge your batteries, you know? You've been pretty sick. Maybe that has something to do with it."

They sat for a long time clinging together. Treet surprised

himself with a sudden outpouring of tenderness for the stricken magician. She was weak, vulnerable; she needed him. He rather liked the feeling, like the yielding nearness of her.

"I think we better go back now," he said finally. "I'll tell them about Nho if you want me to. Crocker won't like it, but there's nothing anyone can do. We'll just have to wait and see."

Only Yarden was cheered by Calin's loss. She took her shoulders and looked her in the eye. "Don't you know what this means? You're free!"

"Yeah," griped Pizzle, "and we're history. We have no compass anymore. No water. No nothing. We're sunk."

"Squelch the doom forecasts," said Crocker. "I've been assessing our situation. We didn't lose all the water. While you've been belly-aching Yarden and I measured out what's left. We've got about twenty liters, by our best estimate, besides what's in our emergency flasks."

"So we postpone the inevitable four or five days. Whoopee."

"Pizzle, you're a crybaby, you know that? You're a spoiled brat of a crybaby," Treet said. "Here we all are, trying to pull together for survival, and all you can think of to do is carp and whine because things aren't absolutely peachy."

"I beg your pardon! The prospect of immediate death makes me a little testy," Pizzle japed.

Crocker ignored him. "I figure if we push ourselves as hard as we dare, we ought to be able to make ten thousand kilometers in four days. That should take us out of this desert—it *can't* be much bigger than that."

"Want to bet?" muttered Pizzle.

"Can we go that fast?" wondered Treet.

"I don't see why not. Didn't you tell me we topped out at four hundred kilometers per hour?" Crocker patted the side of the skimmer he leaned against. "That's flying."

"But that was a race. We couldn't drive like that all day."

"Only short bursts. I figure all we have to do is maintain an average of two hundred and fifty per hour over ten hours travel time per day. We could do that, I think."

"We'd have to double our average," pointed out Yarden. "Before we got sick, we were doing a hundred and twenty-five. I kept track."

"Impossible," said Pizzle, but he stood and came over to join the discussion. "I mean, we'd have to push it to the limit.

And even if we were somehow able to keep from going around in big circles, we still don't know precisely where we're heading."

"We keep the sun at our backs in the morning and aim for it in the afternoon," remarked Crocker. "Just like we've been doing."

"Too bad we can't travel at night and use the stars," Pizzle mused, "like in *Dune*."

"That's another one of your adolescent fantasy stories, I take it?" said Treet archly.

"Only one of the most famous classics of all time."

"Never heard of it."

The company struck camp and proceeded on their way, pushing the skimmers as fast as safety would allow, and changing drivers regularly. The pace wore down muscle tone and reflexes fast. But they soon developed a rhythm of driving and resting, and the kilometers fell away beneath the gleaming, sand-sharpened blades of the skimmers.

At the end of the first day they had covered nearly two thousand kilometers. "We're five hundred short for the day," said Crocker, "but we had a late start. We'll do better tomorrow."

They did do better the next day, covering almost three thousand kilometers of dune-strewn desert. They climbed down from the skimmers in the early twilight gritty, bone-weary, parched, and triumphant. In their sleep that night they relived every dip and swell of the sand-filled wilderness as they slid once more over the endless white void in their dreams.

On the third day disaster struck.

Pizzle was far out ahead of the group—they took turns leading one another so those behind could relax somewhat since it was easier to follow than to forge the trail. Treet was second, watching the high white plume of Pizzle's skimmer weaving its way over the desert landscape when without warning the plume disappeared in a great puff of sand and dust.

Treet gunned his vehicle to the spot and skidded to a stop beside the smoking wreckage of Pizzle's skimmer. Crocker bounded from the passenger's seat and dashed through the clouds of hanging dust to where Pizzle lay spread-eagle on the sand fifty meters away. Treet approached as Crocker rolled Pizzle over.

"Is he dead?" asked Treet. Pizzle's head wobbled loosely on his shoulders. One side of his face was turning a bright red from an ugly scrape, and the heels of both hands were raw and bleeding. It looked as if he'd slid across the desert floor on his hands and face.

"I don't think so," replied Crocker, placing two fingers beneath Pizzle's jaw at the carotid artery. "I've got a good pulse here. He's just out. I don't see anything broken."

Treet straightened and turned back to the ruined skimmer. The smoke was clearing, revealing a twisted pile of metal half-buried in the face of a dune. "Oh, something's broken all right."

Yarden and Calin came skidding in and ran to them. "Is he—" began Yarden, glancing fearfully at the limp body cradled in Crocker's arms.

Holding up his hands, Treet said, "We don't know yet, but we think he's okay. He's scraped up pretty bad—that's all we can tell right now."

Pizzle gave a long, low moan that sounded like a snore. "If I didn't know better, I'd swear he was sleeping," said Treet.

Crocker peered at him doubtfully. "He's coming around." He patted Pizzle's cheek gently. "Pizzle, can you hear me? It's Crocker—hear?"

Pizzle's eyes fluttered open. "O-o-h-h . . ." A hand went to his head. "What happened?"

"You had a wreck," said Treet. "Where does it hurt?"

"All over . . . O-o-h-h. I don't . . . remember . . . a thing," he said, rolling his head from side to side. "I think my neck is broken."

"I doubt it," said Crocker. "But it probably should be. Can you get up?"

"Just let me sit here a minute." Pizzle closed his eyes again. "I must have blacked out."

"Like a light," said Crocker. "Tell us what happened."

"I don't know. I mean—I was driving along, I looked down at the instrument panel to check my speed, and the next thing I know I'm waking up here." He rolled his head again. "Oh, baby! Is my skimmer all right?"

"Total loss," said Treet. "You were lucky." He studied Pizzle closely. His eyes narrowed. "In fact, more than lucky, I think.

The only people who walk away from accidents like this in one piece are drunks."

"What are you saying? Pizzle certainly wasn't drunk," Yarden remarked.

"No, he wasn't drunk. He was *asleep*."

An expression of recognition spread across Crocker's face. "Is that true? You fell asleep?"

Pizzle blanched. "How do I know? Everything's kind of blurry. Maybe I did get a little dizzy just before—"

"Just before you fell off?" said Treet with disgust. He stomped off to examine the smashed skimmer. The machine looked like someone had tried to fold it in the middle. It's sides were crumpled and bowed; its blades stuck out in artistic angles.

"Pizzle, you grouthead!" exploded Crocker. He stood up quickly, dropping Pizzle onto the sand. "Look what you've done!"

A sickly grin warped Pizzle's face. He pushed himself back up on his elbows. "Sorry, guys. I don't know what to say. I didn't mean to. I guess I got mesmerized or something. Rapture of the road, you know? It's never happened before."

"Well, we don't have to worry about it happening again. You'll have to ride with Yarden. You take the prize, Pizzle, you know that?"

"Ease up on him," said Yarden. "He could have been killed."

"Maybe that's not such a bad idea," said Treet, joining them once again. The tone of his voice made the others glance at him. "We've lost the rest of the water. The tent was punctured in the crash. It's all gone."

Pizzle groaned. Crocker swore under his breath.

"We've still got the emergency flasks," Yarden pointed out.

"Well, this is an emergency."

"We're never going to make it," moaned Pizzle.

"Not if we sit around here much longer," said Treet.

"He's right. I suggest we get moving again pronto. We can't get out of this desert fast enough to suit me," Crocker said.

They left, but not before Pizzle had stripped everything of possible use from the damaged vehicle. That took some time, but Pizzle convinced the others that it would likely pay off in the long run. When at last they got underway again, the sun was starting its slide down toward the western horizon and a stiff breeze had picked up, sending sand devils twirling across the flats.

A ridge of cloud appeared away to the south, and the breeze turned into a steady wind. Treet noted the clouds and pointed them out to Crocker. When he looked again, he was amazed to see that the ridge had swelled to a hard, brassy brown bank that was moving toward them fast. He held up his hand and slowed to a stop.

"I think we're in for a storm," he said, indicating the clouds. The wind whistled over the tops of nearby dunes as sand snakes hissed up the smooth dune faces. The sun had become a pale platinum disk in a sky of brittle glass.

"Maybe we can outrun it," said Crocker.

"We can try," agreed Treet.

They pushed the skimmers as fast as they would go, but at the end of another hour the wind had become cold and strong, flinging the sand into their faces, stinging exposed flesh; it became apparent they would not be able to outrun the storm. Crocker cupped his hand and shouted, "Let's find the biggest dune around here and pitch our tents in the windshadow."

Visibility had dropped to a scant few meters by the time they found a place to stop. Copper clouds opaqued the sky and all but obscured the sun, which burned with a ghostly pallor, like a candle shining through burlap. They managed to get one tent up and anchored between the two skimmers when the gale hit.

The wind roared with the sound of a rocket thruster throttled flat out. Overlaying this was a harsh, shushing rasp that was the wind-driven sand in flight. The company huddled together in the crowded tent and listened to the storm. Its howl absorbed all conversation, so they lay back in the dim orange half-light and watched the fabric of the tent stretch and flutter, hoping against hope that their fragile shelter would last the night.

Some time later Treet awoke. The wind had died away to a murmuring whisper. He slipped quietly out of the tent, shoving sand away from the flap with a swimming motion of his hands. He stood and looked around. It was early evening. The sun was down, but the sky still held a leaden glow. Stars burned coolly overhead and the newly-rearranged dunes stood like bleached shadows, silent and immobile, their crests touched with silver.

Treet surveyed their position. One of the skimmers was completely buried in the sand, the other only half-buried. The curved roof of the tent jutted beween them. He climbed to the top of the nearest dune and scanned the horizon, letting his eyes sweep the undulating desert beneath the twilight sky. He had completed a ninety degree arc when he saw the obelisk.

FIFTY

"It's no use," sighed Pizzle. "I've done everything I can think of to do. I don't think it's going to start."

He sat in a ring of scattered skimmer pieces—cowling, chain, sprocket gears, screen mesh, wire, sealed bearings—his face and hands smeared with grease, peering doubtfully into the complicated innards of a dead sand skimmer.

Crocker sat on his heels next to Pizzle, scratching his head and frowning. "I'm sure I don't know what else to do." He drew a soiled sleeve across his brow, jerked his thumb over his shoulder to the skimmer gliding up, and said, "You want to give 'em the bad news or should I?"

"What bad news?" asked Treet as he, Yarden, and Calin, who had become little more than a ghost since her psi deserted her, climbed down from the last working sand skimmer. They had driven to the obelisk Treet had spotted the night before to check it out.

Crocker squinted up into the sunlight at Treet. "We're down to one vehicle. We can't get this other one to start."

"That's bad," said Treet. "But at least we still have one."

"Yeah," said Pizzle darkly. "Keep your fingers crossed and hope it holds out."

"What did you find?" Crocker unfolded himself and stood, squinting in the direction of the obelisk—a narrow white slash in the pale blue sky.

"It's some kind of signal tower—that's my best guess. It's huge—I'd estimate close to two hundred meters tall. The base is one hundred meters in circumference—Yarden paced it off—five sides, twenty meters to a side. There are some funny markings on the base, like numbers or letters, only they're not. The rest of it is completely smooth—some kind of plastic sheeting that covers it to about halfway up, then bare metal beams and struts like a radio antenna all the way to the top."

"Anything on top?" asked Crocker.

Yarden answered, "Some kind of dish—like a satellite dish."

"Could be a microwave reflector," mused Pizzle. "Those have to be pretty tall like that. Any way to climb it?"

"There is a ladder of sorts that begins about five meters off the ground on the south side. But the thing is almost straight up and down. I wouldn't want to go climbing around on it."

Crocker nodded thoughtfully. "Well, let's get packed up here and take a look. The day is getting away from us as it is. We'd better make some good use out of it, or we've wasted a day's ration of water."

The skimmer fairly groaned under the weight of its passengers. All five managed somehow to crowd aboard—along with the tents and the gear Pizzle insisted on bringing in case of a breakdown. They drove to the tower, a short ride of about six kilometers. Crocker parked the skimmer in the shadow of the soaring object and then walked around it.

"Sure is a big old thing," he said. "I think one of us should try to climb it. Maybe we'd see something from way up there that could help us out."

"You mean like an oasis or something? Forget it," said Pizzle. "You're dreaming."

"Or like a river, or green hills, or anything that shows us the way out of this desert," said Crocker.

"Or like a city," put in Yarden. Everyone looked at her. "Is that so farfetched? We're looking at a signal tower of some kind. Whoever built it must have built something else, too. Maybe we could spot it from up there."

"Sure, why not?" asked Treet.

"Then you're going up?" said Crocker.

"Not me. You go up—*you're* the pilot."

"Don't look at me," said Pizzle quickly. "I'm barely functioning without my glasses the way it is. I'd never see anything from up there."

"You were functioning well enough to wreck a skimmer," Treet needled. "Now all of a sudden you're blind."

"I'll go up," offered Yarden. "I'm not afraid of heights."

"Neither am I," remarked Treet. "It's the fall I can't stand."

"You won't fall," said Pizzle. "You'll be extra careful."

"It *was* your idea," added Yarden.

"It was Crocker's idea!"

"No, I mean this morning—when we first saw it. You said

someone should go up and check out the view." Yarden nodded, chewing her lip as she raised her eyes to where the shallow, round dish gleamed from the top. "It probably isn't all that high. I don't mind going."

"I'll go," muttered Treet.

"You don't have to." Yarden smiled at him, then said, "You'll be all right, just hang on tight."

So Treet found himself standing on Crocker's shoulders, reaching for the vertical ladder. "I can't reach it! It's about a finger too far," he called.

"Lean against the base—we'll boost you up."

He leaned full length against the base while the rest of them grabbed his feet and pushed him up higher. There was a single rail next to the indented rungs. Treet caught the bottom of the tubular railing where it joined the plastic sheeting and hauled himself up. The rest was relatively easy—as long as he kept his eyes on the rung just ahead.

He climbed, one hand on the rail, one hand on the rung at eye level, stopping every other rung or so to sweep sand from the indentation. When he finally reached the place where the sheeting stopped and bare metal began, he crooked his arm around the rail and looked out.

A sun-washed whiteness met his gaze on every side, shimmering in heat waves off the sand, melting into light blue in the distance. There was no green, no river, no city, no oasis— nothing but sand dunes and still more sand dunes, looking like the humped backs of white whales from high above.

Treet called down his observation, and Crocker's voice came drifting up to him. "Go higher! Higher!"

Treet gritted his teeth and edged onto the metal superstructure. He could, he quickly found, climb the inside beams at the intersections of joints. This took him higher in a zigzag pattern and gave him good footing and something to hold on to with both hands. In a few minutes he was half again as high as he was when he'd given his first report, but still only halfway up the tower. Far below, the others were mere dark spots on the ground with round white centers which were their upturned faces.

A slight breeze rippled his singleton and stirred his hair. The landscape was a wrinkled ocean whose waves were frozen white ice. Nothing could be seen south, west, north or east— except the same monotonous monochromatic dunescape. As

Treet moved to begin climbing down again, he caught something out of the corner of his eye. He stopped and looked.

Nothing. The heat shimmers were playing tricks on his eyes, he decided. He turned to lower his foot back onto the next joint and he saw it again—off to the southeast, the faintest vertical slashmark on the horizon. He looked again and saw nothing, but tried looking slightly to the left of it and saw it again—the lone spire of another tower barely nudging above the dune line. It disappeared into his blindspot whenever he tried to look directly at it, but became visible when he looked away.

Treet marked its direction and began climbing down. It was a long, slow, muscle-knotting climb, but he finally reached the bottom of the ladder and slid down the base to drop onto the sand.

"Well?" asked Crocker. "What did you see?"

Treet raised a fist of white sand and let it sift through his fingers. "A lot more of this same white stuff, friends."

"I was afraid so," grouched Pizzle.

"*And* . . ." Treet paused, drawing them out.

"Yes? Do we have to guess?" asked Crocker.

"Another tower like this one, I think. Away to the southeast. The same general direction we've been heading all along."

"How far?" asked Yarden.

Treet shrugged. "I can't say. Pretty far. It's hard to tell."

They all looked at each other. "Is everyone thinking what I'm thinking?" asked Crocker.

"We are," replied Yarden, "if you're thinking of following these towers to wherever they go."

"Trouble is," replied Pizzle, "that wherever they go is probably a million kilometers from here. They may not lead anywhere at all. We don't even know if they're still operational, or if whoever built them is still around."

"Do we have any better options?" asked Treet. "We've got four days of water left, and that's at half rations. After that . . . well, we start dehydrating . . . seriously."

"Stop," said Yarden. "All I can think about now is how thirsty I am."

"So let's quit standing around here and get moving. The quicker we find the way out of this place, the better off we'll be."

"You're starting to repeat yourself, Crocker," said Treet.

They climbed back onto the overburdened skimmer and

started off in the direction Treet had indicated. Thirty minutes later—traveling at a top speed of one hundred and ninety-five kilometers per hour—they reached the second tower, an exact duplicate of the first.

"I suppose you want me to climb this one too," said Treet, craning his neck to look upwards. Why did they have to be so blooming *tall?* he wondered.

"If you wouldn't mind—just to be sure," said Crocker.

The view from the second tower was precisely the view from the first in every respect—including the illusive suggestion of a third tower on the southeastern horizon.

"It's there," said Treet as he dropped back exhausted to the ground. "If we keep going this direction, we'll hit it."

A little over a half-hour later they reached the next tower.

"I'm not going up again. I'm not selfish; let someone else have the thrill."

"Not necessary," said Crocker. "We're moving at a forty-five degree angle to the arc of the sun. I imagine we'll find another tower if we keep on going."

Two towers later, they stopped for a drink of water. Fortunately the weather of Empyrion, even in mid-desert, remained uniformly friendly—twenty-five degrees centigrade during the day, dipping at night no more than eight degrees—with a light breeze, when there was a wind at all, so that the travelers did not sweat overmuch, or in fact have to worry about excessive heat at all.

They decided to push on as far as they could go under sun power, and, by carefully increasing the skimmer's speed, were able to pass a dozen more of the strange towers before the sunlight grew too weak to power the vehicle. The sun was low in the sky, throwing the shadow of one of the towers out ahead of them when they stopped.

"As good a place as any," replied Crocker. They erected the two remaining tents and then sat around glumly munching survival wafers and dried eel flesh. They allowed themselves one more sip of water before turning in for the night.

Treet rested for a while, but could not sleep, so slipped out of the tent and, despite the need for conserving energy and body fluids, went for a walk. Walking helped him think, and thinking was what he needed most at the moment.

He thought about their chances of survival—nothing much

to think about there. Then he thought about the towers: incredibly tall and finger-thin, spaced at precise intervals across the desert. What were they for? Who used them? They looked quite old. Perhaps they had been built long ago, their makers dead a hundred generations, their purpose now forgotten. Perhaps, as Pizzle suggested, the towers led nowhere.

The stars came out and splashed themselves over the sky. Treet found a place to sit at the bottom of a nearby dune and lay back to watch the sky. The sand, warmer than the air now that the sun had set, felt good against his back as he gazed up into the alien heavens.

How many times have I seen this sky, he asked himself, and not really seen it? Empyrion's sky was a magnificent creation, like Earth's, but unlike it at the same time. The planet's purer atmosphere made the stars appear much brighter, closer, more readily accessible. But they, like Sol, were just as faraway as ever. But which one was Sol? Which of all those shining flecks of light held his own azure bauble in its gravitational field?

"I thought I'd find you out here."

Treet heard Yarden shuffle up. "You mind?" she asked, when he did not respond.

"Uh, no, help yourself," he murmured, raising his head and then lying back. Here she is, he thought, as much a puzzle as ever. Why can't I get on the same wavelength with her? Maybe it's her sympathetic ways.

"I couldn't sleep either," she said, nestling into the sand beside him. "I thought I'd keep you company." She did not look at him, but followed his gaze skyward. "What are you looking at?"

"Nothing . . . everything. I don't know. Stars. They're all the same, but all different. You never get tired of looking at them. I wonder why?"

"Maybe it's because we know deep down that somehow they represent mankind's future and past and everything in between."

"Huh?"

Yarden smiled in the dark—Treet could tell she was smiling because her voice softened, became warmer. "I mean that when you look at a star you're seeing light from thousands of years ago—that's the past."

"Right."

"And the stars themselves represent the future—going there, visiting them, discovering things, spreading the human race through the galaxy—that sort of thing."

"And everything in between?"

"Well, that's what they represent right now—something to light the night, to give us something to steer by, to look at and wonder at, to plot a life's course by."

"Yarden, I do believe you're a romantic."

"Hopelessly," she sighed. "You are too. I can tell."

"Me?" Treet scoffed. "Never. I've seen too much."

"What's that got to do with it?"

"I mean I don't harbor any illusions about life. It turns out like it turns out. There's nothing anyone can do to change that. Certainly going all starry-eyed over things won't help."

"You don't believe that really."

"Believe what? That getting sappy about life will make it turn out better than it's going to anyway? A man would be a fool to believe it." He paused, and when Yarden did not say anything, he added, "How did we get on that subject anyway?"

"You started it. But the stars *are* nice—like that big one over there. I don't know when I've ever seen one brighter."

"Which one?" he asked.

"There." She lifted her hand and pointed to an intensely glowing star near the horizon to the northwest. "See? So big and bright. Blue-white."

"It's a beauty," allowed Treet. "And as a matter of fact, we haven't seen it before."

"That's strange."

"Not really—we've probably crossed some meridian or equator or something and it's visible now. But it is bright."

"Maybe it's Sol."

"Maybe . . . but I don't think so." Treet's voice sounded as if it were strained through a sieve. Yarden looked at him, but could only see the outline of his head dark against the light sand. "Yarden . . ."

"Yes—" She shared at him in the darkness, trying to see his expression. "What is it?"

He sat up bolt upright. "Yarden, it's moving!"

"What is?"

"That star is moving! It's coming this way!"

FIFTY
ONE

"I don't see any movement." Yarden fixed her eyes on the bright star. "Are you sure?"

"Wait! Hold still, take a deep breath, and look . . ." Treet poised perfectly still for a few seconds. "See? It's getting bigger. That is definitely no star. But whatever it is, it's coming this way."

They watched for a few moments more, and then Treet went to rouse the others. Crocker cupped his hands around his eyes to shut out all extraneous light, watched motionless, and then announced, "You're absolutely right. It's a craft of some sort, and it's headed for us. Judging by the angle of flight, I'd say it was low altitude and only moderate speed."

"Helicopter?" wondered Treet aloud.

"Like a helicopter, yes."

"It's following the line of the towers," observed Pizzle. "Look where it's coming from. Bing, bing, bing—right down the line."

"Pizzle, I do think you're right," said Treet. "Now why would they do that, whoever they are?"

"They're navigational towers," explained Crocker, indicating the dark mass rising up into the night beside them. "The pilot homes in on the towers to stay on course."

"That's a stupid way to fly," said Treet.

"Primitive," agreed Crocker, "but effective."

Yarden broke in, "You don't suppose they are looking for us?" Her stress on the word *they* made the others stop and look at her in the starlight. There was no doubt who *they* were.

"Chasing us? You mean . . ." began Treet. "No, why would they?"

Crocker shrugged. "We'll find out soon enough. ETA is less than twenty minutes by my guess. Maybe we should be ready to make a run for it in any case."

Working feverishly in the dark they struck camp, keeping one eye on the ever-growing light in the sky. They took down the tents and loaded the skimmer, then gathered at the base of the tower to sit and wait. The disk of blue-white light increased by slow degrees until it outshone every other star, and still grew brighter and larger.

Then they heard the engines, softly at first, a mere burring rumble on the night air, like distant thunder. Gradually the rumble grew into a great booming throb that pulsed in heavy waves as it echoed among the dunes. By then they could make out a great dark shape above the light—a huge, black spherical mass that blotted out the stars around it. The bright light emanated from the bottom of the craft, shining down at an oblique angle, playing across the desert as it came. They could see the light striking the crests of dunes, flaring white and sliding down the slope to disappear from view, only to flare again on the crest of the next.

"I think we should get out of the way of that light," cried Crocker. He had to shout above the monstrous thrum of the oncoming engines to make himself heard.

They ran from the tower to lay in the sand atop a small dune near where the skimmer was parked. There they waited. Three heartbeats . . . four—then the mysterious craft was upon them, blacking out a fair portion of the night sky as it glided by, engines roaring, pushing the flying machine past them at a stately pace.

The light swept over the exact spot where their tent had been, flashed over the tower, and continued on. A tremendous black sphere filled the sky above them, below which dangled another, smaller shape that looked like an elongated teardrop. A row of green lights appeared near the front end of the horizontal teardrop, and a dull red glow lit up the rear.

In a matter of seconds it was gone, churning off into the night, the sound of its mighty engines dwindling rapidly, its black smoothness melting into the night once more, the light fading, leaving only the faint suggestion of a red glow behind. Then that, too, was no more.

A feeling of sadness descended over the group with the passing of the craft. No one spoke for a long time.

Finally Crocker broke silence. "What in blue blazes was that?" he asked. Awe, and the stillness of the night after the boom of the craft's engines, made his voice sound thin. "I've never seen anything like it."

"It was an airship," said Pizzle.

"We know that," snapped Crocker, "but—"

"No, he means like a blimp," Yarden offered. "Right?"

"Right. Airship—as in lighter-than. Did you see the size of that thing? Oooeee! Incredible. It must be making a good hundred k's per hour, which for all that mass is doing all right."

"Who were they?" asked Yarden, expressing the obvious question in everyone's mind.

"Calin?" asked Treet, turning to the silent young woman. "I think you can tell us. They weren't Hagemen looking for us, were they?" he said.

Calin shook her head. Her voice came soft in the darkness, touched with wonder. "No, they were not looking for us. They were . . . Fieri."

"Just what I figured," replied Treet. "They didn't even know we were here. We just happened to stumble onto the Fieri air route."

"Amazing, your powers of deduction," quipped Pizzle. "I was about to say the same thing."

"At any rate, that settles the problem of our next move," put in Crocker. "We keep following the towers right to Fieri-land."

"And hope the water holds out," said Treet.

They followed the Fieri towers for three days, passing them at regular intervals every thirty minutes. The overloaded skimmer gave out toward the end of the third day. Tempers frazzled by thirst and the monotony of desert travel snapped when the skimmer lurched, chugged, and shook to a bone-rattling halt.

"That tears it all to hell," said Pizzle, throwing a three-way wrench at the broken vehicle. He'd been tinkering with it for over three hours, and the sand was littered with skimmer pieces. "It's probably some routine maintenance thing that we don't know about. But it's kaput! We're done for."

"Lay down, Pizzy, I'll scoop sand over your head."

"Drop dead!"

"Isn't that what you're suggesting?" Treet said snidely.

"We're not finished yet," said Crocker. "Not even close."

"Oh?" Pizzle turned on him. "I'm overjoyed to hear it. I thought people usually died of thirst when they ran out of water in the desert."

"We're not out of water yet," said Yarden.

"You're right," said Pizzle. "I forgot. We've got a whole half day's ration of water. We could all take baths and wash our hair we've got so much. Whatever shall we do with it all?"

"Cool off, Pizzle," said Treet. "I don't want to hear any more of your spoiled-brat theatrics."

"If I had a stillsuit and crysknife your water would be mine," Pizzle muttered.

"What did he say?" asked Crocker, watching him strangely.

"He thinks he's someone called Paul Dune or something—a character from one of his books. Thirst is warping his brain," said Treet. "Let's leave him here."

Treet picked up his sling, slipped it over one shoulder, and started off. Yarden and Calin fell in behind him. Crocker watched them go, picked up the two slings at his feet, and held one out to Pizzle. "The machine's finished. Even if you knew how to fix it, there's nothing to fix it with. Come on or I *will* leave you here."

He turned and trudged off. Pizzle glanced at the skimmer, hefted the sling onto his back, and shuffled after the others, head down, in his slope-shouldered gait.

Night found them halfway between one tower and the next. But they walked on, having decided to travel by night and therefore minimize evaporation of moisture from their bodies. The hours passed slowly as they dragged themselves over the desert, becoming more aware of the burning in their throats with each and every step.

No one said much. They mostly kept their heads down and conserved as much energy as possible, wasting neither words nor motion. An hour before dawn, the sky showing like oxidized aluminum in the east, they halted, erected the tents, and went to sleep.

Treet awoke from a dreamless sleep feeling like he'd taken a big bite out of a sand dune. He coughed and would have spat, but was afraid to waste the spit, so swallowed instead, which did nothing for the gritty dryness in his mouth. He took up his water flask, jiggled it to test how much remained—only the barest hint of a slosh at the bottom of the flask—and decided to forego the drink he'd promised himself upon waking.

Then he remembered what had awakened him: the sound of an airship's engines.

He rolled to his feet and stumbled from the tent, almost

tipping forward onto his face as he straightened. He was a little light-headed from lack of water and thought perhaps he was hearing things—the aural hallucinations of a dying man. But he was just being melodramatic; he was nowhere near far enough gone to start having hallucinations, aural or otherwise.

He turned his eyes to the sky. It was early afternoon by the sun. A Fieri tower loomed over the dunes to the southeast about four kilometers away. The airship's engines thrummed lightly from out of the northwest, though without its single large head- light it could not as yet be seen. Treet stood squinting into the sky, straining for a glimpse of the craft as the sound grew stead- ily louder.

"Wake up!" he hollered. "An airship is coming! An airship! Quick, wake up! We've got to try to flag it down!" he hollered, dashing from one tent to the next to rouse the others. By the time they tumbled out upon the sand, the shape of the Fieri airship could be vaguely discerned—a rust-red disk in a cerulean sky.

"This is it," said Crocker hoarsely. "We've got to make them see us. It's our only chance."

"If we only had a signal flare—" griped Pizzle.

"Take down the tents. We'll wave those," commanded Crocker.

Pizzle dived into the tent, fished out his sling, and dumped it out in the sand. He grabbed up a small canister and some other objects and started fiddling with them.

"Now what are you doing?" asked Treet in exasperation. "We could use your help."

"Shut up and leave me alone!" snapped Pizzle. "I've got an idea."

The Fieri's craft loomed closer. Now they could see its bulk casting a rippling shadow over the dunes.

"There!" said Pizzle shortly. "I hope it works." He held up his handiwork for all to see. Attached to the canister were several wires and a broken piece of a solar cell.

"What is it?" asked Treet.

"A smoke bomb. This is from the skimmer I wrecked—it's filled with solid fuel, and the cell ought to heat up the wires and blow the fuse inside. It might be enough of a spark to touch off the fuel. I figure it should smoke two or three minutes."

"Pizzle, you're a wonder," said Treet. "Want us to do any- thing?"

"Yeah. Stay out of my way."

"You better get it going right now. That airship will be here any minute."

Pizzle climbed a dune and hunched himself over the canister, holding the solar cell by the edges, tilting it toward the sun. In a few moments a hissing sound came from inside the canister. "It's getting hot in there."

"Look!" cried Yarden. "The airship is almost here!"

Treet glanced skyward and noted the looming shape of the Fieri airship. "It that thing going to work?" he hollered.

"Shh!" warned Crocker. "Give it a chance."

The hissing grew louder. "Go baby, go-o-o," coaxed Pizzle. "Do it, do it, do it. Make your papa proud."

"It's not going to work," said Treet.

Yarden looked at him with worried eyes. Calin stood silently, watching with a stricken expression. Crocker pounded his fists against his thighs, his face intense, looking like a gambler whose winnings were riding on a heavy-odds underdog.

"Will you shut up!" cried Pizzle. "It'll work—just give it a second."

"The ship is almost here!" said Yarden. "Ooo, come on, come on . . ."

The canister hissed loudly and gave a muffled pop. Yellow smoke erupted from the top of the canister along with sparks and a sharp sizzling sound. "There!" said Pizzle triumphantly. "I told you it would work."

But the words were no sooner out of his mouth than the sizzling stopped. The sparks fizzled and died; the smoke evaporated. "No!" cried Pizzle, diving for the canister.

"So much for the miracles of modern science," said Treet, already dashing away. "Get those tents!"

"I can get this going again, I know it." Pizzle jiggled the wires and tapped the canister. He held the solar cell to the sun.

"Forget that!" barked Crocker. "Find something shiny to flash. The rest of us will signal with the tent fabric and hope to God they see us!"

The airship was almost directly overhead by the time they started waving the orange tents from the top of the tallest nearby dune. Treet could make out individual windows in the bulbous, teardrop-shaped cupola suspended below the gigantic gas-filled sphere of the airship. But if anyone aboard was watching, he couldn't see a face. The thundering engines reverberated across the desert, bouncing sand from the dunes below, vibrating diaphragm and eardrum alike with their deep, sonorous sound.

As the giant airship's shadow slid over them—a rusty moon eclipsing the sun—Treet shouted, "We're too much underneath it! They'll never see us!"

He snatched the tent from Crocker's hands and fled into the sunlight again, sliding, slipping, rolling down the side of the dune. He ran hard, trying to keep up with the craft, waving the tent fabric over his head, yelling, falling, sprawling, getting up, and running again.

The airship floated on without so much as a tip of a trailing stabilizer to them. In a little while the Fieri craft became a mere blip in the sky, leaving only the purr of the engines behind.

Treet lay panting in the sand, watching the airship disappear once again. He felt stunned and sick and foolish. To think they would die out here now after all they had been through. That airship had been their last real hope, and it had just vanished over the bleak horizon. The cursed white desert—nothing but bleached dunes beneath a waxy blue sky—would soon cradle their bones in its vast desolation.

The unfairness of it! Treet wanted to cry, but it would be a waste of precious tears and would do no good. He rose slowly and ambled back to where the others sat waiting, their expressions mirror-images of his own dejection.

"Well, we're awake now," Crocker was saying. "We might as well get moving."

"Why?" grumped Pizzle. "What difference does it make whether we die here or fifty kilometers from here? It's all the same to me."

For once Crocker did not snap back at him; he didn't even bother to reply, just turned sad eyes toward him and shrugged. The resignation in that heavy lift of the pilot's shoulders cut at Treet's heart like a razor. Never had he witnessed such an elegant statement of despair. He looked away, a lump the size of a melon swelling in his throat.

Yarden jumped to her feet; her dark eyes narrowed in quick anger. "I defy you to give up on us!" she shouted. Treet swiveled around to see her face livid with rage, fists clenched and shaking. "It is a sacrilege!"

Crocker looked properly chastised, but Pizzle glared back defiantly. "Bitch!" he spat.

Yarden's slap sounded like the retort of a gun. The white

imprint of her hand on Pizzle's cheek was already turning deep red before Pizzle knew what happened. A rich interplay of emotions—shock, bewilderment, outrage, innocence, guilt—pinwheeled over his homely features. He settled on an expression of unalloyed astonishment. "You hit me," he observed softly.

Yarden's eyes flared, but she answered coolly, "I'm not sorry. You deserved it. Get on your feet, and let's get moving."

Calin rose and came to stand beside her, saying nothing, but showing quiet courage in the gesture. Treet, still on his feet, took a half-step closer. The three of them waited, looking down at the two men.

"Looks like we're bound for a little more sightseeing, Pizzy old boy," said Crocker. He got up slowly, patting dust from his clothes.

Pizzle climbed to his feet, now contrite and apologetic. "Okay, okay," he said. "Why's everybody always taking these things so seriously?"

Yarden's lips remained pressed firmly into a straight line. But the hard light in her eyes softened, and satisfaction radiated from them. She spun on her heel and stalked down the face of the dune, starting off once more across the desert.

FIFTY
TWO

Yarden's steely determination carried them three more days. On the fourth no one got up. They lay in the tents, too weak to move, too demoralized to care, merely waiting for the end, hoping it would not be too painful.

Treet drifted in and out of consciousness. The last two days had been cruel torture. Simple thirst had ceased, only to be replaced by a most compelling agony: his tongue swelling in his mouth, every tissue giving up its stored water, internal organs shutting down for lack of moisture. He and the others had nevertheless stumbled on doggedly, dimly aware of where they were and what they were doing.

Nothing mattered. Beyond care, beyond regret, beyond every other human response, now only the slow, inexorable approach of death held any interest for him. To be alive and know you were dying and know too there was nothing you could do about it, thought Treet in one of his lucid moments, was surely the worst trick of a whole universe full of lousy tricks.

By the fevered whispers and the soft sighing moans emanating from those around him, Treet knew that he was still in the land of the living. But as the day progressed, the hours dragging by in leaden succession, each one too long and too laden with the thick, foul presence of death, the moans and whispers gradually ceased.

The bright orange light inside the room was fading when Treet roused himself from a trancelike stupor in which he imaged the deep pulsing thunder of airship engines as the great spheres passed, one after another, oblivious overhead. He rolled weakly, painfully onto his side and listened. He heard a droning buzz and could not place the sound. He listened for a moment, and the sound resolved itself into voices—Yarden was talking to someone in the hallway outside. They were talking about him.

"He is dying," she said. "We're all dying, don't you see. It's okay though—really it is." She was obviously trying to convince herself as well as her companion that death was an acceptable outcome of their ordeal. "Actually, I could have predicted it from the beginning. Failure is nothing to be ashamed of. It happens. Anyway, we all have to die sometime."

There was more that Treet could not get. Such stupid talk, thought Treet. Odd coming from Yarden. She was the one who had used every ounce of her own stubborn will to urge them all on when nothing else would have kept them going. Now here she was telling whoever she was talking to, most matter-of-factly, that it was perfectly proper to lay down and die. That wasn't like Yarden at all.

Tears came to Treet's eyes, hardly more than a mist wetting his hot, dry eyes. I've lost her, he thought. I should have told her I loved her. Not that it would have made any difference—but no, it always made a difference. I should have told her. Now she would die without knowing . . . but it didn't matter. He would die without saying it, so they were even.

"You know what burns me," Yarden was saying to her listener. Her voice came from just outside the curtained door. "I could have sworn that Orion Treet and I were friends—more than friends, if you know what I mean. I mean, I did everything I could to let him know how I felt. A girl can only do so much though. It was up to him to meet me halfway, but he never did."

"I can't understand it," the stranger's voice replied. "It was obvious to everyone else how you felt about him. But look at it this way—you're probably better off the way you are."

"Dead?" Yarden asked in mild surprise.

"No, I mean better off without him. He wasn't much after all. You could have done much better. You were young, you had lots of other opportunities."

"Had," huffed Yarden softly.

"Yes, had. Well, like you say, it can't be helped. You certainly did all you could. No one could have done more, I must say."

Treet groaned. Why were they talking like that? It was life and death they were talking about, not the price of eggs in Egypt. This was *his* life, *his* death—he wanted it treated with a little respect.

"Stop it . . ." he murmured.

But the voices went on talking in that odd, insane way. He could no longer distinguish the words, but he heard their buzz and at one point recognized Calin's voice among them—a man's voice, too, but not Crocker's or Pizzle's—his father's voice. They were all talking about him, about his miserable life and even more miserable death—he knew it and resented it. "Stop!" he said again, his voice rasping in a dry throat, the mere rush of wind over desert sand. "Stop, damn it!"

Treet pushed himself up on his elbows and inched toward the tent flap. His muscles, stiff and unyielding, trembled and resisted the feeble effort, which was, he knew, his final mortal act. They can't talk about me like that, he thought. I'm dying. It isn't right . . .

He flopped forward and reached the door, pushed his head through the curtain. Though it nearly exhausted his ebbing strength, he stretched his arms forth and hauled himself halfway through the opening, where he stopped. The air was cool on his skin, the light dim. Either it was getting dark or his eyesight was going, probably the latter. He didn't care. The voices stopped as he emerged from his room, he noted with grim satisfaction.

Good, he thought, I've given them something to think about. They didn't know I could hear them; now they'll think twice before writing anyone off quite so casually. But there was something else he wanted to do—one final thing. It was why he'd crawled out into the hallway. What was it? His head was no longer clear; the thoughts wouldn't come.

Fog-wrapped images played before him. He saw once again the face of his father, looking at him in frank disgust over a priceless M'yung Dynasty perfume jar smashed into smithereens. He was seven years old and had not meant to break the ancient thing; it slipped while he was looking at it. "You'll never learn, will you?" said his father. "You're hopeless."

It would have been better if his father had hit him, walloped him a good one for his clumsiness. That he could have accepted. But the once-and-for-all pronouncement was too severe and unremitting. There was no appeal.

"I'm sorry," breathed Treet. "S-sorry . . ."

The drone of the voices returned again, more insistent. He'd given them something to think about. Treet smiled, feeling his lips crack as the skin stretched. He tasted blood on his tongue. The taste brought him around somewhat—at least to the point of remembering why he had crawled from his death-bed. He had a message.

"Yar-den . . . I . . . love you."

Again the voices buzzed over his head. Dark spots swam in the air above him. Flies, he thought. Not voices . . . flies. They were only flies all along.

Pizzle heard the sound of his heart beating in his brain. It thumped with a droning monotony on and on and on. Beating, beating. Growing louder and ever louder. The sound reminded him of the Fieri airship's engines beating in his dreams—the airship that had passed over them, thus condemning them to death. The sound made him angry. His anger propelled him up through unconsciousness, fighting through layers of heaviness like a swimmer ascending from cold, obscure depths.

With an effort he pushed himself up on his elbows; Crocker lay beside him. Treet lay half in, half out of the tent. Both were still, barely breathing, the light inside the tent making their faces livid and grotesque.

He licked his lips with a thick, dry tongue. The sound of the thrumming engines persisted. Now it came from outside. The sound became a hateful thing—a mocking, ugly thing. He would silence it.

With a groan he lurched over Treet's body and out into bright sunlight, where he lay on his back with his arm flung over his face. But the sound, the sound of the airship engines, grew louder. He roused himself to look up.

The hot white sun dazzled his eyes. When his eyes could take the light, he saw an empty, uncaring sky, the blazing disk of the sun the only feature. As he watched, the sun went into eclipse. How strange, he thought, to witness a solar eclipse. I'm dying and I see an eclipse.

Since when do eclipses make noise? he wondered. Wait . . . wait . . . this is not right . . . Muddled thoughts surged around in his head. What is it? What is it about this that is not right?

Pizzle was on his feet now, swaying, peering through his shielding hands at the sun. An airship! It had to be. He had one more chance. One more chance to show the others, one more chance to survive.

He staggered to the tent and thrust his arm in, dragged out the sling, and opened it. Out tumbled the smoke canister he'd made. He picked it up and knelt over it. His eyesight wavered, but he forced himself to concentrate on jamming the wires down inside the container. He held the fragment of solar cell toward the sun and felt the wires grow warm in his hand.

Last time it had failed and he had let everyone down. It would not fail this time; he would not be the butt again.

"Go-o-o," he cooed, his voice a breeze through dry grass. "Ple-ease, go-o-o."

A fizzing sound came from the canister. "Go-o-o!" He willed the canister to ignite.

Smoke started pouring from the top of the cylinder. But it wasn't enough. The hole in the top was too small and only a thin, wispy trail of gray smoke emerged.

"No!" he cried, jerking the wires out. Pizzle grabbed the top of the canister, but the cone-shaped top was hot and the metal seared his hands. He yelped and dropped it in the sand.

He scooped it up again and scratched at the top, heedless of the hot metal or the pain. His fingernails tore, but the lid refused to budge. "Arghh!" he roared, scrabbling with his bloody fingers on the burning canister.

His hands were blistered now. The airship was closer, almost directly above him. He held the smoke bomb in the crook of one arm and braced it there, screaming in pain. "Ahh-hh!" He placed all four fingers on the ragged edge of the lid, gritted his teeth, and pulled. "Off! O-off-ff!" he cried in agony.

The stubborn lid finally loosened and spun off. Oxygen flooded in to touch the solid fuel inside, and the canister erupted like a small, mobile volcano.

F-f-f-whoosh!

Smoke and fire spurted out in a huge fireball that rolled up into the sky. Pizzle fell back, reeling, dazed, his face burned and blackened, his hair smoking.

The orange-and-black fireball rolled heavenward—up and up—higher and higher, passing right in front of the airship.

Pizzle rubbed the ashes of his eyelashes out of his eyes and looked up. The airship's shadow passed over him, and he saw it glide by. He fell back, exhausted by his futile last attempt.

It was then that he noticed the absence of sound.

He had gone deaf?

He shouted and heard his voice croak. No—not deaf! The

engines had stopped! He squirmed and rolled over on his stomach, raising his head weakly. The airship, totally silent now, was heeling majestically around. It was coming back!

Pizzle lay facedown in the sand and cried.

FIFTY THREE

"What do you think that is?" asked one of the Fieri pilots idly. He leaned over his instruments, gazing down at the immense white sheet of desert beneath them.

"Where?" his copilot responded.

"There—just off beamline to the south. I thought I saw something—a glint of color. It's gone now."

"You'd better tell Bohm."

"I don't know. It was probably nothing. You look too long and you start seeing things down there."

"I know what you mean. Still," the young man peered down at the dunescape as it rippled beneath the airship, "let's take it down a bit closer and see. Bohm's instructions are explicit."

"Do you really think they saw something?"

"Oh, they saw something. But they should have turned back to check it out."

"Would you? Look at it down there. As many times as I've flown this route I've never seen anyth—" He stopped in midsentence to watch a bright red-orange and black ball of flame billow up right in front of the craft. "Now that was something! I'm turning back. Get Bohm—I think we've found what he's looking for."

The Fieri airship hung like an enormous rusty moon above the two forlorn tents of the spent travelers. The rescue party had wasted not a second, deploying the survival cylinder the moment the airship hovered to a stop over the tents. Fieri physicians hit the sand running and quickly reached the dying wayfarer whose signal had alerted them. In the next fevered seconds, electrolyte fluids were administered and the condition of the patient was carefully noted. He was placed in the cylinder and whisked back to the airship, while the rescuers turned their attention to the women in the first tent.

The Fieri spoke softly to themselves, wondering how the fugitives could have come so far in the desert, remarking on their unusual, old-fashioned clothing, coaxing their patients to live just a little longer so they could be cared for properly aboard the airship.

They had been startled when one of the refugees, lying half out of the second tent, partially revived before they had a chance to minister to him.

"Get him out of the sun!" said Bohm, director of the rescue operation. "Quickly! Get him a stabilizer!"

"He's saying something," said Jaire, a young female physician. "Flies? I don't understand it."

"He's delirious. Here—you two," Bohm directed two aides, "help Jaire get him wrapped up. He will go after these two."

"There is one more inside this tent," said one of the aides.

"Bring him out. I'm almost finished here. Take these two to the cylinder. Gently, now." He touched a triangular tag dangling from an epaulet. "There are five. Three alive so far. Two are on their way up now. I want them started on fluid replacement and stabilization."

The Fieri leader hurried to the next tent, glancing at Treet as he passed. He peered into the face of the fugitive and whispered, "Infinite Father, guide our hands and minds; help us save them."

When all had been brought aboard, the airship, its engines booming echoes into the dune valleys, moved slowly off, gaining altitude as speed increased, leaving behind two orange tents and a scattering of footprints in the sand.

Considering what one had to go through to get there, death was not so bad. At least it was peaceful and the body no longer ached. There was even a muzzy sort of awareness—call it a phantom persistence of being that allowed inconsequential thought—little more than *I am . . . I am . . . I am . . .* over and over and over.

Most surprisingly, death was not black. It was red. Rather,

it was vermilion with clear blue highlights. And it was anything but the everlasting silence Treet had always believed it would be. Death was a clattering din, truth be told. There was a droning hum that drummed like an irregular heartbeat, an aggravating click like that of many steel balls smacking together simultaneously, and the sound of static electricity snap-crackling as from an oversized Leyden jar.

Were these the sounds of his own dissolution? He did not know. If not for the noise, he could have gotten used to it. But the incessant racket kept him from the quiescence of his insubtantial thoughts.

Treet opened one eye a crack. Surely that wouldn't hurt anything—being dead and all, one was allowed certain license, and as yet no one had read him any rules regarding the conduct of a corpse. He supposed that on opening his eye he would see that oft-described sight of his own empty husk of a body splayed where his soul had left it, staring blankly up into everafter, a poor advertisement for the tenacity and resilience of the human species.

Instead he saw a woman with long henna-colored hair tied back to grace a slender neck, bent as she peered into the screen of a machine, not much bigger than a common calculator, which was emitting all those annoying clicks. Treet liked what he saw, so he opened the other eye—fearing that so flagrant an action might cause an immediate forfeiture of his corpse status, but being unable to help himself anyway.

The woman sat perched atop a tall stool. She was dressed in a smock of sea-foam green with a loose, open jacket edged in blue. The jacket had deep pockets and a blue belt tied at the side, accenting the slimness of her waist. Her long legs were sheathed in soft white boots that laced to just below her pretty brown knees. Sunlight from an oval window flared her hair, making a halo of red gold around her head. A wisp of cloud trailed by the window, giving the impression of flight.

This must be an anteroom of the afterlife, thought Treet, complete with angel and cloud city.

Directly over him a cone-shaped instrument hummed and crackled with static electricity as a ruby light glowed from within it. He lay on a flat, padded table, his head held in position by a contoured pillow something like a sandbag. A white, gauzy cloth covered his loins or he would have been completely naked. Yet he was not cold. In fact, his skin glowed with the rosy hue of a sun-worshiping health freak, rather than the insipid pallor of the recently deceased.

The rest of the room, from what Treet could see without moving his head, was kept in shadow. But the shadows were uncluttered, and apparently he and the angel were alone. He worked his mouth and found that it moved quite easily, although it took a few moments for his voice to emerge. And when it did, he did not recognize the raspy wheeze as his own.

"Are you real?" he asked. The gummy film on his tongue tasted as if something nasty had crawled in his mouth and died.

The angelic being turned from the clicking screen and fastened concern-filled eyes on him. Her eyes were the exact color of her hair—ruddy brown with flecks of gold. Delicate arched brows drew together, and her lips pressed firmly in a frown of competent care. She reached a long-fingered hand toward him and placed it on his chest. Her hand was warm on his skin.

"Am I . . . dead?"

The frown turned into a light-scattering smile. "No," the angel laughed, her voice soft and full and throaty. "You are not dead, nor will you be for a very long time." Her speech was understandable, though colored with a light dialectal lilt which made it seem decidedly otherworldly.

"Oh," Treet whispered.

The angel touched his face with the back of her hand. "You sound disappointed."

Treet only stared upward into the lovely, flawless face, noting the sweep of her dark lashes and the silky smoothness of her cheek. He wondered what it would be like to look upon such perfection for an eternity. "No," he croaked finally, "not disappointed."

Just then a door opened somewhere in the room behind them. Treet felt a rush of cooler air that entered with the new arrival. "So, Jaire, our Wanderer is awake, eh?" said a sharp, trumpet tenor. "Has he said anything?"

The woman, Jaire, glanced up and smiled as a man with a cap of white frizzled hair came to stand beside her. Though he appeared well-aged, his muscles were firm, his skin supple. Vitality burst from his quick blue eyes like z-rays from uonium. Apparently there was no way to contain it—the life in the man simply overwhelmed its slight but sturdy container.

"Yes, Bohm, we have been talking about life." She winked at Treet. "He has decided to remain on this side of the Transformation."

"Was there ever any doubt?" said Bohm. He placed a ready hand on Treet's cheek, glanced at the cone-shaped instrument, gazed into Treet's eyes for a moment, and then declared, "The life force is stronger—no question about it." He looked at Treet and said, "Your Creator has seen fit to grace the world with your presence a little longer. Ours is the benefit."

Treet swallowed, then gagged. His tongue felt twice its size and sticky. A green cylinder appeared in Jaire's hands, and a curved straw was placed at Treet's lips. "Drink slowly," she instructed.

A cool, slick liquid slid down his throat, which felt like baked cardboard. "Thanks," he whispered, and drew in another lengthy sip. "What about the others?"

"Your friends are resting comfortably," said Bohm as Jaire pulled a thin sky-blue coverlet over Treet. "They are still asleep at the moment, but should awaken before we reach Fierra. Please, don't worry about them. Think no negative thoughts. Your trial is over. All will be well."

A little pinging sound came from another room. "Ah!" said Bohm, turning away. "Another has awakened to join us. I will look in and return when I can. Rest well, Wanderer." He patted Treet's shoulder as he went by. The door whished open, and he was gone.

"Bohm is a busy fellow," observed Treet, noticing the light in Jaire's clear eyes as she watched him. "We're on our way to Fierra, which means you must be Fieri."

"Yes," she replied, pleased, and a little surprised, Treet thought. "You know our ancestral name. Now you must tell me yours."

"My name is Orion Treet."

"Two names? Which do I call you—Orion or Treet?"

"Either."

"Then I will choose Orion. It has a mysterious sound." Her eyes sparkled merrily. "What does it mean?"

"What does it mean? Oh, it's the name of a great hunter whose image is remembered in the stars."

"A good name for you then," she said. She gazed at him with open admiration, making Treet feel like a rank impostor for presuming to use his own name. She reached down, pulled the coverlet up beneath his chin, and tucked it around his shoulders. "Bohm has said that you should rest. I will leave you now."

"No, don't. I wa—"

"I will be close by should you need anything. Rest now. Anyone who has come across the Blighted Lands needs all the rest he can get. Think no negative thought."

Jaire left quietly, and the lights dimmed as the door whished once again, leaving Treet in the soft light from the oval window. He closed his eyes. Yes, it felt good to rest. He would doze for just a moment before getting up.

FIFTY FOUR

The moment must have been a long one, for when he awoke again, the sky through the little oval window showed steel-blue dusk. He felt better than when he woke up the first time, so raised his head slowly from the table. The movement made him slightly woozy, but it passed almost immediately and Treet swung his legs over the edge of the table and stood up, draping the coverlet over one shoulder like a toga.

He tiptoed to the window and looked out. From his vantage point he surmised that he was in a Fieri airship, flying eastward at an altitude of about a thousand meters. It confirmed what he already knew to be true—that they had been rescued from the desert at the point of death by the Fieri and were now en route to the Fieri settlement.

Below, he could see a slice of landscape—not oyster white and dry as bone, but dark green and lush, and not the washed-out green of the hill country either—fertile looking, with gently mounded hills and shallow valleys filled with small round-topped trees. The silver blue threadwork of a river wriggled beneath the airship as it pushed its way through the lowlands. The rest was cloudless sky, sinking into twilight.

Treet heard the door slide open behind him and tightened his hold on the folds of his improvised toga. He turned to meet Jaire, standing in the doorway. "You are up, Orion. Good. Bohm thought you would be." She held out her arms, and he saw that she carried clothing. "I brought these for you to wear." She stepped closer, placing the bundle on the table. "When you are dressed, come out. I want to show you something."

"Thank you." Treet nodded. "I will."

He stared at the place she had stood long after she had gone. There was a woman worth getting to know on more intimate terms, he thought. I should be so lucky.

He shrugged off the toga and sorted through the pile of clothing she'd brought for him. There was a pair of loose-fitting underwear which he donned at once, and a pair of trousers of a softspun, loosely woven material, sandy colored, with a voluminous, three-quarter sleeved shirt to match. He put on the trousers, the pantlegs of which stopped well short of his calves, and then tried the shirt, discovering that it had no buttons. The next item from the pile was a wide, plum-colored sash. He took the shirttails and overlapped them around his waist—noticing that he'd lost every ounce of the life-support system he'd carried with him for the last thirty years—stuck the tails into his trousers and tied the whole works with the sash.

Next he perched on the edge of the table and drew on high boots, dove-gray in color, and made of a canvassy material. He pulled the corded laces tight and wrapped them around the top of the boots, stuffing the few centimeters of pantleg into the boot tops before tying the laces just below the knees. He stood, bounced on his heels a few times to get the feel of his boots, and decided he was ready to join the human race again.

He approached the door and put out a hand, only to have the thing slide open of its own accord. He stepped through to meet Jaire, waiting for him with her back turned, leaning a graceful hip against a rail. She tossed him a glance over her shoulder as he moved to the rail and saw that they were on a circular balcony overlooking a large, circular room. At intervals, short flights of stairs joined the balcony from below, where three male Fieri—each dressed similarly to Treet, except for the fact that they wore their shirttails out—engaged in various tasks related to flying the airship.

"Come with me," Jaire said, moving off along the rail. "How do you feel?"

"Much better," Treet said, taken aback by the grating rasp of his voice. "Though I sure don't sound like it."

"Bohm says that will pass." She put a hand to his elbow and led him around the circular railing to a bank of windows which curved both above and below the balcony, following the contour of the bulb-shaped nose of the craft.

"This is my favorite way to see Fierra," explained Jaire, "at dusk, just as the light of the city begins." They stopped at the first window. "See?" She indicated the view with a sweep of her hand. "Isn't it beautiful?"

Beautiful was not a strong enough word for it. Enchanting, was closer. Below them, unfolding as the airship descended slowly toward it, was a vast, gleaming city, winking like crystal in its own light. Treet's first impressions was of an entire plain sprung up with sparkling faerie castles, or of a glowing cathedral stretching endlessly for kilometers in every direction. It was a city of light—like nothing he'd ever seen, except perhaps in a dream.

He'd had the idea—from something he'd read in Feodr Rumon's *Interpretive Chronicles,* most likely—that the settlement of the Fieri was a simple encampment of mud huts or skin tents, more a wide place in the wilderness than an actual walls-and-pavement city. But this . . . this vision of splendor was simply beyond all expectation or imagining.

The airship swung closer, and Treet saw tall, freestanding towers with spires like needles, their points glowing like fiber-optic threads. He saw the sweeping arches of numerous bridges spanning a river that flowed through the city to merge with an enormous, shining lake—shining because fully half the city appeared to be built right out over the water. The mirrored surface glittered with golden light from wings and causeways stretching between luminous mansions. The jetties connecting these floating palaces were so numerous that they formed a glittering webwork—nets of light flung out over the royal-blue deep.

There were pavilions and courts and halls, groves and gardens and bright arcades joining plazas and parks. Meandering, tree-lined avenues wound through expansive residential districts whose dwellings radiated soft rosy light from high round domes.

Treet's eyes blinked in a prolonged visual gasp as his mind sought words to describe what he saw. Then they were descending to a great square marked by rows of blazing pylons. Flood-lights played over the spherical shapes of airships anchored in a hollow square formation.

Treet became aware of the voices of the airship's pilots as they communicated with the ground crew. Their forward progress halted, and the ship slid down vertically to its berth. The pylons rose up; the airship hovered, then kissed the ground . . . once . . . twice . . . coming to rest like thistledown upon a new-shaven lawn.

"What do you think of Fierra?" asked Jaire, regarding him with bright, amused eyes.

"I do believe I've died and gone to heaven," replied Treet in an awed whisper. "It's totally . . . unbelievable!"

His answer pleased her, he could tell. He was properly impressed and didn't mind letting her know. She smiled, took his elbow, and guided him away from the window toward the nearest ramp of stairs.

Bohm met them at the railing, beaming with keen intensity. "You look well, considering your test," he said. "I would easily mistake you for one of us—a Mentor, perhaps. Still, I hope you won't mind being noticed."

"Will I be noticed then?" asked Treet, catching an undercurrent of meaning in the old man's words.

"Most certainly you will be noticed. I have communicated with the Mentors. They are most anxious to greet you personally." He paused, waiting for Treet's reaction. When it was not forthcoming, he hurried on. "But all that can wait until you are feeling up to it. You and your companions are to be our guests, Orion Treet. I ask only that you recuperate and enjoy Fierra."

"I am in your debt." He turned toward Jaire and said, "I think I would recuperate much faster if I had someone to show me your impressive city."

"My father has already requested the honor," she said, linking her arm in his. "I will take you to my parents' pavilion on the lake—that is, if you wish."

"I wish." Treet smiled, then remembered his neglected companions. "Unless, of course, my friends and I would be too—"

"I have made separate arrangements for your friends," interrupted Bohm. "You are not to worry about them. They will be well cared for."

"Yes, I'm certain of it," agreed Treet. "It's just that I haven't seen them since we were rescued. I ought to check on them at least. Where are they?"

"Come with me," said Bohm, already leading the way. "If it will help ease your mind, I think you should see them."

One by one, Bohm led Treet into small rooms along the circular balcony. Each room had a padded table like the one Treet had awakened on, and the same conical hood above, making the same crackly static sound over the inert body of one of his companions. All were peacefully asleep—Pizzle was even snoring—and all appeared none the worse for being dragged bodily back from the very threshold of death's dark and silent gate.

The sight of Yarden comatose on the table sent a pang of guilt through his midsection.

"I hate to leave them," said Treet as he crept from her side.

"Maybe I should wait until they wake up and we can talk about this."

"If you prefer," said Bohm. "But that really isn't necessary. Besides, it could be several hours before they respond." He gave Treet a fatherly pat on the arm. "Please, allow me to take care of them for you. Go with Jaire, and do not concern yourself about their welfare."

Treet hesitated, but there was no reason to doubt Bohm's word. "All right, I'll leave them with you for the night."

"I will send word to you tomorrow about when you can all be together." Bohm ushered them down the stairs through the airship's command station, through an open hatchway, and down a short ramp to the landing field. The gigantic spheres of Fieri airships, looking like colossal mushrooms, each one tethered to a pylon, met his gaze as he set foot on the grassy field. "Good night, Wanderer. May you find in Fierra all that you are looking for."

"Good night. And thank you . . . thank you for saving my life," said Treet as Jaire took him into the softly glowing night.

FIFTY FIVE

"**I** think I'm going to like it here," said Treet. He and Jaire were riding along the wide boulevards of Fierra in a low, driverless two-seater which had met them at the airfield. Jaire had pressed a code into an alfanumeric pad and off they went, cruising silently through the city, guided by the vehicle's internal navigator.

Everywhere Treet looked he saw handsome people, some in silent cars like the one he and Jaire were riding in, but most afoot, going in and out of the glowing, dreamlike buildings, or thronging the generous walkways. Treet did not know which impressed him most—the Fieri or their architecture.

The people were on the whole tall and statuesque, with well-proportioned limbs and torsos, graceful in movement and aspect, their features fairly formed and expressive. In general appearance, they resembled the ancient Etruscan sculpture Treet had become enraptured with as a student—gods come to life. The women possessed a willowy femine allure that complemented the unadorned masculine vigor of the men. A more elegant race would be hard to find anywhere.

The architecture, on the other hand, was equally attractive in its own way. Whether clustered together in metropolitan communion, or standing alone on a favored acre, the buildings were individual works of art—given to upsweeping lines and simple, flowing curves, subtle tapers and clean edges. Apparently the Fieri were fascinated with spires, for nearly every structure possessed at least one, and usually more than one of the blade-thin towers. The effect was of an entire city straining heavenward, poised for imminent flight to the stars.

Most arresting, however, was the fact that the buildings themselves glowed. They were not transparently luminous, like some type of exotic glasswork, for the buildings appeared solid enough; but those same solid surfaces gave off soft, steady light.

Most of the Fieri habitations radiated a subdued rose-colored glow, but others shone topaz, pearl, and marbled blue and green, richer than the rarest peacock opal.

"What makes the buildings glow like that?" asked Treet, waving his hand toward a block of lambent residences. "Some kind of stone?"

"You're very astute," replied Jaire. "We use sunstone from the Light Mountains in the north. Nearly everything in Fierra is made of sunstone."

"It certainly creates an effect."

The car whisked them along through the city toward the lake—now crawling slowly through heavier traffic, now speeding over seamless causeways, the sponge-vinyl tires whispering on the pavement, the wind cool on their faces as it swirled around the low windscreen. The sky overhead faintly gleamed with relument luster—a ghostly aurora of reflected glory—making the night seem alive.

Treet took it all in—as much as he was able—in silence, too dazzled to speak, letting the panorama unfold around him as he moved through it until he was almost drunk with wonder. The alien beauty of the place made his head swim, and he sopped it up greedily. Soon, though, he felt his eyelids growing heavy as sleep snuck up to overtake him. He struggled to stay awake, but the long days in the desert had eroded his strength, and he had reached the end of his endurance for the day. Finally he let his head flop loosely on his chest and sank into sense-numbing slumber.

He was still asleep when they reached their destination: a spacious pavilion built on stilts over the lake, connected to the shore by a wide, curving jetty which served neighboring pavilions as well. The car crept to a halt in front of Jaire's parents' pavilion, and they were greeted by a slender young man who looked enough like Jaire to be her twin. Treet roused himself just enough to help them bundle him from the car and into the house.

He walked mechanically through a brightly lit interior, the details of which were fogged with sleep, and allowed himself to be stretched out on a soft pallet in a dark room, one side of which was completely open to the lake. There he was left alone, and he soon drifted to his dreams once more.

• • • • • •

The sun had turned the lake to burnished platinum by the time Treet awoke. He stirred and sat up suddenly when he remembered where he was. He looked around at a large square room devoid of furniture except for the bed and a stand on which were hung several outfits of clothes like the one he wore. The walls were buff-colored with broad borders of cinnamon, textured with an indented pebble grain. Two facing walls bore a curious printed design: a triangle with wings outspread, glowing from its center, sending out rays that become tongues of fire. The same design was printed over the curtained door.

A fresh breeze ruffled the loosely woven curtains at the open end of the room and flicked up small waves to lap against the pilings. Out on the silver-white water the curved scarlet sails of a sleek windrunner leaned into the breeze as the boat slashed through the water.

Without thinking about it, Treet found himself leaning his elbows on a balustrade on the walkway outside his room, staring out over the lake. The shoreline stretched in a long scimitar sweep into the distance; he could not see the opposite shore from where he stood, but reasoned that the body of water before him was more inland sea than lake. The air smelled fresh and clean, and Treet detected the citrus scent of orange blossoms.

His stomach growled, and he realized he had eaten nothing for quite some time—nothing that he could remember anyway. So he moved off along the balsutrade in search of some nourishment. At intervals above him were balconies with canopies affixed to crossed poles. No one appeared on any of the balconies as he passed by.

Treet reached the far side of the great house and turned the corner, continued on along a blank, sun-baked wall, turned again to pass through a breezeway between two freestanding wings of the house. A walkway joined the upper stories. He walked twenty paces and entered a huge courtyard, covered by a bright yellow canopy.

There Treet stopped. The pavilion was built around the courtyard, and it was easy to see that it was indeed the center-piece. Rooms opened directly onto it from every quarter, both on the house's upper and lower levels. Every square meter of the courtyard was filled with plants of the most outlandish varieties. The yard was a veritable jungle of exotic vegetation: all in shades

of deep blue-green, with waxy leaves and spiraling, fleshy-pod-
ded tendrils and wild iridescent flowers.

The canopy overhead formed a lemon-tinted sky and was
made of the same open-weave cloth as the floor-length curtains
in his room, allowing the sun's rays to fall through the loose
pattern of the weave. It rippled like a parachute in the breeze off
the lake, causing hot, bright spots of sunlight to flitter like
phosphorescent butterflies over the plants and shrubs and painted floor tiles of the courtyard.

Treet gazed at the lush profusion around him and took a
step forward, nearly treading on the tail of a creature which at
first glance appeared to be the largest black leopard in captivity.
The animal turned its massive head toward him, winked huge
green eyes, and lazily withdrew paws the size of dinner plates. It
yawned at him, showing a furrowed pink tongue and a double
row of shining white triangular teeth like shark's teeth, then slid
down to lay on its lightly spotted stomach, stretching muscled
legs out into the greenery, effectively blocking the pathway beyond.

Taking a long, slow step backward, Treet attempted to
remove himself from the animal's presence. He backed two
paces and bumped against something that felt like a fur-covered
fireplug. Looking down, he discovered another creature identical to the one directly in front of him. This second one raised a
paw and took a swat at him, missing by only millimeters. Before
he could dodge away, the next swipe hit his thigh and spun him
around and down. The great leopard thing grinned at him and
put its head forward, licking velvet lips.

"Hsoo!" Jaire shouted from the upper gallery. Treet glanced
up to see her staring down, hands on hips. "What do you think
you're doing? Let him up at once. He's a guest!" She dashed for a
stairway.

The giant panther cocked its head and came closer to
nuzzle his prize, sniffing Treet indiscreetly. "Hey!" cried Treet
involuntarily. The next thing he knew he was being licked in two
directions at once—one beast slurping left to right, the other
right to left. "Hey-y-y!"

"Jomo! Hsoo! Stop this instant! He's a guest. Leave him
alone and let him up." Jaire arrived in a flurry of exasperation,
grabbed the foremost of the two creatures, and dug her hands
into its thick black pelt, pulling with all her might. The animal

allowed itself to be diverted and moved off sedately. "You, too, Hsoo. Go take a swim or something. You're not to bother Orion again."

Treet watched the two animals lumber off, their hides bunching and smoothing over rippling muscles. "I'm glad they weren't hungry," he remarked.

"They're such nuisances sometimes, but don't worry. They eat only fish, so they're not really dangerous."

"Except to fish."

Jaire laughed, filling the air with a shimmery ring. "I don't think they'll likely mistake you for a fish. Wevicats are highly intelligent. *Too* smart I often think. Jomo and Hsoo know what effect their appearance has on strangers. They were playing a joke on you."

"I'll remember to laugh next time," said Treet, trying to think of another question just to keep his beautiful companion talking. I could listen to that lilt forever, he thought. Jaire led him along the green pathway through the courtyard to a wide entrance on the ground floor. "Are there any more creatures lurking around I ought to steer clear of?"

"Only old Bli, but he's a rakke."

"A what?"

"Rakke—a water bird. He's ill-tempered, but likes to stay close to his perch in the sun, so you probably won't run into him." She looked at Treet closely. "I know I'm not supposed to ask, but don't they have animals in Dome?"

"Dome? You mean the colony—Empyrion?"

"This is Empyrion." She waved a graceful hand to indicate the whole world. "What do you call the Dread City?"

Treet stared at her and scratched his head. "Are we talking about the same place? The colony? Bubbletown?"

Jaire nodded uncertainly. "Y-yes . . . I think so."

"Is that where you think I came from?"

"Where else?"

I could tell you, but I don't think you'd believe me, thought Treet. Instead he replied, "Who said you weren't supposed to ask me about it?"

"My father," she replied. "In fact, he's waiting to see you. I was on my way to find you." They entered the pavilion and moved across a spacious, polished floor to a smaller receiving room.

"Ah, at last I meet my guest. Welcome to my home, Orion

Treet." The voice was *basso profundo,* a rumble of rich and operatic sound. Treet glanced up to see a very large man dressed much as he was with the addition of a long sleeveless coat over his shirt. The pattern worked into the sea-green cloth was light gold—intricate interwoven arabesques that glittered dully. His tall boots were dark brown, matching his dense, curly beard. There was a thick band of lustrous gold metal around his neck.

The man crossed the room in three strides, moving quickly for a person of such size. He held out both hands to Treet as he came close. Treet did not know what to do, but reached out and took the hands—and had his own wrung severely. "I am Talus, Mentor of Fierra. My daughter you have met already; this is my son, Preben."

Treet blinked and saw that a younger man accompanied Talus. The younger man was an exact duplicate of Jaire, only done up in male flesh, with unmistakably male features and attributes.

"My brother," Jaire said, "you met last night, though I don't think you would remember."

Treet gripped Preben's hands too, and said the first thing that came into his head. "Yes, I've met you both before—by various names: Zeus and Apollo, Poseidon and Ares, Odin and Thor . . ." He realized what he was saying and broke off. "Forgive me for rambling on. I—ah, did not mean any disrespect."

Talus nodded gravely, studying him. Measuring me for a straitjacket, thought Treet. But then his host smiled and laughed, the sound a merry earthquake. "Your words are strange, but there is no offense in them. I think the Mentors will enjoy you."

"Were they friends of yours?" asked Preben.

"Zeus and Apollo? Yes, in a way," replied Treet, feeling more at ease. "They were friends of my youth."

"How are you feeling?" asked Talus. "My daughter tells me that you were very near death when they rescued you. No one to my knowledge has ever traveled across the Blighted Lands and lived."

"I guess we were lucky." Treet shrugged. "We didn't have much choice."

"Luck? Ha!" Talus said sharply. "The Protector Aspect was full on you, or you would not have survived." He softened, apparently remembering the welcome he'd just extended. "But we will discuss all that later. I imagine you are hungry, so let's not waste time better served eating."

Jaire chimed in, "I've already prepared the food. Mother will be waiting for us."

"I will serve," said Preben. He ushered them through the wide entrance, through a great hall to a smaller room at one end. Inside, at a huge table covered with a cream-colored cloth edged in silver, a slightly older, more mature Jaire was arranging an overflowing bower of plants in a basket with deft, quick motions of her hands. "Mother," announced Preben, "our guest has joined us."

The woman looked up, a smile lighting her eyes. "Welcome! I see you have met my family. Now I too have the pleasure of meeting you. I am Dania."

Treet suddenly felt quite formal. "Yours is a most gracious home," he said stiffly. "I hope my presence is not an intrusion."

She smiled again, looked at her husband, and then back at Treet, saying, "Such intrusions are all too rare here at Liamoge." She absently tucked a wayward flower back in place and straightened. "Sit here in the honor seat," she patted the back of a graceful chair, "that I may serve you myself."

It was an awkward moment for Treet, being seated by a woman while the others stood looking on. Dania then took up an oval platter and, as Preben offered each in turn, began filling it with food from the various vessels on the broad table. She placed it before him and reached for her own platter. Treet waited until all were seated, using the time to study his plate.

There was sliced meat—pink like ham or rare roast beef—pale yellow cheese, a salad of chopped pulpy fruit, miniature loaves of dark bread, chunks of fish marinated with vegetable pieces in a pungent sauce, steaming lumps like orange speckled potatoes, something that looked like pasta in the shape of a horn (stuffed with cheese, bread, and spiced meat and covered with red gravy), and four tiny cakes glazed with green frosting. It all looked delicious to Treet; he sucked his teeth to keep himself from drooling.

When all had been seated, Treet picked up his fork—a two-pronged utensil with a carved stone handle. He was about to spear a slice of meat when Talus raised both hands and, with eyes fixed on a point on the ceiling, said, "Receive our thanks, faithful Provider. Your blessings spill over us like the rains in Rialea, and we praise Your many hallowed names." Lowering his eyes once again, he smiled and said, "Eat! Enjoy! The blessing of the Provider is given."

They all dug in. Treet ate with abandon, giving himself to the task with an enthusiasm that would have been considered rude in polite company, if not for the fact that his hosts matched him nearly stroke for stroke. Forks flashed, and teeth chewed, and food dwindled on the platters. No one spoke until Talus, midway through his second helping, said, "Life is good always, but best at table. Don't you agree?"

"Mosht shertainly," Treet mumbled around a mouthful of bread. The food was excellent—apart from the fact that even leek gruel and dried crusts would have tasted like *haute cuisine* after weeks of dried eel. Despite his long deprivation, Treet's taste buds registered a meal that would have thrown the staff of any five-star restaurant into contortions of envy.

Talus rose, grasped a large pitcher, and proceeded around the table, filling tall white-gold goblets with a light green liquid. When he finished, he replaced the pitcher and, still standing, lifted his goblet into the air. "To new friends!" he cried, beaming at Treet from behind his bushy beard. "There is nothing so fine as a new friend, for in time they become the most precious of all the Comforter's gifts—old friends!"

He put his goblet to his lips and drank deeply. All at the table followed his example. The liquid was tart and refreshing, like lemon water, but leaving a piquant hint on the back of the palate, like anise. Treet let the beverage roll over his tongue and kept his nose in his cup after everyone else had come up for air.

Preben stood and said, "To new friends! May they stay long, and leave only to cheer us with their quick return."

They all drank to Preben's toast and then turned to Treet. He stood, and in order to give himself more time to think of an appropriate toast for the occasion, picked up the pitcher and proceeded to fill the goblets of the others himself. Talus protested gracefully, but smiled with satisfaction as Treet worked around the table. He refilled his own goblet last and lifted it high. "To new friends," he said, looking at each one in turn. "May hearts beat fondly, life flow richly, and time pass slowly when they are together."

They finished the meal with a sweet cordial that tasted of spiced cherries. Jaire and Preben dismissed themselves, confessing pressing errands, and Talus and Dania led Treet to a grouping of cushioned chairs in a nearby corner of the courtyard. They sat down together, and Treet waited patiently while his hosts gazed at him for some moments in silence.

Is this where they give me the bad news? he wondered. Sorry, big fella, we're going to use your brain for fish food. He had been waiting for the other shoe to drop ever since he had awakened aboard the airship. Surely, no one was as kind, thoughtful, charitable as these Fieri—especially to strangers. There had to be a catch somewhere. They wanted something from him, or they intended using him in some way. But what could they want? How could they use him?

FIFTY
SIX

Talus fingered his beard and slumped in his chair, looking like a king settling back on his throne for a season of thought. At last he spoke, his voice a low rumble in his deep chest. "I imagine there is much that you have to tell us," he said.

Here it comes, thought Treet; this is it. He tried to gaze unconcernedly back.

"Here I must ask your indulgence."

Yep, thought Treet, they're up to something. "What indulgence is that?" he asked innocently.

"Only this: that you save your story for the College of Mentors. We would all very much like to hear it, and it is our opinion that repeating it too often will distort it."

That was nothing like what Treet had been expecting. He said, "If that's what you want, Talus. However, I want you to know that I wish to keep nothing from you. Whatever I can tell you, I will tell you freely."

"Could you come with me this evening?"

"This evening?"

Dania remarked, "If you knew, Orion Treet, how much this request chafed Talus, you would understand his eagerness. The Mentors are curious boys, despite all their dignity. If it had been up to them, they would have had you before them the moment you stepped from the balon. But the Preceptor thought differently, so you were brought here that you might refresh yourself first." She paused and glanced at her husband, then back at Treet. "You are not to meet with them until you feel ready, and that you must decide for yourself."

This is weird, thought Treet. Are they trying to smother me with kindness? Is this some sort of test? What are they after?

"Dania is right to remind me of the Preceptor's wishes. I merely thought . . . if you are feeling well enough . . . that you might—"

"Talus, leave our guest alone. You are as bad as Jomo and Hsoo in your own way."

Treet smiled emptily, looking from one to the other of them. He made the best answer he could. "I have no wish to leave your gracious home so soon. But I would be happy to repay the kindness you've shown me in any way I can. If answering your questions will help, so be it."

He tried to be sincere—he certainly was not misrepresenting his true feelings. He was grateful to be alive and happy to help those who had helped him. But he felt awkward at the same time, as if he were betraying someone by being too cooperative or aiding and abetting a suspected enemy. Why should I feel that way? he wondered.

The answer came back: perhaps I just don't understand true generosity of spirit when I see it. I'm not used to it; it makes me nervous, and things that make me nervous make me wary.

"There is one other thing," Treet added. "I'd like to see my friends as soon as possible."

"They are being cared for," said Dania. "I chose the receiving homes myself. Their welfare must not concern you."

"Their welfare, no—I know they're in good hands. It's just that they may worry about *me*. They might wonder where I am, or think I've deserted them or something, you see."

"Think no negative thought in this regard," said Talus. "All is well, I assure you."

"Still, I'd like to see them," said Treet. Talus and Dania glanced guiltily at one another. "Is there some reason I can't?"

"The Preceptor has asked that you be kept apart from one another. We are obeying these instructions," Talus admitted.

"Oh." His frown must have given away his negative thoughts.

"Please, trust us in this," said Dania quickly. "Our Preceptor is a very wise and revered leader. Your welfare is our only concern. You'll see."

"You mean I can't see anyone until after my interview with the . . . College of Mentors, is it? Anyway, I can't see them until then?"

"It would be best." Talus nodded gravely.

"What if I refused?" Treet didn't like saying that; it seemed like a dirty trick. But he had to know.

"That would be unfortunate . . ."

Ah ha! thought Treet. At last we come to it. The velvet dagger in the neck. "I thought so," replied Treet. "I should have kn—"

Before he could finish, Talus continued, ". . . because it would disappoint the Preceptor. She knows what you have gone through, and she has suggested this rule for your welfare."

"What do you mean exactly?"

"She understands what life must be like in Dome. She is anxious that none of you feel threatened by the others." To Treet's puzzled look, he said, "She wants each of you to be able to speak freely and openly with us. To ensure that, she has asked that you be kept apart until each has had opportunity to speak."

Understanding dawned slowly on Treet. "You mean that if one of us had some hold over the others, he wouldn't have a chance to reassert his power or make threats or whatever. I see. Yes, very smart." Smart from several points of view. They wouldn't be able to compare stories either, if by some chance they meant mischief—spies on an espionage mission, for instance.

"It is for the best," offered Dania. "I hope you see the justice of it."

"I guess I do," replied Treet. "Very well. Let's do it tonight then. We'll get it over with, and that way I can see my friends that much sooner."

Talus leaped to his feet so fast it made Treet jump up too. "Good! Good! I will notify the Clerk of the College at once, and he will arrange it." He bounded off, leaving Treet a little dazed, wondering what he had acquiesced to.

Oh well, not to worry—think no negative thought, he reminded himself. I'll find out soon enough.

Treet spent the rest of the day in the agreeable company of Jaire, who looked after him like a combination nurse-and-private-tour-guide. She led him from room to room in the great house, showing him the various *objets d'art* and items of interest in each. Treet's respect and admiration multiplied as the day went on. It was clear that the Fieri were possessed of immense artistic talent and took that talent and their art seriously. For every room contained at least one object—a carving or painting or metal etching—which would have been a museum centerpiece anywhere on Earth.

The house itself was a work of art: large, spacious, conceived on a grand scale, yet not overbearing or gauche for its size. The furniture—what there was of it, for the Fieri apparently liked their interiors Spartan—and other appointments were simply designed in the same clean, uncluttered style. Each piece of furniture or work of art became an integral part of the room. And each room appeared exquisite in conception and execution individually, and at the same time part of a greater whole.

About the time they completed the tour, Treet heard Talus' voice booming from the lower level. "Jaire! Bring our guest to the entrance. The evee will be here soon."

"We have to go now," said Jaire apologetically, looking at him candidly with her deep brown eyes. "I hope you were not bored by my discourse."

"Most enjoyable. I would not have missed a moment of it. I only wish I didn't have to leave so soon."

"My father is anxious for you to make your appearance. For many years he has been urging the Mentors to establish contact with Dome," she said as they made their way to the main entrance of the pavilion. "He thinks it would be highly beneficial."

"I see," said Treet thoughtfully. "I don't see how I can help, but I'll try. Tell me about these Mentors."

Jaire shrugged. "What can I tell you? They are men and women who serve Fierra."

"What do you think they want to hear from me?"

Jaire did not have time to answer, for they had descended to the entrance. Talus came forward, snatched Treet by the arm, and all but dragged him outside where one of the Fieri's small driverless vehicles was at that moment rolling to a stop—this one slightly larger than the one that had brought Treet to Liamoge.

Preben stepped forward and opened the single door on the side of the sleek car, helped Treet and Talus climb in, and then entered himself, folding down a jumpseat in front. With a nod from his father, the young man entered the destination code into the keypad on the dash, and the car slid quietly away.

The sun was lowering and would soon dip beneath the western rim, leaving the sky whitewashed blue and radiant, but fading quickly. The evee swept along the causeway over smooth, chrome-colored water, past numerous pavilions—some larger, some smaller than Talus' home, but all the same lackluster gray. The sunstone gave no hint of its coming transformation.

Closer to the heart of the city, traffic thickened. Other driverless vehicles sped along beside them. Treet noticed that the evee adjusted its speed according to the traffic patterns around it. Most of the vehicles appeared to be heading toward the same destination: a great seven-sided obelisk surrounded by a half-circle of smaller obelisks and set on an expanse of rising land amidst a carefully tended grove of miniature trees.

The evee swung into a long circular drive at the foot of the rise below the edifice, and they disembarked, joining the throng moving up the hill. With the lowering sun directly behind the obelisk, scattering the last of the sun's rays, the slim spike seemed to become a spacecraft lifting from its launching pad on a burst of white fire. Men and women were disappearing behind the standing ring of smaller stone obelisks, and coming closer Treet saw that a steep hollow had been dug in front of the main structure, forming an open-air amphitheater. Fieri were streaming down into the amphitheater, taking seats along the stair-step sides.

Treet and his companions approached the standing stones, passed between them, and descended into the amphitheater. Only then did Treet remember that he was the featured speaker for the evening. The realization gave him a sudden case of stage fright. His palms grew clammy, and his stomach fluttered; his feet stumbled as he moved down the narrow aisle. He felt instantly awkward and forgetful, afraid to open his mouth—whatever might come out was beyond his control.

Talus apparently sensed his discomfort, for he put a large hand on Treet's shoulder, leaned close, and whispered, his voice small thunder, "Be at ease. All you see here are your friends. They wish you well."

"I wish there weren't so many."

"Ordinarily there would not be this large a gathering. But you and your friends have stimulated our interest, so we are meeting in the amphidrome tonight. I'll stay with you every moment."

They made their way down to the floor of the amphidrome and found seats on the first row. Preben excused himself and disappeared as two men came hustling up, one white-haired, the other dark-haired but with a beard graying in the center and at the edges. Both wore faded blue cloaks over their clothes. The white-haired one Treet recognized as Bohm, whom he had met at the airship. Bohm spoke first, greeting Treet and Talus, and presenting the stranger to Treet. "Orion Treet, allow me to introduce you to Mathiax, Clerk of the College of Mentors."

The man's bright eyes glittered with excitement as he extended both hands, palms upward in the manner of the Fieri. Treet took the hands and squeezed them, saying, "I am pleased to meet you, Mathiax."

The Clerk nodded and glanced at Bohm, his expression stating emphatically, Oh, this is really something. He even speaks our language! Treet felt like a lab specimen on display, a feeling that escalated with each passing second. But when Mathiax replied, it was in the warm, intimate tone of one trusted confidant to another. "You must forgive us our ebullience at your expense. We sometimes forget ourselves in our haste to embrace new awarenesses."

These people are so polite, considered Treet, so formal, so different than I expected. It's hard to believe they share the same common ancestry as those who live in Dome.

"I am only too happy to—ah, serve in any way I can."

Mathiax nodded happily and said, "We will begin in just a few minutes. I want to be certain all are here, so if you will excuse me . . . Talus, you will act as Prime Mentor this evening. I will give you the signal when it is time to begin."

With that he and Bohm left, hurrying off together. Treet heard the Clerk say to Bohm, "Yes, I see what you mean . . ." as they passed from earshot.

"Please be seated," said Talus, lowering himself to a seat. He patted the one next to him with his hand. "Relax. There is nothing to be concerned about. You will do well."

Treet sat down absently, scanning the rapidly filling amphidrome in the process. "How does this work?" he heard his voice asking.

"This?" Talus waved a hand to the rows of spectators. "A conclave is a general session of all Mentors and certain invited guests who have an interest in the subject area under investigation."

"Am I under investigation then?"

Talus wagged his head earnestly. "No, no. We only want to hear what you can tell us."

"What can I tell you?"

"What you know." Talus seemed about to elaborate further when Preben arrived with a blue cloak for his father. The big man put it on and was about to sit down once more when the clear pealing tone of a bell rang in the air, a pure and beautiful note as if rung from a crystal bowl. "Ah, that is the signal." He smiled and rubbed his heavy hands together. "At last we can begin."

Talus stepped out onto the floor of the amphidrome and held up his hands. The audience grew silent instantly, as if the sound had been switched off a holovision. He raised his re-sounding voice in a brief invocation to someone or something called the Seeker Aspect. Treet did not catch all the words—he was too busy wondering what he would say to all these people who had turned out to see him. Had he known he would draw such a crowd, he might have prepared a speech, or maybe sold tickets.

Then Talus was saying his name and waving him forward. Two high-backed stools were produced by aides in green cloaks. As Treet climbed into the nearest one, his aide pressed a dia-mond-shaped tag onto the front of his shirt. In the center of the tag a glittering bit of glass or crystal winked in the early twilight. The obelisk rising behind them held a golden luster as if the sun were striking its surface, though the sun had set behind it. The sunstone was beginning its night's work of converting Fierra into a city of light.

Talus nodded at Treet encouragingly. Treet turned his eyes to all the faces peering down at him from the rising gallery, fierce in their intensity, expectant. What could he say to them? What had they come to hear?

"Go on," whispered Talus. "Don't think about it, just say what the Teacher puts into your mind to say."

Okay, thought Treet. Here goes nothing. He swallowed hard and opened a mouth gone suddenly dry. "I am—" he croaked, and heard the echo of his amplified voice ripple through the amphidrome. The Mentors waited, leaning forward in their seats. He took a deep breath and plunged in headfirst.

"My name is Orion Treet, and I come to you from a world beyond your star . . ."

FIFTY SEVEN

When Treet finished speaking, it was very late. The sky over the amphidrome glimmered with its ghostly aurora, through which the stars winked like jewels from behind a shimmering veil. The assembled Mentors sat in awed silence, gazing upon this mysterious stranger who had materialized in their midst. Treet expected questions to come thick and fast, but the crystal bell tolled once more and the entire gathering rose and began climbing the steps, filing quietly from the amphidrome to disappear into the night.

Treet breathed a long sigh of relief for having survived his ordeal. He'd told them, as simply as he knew how, nearly everything—which was more than he'd planned on telling, certainly. But once he'd gotten started he hadn't known where or how to stop, so he dumped it all out—everything from the arrival of their transport to their rescue by the airship.

Talus rose from his stool on Treet's right hand and came to him. "Do you think they'll vote for me?" asked Treet.

"I do not understand," said Talus, shaking his head slowly. "Much of what you said I do not understand."

"Never mind. What about the parts you do understand?"

"Those I find most disturbing."

"You don't believe me?"

"No, I believe you. No one could speak as you do if it were not true. And that is what troubles me."

"I think my friends will tell similar stories," pointed out Treet.

"Again, I believe you. Understanding—that is another matter entirely."

Just then the busy Clerk came running up. He shoved a folded card toward Talus. "This has just come from the Preceptor."

Talus took the card, unfolded it, glanced at it, and handed it to Treet. "Your presence is requested. At once."

Was it something I said? wondered Treet

They whisked along the near-deserted streets of Fierra. Over delicate arches and through brightly lit tunnels, past open markets and blocks of dwellings, along thoroughfares lined with glowing pylons they went—Talus and Treet accompanied by Preben and Mathiax. Treet could tell by the long sideways glances he was receiving from the others that they were dying to ask him some of the millions of questions that were bubbling up inside their brains like lava from a hot volcano. Mercifully, they let him sit quietly and watch the enchanted city slide past.

"There is the Preceptor's palace," said Mathiax, pointing to a many-tiered pagoda rising from a clump of trees ahead. The evee slowed as it turned into a narrow lane, and the Preceptor's palace swung full into view, glowing, thought Treet, with a rosy luster like those floodlit castles that were so popular with the postcard crowd. The drive ended a few meters inside the grounds, and the vehicle stopped. The passengers got out and made their way across a wide, dark lawn, spongy underfoot with thick vegetation.

Two Fieri, one male and one female, met them at the open entrance to the palace. Both were dressed in a high-necked jacket with deep sleeves and a large triangular patch of bright silver over the heart. On the patch was a symbol Treet could not make out. It looked like a ring of circles, each one blending into the next, yet somehow separate from the others. The image appeared to be spinning so that each time he tried to look directly at it, the symbol blurred and shifted.

The male attendant held out his hand, and Talus placed the folded card on his palm. "Thank you for attending our request," said the woman. She smiled warmly. "You will find our Preceptor awaiting you in the audience room. I will be glad to show you the way."

"No need," said Mathiax. "I know how to find it."

"As you wish," she said and waved them through.

The Clerk led them up three levels on a sweeping spiral staircase to an enormous room that took up nearly the entire third level. "This is the reception hall," explained Talus as they trooped across the threshold. The interior of the hall was lit by several large columns of sunstone, which cast a soft, rose-tinted light all around.

Treet thought, upon entering the reception hall, that the room was empty, but then saw a tall, slender figure standing before heavy, floor-to-ceiling curtains worked in designs of green and gold. The Preceptor wore a short copper-colored robe over silver knee-length trousers. The robe was cinched at the waist by a silver belt; silver boots met the trousers at the knee. Yellow sunstone chips glimmered in a wide silver band around a graceful throat.

The Preceptor waited for them to come close, her long, fine hands clasped in front of her, gazing intently at them as they crossed the polished expanse of floor, their footsteps tapping the stone. She smiled as they came to stand in front of her, extending her hands to Treet, and then to the others in turn, saying, "I realize you must be tired. You do your leader a kindness by coming at this late hour. I won't keep you long."

She stepped lightly to the curtain and pulled it back. The audience room was a small chamber concealed behind the draperies. They filed into the room, and the Preceptor entered, waving them to long, low divans arranged in the center of the room. She seated herself across from Treet and gazed at him with intense violet eyes that probed his directly. He realized that if he remained very long in this woman's presence, he would have no secrets left. Those eyes—hard and bright as amythests, set in a face of intriguing angles above a straight, aquiline nose and a strong, almost masculine jaw—would pierce like lasers anything that did not yield instantly to them.

"I listened to your story," she began. "I was much amazed by all you said."

"You heard me?" It was a dumb question, but it was out before Treet could stop it.

She pointed to the badge still stuck to the front of his shirt. "My crystal is tuned to receive sympathetic vibrations. I heard every word." She studied him for a moment, as if making up her mind about him. Then she said, "No one has ever come across the Daraq. The few who risk the journey die in the attempt. We find them, but always too late."

"Others have come before us?"

"Not many. And not for a very long time. But the Protector

went with you, and the Sustainer watched over you until we could send a balon to rescue you. Therefore, we can assume that the Infinite Father has a purpose in sending you here."

Treet sat still. He had nothing to say on that score. The Preceptor continued, "We must find out what that purpose is so that we may fulfill it. Would that be agreeable to you?"

"Yes, of course," said Treet. "What do you want me to do?"

"Stay with us, learn our ways. My kinsmen Mathiax and Talus will guide you, and all of Fierra will be open to you. Then, when the All-Wise reveals His purpose, teach us."

"That's it? That's all you want me to do?"

The Preceptor nodded slightly. "Yes. What more is required than that we fulfill our spiritual purpose?"

"Can I see my friends?"

"If you wish. Your love for your friends is commendable. But it would be better if you wait until each of your friends has spoken before the Mentors. However, this is a request I make, not a precept. You are free to do as you will."

"Talus explained your request to me. I accept it, although I'd like to point out that I hold nothing over any of the others."

"But they might hold power over you."

Treet considered this, and rejected it. "No, there's nothing like that at all. I'd know about it, wouldn't I?"

"Perhaps not. Power comes in many subtle forms, some most difficult to recognize."

Treet saw that he was getting nowhere, and decided to abide by the Preceptor's request. "I don't mind waiting. May I send a message to them?"

She shook her head imperceptibly. "They already know that each of the others has been saved and that all are being cared for. I know it is difficult, but have patience—you will all be together again soon."

It occurred to Treet that he'd heard a similar promise recently; Supreme Director Rohee had mouthed words to the same effect, and look what happened. He had been lying. Was the Preceptor also lying? Before Treet could wonder further, she rose, signaling an end to the audience. Mathiax, Talus, and Preben, none of whom had said a word throughout the interview, stood and extended their hands. The Preceptor clasped hands and spoke a few intimate words with each one before they were ushered from the private chamber, back across the empty reception hall, and down the spiral staircase and out into the dwindling night.

It will be dawn in a few hours, Treet thought. And in a few hours I resume my career as a sponge.

He should have been ecstatic at the prospect of probing into the secrets of the Fieri—delving into exotic cultures was his life, after all—but there was something missing. Something had a name, and the name was Yarden.

He walked out onto the darkened lawn, heavy with bitter disappointment. He puzzled over the feeling and realized that subconsciously he had been hoping up to the very moment of their dismissal by the Preceptor that he would see Yarden. He would turn a corner and she would be there, or he would enter a room to find her waiting. The whole time he had been with the Preceptor, he had been hoping Yarden would step unexpectedly from behind the curtain.

Without knowing it, he had been waiting to see her. Now he knew that he would not—at least not for several more days. The thought depressed him.

By the time they reached the waiting evee, Treet was in such a black mood that he sat sullen and silent all the way back to Liamoge, staring blankly at the bright wonders of Fierra. They had, for the moment, ceased to hold any charm for him.

FIFTY
EIGHT

"The thing you keep forgetting," said Mathiax, looking directly at Treet, his fingers combing through his graying beard, "is that each and every Fieri is aware of the Infinite Presence at all times. We are permeated with this awareness—it informs all we do."

Treet thought about this. Yes, in the last several weeks he'd certainly seen evidence of this awareness Mathiax was talking about. "I understand your religion is very important to you, but are you telling me that it even influences your technology?"

"Why not? Why should that be so hard to accept?" Mathiax leaned forward and tapped Treet on the arm. "Let's walk a bit further—it's good for the brain."

They were sitting on an empty stretch of beach by the silver lake. They had been walking most of the day, stopping to rest and discuss, moving on when they reached an impasse in communication or came to a subject which required additional thought in order to translate it into terms Treet could properly understand. Mathiax was a quick and able teacher, and it had been his idea to take Treet out away from the city to walk along the lakeside for part of each day's session. "Less distraction," he'd said. This gave Treet time to assimilate what he'd seen and heard before returning to Talus' pavilion.

In three weeks' time Treet had learned much about the Fieri. Most of it had to do with their simple religion. Apparently everything the Fieri did or thought was in some way rooted in this intense spiritual awareness Mathiax had been describing. The Fieri religion was not difficult; its central tenet could be summed up quite simply: A Supreme Being existed who insisted on concerning Himself with the affairs of men in order to draw them into friendship with Him.

That was the basic idea, plainly stated. The Fieri believed that this Being was a pure spirit who expressed Himself in many different personality modes or Aspects. They recognized any number of the Aspects—Sustainer, Protector, Teacher, Seeker, Creator, Comforter, Gatherer, and so on. But all were merely individual expressions of the One, the Infinite Father, as they called Him.

Treet got the idea that they were a little reluctant to pin the Deity down to one name or expression. They preferred a much more flexible and elastic approach. But although they spoke of Him in many different ways, depending on what they wanted to say about Him, it was always understood that to invoke one Aspect implied all the rest. The Infinite Father was One, after all, indivisible and ultimate in every sense.

This was the Fieri doctrine—not complicated or obtuse, but ripe with enormous implications. For once a person accepted the idea that the Infinite Father of the entire universe actually desired commerce with individual men, literally no sphere of mortal endeavor was untouched. Each and every thought and action had to be examined in light of an expressed partnership with an infinite and eternal patron.

These were not utterly new ideas, Treet knew. There were several Earth religions that espoused the same general themes. The difference here, as far as Treet could tell, was that the Fieri's beliefs had created a vital, thriving society of nearly eight million souls in love with truth and beauty and kindness to one another. Nowhere else he'd ever heard of had that happened on so great a scale.

In Treet's experience, personally and scholastically, theocracies produced miserable societies: stubborn, resistant, suspicious, intolerant, highly inequitable, and so hidebound they could not function in the face of change or conflict.

The Fieri had apparently avoided all that and stood at a pinnacle of social experience unique in human existence. They had discovered Utopia, had been smart enough to recognize a good thing when they saw it, and had worked at making the vision reality. For this they had earned Treet's respect and admiration. Orion Treet also recognized a good thing when he saw it.

The one item that puzzled him in all this, however, was how such a society could have developed at all, considering how they had originated. The Fieri were part of the same population of the colony ship that had landed on Empyrion in the beginning.

According to the colony's official historian, Feodr Rumon, a group of dangerous malcontents had been cast out, or had left of their own accord, but under protest. Exactly what had taken place wasn't clear; Rumon's *Chronicles* were slightly schizophrenic on this point. Still, the proto-Fieri had been forced from the safety of the colony and condemned to wander the wild wastes of Empyrion.

But the homeless nomads had somehow transformed themselves into a culture that in almost every respect surpassed the highest achievements of any Earth had ever seen. At least, in three weeks of scrutiny, Treet had not discovered any flaw. Theirs was a perfect society: no poverty, no disease, no crime, no homeless, no idle lonely old.

Now he and Mentor Mathiax walked along the coarse, pebbled beach of the inland sea the Fieri called Prindahl. The wide water shone flat and metallic beneath the white sun, a quicksilver sea over which the knife-hulls of boats with sails of crimson and ultramarine raced, trailing diamonds in their rippling wakes. Closer in, the sky held the gliding bodies of long-winged birds, rakkes, diving and soaring, feathering the gentle wind to rise high and then plummet to shoals of sparkling yellow fish.

A little distance away, graceful Fieri children frolicked at the water's edge with their wevicats, dark and feral beside the angelic youngsters. Together the huge, lithe animals and their diminutive masters abandoned themselves to play, tromping the shallow water into foam, lost in laughter and the joy of the moment. The children's voices rang clear like notes struck from silver bells.

Treet watched the boats and the birds, creatures of the wind, so fast and free. He listened to the sound of the children playing. A pang of envy shot up in his bones, an ache for something he'd scarcely been aware of lacking: peace. Not merely the absence of tension or conflict, but the complete unity of body, mind and spirit, the total harmony of life in all its parts. That is what the boats and birds and children symbolized: creatures at rest within themselves and in harmony with their environment. Not fighting it, but accepting it, shaping it and being shaped by it to live in it and beyond it.

That, Treet decided, was exactly what the Fieri were about as well: transcending the conditions of their existence by the force of a unity of spirit so strong it re-created all it touched. They had discovered the secret of this harmony, and he envied them.

For most of his 153 years, Treet had thought it was freedom he was after. He realized now that it was harmony. Without inner harmony, no amount of external freedom would ever make one free. One would always be a slave to selfishness, to pettiness, to passion, or to any of a jillion other afflictions of the soul.

This spiritual harmony had finally to rest on something absolute—this was what Mathiax had been trying to tell him for the past weeks. The Fieri peace was not the absence of something negative, but the presence of something positive—a solid force knitting the center together, and around which everything else moved: a starmass whose gravitational field held all lesser bodies in their orbits, described their movements, kept them spinning in their flight.

For the Fieri, that solid force at the center of everything was the Infinite Father.

"Tell me something," said Treet, breaking the long silence that had wrapped them as they walked. "What do you remember of Dome? Why did the Fieri leave?"

Mathiax pursed his lips and scowled. He took a long time to answer, but at last said, "No writing has come down to us from the Wandering. But in earlier times, the old rememberers said that a great change swept through Dome—a change that left it forever twisted. Those in power no longer respected life; they respected expediency. Any who argued for life over expediency fell under suspicion, were persecuted and eventually driven out. For Dome to exist, it was said, all had to yield to the greater good. The Fieri—only our name and these few memories come down to us from those times—said that what could not be good for one individual, could never be good for the whole. If one person suffered, all suffered. The rulers of Dome could not accept this. Persecution began—terrible suffering for all who stood with us. Rather than retaliate in kind or endure the injustice of persecution, our forefathers left their homes."

"And then?" Treet weighed this version of the story with the one he'd read in the colony's official records.

"We wandered. Empyrion was a vast, rich world designed by the Creator for sustaining life. The land welcomed us, and our people roved the world and learned its secrets. Later, much later, we built great cities on fertile plains and raised a strong people under peaceful skies . . ." Mathiax drifted off. The

Clerk's gray eyes gazed far out across the lake, remembering things he'd never seen.

"What happened?" Treet asked softly.

"The Burning . . ." Mathiax made a choked sound deep in his throat, and Treet turned toward him. Tears streamed down the man's face.

Afraid to speak lest he intrude on the Mentor's sorrow, Treet looked out across the lake to where the boats were but smears of color in the distance.

After a moment, the Mentor came to himself again and wiped his eyes. "These are things which cannot be remembered without sorrow," he explained.

"I understand," replied Treet. "If you'd rather not talk about it—"

"No, no. You will hear it. But perhaps I'm not the one to tell it." Mathiax turned, and they began walking back to the waiting evee. The lesson was over for the day, and Treet had more than enough to think about.

On the way back to Liamoge, Treet felt again the sense of urgency he had begun experiencing at odd times in the last several days: a straining forward, a quickening of the blood, a momentary catch in the heart's rhythm, a skipped beat in the anticipation of an unknown event speeding toward him. He wondered, not for the first time, if the feeling was in some way connected with the *purpose* the Preceptor had spoken of. A purpose he did not recognize yet, but felt drawing inexorably nearer with every passing hour.

Treet did not wonder about his purpose; he figured he'd know it when he found it. Or rather, when *it* found him—the sense of being pursued was that strong. The urgency puzzled him, however. While content to let whatever was pursuing him catch him, he also felt that time was in some sense running out—for him, for the Fieri, for a person or persons unknown. And if he did not act soon it would be too late—although what *act* or *too late* meant Treet could not guess.

All this provided Treet with the overall impression of being impelled toward a far-off destiny, a fate already chosen for him from the first—although he believed in neither fate nor destiny.

Still, he sensed that events beyond his control were aligning themselves around him like lines of magnetic force, and he was powerless to prevent it.

And now, as he and Mathiax sped along the seamless causeway over sparkling Prindahl toward Talus' pavilion, Treet allowed the surge of confused emotion to play over him, savoring the heightened awareness emerging from the muddled wash.

Yes, something was about to happen; it waited only for him to set it in motion. I am the catalyst, he thought. It's up to me. But will I know what to do when the time comes?

FIFTY
NINE

When they reached Liamoge, there was a large, multi-passenger evee waiting outside the entrance of the pavilion. Treet walked briskly through the entryway and into the main hall where Talus and Dania stood talking to several guests. One of the guests turned as he entered, and Treet found himself looking into the face that had begun to haunt his dreams.

"Yarden!" He stared, afraid to move lest the vision vanish.

She approached him slowly, almost shyly, he thought, until he saw that she was studying him closely. "You've changed," she said. "But I don't know how."

"You haven't," replied Treet. The others had stopped talking and now looked on. He told Talus, "Excuse us for a moment. We—"

Dania answered, "You have much to say to one another. Walk in the courtyard; no one will disturb you."

They walked through the hall and into the deep green confusion of the courtyard. He had so much he wanted to tell her—he'd been saving things up for months, it seemed—and now that she was here, he could not think how to begin. His mind went blank. After a few steps they slowed, turned, and gazed at one another.

"How have you been?" he asked. No, that's not what he wanted to say at all. Just say it!

"Well," Yarden answered, looking away. "And you?"

"Fine . . ." This was getting them nowhere. He glanced down at his hands and noticed that they were quivering. "Look at my hands—they're shaking."

Yarden placed her hands over his. "They're cold too." She stepped closer to him, raised her eyes. "I've missed you, Orion," she whispered. "I've missed you very much."

Then, without his knowing how exactly, his arms were filled with her warmth. "Yarden . . . I began to think I'd never see you again. The last time we were together . . . I was afraid—"

"Shhh," she soothed. "Not now. Just hold me."

Treet stood with his arms wrapped tightly around her, cradling her softness. They stood for a long time without moving, without speaking, letting their embrace find its own eloquence. At last Yarden pushed back to look at him. She raised a finger to trace his chin. "Funny, I'd forgotten about your beard," she said.

"I'd forgotten how beautiful you are." Her long dark hair was smoothed back from her face to fall in a loose cascade behind her shoulders. Her eyes, jet beneath sweeping brows, hinted at depths unexplored. She put her cheek against the hollow of his throat, and he smelled the freshness of her hair. "I never want to let you go."

"I could tell when you were thinking about me," she said almost absently.

"I wondered if you would know. What did you get?"

"I'm not going to tell you. But it let me know that I was right about you."

"I thought you considered me an ogre."

"Crusty, conceited, and too independent for your own good, but not an ogre."

"Coming from you, ma'am, that's a compliment." Still holding her, he led her to a grouping of chairs in a far corner of the courtyard. They sat together in one of the larger chairs. "I thought I had so much I wanted to say to you, but I seem to have forgotten everything. It hardly matters though."

"But I want to hear it. I want to hear about every minute of these last weeks."

"All right," agreed Treet. He pulled her close and began relating all that he'd experienced since stepping off the airship that first night. When he was through, Yarden straightened and turned toward him, drawing up her legs and crossing them.

"Now it's my turn," she said. Her story was nearly identical to Treet's. By the time she came to, the airship that had rescued them had landed. Still very drowsy, she was taken to the home of a young Fieri woman named Ianni.

"I was half-asleep for the first two days," said Yarden. "But Ianni understood and did not press me too hard, although she was very excited to learn all about where I'd come from, how I'd gotten here—everything I could tell her." She paused in her recitation and said, "Oh, Orion, aren't these the most wonderful people you've ever encountered? They are so loving. Fierra is simply incredible . . ."

He agreed that he'd never seen anything close to it, and she continued, "Ianni took me everywhere. She is an excellent teacher, very sensitive. She introduced me to everything Fieri. We were up every morning at dawn and went to bed late every night." Yarden told him of their long days of discussion and travel around the city, about visiting the Preceptor and sailing out across the lake one night under the stars. She ended by saying, "I've seen the most amazing things, eaten the most delicious food, been exposed to wisdom and kindness I never dreamed existed!"

"So have I," murmured Treet, pulling her close once again. "But that's not all. I learned that . . . I love you."

He would have said it again, but her lips were on his, her arms around his neck. He drank in the heavy, honeyed sweetness of her kiss. He returned it with all the desire that was in him, demanding more and more of her, of himself, until they broke apart, breathless, clinging to each other.

"Yarden—"

Just then a shout came from the other side of the courtyard. "Hey! Where is everybody?"

"Pizzle!" Treet felt as if someone had dumped ice water on him.

A moment later the scraggy, jug-eared head poked through a tangle of foliage directly in front of them. "There you are! Hey, don't get up—I'll join you." He slid a chair up and plopped in. "Boy, isn't this some place they got here? I never would have imagined it could be like this—not after seeing the inside of Dome. You guys look great! Just great! I was starting to wonder whether we'd ever get back together. Not that I worried about it—there is just so much to do here, you know. Unbelievable!"

He sat there beaming at them and shaking his head. "It's good to see you, too, Pizzle," said Treet. He'd forgotten what a bother the egghead could be, but was quickly remembering.

"I understand we have you to thank for saving our lives," said Yarden. "You flagged down the airship that rescued us."

"Yes, we owe you a lot," added Treet. "How are your hands? Mathiax said you were burned pretty bad."

Pizzle held up his hands and wiggled his fingers. "Never better. These Fieri are genius doctors—I don't have a single scar to show for my heroism. But to tell the truth, I thought we'd had it out there in the desert. I figured I'd jigged my last jig. I know I was more dead than alive when they picked us up, 'cause I don't remember much about it. Seems like it happened a hundred years ago."

"I know what you mean," agreed Yarden. "So much has happened in such a short time it all seems like a bad dream— like it happened to somebody else. I'm just thankful we all made it."

"Speaking of which," said Treet, "have you seen Crocker or Calin yet?"

"Crocker's due here any minute. That's what Talus said. I don't know about Calin." Pizzle grinned, putting all his teeth into it. "I'll tell you what—isn't this some place though?"

"I've never seen anything to compare," agreed Treet.

"If you're here and Crocker's coming," Yarden said, disentangling herself from Treet's embrace, "it must mean that you've spoken before the College of Mentors."

"Correct. Very attentive audience, I must say. I take it you two have done your bit?"

"I spoke yesterday," said Yarden. "I talked myself hoarse, and they would have sat there all night long. When I finished though, not a word—they just got up and went away. Strange."

"They did the same with me," said Pizzle. "I guess it's their way."

"I think they plan some sort of free-for-all later. Right now they only want the facts as we see them."

"You don't think they believe us?" asked Yarden.

"Oh, they believe us," replied Treet. "But we've really upset them more than they let on. They don't know what to do with us—that is, with the information we bring with us." Treet paused and pursed his lips thoughtfully. "I've observed a few lapses in the Fieri code of impeccable conduct. If you're interested, I'll tell you what I think they mean."

"I'm all ears," said Pizzle happily. He was living every SF fan's keenest aspiration: high adventure on a distant planet.

"Well, here goes. One: our reception here was odd, to say the least. We're packed off to private residences, rather than greeted by their representatives of law and order. Why? For all they know we could be killer commandos come to take apart their city stone by stone. It's as if they want us to think our coming was no great shake at all—yet, our appearances before the College of Mentors indicates a considerable degree of healthy concern."

Yarden opened her mouth to speak, but thought better of it and nodded for Treet to continue.

"Okay? Two: Talus imposes a gag order on his own family in order to keep me from talking to them. He's a Mentor—which I'm sure you've figured out is pretty high up in the Fieri chain of command—and he set great store by my speaking before the assembly just as soon as possible—my second night here, in fact. Yet, he's asked me no questions and has not really spoken to me since that night—except to say hello and good-bye and have some more salad.

"Three: After my little speech, Mathiax, not Talus or Jaire, becomes my official tutor. We spend the next weeks wandering around this incredible city of theirs while he fills my head with stories. But every time I begin to make a comment or observation about what I see, or compare it to Dome, he cuts me off—doesn't want to hear it. It's like he wants me to soak it up, but not let anything run out."

"Same for me," offered Pizzle.

"Four: when I speak to the Preceptor, she doesn't ask me a single question about where I come from or what I'm doing here. Instead, she tells me to discover my spiritual purpose. What's that mean? And what's that got to do with any of the rest of this?"

"The point?" asked Yarden.

"The point is, I know the curiosity must be killing them, but for some reason they're going to great lengths to cover up the fact, or at least not to let it influence them in their treatment of us. Hence, they are rolling out the red carpet for us, but in a very casual, almost secretive way."

"So?" wondered Pizzle, chin in hands.

"It's obvious, I think. They are uncertain—not to say suspicious—of us. On the one hand they treat us like we're just folks, long-lost cousins come to visit—"

"On the other hand, they don't want to risk offending us in case we turn out to be emissaries from on high." Yarden finished his thought for him.

"Exactly."

"So they bend over sideways trying to make us feel at home," said Pizzle, "getting us to understand what they're all about, showing us how great everything is here so that when we decide to do whatever we've come here to do, our actions will be tempered with the knowledge of what we've seen."

"Something like that," agreed Treet.

Yarden frowned. "They're highly intelligent, highly compassionate people. What would you expect them to do?"

"I don't know, but it strikes me as slightly screwy. The reception we got at Dome made more sense."

"Cynic," said Yarden. "Looking for the cloud behind the silver lining."

"I might add that they are desperate to convince us of their sincerity, and the integrity of what they have here."

"I'm convinced," said Pizzle. "They have nothing to fear from me. I only hope they let me stay."

"Sure." Treet nodded thoughtfully. "That would be great, only . . ."

"Only what?" asked Yarden, regarding him with a sidelong glance.

"Only it may not be that simple."

"**W**ell, well, Crocker, you look your handsome, dashing self," said Treet. "I see Fieri food agrees with you." The three had rejoined Talus and his party in the reception hall, now nearly filled with people—most of whom were watching their visitors with keen, if scantily disguised, interest. They found Crocker standing with a group of Fieri talking about airships. The group broke apart discreetly as they approached.

At the sound of Treet's voice, Crocker looked up, smiled broadly, and reached out to take their hands, then hesitated and withdrew awkwardly. The light died in his eyes. "After all those weeks in the desert together, I didn't think I'd be so glad to see your scruffy faces again. It's good to see you. What's it been? Six months?"

"Seems like it," said Pizzle. "They give you the grand tour?"

"I've examined every bit of real estate from lakeshore to kumquat grove, and I'm here to tell you I've never seen anything like this place in all my worldly days. What they have here—it's a monument to genius, that's what it is." Crocker's words were warm and even enthusiastic, but his tone lacked conviction—as if he were reading a written speech he'd grown tired of reciting.

"I agree," replied Yarden. She reached out and pressed Crocker's hand, scrutinizing him closely. "Still, I'm glad we're all together at last."

"Not quite all," said Treet. "Calin isn't here . . . Ah, Pizzle, you and Crocker hold forth. Yarden and I will go and see what we can find out about Calin." He pulled Yarden away with him and they wound through knots of convivial Fieri, who stopped talking and watched them as they passed by.

"You're not worried about Calin," said Yarden when they reached a far corner of the room. "You're worried about Crocker."

"Did you see that? He slammed the door shut so fast, I'm surprised he didn't pinch his fingers when he yanked the welcome mat out from under our feet."

She confirmed his observation with a sharp nod. "I saw. It was definitely not the Crocker I know."

"You told me I'd changed—"

"Yes, but not like that. Something's happened to him."

"Sometimes severe trauma warps a person. They feel guilty for surviving, or that they have to mend their ways somehow."

"I don't think that's what's ailing Crocker. After all, he didn't survive at the expense of any of us. We all made it together."

"Maybe he knows something we don't know."

"Could be, but what?"

"Do you get anything from him?"

Yarden scrunched up her face in concentration. After a moment she said, "No, nothing. But then, Crocker and I have never been on the same wavelength. I've never received good impressions from him about anything. He's opaque to me." She looked at Treet seriously. "What did you mean when you said it may not be that simple?"

Treet ran a hand up and down her arm and gripped her hand. "I'll tell you later. Right now let's check on Calin and then get back to Pizzle and Crocker. I have a sudden funny feeling we're about to have a rude awakening."

Talus greeted Treet and Yarden with gusto, clapping them both in fierce bear hugs. It occurred to Treet that the big man's smile looked pasted on. When Treet described his concern for the missing member of their party, Talus replied, "I understand. But you need not fear for her welfare. She is well . . ."

"But?"

Talus filled his bellows of a chest with a deep breath. "Your companion has shown no response to our continued efforts at reaching her."

"What do you mean, no response?" asked Yarden.

Talus' eyes became grave. "She remains listless and will not speak. Although we have tried to engage her interest in activities and conversation, she does not reply or acknowledge our advances in any way."

"She's okay physically?" Treet fixed Talus with a direct stare. "She eating and sleeping and all that?"

"Oh, yes, although she eats very little. Still, we can find nothing wrong with her." Talus spread his hands in an expression of genuine helplessness. "She will not speak to anyone."

"Talus, there's something I should tell you about her." Treet paused, looked at Yarden, who gave him silent encouragement, and then plunged ahead. "Calin is not one of us—that is, she's not a Traveler. She's from Dome."

Talus pulled on his curly, ram's fleece of a beard and puffed out his cheeks. "I see," he said finally. "Yes . . . that might explain her behavior. But," he looked up decisively, "it would not have altered her care. We would have done nothing differently."

"I appreciate that, Talus," said Treet. "But it might be best now if we could see her. If she knows we're still here with her, she might snap out of it. For all we knows, she thinks she's landed in the enemy camp and you're all waiting for a chance to kill her."

Talus wagged his head back and forth with a heavy frown. "No one could believe such a thing of us."

"She's from *Dome*."

"She's also lost and very, very frightened, Talus," pointed out Yarden. "You have to remember that neither she nor anyone she's ever known has ever ventured outside Dome and lived. We had a similar experience with her out there—the landscape overwhelmed her and she went into convulsions. If we could see her—"

"Don't say no, Talus," put in Treet. "I know what your Preceptor has advised, but she did say it was only a recommendation. We're free to choose our own way in this, right?" Talus nodded slowly. "Well, I'm choosing for Calin since she can't choose for herself. I say she'd feel better if she could see us, be with us."

"If she would speak—"

"She won't. Anyway, what do you need her for? You've already heard from the rest of us. That should give you enough of whatever you're looking for."

"But she's from Dome! She could tell—"

"Look, let us go to her, or bring her here. Maybe when she gets over it, she can talk to you." Treet could see his argument was succeeding. He pressed it home. "Think it over. You'll never get anything from her any other way."

Talus admitted defeat. "It is as you say. Yes, I'll have her brought here, and we'll hope that she responds to your care. The love of friends is a powerful remedy. I'll do as you suggest."

"Thanks, Talus. You won't regret it," Treet assured him. Talus moved off to fulfill the request, and Treet turned to Yarden. "That's done. Now we should rejoin the others and figure out what to do next."

"About whatever it is that you think is going to happen here tonight?"

"Right. I don't know what form it's going to take, but I suspect a major confrontation."

Yarden scowled at him. "You make it sound like they're going to throw us to the lions."

Treet gazed around the throng, noting the humming undercurrent of tension in the voices and the sharp tang of anticipation in the air. "Could be, Yarden," he muttered. "Maybe they are."

SIXTY
ONE

Treet could tell when the Preceptor arrived—excitement rippled through the room, voices grew hushed and then resumed their chatter but at lower decibels. The assembled Fieri, most of them Mentors, Treet suspected, formed a phalanx around them, hemming the travelers into a corner of the reception hall. "This is it," said Treet, looking around. "The moment we've all been waiting for."

"I'm still skeptical," said Pizzle. "They don't . . . hey, they're all looking at us!"

"Don't say I didn't warn you, okay?" Treet turned to face the Fieri, who, as Pizzle had said, were indeed regarding them intently. A path opened in the wall of people as the Preceptor drew near.

She came to stand before them, dressed in shimmering black with a close-fitting cap of silver that hugged the crown of her head. The cap was trimmed with yellow chips of glowing sunstone so that she fairly radiated a golden halo. Her amethyst eyes gave no hint of her intent, but the set of her jaw spoke of determination, and there was gravity in her step.

Talus, Bohm, and Mathiax closed ranks behind her. Each of the men shared their leader's seriousness. All talk in the hall fell away as the Preceptor came close and stopped before the travelers. She inclined her head toward them in a dignified greeting.

"You honor us with your presence, Preceptor," Treet told her. His companions remained silent.

The Fieri leader smiled gravely and answered, "You speak so lightly of honor, I wonder if you know what it means."

Treet was taken aback by this reply, but recovered and said, "I meant no disrespect, Preceptor. I am cert—"

She waved aside the apology. "Please, I spoke out of frustration. Take no offense. I only meant that the Infinite Father alone is worthy of honor." She paused, folded her hands in front of her, and said, "My friend Mathiax has informed me that you inquired about our past, about the Wandering and the Burning. He did not answer you because I asked him to allow me to tell you in my own way." She raised her hands to indicate that here in this place, before all these people, was the way she had chosen.

"I understand," offered Treet. His stomach tightened, and his pulse quickened. Yarden pressed nearer to him; her hand closed over his and squeezed.

The Fieri formed a silent wall of faces. Their anticipation charged the atmosphere in the hall until it fairly crackled. Did they know what was about to come?

The Preceptor closed her eyes, her hands frozen in the gesture she'd begun. A sound came from her throat: a long sighing moan, aching with sadness and melancholy.

"Hear the story of the Fieri," she began abruptly, eyes still closed, head tilted back slightly. "The Infinite Father awakened His people in the midst of folly and led us out from the dark cities to roam fair Empyrion and make a new home where light could rule. So we wandered."

"We wandered," replied the Fieri in unison. Treet realized that the story was a litany all Fieri knew by heart.

"In the West we found the fields of living crystal, and in the East the mountains of light where our fathers dug the first sunstone; in the North we saw the Blue Forest, alive with her creatures, magnificent and old; in the South we found gentle hills and clear running water, and the Marsh Sea with its floating islands where the talking fish birth their young. And we wandered."

"We wandered."

"When we had learned the secrets of our world, the time of wandering came to an end. We harnessed the living crystal for power, and quarried the shining sunstone. Our fathers built great cities of light and lived under the sun in harmony with all things. We remembered our brothers in the dark cities and sent emissaries to them, bringing our most precious gifts to share. They welcomed us, and greedily learned all we could teach them, then turned against us, using the knowledge we had given them to make weapons. They covered their cities with crystal and became Dome."

"The cities of darkness became Dome," the chorus replied.

"They turned jealous eyes upon us. In darkness they cursed

our light and dreamed our destruction. The fever of hate inflamed them, and they went mad in their delirium. Then, when the evil in them grew too great . . ." The Preceptor's voice cracked with emotion. All in the room held their breath. "Then came the Burning."

"The Burning," answered the chorus in a hushed whisper. The effect was chilling. Treet stood spellbound.

"The Burning," the Preceptor sobbed. "Fire fell from the clear sky without warning, raining down on the cities of light, destroying them in clouds of smoke that blotted out the sun, consuming even the stones. No one survived. Young and old alike perished in that terrible day. It was over in a moment, but the black smoke rolled up to heaven for many days to become a shroud to cover the sky. On that day, our bright homeland became the Blighted Lands, a desert where no living thing could ever survive."

Tears escaped from under the Preceptor's closed eyelids. She let them fall and in a little while resumed. "But the Fieri survived. A very few, it's true. Some of our people were working the crystal mines in the West when the Burning took place. Others were away in the mountain quarries to the North. These few survived to wander once more.

"A dark epoch followed. Sickness became our constant companion: our men grew old too quickly and died suddenly; those of our women who were not barren gave birth to dead babies or produced monsters from their diseased wombs; our flesh withered while still young; little children lost teeth and hair, they vomited blood. Our proud ancestors became a nation afflicted with sores and running wounds.

"All that we knew passed away; all that we loved died. The treasures of our great civilization fell into dust. We lost the knowledge we had worked so hard to discover—we lost everything to the dark time.

"Yet, we survived."

"We survived," came the murmur from the chorus.

"We lived, for the Infinite Father heard our people and took pity on them. As they wandered the land, sick and sore, the Seeker found them, the Gatherer brought them together, and the Sustainer led them here, to the shores of Prindahl, where we were given a new beginning."

"Glory to the Infinite Father!" said the Fieri behind her.

"He bound our wounds and healed our sickness. He gave

us the light of hope to guard us, and taught us a deeper love than any we knew. The Infinite Father raised us from the ashes of death, and He claimed us for His own."

"Praise to the Infinite Father!"

The Preceptor opened her eyes and regarded the visitors with unutterable sadness and compassion. Treet was overwhelmed with a rush of jumbled emotions—outrage at the crime that had been visited on these noble people, grief for their loss, wonder at the meaning of the Preceptor's words, and astonishment at their incredible will to survive. For what she had described was a nuclear holocaust.

Out of jealousy and spite, the inhuman monsters of Dome had leveled the bright cities of the plain with atomic weapons. They had turned once-fertile soil into a wasteland scorched white and sterilized by radiation.

As one who had passed through that man-made desert, Treet felt the cruel injustice of it like a hot brand in his heart. It was some time before he could speak. "Such horror . . . I never guessed . . . ," he murmured.

"The worst that could ever happen to any living thing happened to us," said the Preceptor. "But the Infinite Father in His love sustained us."

"Sustained you? He let it happen in the first place!" snapped Treet without thinking. Every eye in the place turned on him.

"How so?" the Preceptor asked softly. They might have been the only two people in the room.

"He could have saved you, but He didn't. He let it happen," mumbled Treet, dreadfully sorry he'd said anything at all. He felt Yarden tugging at his sleeve.

"We did not know the Infinite Presence then."

"But He existed, didn't He?"

"Yes, and He revealed Himself to us through our pain. He taught us with our tears."

"It seems a hard lesson," remarked Treet finally. "Too hard." Yarden tugged again.

"No, you do not understand. Our pain was His pain first. If we grieved, how much more did the Comforter grieve. He became our sorrow; the death of our loved ones was no less death to Him, the Light of All Life. He took our sorrow to Himself and transformed it into love and gave it back. That is His glory."

Treet caught only the barest hint of what the Preceptor was saying, but he let it go. "You've stayed away from Dome ever since?"

"The Protector gave us Daraq, the desert, as a shield. Dome will not cross the Blighted Lands. Now they live turned in among themselves. Their disease will not be healed. It festers within them; it devours them and will in time destroy them. We leave them to their madness."

Treet stared at all those around him and knew in that instant why he had come here to this place. Words bubbled up from inside him and fought their way to his tongue. He felt like shouting, like hiding, like running from the hall screaming, like weeping and singing all at once. He began to tremble and felt Yarden's hand on his arm.

He clamped his mouth shut, determined not to make a bigger fool of himself than he already had. But his mouth would not stay shut. Hot pincers gripped his tongue, and the words came of their own accord. "The horror is starting again!" His voice grated in the hushed room.

The assembled Fieri looked at him strangely. The Preceptor nodded and said, "Speak freely. Tell us what has been given you."

Treet drew a quivering hand across his damp forehead and said, "You know that I—that is we," he included those with him, "escaped from Dome. But while I was there I saw the signs—the madness you spoke of just now—it's all beginning again. Already the leaders of Dome are searching for you, fearing you without reason. It's only a matter of time before they overcome their fear and come for you."

His words sent shockwaves of surprise coursing through the assembly. "Treet!" came Yarden's urgent whisper. "What are you doing?"

The Preceptor merely nodded once more, pressed her palms together, and brought her fingertips to her lips. Treet waited. Needles pricked along his scalp from nape to crown.

She leveled her eyes on him. "What will you do, Traveler?"

The question was not what Treet expected. "Do?" He looked to Talus and Mathiax for help. They merely peered back at him with narrowed eyes waiting for his reply. "I'm sorry—I don't know what you mean."

"Your purpose has been revealed to you," the Preceptor explained. "Now you must decide what to do."

"Why me?" Treet sputtered, looking around helplessly. "I mean, this affects every one of us. We all—"

"*You* must decide," said the Preceptor firmly.

"I'm going back." The words were out of his mouth before he could think, but once said he realized he'd been waiting to say them since the moment he'd set foot in Fierra, perhaps even before. "The signs are there—I've seen them before. We've got to stop Dome or they'll destroy everything. Come with me."

The Preceptor regarded him silently and then said, "We have seen what war can do; we carry in our hearts its terrible wounds—wounds which can never heal." She shook her head. "No, Traveler, we will not go with you. We will not fight Dome."

"But they wi—"

"The Fieri have vowed eternal peace. We will never lift a hand against another living being."

"They will annihilate you," Treet said wonderingly.

"So be it." The Preceptor's eyes glittered in the light. "It is better for us to join the Comforter in the pavilions of the Infinite Father than to increase the hate and horror of war by participating in it. We have vowed peace; let us live by our vow."

Treet could not believe what he was hearing. He looked to Mathiax and Talus for help, but they merely looked back emptily, their faces drawn in melancholy. "You will die by your vow," he said, shaking his head.

The Preceptor turned and moved away. The ranks of Fieri broke and the hall began to empty. Treet watched them go and then turned to his companions. Each regarded him with expressions of incredulity and contempt mixed in equal portions.

Crocker said, "You put both feet smack in the brown pie this time. Coo-ee!" He strode off.

Pizzle shrugged. "What can you expect from a guy who's never read *Far Andromeda?*" He shuffled away, following Crocker out into the courtyard.

"I'm going to my room," Yarden said icily.

"What did I say?" whined Treet. "Yarden, listen!" He hollered at her retreating figure, but she did not turn back. In a moment he was all alone. No one has any use for a doomsayer, he thought; and that's just what I am.

SIXTY
TWO

"You're insane, Orion Treet! Is this some kind of kinky death wish? Is that what it is?" Yarden seethed. Anger flared her dark eyes with flecks of fire and honed her words to piercing points like needles of ice. Treet had never seen such fury in a woman and stood back in awe, as from a flame-sprouting geyser.

"Yarden, be reas—"

"Be reasonable yourself! If you weren't so infatuated with that gigantic ego of yours, you'd see how crazy it is!"

Treet flapped his tongue in response, but his reply was lost amidst Yarden's fresh tirade.

"It's a fool's errand. You'll get yourself killed for nothing. You have some kind of misguided messiah complex, and you think you'll change Dome. But you won't. They're *evil*, Orion. Through and through evil—rotten with it. I won't stand here and listen to you delude yourself."

"It's not that bad, Yarden. Honestly, do you think I'd—"

"Think you'd walk into that nest of vipers unawares? Yes, I do. You don't know them for what they are. You did not see them like I did. Please, listen to me. Stop this stupid, stupid plan of yours now. You don't have to do it. No one will care whether you go or not. No one will think less of you for not going. Give it up."

"I can't give it up! Can't you see that?" He'd tried the calm-down-cool-off-let's-talk-about-it approach, and it had proven about as effective as a pup tent in a hurricane. Yarden's reaction mystified him. She had blown up instantly, without warning. He hadn't seen it coming. "Someone has to do something about Dome or the holocaust will begin again."

"You have no proof of that."

"I know what I've seen. I know the pattern from history—I've seen it time and time again. The machinery of war is already in place. We've got to stop them before they get full control of it."

"How do you intend to stop them?"

She had him there. He had no idea. "I don't know, but I'll find a way. Come with me."

"No! I won't be a party to your suicide. I love you. I won't watch you kill yourself."

"I'm not saying it isn't dangerous. I know it is. I'll be careful. But dangerous or not, it's got to be done. Don't you see that?"

"No, I don't. The Fieri have lived for two thousand years avoiding Dome. Why should that change now all of a sudden?"

"It's the age-old pattern, the cycle of hate. Dome despises the Fieri, and over time that hate builds up until they can't contain it anymore and it explodes. Last time they incinerated the Fieri cities—changed a million kilometers of fertile farmland into a sterile desert waste; they blasted three generations of civilized human beings into sizzling atoms in less than two seconds. They'll do it again unless they are stopped."

Yarden stared at him. Her lips were compressed into a thin, straight line. Her face was clenched like a fist, teeth tight, jaw flexed. "I can't believe you'd do this to us," she said finally.

"To us? You think I want this?"

"Yes. In some strange way no one will ever understand, you do want this or you wouldn't insist on going."

"Yarden, I don't *want* to go. I'm no hero. But someone has to go, and there's no one else. You heard the Preceptor. None of the Fieri will go. Fine. I'm not bound by any sacred oath. Besides, I promised I would go back."

"You what?"

"I told Tvrdy I'd return. They're desperate for help, and they're waiting for me to bring it. I told them I'd come back with help, and I meant it. That's why we left, remember?"

"I don't believe this," Yarden huffed. "After all you've seen here, you can still think about returning?"

"They're waiting for me—us—to come back with the help they need."

"They're using you, Treet! Open your eyes. Suppose you helped them overthrow Jamrog—what makes you think Tvrdy would be any different, any better than the fiend he replaced? They scream about injustice and brutality. Yet, when the new regime comes to power they show themselves worse villains than the villains they replaced: more brutal, more unjust, more repressive. It's the politics of terrorism—you end up replacing one terrorist with an ever bigger terrorist!

"Wake up, Treet; they're using you. You owe them nothing. You're not bound by anything—except your own inflated ego!"

"You don't know—"

"Give it up," Yarden pleaded. "Please, give it up. You don't have to go. You don't owe them anything. What goes on in Dome doesn't concern us any longer. We're free. Forever free. The life we've always dreamed of—that all mankind has always dreamed of—is here. And it's ours for the asking. Please, Orion, stay with me. We'll be happy."

"I want nothing more. You have to believe that, Yarden. But what happens inside Dome *does* concern us. Can't you see that? Dome will strike again; they can't stop themselves, so they have to be stopped and there's no one else to do it. I have to try. I don't want to, but I'm going." He moved toward her, raising his hands to touch her. She stiffened and turned away.

"I'm leaving," she said.

"No, wait. Don't go, Yarden. Let's talk about this."

"You've made up your mind. There's nothing more to talk about."

He watched her rigid form move through the doorway and disappear in the darkened corridor beyond. He knew that everyone in Talus' pavilion had probably heard them fighting, but he didn't particularly care anymore. He sank into a chair and shook his head wearily. Of all people, he expected Yarden, if not to support his decision, at least to understand it. Instead, she had reacted in the worst way possible.

Was she right? Was he being a stubborn, egomaniacal ass? Had he misread the signs entirely?

He thought about this, remembering the haunted expressions he'd seen on the faces of Dome's inhabitants: that vacant, sunken-eyed hopelessless that in the strange alchemy of repression was transmuting the simple desires of an abused people into a volatile ether awaiting the proper spark to ignite it. The spark would be a leader who, to slake his unquenchable greed and power lust, would turn the force of firestorm toward the innocent Fieri. The Fieri would become the hated enemy whose destruction would be presented as the panacea for all Dome's ills.

Treet knew that torturous trail for what it was. He'd seen the bloody cycle repeat itself too often in history not to recognize it now. The mystery was, why did no one else recognize it?

He would have gladly agreed with Yarden if there had been even the smallest particle of doubt in his mind, if there was any other logical explanation for what he had seen and heard. But he knew in the marrow of his bones he was right, and his scholarly integrity was too keenly developed over too many years to allow him to back away from his assessment just because it was inconvenient or threatening.

He was right. Dome would attack again, probably very soon. Something had to be done. It was all well and good to appeal to two millennia of peace and invoke a sacred oath of nonviolence. But the rabid, power-mad rulers of Dome would not think twice about violating peace or sacred oaths when they could conceive of neither.

As soon as Dome whipped themselves into enough of a killing frenzy, they would strike. They would venture out from under their enormous crystal shell with death in their hands; they would seek out the Fieri and annihilate them. They would do this, Treet knew, because, as it had happened time and time again on Earth, the mere presence of the Fieri challenged their warped existence the same way a single ray of light jeopardizes whole realms of darkness. Dome could never be reconciled to the Fieri—the differences between them were too great.

The problem was classic: how do you appease an enemy who will not be appeased by anything less than your death?

If the Fieri could accept annihilation out of religious conviction—as the Preceptor had pointed out, they knew the horror of war better than anyone else and had vowed that they would never increase that horror by participating in it—so be it. Treet had taken no such vow.

Besides, there was a chance that Dome could be diverted from its present course if he acted soon enough. And he wouldn't be alone: Tvrdy and Cejka and their followers already struggled to dismantle the war machine, or at least halt it. Perhaps with help they could succeed—perhaps not. But in any case there was absolutely nothing to lose. If they failed, there would be no life for the Fieri anyway.

One day soon Dome would again fill the skies with fire, and there would be no escape. To think otherwise was utter delusion. Besides, what kind of life would it be to awaken every morning wondering if this was the day the world would end? What kind of happiness could exist as long as the specter of inevitable destruction loomed larger every moment? What kind of feast is it where hooded death sits at the head of the table?

He had to go. There was no other way.

"I think you're nuts, too," said Pizzle when Treet saw him in the courtyard the next morning. "If you think you're going to talk me into going back with you, then you're more than nuts—you're psychotic."

"I knew I could count on you, Pizzle. True blue."

"So sorry! I've just never been much of a martyr. Aversion to suicide is one cultural trait I approve of. It's very practical."

"I wouldn't expect you to be anything but practical. That's you all the way—good old pragmatic Pizzy." The sarcasm in his voice finally got to Pizzle.

"Look, if you want to toddle off on some lunatic crusade, go right ahead. Who's stopping you? Anyway, you should thank me: a coward like me would only slow you down. You could save the world a lot quicker without me hanging on your back."

"You're right about that. But, loath as I am to admit it, Pizzle, you've got a cool head on your shoulders when you choose to use it. You'd be a help."

"Right. And this head is staying fixed on these shoulders. Thanks, but no thanks."

Treet got up and looked down at Pizzle with dismay. "You don't have to make up your mind right now. Think it over, I'll be back."

"Suit yourself." Pizzle shrugged and looked myopically up at him. "But I'm not leaving Fierra. Ever. Jaire is taking me sailing today. You know what? I've never been sailing in my life. I've never been alone with a beautiful woman either, as a matter of fact. And this is just the beginning. I intend to start doing a lot of things I've never done before. I'd be a fool to leave this, and so would you."

"Don't you think there's the slightest chance you could be overdramatizing all this?" Crocker sat across from Treet, leaning toward him, resting his forearms on his knees. The courtyard was cool and quiet in the midmorning sun. The yellow canopy made them both look slightly jaundiced.

Treet shook his head slowly. "No. I wish I could make myself believe I was wrong, but I've seen too much, I know too much. Pretending it doesn't exist won't make it go away."

"I agree," said Crocker. "If you feel that way, I think you should go."

"You do?" Treet looked at the pilot closely, studying him for any trace of the odd aloofness he'd displayed since the travelers had been reunited. Crocker seemed himself, but Treet remained wary. "Why do you say that?"

"Well, if you can have an opinion, why can't I agree with it?"

"I mean, why do you think I should go? No one else does."

"No big secret there, Treet. I just think a man has to do what he thinks is right no matter what."

"Code of the wild west, eh? A man's gotta do what a man's gotta do."

"Go ahead, make fun of the only person who believes in this crazy scheme of yours."

"You say you believe and you still call it crazy. Thanks a lot."

"I'm willing to go along with you."

That stopped Treet cold. "You what?"

"I'll go with you—back to Dome. What's the matter? Isn't that what you want?"

"Sure, but—"

"But what? Isn't that what this little conversation was leading up to—asking me to go with you?"

"Yeah," Treet admitted, feeling unsettled, but not certain why. "I *was* going to ask you to go with me."

"So I saved you the trouble. This way, if anything goes wrong you won't have to feel responsible. You didn't recruit me—I volunteered."

"You really want to go, huh?" Crocker's reaction was so different from what he'd received from Yarden and Pizzle, Treet was suspicious.

"It's not a question of *wanting* to go. But let's just say your little speech last night convinced me. Something has to be done, or we might just as well lie down in a deep hole and pull the sod over our heads. I'm not ready for that yet. If there's a chance we can prevent it, we've got to try. That's how I see it."

"Crocker, you're a wonder," said Treet. "I figured you'd laugh in my face like Pizzle did."

"Pizzle's a spineless, self-seeking coward! He's not worth spit," replied Crocker with a vehemence that surprised Treet. Crocker and Pizzle had been the best of friends throughout their desert ordeal. It wasn't like Crocker to denounce him so strenuously.

Treet got to his feet, and Crocker slumped back in his chair, staring up at him. Treet said, "Thanks for the vote of confidence. I'm going to look in on Calin. We'll start making plans for the return trip in the next day or two."

"Fine." Crocker nodded slowly. He looked gray and exhausted, as if wilting before Treet's eyes. "I'll be here."

Treet left the courtyard quietly and made his way to Calin's second-floor room, knocked once, and went in.

SIXTY
THREE

The room was dark, the woven draperies drawn, letting in little light from the open balcony beyond. The muted plashing of water mumbled like liquid voices, and the lake breeze soughing through the drapes made the room breathe as if alive. Calin lay on a low platform-bed on her side with her knees drawn up to her chest. She did not move when Treet came in, and at first he thought her asleep. As he came to stand over the bed, he saw that her eyes were open, staring into the dimness of her room.

"Calin," he ventured. No response. "It's me, Treet. I came to see how you're doing. Mind if I sit down?"

He sat on the edge of the bed, stretching his legs in front of him and leaning on his elbow. "You know," he said, trying to keep the anxiety out of his voice, "you've got our hosts climbing the walls. They can't figure out what's wrong with you. If there's anything you want to tell me, I'd like to listen."

Treet waited, heard the faint ruffle of her shallow breath. "I know you can hear me, Calin. And I was hoping you'd talk to me. If anyone has a right to hear from you, I guess it's me. After all we've been through together, if you can't trust me, you really are out of luck."

He grimaced at that last part, but Calin gave no indication that she'd heard him at all. He blustered ahead. "I was hoping you would at least talk to me . . . I, uh—I've got something to tell you."

The Dome magician might have been in some kind of cataleptic trance for all the interest she showed in his news. Treet had heard of people who could simply will themselves to die, and wondered whether Calin had the knack.

"Anyway," he told her matter-of-factly, "Crocker and I have decided to go back to Dome. There's unfinished business back there, and it's important we go as soon as possible. I don't know how we're going to get there yet, but . . ." He paused, then added impulsively, "I was wondering if you wanted to go back with us?"

Treet surprised himself with the question. When he entered the room he had no idea of asking her, and even as his lips formed the words he did not seriously consider that she would be able to respond to it.

But to Treet's amazement, Calin rolled over and looked at him. She blinked her eyes, and Treet saw her presence drifting back as if from far, far away. Her hand made a motion in the air, and Treet followed the gesture and saw a low table at the foot of the bed. A carafe of water and a cup sat on a tray. He poured water and lifted her head while she drank.

When she had sipped some water, Calin said in a creaky whisper, "Please . . . take me with you. I want to go back . . . back home."

He stared at her for a moment, considering what he'd done. "Well, uh—I . . ."

"Please." She clutched at his sleeve pathetically. "I will die here."

What she said was likely true. One way or another she would die here. So, on impulse, he agreed. "Good. I want you to go with us. I need you, Calin—you're my guide, remember?"

The mention of her old function brought a sad, lost smile to the young woman's lips. "Your guide," she said. "I will be your guide again."

"Yes, but before we go anywhere you're going to have to pull yourself together. Okay?" He went to the draperies and yanked them open. Bright sunlight streamed in. "First, let's get some fresh air in here." The breeze floated in, balmy and inviting. "There, that's better." He came back to the bed. "Let's see if we can get you on your feet."

She pushed herself up slowly from the bed. Treet put an arm around her and lifted her effortlessly. She was nearly as weightless as a shadow. This shocked him more than seeing her in her cataleptic state. "We've got to get some food into your stomach. You're withering away to nothing, and it's a long trek back to Dome."

Calin moved easily enough once she got going, and Treet knew that she had snapped out of whatever self-induced spell she'd been under. The simple mention of going home had done it. Though he could in no way imagine such an attachment, for

Calin the twisted, teeming warrens of Dome were home, and she missed it.

In the smaller dining hall they found food laid out. Treet broke the magician's fast with good bread and soft fruit, then offered her some cold, sliced meat which she gobbled down. Treet ate too, chewing thoughtfully, watching Calin and pondering about all that had happened in the last twelve hours or so:

He had somehow volunteered for a kamikaze mission behind enemy lines, alienated the one person in the entire universe who loved him, antagonized a very useful comrade, become nursemaid to a hothouse flower that couldn't live in the real world . . . not to mention loosing the fear of war among the most amiable, peace-loving people that ever lived.

And all this without meaning to, which, for a man who never put on his underwear in the morning without a strong conviction, was highly uncharacteristic of him to say the least. What could I have accomplished if I'd set my mind to it, he wondered.

He heard the low vibration of Talus' voice somewhere close by and got up, saying, "Stay here and finish eating. I'm going to talk to Talus. I'll be right back."

Talus was standing with two other Mentors: Bohm and Mathiax. The three formed some sort of triumvirate of Fierran leadership which Treet hadn't figured out yet. They looked up as Treet came toward them. Talus stroked his beard, and the others crossed their arms over their chests and studied him coolly.

"I guess I stirred things up here last night," he said. "I'm sorry if I embarrassed you."

"If you are right about what you said," replied Talus slowly, "you need have no concern for my feelings."

Mathiax said, "As a matter of fact, we have been talking about how to aid you."

"I thought the Preceptor made it quite clear that I could expect no help from the Fieri." Treet glanced quickly at the three grim faces.

"That is so," answered Talus. "We have no wish to violate a precept, but Mathiax here has suggested that perhaps a greater precept claims authority in this special case."

"What might that be?"

Mathiax answered, "The most fundamental precept of our

people requires that we extend ourselves to the aid of another whenever and wherever and in whatever way required."

"You have no obligation to me," said Treet.

"Oh, but we do," said Bohm. "We do because we choose to, and will always choose to. To refuse aid when aid could be offered would be a greater error than breaking the vow. Our precepts make us Fieri, not our vows. Even so, we need abandon neither."

"What Bohm is saying," explained Mathiax, "is that there might be a way of helping you, while at the same time observing our vow of peace."

Treet frowned. "I'd be grateful for whatever you could do, but," he shrugged, "going back is something I've chosen. You don't have to feel obligated."

Talus and Mathiax shook their heads sadly. "You still don't understand," said Mathiax. "Never mind. It doesn't matter. We have decided to offer you transportation. One of our balon routes lies just north of Dome. Ordinarily our navigators avoid flying within sight of Dome, but if one of them happened to let his balon wander a few hundred kilometers to the south, no harm would be done."

"I see. Yes, and if I happened to be on that balon, it might even touch down momentarily. No harm in that certainly."

The three Mentors shared sly smiles between themselves and nodded. "Thanks," said Treet. "You've helped me more than you know."

Talus put a large hand on his shoulder. "It was a difficult decision. But the truth was in you last night, and that we cannot ignore. May the Protector go with you."

"I have a feeling I'm going to give your multifaceted Deity a workout before this is over," said Treet lightly. "I'm going to need all the help I can get."

SIXTY
FOUR

Events spun past Treet with dizzying rapidity. Plans were laid and provisions secured for the return to Dome. Despite their vow of nonaggression, the Fieri willingly involved themselves in all phases of Treet's preparations. Bohm provided detailed maps of the balon route and the area where the travelers would be dropped off: along the river about twenty kilometers to the north of Dome.

"It's very simple," explained Bohm, stabbing a finger at the map. "The route lies between Dome and the Blue Forest. You will land here—where the river ends its slow curve around Dome's plateau. Then you can either move southwest away from the river, or follow it to here and turn in westward. It's roughly the same distance either way."

"You're sure it'll be all right? What if Dome sees the balon? I don't want to endanger your crew."

"They have been informed of the risks, and they all want to help. But to tell you the truth, we've never had any indication that Dome has ever seen one of our balons. At least not in the last five hundred years—as long as the airships have been flying."

"Is that so? How did you travel before that?" wondered Treet, suddenly interested.

Bohm smiled and laughed. "Oh, I thought you knew. You used them yourself, I understand."

"The sand skimmers?" Why did that seem so odd?

"Of course. In the very early days we traveled overland to the crystal mines. But that is tedious—despite the speed of skimmer blades."

Treet nodded. "Then the skimmers we found in Dome belonged to you, to Fieri I mean. They were yours."

Bohm looked surprised. "Yes! Certainly they were. Who else would have made them?"

What a lump I've been, thought Treet. A cheese-headed

lump! Dome had no use for sand skimmers. Why would they develop vehicles to traverse a desert they never entered? That brought up an obvious next question: "How did the skimmers get there, Bohm?"

The old man frowned and said, "They were captured—must have been. Though I can't recall ever hearing about anything like that."

"It's at least five hundred years ago, as you said, maybe longer."

"Yes." Bohm nodded thoughtfully. "Still, if you are interested, there would be a record of any such event in the Annals. As Clerk, Mathiax would be able to find it. Shall I have him look?"

"No, it's not important. I can guess what happened. It was an interesting fact, that's all."

Mathiax had a slightly different interpretation of that fact when Bohm told him about it later. The Clerk had joined them at Bohm's house near the airfield, and Treet confirmed the story by describing the skimmers in detail from shining blade tip to trailing solar panel. Mathiax listened, eyes half closed, nodding and grunting agreement.

"It is strange how the Provider works, is it not?" he said when Treet and Bohm had finished. "I had not stopped to consider it before, but now that you bring it up, I see the hand of the Infinite in this."

"Oh?" Treet didn't see it himself, but as a scholar he respected the Fieri's beliefs about their Deity.

"Yes, it's obvious. Don't you see?"

Treet gazed blankly back at his friend and said, "Frankly, no. But I'm not used to looking for such things."

"You should get used to it, Orion Treet. The Infinite Presence has chosen you for a task. When He chooses someone, He makes it possible for His agent to carry out the task for which he was chosen. You see?"

"You mean to tell me," replied Treet skeptically, "that five hundred years ago your Infinite Father arranged to have sand skimmers captured just so I'd have transportation when I needed it?"

Mathiax considered this for a moment and then agreed. "It amounts to that, yes."

"But what happened to those who were riding the skimmers at the time? They would have been imprisoned—killed, more likely. I'd call that a heavy price to pay just so I could have a ready getaway."

"We do not presume to fathom the ways of the Provider. It could be that those who were captured had their own tasks to complete. But we recognize that the Creator works in all times and places, turning even the very worst of circumstances to His purpose."

"It is so," agreed Bohm. "All praise!"

Two days later, they were ready to leave. Treet awoke on the morning of their departure heartsick. He had not seen Yarden since the night of their argument. He had looked for her, expecting to find her at Talus', and was told that she had returned to Ianni's house. He sent messages to her which she ignored. When, on the night before the balon was to leave, he had Jaire take him to Ianni's, they found the place empty. Yarden was not there.

Treet was forced to conclude that she was avoiding him, refusing to see him or speak to him. He considered delaying the trip another day or two on the off-chance that he might find a way to see her and talk to her again, but what was the use? She doesn't want to see me, he told himself. If I stayed another month she'd find excuses not to speak to me. It's over for us. I blew it. I might as well go now; there's no reason to stay.

And there was at least one very good reason to leave as scheduled: fear. Treet was afraid that if he didn't go now, he'd lose his nerve. The thought of actually returning to Dome and finding a way to do what he had to do there had become almost overwhelming. He couldn't think of it all at once, only in small chunks—hiking to the colony, making contact with Tvrdy, losing himself in the colony underground . . . the rest became fuzzy. But vagueness at this point he considered a blessing.

As the hour of departure neared, Treet grew more anxious. He wanted just to be gone, or at least moving. He couldn't stand the waiting any more. Each moment brought something that reminded him it was not a holiday vacation he was undertaking. He looked upon every Fierran vista as the last. See that? he told himself. You'll never see it again. He did not add that if his quest failed *no one* would ever see it again, but knew it just the same.

Crocker's mood could not be guessed. Treet checked with

him several times prior to departure, and each time Crocker appeared preoccupied and busy with his own preparations, though what those might be, Treet could not guess and Crocker didn't say. Treet left the pilot to himself, thinking, There'll be plenty of time for catching up later.

Now Treet stood next to a gleaming pylon on the edge of the airfield, the rising sun stretching his shadow across the expanse of close-cropped green lawn where the enormous red sphere of the balon, the Fieri airship that would take them to Dome, glowed against the pale blue sky. The oversized beachball shapes of balons tethered to the ground formed a bulbous, multicolored mushroom hedge around the field. Beneath the yoke-shaped gondola, the ground crew moved with unhurried efficiency. The wide loading ramp was down, but Treet didn't feel like climbing aboard just yet. He waited.

In a little while he heard Talus' resonant tones rolling across the field and turned to see Crocker and Talus striding toward him. Crocker had his kit slung over his shoulder and a grim, determined look in his eye. "Morning, Treet," he said, glancing toward the balon. "Good weather for flying."

Talus clapped Treet on the back and said, "This day has come too soon."

"You're right, Talus. I feel like I'm turning my back on the treasure of a lifetime. I'm going to miss you all very much."

"You won't change your mind and stay with us?" the Mentor asked earnestly. Crocker's head swiveled sharply to note Treet's reply.

"Thanks, Talus, but no." Treet shook his head wistfully. "I can't stay."

The big man regarded Treet with utmost compassion. "Follow the light that is in you, Traveler Treet. The Protector will watch over you, the Sustainer will keep you, the Comforter will give you rest. Go in peace and in peace return."

Treet didn't know what to say. No one had ever given him a benediction like that before. "Uh—ah, thanks, Talus. That's really nice."

Crocker made a sound in his throat, turned, and walked toward the balon. Talus watched him for a moment and, lowering his voice, said, "I wonder about that one. He is too much involved with himself."

"Crocker? He's okay—just a little nervous maybe. This isn't a joyride we're going on, you know." Treet spoke lightly, but his heart felt the implied foreboding of Talus' words. "What about Calin? I thought she was coming with you."

"Jaire will bring her." He gave Treet a knowing look.

"Maybe I should go—"

"It will be all right. We have a little time yet, and Mathiax has something for you."

As if on cue, an evee approached and came to a halt on the grass a few meters away. Mathiax climbed out and joined them. "I see all is ready . . ." He hesitated, then added, "I wish we could do more."

"You're doing enough," Treet reassured him. "You said yourself this is my task. I'll be all right."

"You may depend on it," the Clerk said solemnly.

An awkward silence grew between them, so Treet spoke up. "Talus said you had something for me."

"Oh, yes!" He pulled a folded card from his purple vest and handed it to Treet. "The Preceptor asked me to give you this. You are to read it after departure—alone."

Treet tucked the card into the pocket of his brown Fieri jacket. "Thanks. I will." Silence overtook them again. "I—uh, guess this is good-bye." The two men extended their hands to him in the Fieri manner, and Treet gripped them tightly. "Good-bye," he said, his throat tightening inexplicably.

"The Infinite Presence goes with you," said Mathiax. "Trust in Him to lead you."

"I'll try." Reluctant to take his eyes from their faces, Treet stepped backward from them and collided with someone standing a few paces away. "Sorry!" He turned, his hand frozen in midair. "Yarden, I—"

She was dressed in a white sleeveless jacket with white trousers and boots. Her black hair hung loose, gleaming with blue highlights, feathered by the breeze. His heart lurched in his chest. She said nothing but drew him aside with her. When Treet looked back, Talus and Mathiax were climbing into the evee to leave. They continued walking.

Halfway to the balon she stopped and faced Treet. "I haven't come to say good-bye, if that's what you're thinking."

"Why have you come, Yarden?" He ached to take her in his arms and hold her, to bridge the distance yawning between them.

"I came to give you one more chance to call off this asinine scheme of yours. Stay here, Orion. Stay with me. I . . ." Her cool, matter-of-fact manner faltered. The next words were spoken from her heart. "I need you. Don't go . . . please." She searched his face for a sign that he would amend his plans, but found only resolution. "That's it then. You won't change your mind."

Treet looked away. "I . . . Yarden, I can't."

"Then I won't either!" she snapped. "When you leave, it's good-bye."

"I'll come back."

"I won't live like that. No, it's forever. I never want to see you again." She stepped away from him, and he felt as if he had been jettisoned into deep space without a suit.

"Yarden, don't go! Please!"

She turned away slowly and began to walk across the field, spine straight, shoulders squared.

"I love you, Yarden!" Treet called. Her step halted, and her shoulders slumped; her head dropped momentarily. Treet saw a hand rise to her face, but she did not turn back. In a moment she continued on as before, but more quickly.

Treet stumbled toward the waiting balon. When he reached the ramp, Yarden was a small white figure against the green of the field. He watched until she passed behind a pylon and disappeared, then blindly pulled himself up the ramp and into the airship.

SIXTY
FIVE

Treet spent most of the flight cloistered in his quarters aboard the balon, emerging only occasionally to check with the navigator on their progress. The first time he went down to the bridge, they were high over deep folds of thickly forested mountains whose creases sparkled with freshets and silver cascades. Only a few hours later they reached the outer fringes of Daraq, the great desert shield.

Leaning with his elbows on the rail at the curving observation window, he gazed down on the glistening humps of white sand, watching the tiny round shadow of the balon dip and glide as it rippled over the wrinkled dunescape. Calin crept catlike up beside him and stood with eyes fixed on the spreading whiteness far below. Treet wondered if she knew how the desert had been made by her own people long ago. No, the Fieri would not have told her; they would have spared her that.

Still, something in the way Calin stared at the endless waste sliding away beneath them told Treet that she grasped part of the truth. "It is so dead," she whispered after a long while. "So dead and sad. I feel a sorrow I did not feel before."

"We were busy before," offered Treet, "just trying to stay alive."

Calin did not say anything, but Treet knew she did not accept his explanation.

He left her at the rail and returned to his quarters, threw himself down on his flight couch, and pulled the folded card from his pocket for the sixtieth time, opened it, and read the fair, handwritten script.

Traveler Treet, you stand at the center of events beyond your knowing. I ask the Infinite Presence in your behalf, not for strength, but to give you wisdom, that you may know what to do when the time comes for you to act. You suppose your arrival upon our world to have been chance; yet, though the designs of the Creator are most complex, every thread is woven in its place with His full intent. As you have said, you come from a world beyond our sun—a world we remember only as the shadow of a dream of long ago. Your presence reminds us that we cannot forget the lessons of the past. We *are* our past. I ask you to remember this. And also to remember for us who we were, for this we are beyond remembering. Know that you are the perfect agent for the task before you. Mathiax has told you, but still you doubt. Put your unbelief aside, and do not be afraid. You are well chosen.

The Preceptor

The trip lasted four days, and most of that time Treet spent thinking about what the Preceptor was trying to tell him in her enigmatic way. There was encouragement, yes, but something else less easily defined. At heart, her message seemed to be hinting that the key to succeeding in his task lay in understanding Empyrion. This understanding, she seemed to be suggesting, was to be found in his knowledge of his own world. Perhaps that's what she meant by making reference to his world beyond their sun. As for the part about remembering, he didn't get that at all.

And what did she mean, "we *are* our past"?

Maybe she simply meant that the Fieri were shaped by their past. Isn't everybody? Yes, but the Fieri were products of a past they could not remember. Their memory had been effectively wiped out in the holocaust.

But he, Treet, could remember. He knew, probably better than anyone else alive on Empyrion at the moment, the origins and history of their race. The Preceptor was asking him to remember for them the things they could not remember themselves—their past.

Was this so important? Ultimately, what did it matter? They could not change the past. Even if they all remembered perfectly the events which had led their ancestors out from Dome, or before that their colonizing journey from their original home, Earth, what could they do about it but accept it?

Adopting his familiar role as historian, Treet settled himself for some serious thought on the problem and finally came to the conclusion that for the Fieri, being shaped by a past beyond memory meant that they could never be certain about their future. As odd as that might seem on the surface, there was ample precedent in history for such a notion. Many ancient

Earth cultures believed that the past actively influenced the present and future. Nothing extraordinary there.

But what if one was cut off entirely from the past? That, perhaps, would mean a fairly one-dimensional future, a flat future, devoid of the richness and texture of the informing past. Also, the mutiplied chance that the past, in some way, because it was unknown, could repeat itself and they would be powerless to stop it.

The more he thought about it, the more unhappy Treet became with this line of reasoning. It did not account for much that he had seen in his too-brief stay there. There was something else that it did not account for: the curious reception given the travelers.

This had bothered him from the first.

If the Fieri were really as ignorant of the past as he supposed, why didn't they pump him for information day and night? They had in Treet a mobile data bank packed full of just the sort of fascinating tidbits they—according to his theory—ought to want to know: details of their home planet, their colonist patriarchs, what the colony must have been like in the early days, what caused the tragic split with Dome.

Inexplicably, the Fieri (and Dome, too, for that matter) appeared manifestly uninterested in any details of that sort. This perplexed Treet utterly—until he tried to put himself in their place. How would he react if a strange humanoid showed up on his doorstep one morning saying, "Hi there, I'm from another world and time, and I was just passing through the universe and thought I'd drop in. By the way, I can solve the riddles of the ages. Want to know the origins of life on your planet, huh? Go ahead, ask me anything."

All things considered, the Fieri reacted quite intelligently. Back home on Earth the supposed visitor would have been enrolled in the nearest noodle nursery before you could say DNA. Everyone he'd met on Empyrion so far seemed to consider him just an ordinary tourist and this, Treet decided, was what bothered him the most. Treet and his companions were from Earth! Yet the inhabitants of Empyrion seemed universally unimpressed.

Perhaps, he concluded, they simply had no way of comprehending it any more than he would have of comprehending the time traveler who appeared on his doorstep. Yet, the canny

Preceptor had put her long, well-manicured finger on it—Treet's veracity was of crucial importance to the survival of Empyrion. If indeed he was who he said he was, then somehow, some way it was up to Treet to do what only he could do.

But what?

Orion Treet, now on his way to confront his peculiar destiny, had absolutely no idea.

Late in the afternoon of the fourth day, the balon began its descent. Treet joined an excited Crocker at the railing and watched the airship gently lower itself from an opal sky. Below them, stretching northward to the broad, unvarying horizon, lay a heavy carpet of forest so dense and deep and dark it looked blue.

Emerging from the leading edge of the Blue Forest was the shining course Pizzle had dubbed Ugly Eel River. Along that river to the south, Treet knew, lay the glittering, multipeaked monstrosity of Dome, sparkling beneath the white sun of Empyrion like a diamond mountain. Treet glanced at Crocker and saw that the pilot stared into the southern distance as if hypnotized.

"I don't see it, do you?" said Treet.

Crocker pulled himself back and replied, "No . . . still too far away. It's down there though."

"You don't have to go. Calin and I can find it. You can stay on board—"

"No!" Crocker's face distorted in genuine anguish. Treet noted the reaction with alarm.

"Hey, it's okay—either way. I only wanted you to know that I'm not forcing anyone to do anything they don't want to do."

"You don't get rid of me that easy." Crocker forced a smile that looked like a death rictus. Treet felt a chill creep up into the pit of his stomach from the soles of his feet.

"I don't want to get rid of you, Crocker," he replied.

They watched the landscape drift closer, gaining definition with their descent. The river widened as they approached and eventually slipped beneath them and out of view. The pale turquoise hills that formed their landing field were as uniformly desolate as he remembered them, the turf just as wiry and tough. The balon dropped vertically the last thousand meters and bounced like a bubble on a forlorn hilltop. The wide hatchway opened, and the ramp descended to the ground.

The travelers watched the balon float away silently, rising straight up in the air. Then, when sufficient altitude had been reached, the engines cut in, pushing the spherical craft onto its northwestern course. There had been no fanfare for the travelers' leaving. They had said good-bye to the Fieri and climbed down the ramp, followed by a small, three-wheeled cargo carrier. The carrier was self-guided, programmed to follow the trailing member of their party at a distance of four meters.

Treet glanced at the map in his hands and oriented himself to the river, which he could see as a dark line curving away to his left a kilometer or so distant. "It's straight ahead, friends. We can walk a couple of hours and make camp for the night. With any luck, I figure we'll reach Dome sometime tomorrow afternoon."

"Suits me," said Crocker, staring off into the distance. Without another word he started walking.

Treet watched him, then said to Calin, "I'm a little worried about him. He's not himself."

The magician's eyes flicked from Treet to Crocker and back again. "I sense fear . . . and—I don't know . . ." She bent her head. "I'm sorry."

"Don't be. It's not your fault. I'm a little scared myself. How about you?"

Calin nodded and hugged herself. Standing there among the featureless hills, small, vulnerable, it was the gesture of a lost child. Treet gathered her into his arms. "It's going to be all right. Believe me. Nothing's going to happen to us."

They held each other for a moment, and Treet remembered how she had put her childish trust in him at the beginning of their odyssey. Now here they were again, about to reenter a strange, forbidding world. Her world. He would need her there just as much as she needed him outside it. Treet pulled her close and then, quite without premeditation, put his lips to hers.

The kiss was brief, but it lingered in his mind for a long time after. He took her hand and they followed Crocker, who had disappeared momentarily into a fold in the hill line. At their movement, the robo-carrier whirred. Its lenses swiveled in its sensor panel, fixing the proper distance and when four meters stretched between them, its wheels rolled forward and it came tagging along behind.

SIXTY
SIX

Crocker unrolled his sleeping pallet as soon as he'd finished eating. They had hunched together over the small pellet-fuel fire they'd made to warm their food. The Fieri had provided them with all they could think of to ease the rigors of the hike. Even though it was only twenty kilometers, they were outfitted for a journey across the entire continent. Treet wished they had been so provisioned on their first trip.

Their meal had been simple, filling, and eaten in almost total silence. Calin nestled close to Treet, and they sat together across from Crocker, who ate with his head down, dipping his hand mechanically into his bowl. It seemed to Treet that the pilot was avoiding eye contact with him, but he put it down as fatigue and jitters about what lay ahead of them. The times Treet attempted conversation evoked no response. Crocker sat with his long frame bent over the bowl balanced on his knees, staring alternately into the fire and then into the darkening sky.

By the time they finished eating, night covered them with its blanket of stars. Treet and Calin followed Crocker's example and fished their pallets from the robo-carrier and unrolled them next to the fire. The pallets were made of a soft foam bottom layer bonded to double layers of a heat-reflective blanket material. Weary travelers would slip between these blankets and sleep comfortably all night.

But Treet did not sleep well. He lay for a long time listening to the enormous silence of the hill country, watching the impossibly bright stars glaring down at him from a firmament that shone like the inside of a burnished iron bowl.

He could not stop thinking about what lay ahead, could not help but think that he was hopelessly unequal to the task and foolish for even considering that what he might do could make any difference. He had no plan, no weapons, no help that he could count on. Visions of futility shimmered in the flames beside him as he lay on his arm, gazing into the fire.

The fire had burned itself out when he awoke again. The night was bright with stars, and he sat up. Calin kneeled over him; her touch had awakened him—that and an odd sound: someone moaning pitifully.

"What?" he asked. "Crocker?"

The pilot groaned again, this time a deep, guttural sound like that of a wild animal—a wolf perhaps, readying itself to attack. Treet pulled his feet from the pallet's envelope and went to Crocker, put his hand on his shoulder, and jostled him gently. "Crocker, wake up. You're having a bad dream. Crocker?"

The man growled again, savagely, and came up, muscles tense and rigid, teeth flashing in the cold starlight. "No!" he shouted. "No! Ahh!" His eyes bulged. Sweat glistened on his forehead.

"Take it easy, Crocker," said Treet. "You're having a nightmare. It's over now. You're here with us. You're safe."

In a moment Crocker relaxed, the tension leaving his muscles all at once. "I—don't know what came over me," he said, shaking his head and rubbing his neck. "It was like a—I don't know—like I was frozen inside a block of ice, or fire, or something. I couldn't break out. I was dying."

"It was only a dream. You're okay now. Take a deep breath."

He lay back down and was asleep seconds later. Treet was not so lucky. He lay awake waiting for Crocker to dream again, but heard only the heavy, rhythmic breathing of deep sleep. After a while he felt a light touch on his arm and glanced up to see Calin's face above his. "No, I'm not asleep," he said softly.

The magician came around and bent close to him. Treet lifted the blanket and let her slide in beside him. He wrapped his arms around her and held her body close. The comfort in that simple act sent waves of pleasure washing through his soul. Entwined together, they slept until morning.

Crocker sat watching them when Treet awoke. The sun was barely touching a pearl-gray eastern sky, and a light wind stirred the longer blades of grass on the hilltops. Treet came fully awake the second he saw Crocker's face—half of it was smeared down, as if someone had run a torch over the left side of a wax mannikin's face. His eyes were lusterless, dead. His mouth pulled down on one side and up on the other in a ridiculous, ghoulish grimace.

"Crocker!" Treet cried. Calin started from sleep and looked up, cowering.

Treet disentangled himself from his bedroll and got to his feet. The pilot looked at him dully and then began to laugh. It was a ghastly sound—hollow, disembodied, half mocking, half pitying. He stopped abruptly, like a recording switched off.

"What's wrong with you? What's so funny?" asked Treet, shaken. Calin cringed.

"Wrong? Nothing's wrong." His voice was soft. Too soft. "I was just thinking . . . what a shame to waste it . . . eh?"

"Waste what? What are you talking about?" Treet took a step closer. Crocker threw up a hand to stop him.

"Your girlfriends—I don't see what they see in you."

Jealousy? Was that it? Crocker had never shown anything like that before. "Look," Treet said, "you had us worried last night. You had a nightmare—remember?"

Crocker rose, yawned, stretched his arms out wide. Treet noticed the tremendous reach of those long arms. "I slept like a baby." His lips twitched into a wolfish grin. "So did you, it looks like."

"She was scared," said Treet, then wondered why he was explaining. "So was I. You really had us going."

"Speaking of going . . ." Crocker stooped, rolled up his pallet, and stuffed it into the carrier. "Let's get it over with."

He watched while Treet and Calin put away their bedrolls, then turned and headed off. When he had passed from earshot, Treet whispered to Calin, "We've got to keep an eye on him. Something's wrong."

She nodded, but said nothing, and they started off once more.

By midmorning they had reached the halfway point, Treet estimated. They sat down on a hilltop to eat some dried fruit. "We ought to be able to see it soon," he said.

Crocker nodded, chewed silently, and swallowed.

"We should probably talk about how we're going to get inside."

"Plenty of time later," said Crocker.

"Okay. Sure. Later."

When they moved on, Crocker fell behind them, shuffling

along flat-footedly now, where before he'd swung his long legs
in an efficient, ground-eating stride. Calin hung close to Treet's
left hand, glancing back at regular intervals. Treet refrained from
looking back, but once, when he could stand it no longer, he
peered over his shoulder to see Crocker's mouth working silently, as if he were debating with himself. Crocker stopped when he
saw that Treet was looking.

They stopped a few hours later for their first good look at
Dome. The sun was high overhead, blazing in the crystal facets
of its enormous webwork with white brilliance. From this distance, it would have been easy to mistake the structure for a
glass mountain whose peaks and tors glittered as the sun's rays
played over its polished surface. From a closer vantage point,
individual sections of dome clusters would be seen, giving Dome
the appearance of a mound of soap bubbles dropped on an
endless flat lawn.

"There it is," said Crocker through his teeth. He turned to
Treet, but looked through him.

Treet glanced away. "We can be there in a couple of hours.
We'll have plenty of time before sundown to find a way inside . . . *if* Tvrdy is still watching, that is."

They started down the hill to the last valley before the
long, gradual climb to Dome's low plateau. Crocker fell behind
again, and Treet halted when he reached the bottom of the hill
to wait for the pilot to catch up. Crocker waved him on. Treet,
with Calin stuck like a second shadow to his side, continued on,
growing increasingly worried. Something was terribly wrong
with Crocker, he knew. What? Nerves? Treet was nervous himself; it wasn't that. It was something deeper, more sinister.

After walking for an hour or so, now beginning the trek up
the slope to the plateau, Treet looked around to see Crocker, his
back turned, standing over the carrier. "Anything the matter?"
he hollered back.

"Yeah, this robot is jammed up. It can't make the climb.
We'll have to leave some of the gear."

"Stay here," Treet told Calin under his breath.

Calin, staring down at Crocker, nodded. As Treet turned
away, he felt her hand on his sleeve. "Be careful," she whispered.

"What's the problem?" he asked as he joined Crocker. The
man was sweating through his clothes.

"I don't know. I heard it laboring, and I looked back and it
was stuck."

"We've had tougher climbs than this. It always made them before."

The pilot shrugged. "Maybe its gears are shot."

"Let's take some of the stuff out and see if that helps." Treet bent over the carrier and started undoing the straps that held down the webbing. "Are you going to stand there or are you going to help?"

Crocker stood rock still.

Treet stooped, pulling articles from the three-wheeled robot. "Well?" He looked back just in time to see Crocker's arm swinging down in a murderous stroke, sunlight gleaming on the object in his hand. Calin screamed.

Treet ducked, but the blow caught him on the top of his right shoulder, missing his head, but smashing the median nerve into the clavicle. His arm fell to his side, paralyzed. Blinding pain flared from the shoulder a microsecond later.

Treet collapsed and rolled on his back to avoid the next strike. He started screaming. "Crocker! What are you doing! It's me, Treet! Treet! Crocker! Stop! Sto-o-p-p!"

The metal bar blurred in the air. Treet squirmed on the ground, dodging away as best he could, as the improvised weapon dug a little furrow in the dirt bare centimeters from his left temple.

Treet heard another shout and saw Calin flying to his aid, arms flailing. She attacked her heavier adversary with her claws, raking red welts into the side of his face and neck. The pilot threw her off, but she was at him again, scratching like a she-cat. A slashing backhand blow sent her spinning into a heap.

The diversion had allowed Treet to get to his feet, however. He lunged toward Crocker, his useless arm dangling. He thought to knock the mad pilot off-balance and somehow wrest the bar away from him.

Crocker, with the quickness of the insane, roared and jumped to the side, wielding the short length of metal in a deadly arc. The swing grazed Treet on the lower jaw, tearing a ragged gash along the jawline. Blood spilled down the side of his throat. "Crocker," he said, gulping for breath, "in the name of God, give it up."

The pilot lunged again, a strangled, inhuman sound bubbling from his throat, his eyes flecked with blood. With dreadful clarity, Treet's pain-dazzled brain registered that Crocker meant to kill him. His only hope now was flight; he could try to outrun his assailant and escape, or at least put some distance between them until Crocker came to his senses.

He turned to flee, shouting, "Run, Calin! Run for it!" The magician had circled around Crocker and now stood only a meter or two to Treet's right. She did not move. Her eyes were half-closed and her face rigid in concentration. "Calin!"

Treet flung out his good hand, snagged Calin by the arm, spun her around, and shoved her forward all in the same motion. He felt a sharp jab in his upper back, and then the force of the thrust wheeled him sideways. He tripped over himself and fell headlong to the ground.

He landed on his right side. His dead right arm failed to break his fall, and he hit hard. The air rushed from his lungs in a terrific gasp. Black circles with blue-white edges dimmed his eyesight. He heard himself yelling for Calin to run for it.

Standing over him now, Crocker, with a mighty snarl of rage, brought the metal bar down with both hands from high over his head. Too late to dodge, Treet threw his left hand up to divert the blow, expecting to see his forearm splinter as the heavy bar slashed down upon it. The second stroke would crush his skull like an eggshell.

Instead, he saw the metal bar fall with lethal accuracy only to glance aside at the last second. One instant it was a deadly blur descending toward him, the next it was sliding away. He was untouched.

Crocker appeared dazed. The weapon dangled in his hand. Treet threw himself at it, grabbed. With only one hand, Treet could not hope to hang on. The weapon slid by centimeters from his fingers as Crocker's superior strength overcame his single-handed grasp. The pilot kicked out; Treet's knee buckled and he toppled.

The pilot staggered back, clenching the bar in his upraised hands. Howling, he swung the bar down. Treet's eyes closed reflexively. Again the bar bounced harmlessly aside before impact.

Crocker roared in pain—like a berserk rogue elephant stung by the dart of a keeper. He whirled away.

"Calin!" Treet struggled to his knees. The magician stood with one hand upraised, her eyes closed, sight turned inward. Treet recognized the posture as her trance state. "Calin, look out!"

Crocker's furious lunge drove the end of the metal bar into

Calin's neck. They both fell together, Crocker sprawling head-long over his victim. The metal bar rolled on the ground. Treet scooped it up with his left hand and swung blindly at Crocker's huddled form.

The bar, awkward in his hand, slipped as he struck out, catching the pilot on the hip. Treet glanced down and saw his hand dripping red; the bar was slick with Calin's blood.

Crocker gathered his long frame to spring. Treet braced himself, raising the bar. The pilot rushed forward with a howl, his face twisted almost beyond recognition: eyes bugging out, mouth gaping, jaws slack, tongue lolling. The bar thumped inef-fectually on Crocker's chest and bounced out of Treet's grasp as he stumbled backward.

He lay facedown, panting, knowing that even as he thought it, the metal bar was closing on his skull. He waited. Rather than the sound of metal singing through the air to splat-ter his gray matter over the turf, he heard an odd grunting noise and the faint whir of a machine. Treet glanced up to see the demented pilot limping away, the little robo-carrier rolling after him.

Crocker's body jerked spasmodically, arms loose, legs stumping woodenly, shoulders rolling. He looked like a puppet whose strings were fouled. As he lurched along, a loathsome gagging sound came from his throat. With a shudder, Treet realized the pilot was weeping.

On hands and knees he crawled to Calin's side and gath-ered her up. The wound was deep. The bar had been plunged into the soft flesh of her throat and ripped upward, leaving a ragged hole. Blood streamed from the hideous wound; her jack-et was drenched in crimson and sticky to the touch.

"Calin," Treet huffed, his stomach turning itself inside out. "You're going to be all right. He . . . he's gone."

She opened her eyes slowly, and from her unfocused stare Treet knew that she could not see him. "Hold . . . me," she whispered airily. Her larynx had been crushed, or torn apart. "S-s-o . . . da-ark . . ."

Treet drew her close, cradling her head against his chest. "You'll feel better in a moment," he told her, hating the lie. "Just rest."

Calin's lips parted in the gesture of a smile. "Nho," she wheezed. "Nho . . . came . . . back."

"That's good," he soothed. "Now rest."

She swallowed, pain convulsing her features. When she opened her eyes again, Treet saw the effort it had cost her. Still, she struggled to speak.

"What is it?" He put his ear to her lips.

"Ahh . . . I am . . . magician again . . ." She sighed, so lightly that Treet thought she had fallen asleep. When he looked he saw the empty, upward gaze, her dark eyes clouding with death.

SIXTY
SEVEN

Treet closed her eyes and kissed Calin's forehead, smoothing her tangled hair from her face. He sat for a long time, cradling the body, rocking back and forth, oblivious to the tears streaming down his face, murmuring, incoherent in his grief.

Slowly the warmth seeped from the body; Calin's limbs grew cold, and at last Treet let her go. He laid her gently down, pulling his jacket around her to hide the thickening stain on her clothes. "I'm . . . Calin, I'm sorry. . ." he told her, lifting his face to the sky. "So sorry . . . I should have known . . . seen . . . protected you. I'm sorry. Forgive me, Calin."

Time passed—how much time he did not know. But his shadow stretched long when he finally raised his head and looked around at the vacant hills, thinking, I can't leave her here like this. I have to bury her.

Where? He had no tool to dig a grave—only his bare hands, and the turf was too thick, too dense. He turned his eyes toward Dome. Then, carefully gathering the body into his arms, Treet stood and began to walk.

Night was far gone by the time Treet reached Dome. All the muscles in his back and legs had long ago twisted into throbbing knots, but he had walked on, ignoring the pain, his senses numb, heeding only the stubborn will to put one foot in front of the other and move on.

The sun had set in a ghostly yellow fireball, tinting the Western sky briefly before night extinguished the golden glow and plunged the lonely hills into darkness. Dome loomed larger with every aching step, the conical peaks and bulging humps holding the sky's last light long after the sun had sunk beyond the hills. Now its hulking mass brooded in the dark, except where starlight glinted cold from the planes of the crystal shell.

At the foot of Dome's foremost cluster, where the fiber-steel and crystal sank into the earth, Treet lay Calin's body down. The grass grew long around Dome, and the earth was soft. Treet pulled, and the stiff grass came up by the roots, dragging large, heavy clods with it. He cleared an oblong swath and dug his fingers into the soil, smelling the deep, rich scent.

The stars bled dim light over him. With nightfall a haze had crept into the upper atmosphere, casting a pall over heaven's face. With his fingers he gouged out a shallow depression, scooping the earth away in clumps. His fingernails tore and bled, but he toiled on until he had carved a rough grave beneath Dome's roots.

He slid Calin's body into the grave, knelt over it, and, placing a hand against her cold cheek one last time, said good-bye. He started crying again as he heaped dirt over the body, watching her pale, smooth flesh disappear under the dark earth. When he had finished, he replaced the grass atop the mound and stood, brushing the dirt from his hands and knees.

He turned to go, but felt that there ought to be some sort of ceremony; some words, at least, should be said. He stared at the rude mound, but could think of nothing suitable to say—until it occurred to him to recite the benediction Talus had given him.

Raising his face to the dim stars, he imagined the magician's spirit hovering nearby. He said: "Follow the light that is in you, Calin. May the Protector watch over you, the Sustainer keep you, the Comforter give you rest. Go in peace." After a moment he added, "Infinite Father, receive this one into your care."

He turned away and began walking around Dome's vast perimeter.

Dawn found him standing at the edge of the canopy formed by the superstructure supporting the landing field. He entered, moving among the heavy fibersteel pylons as through a dark forest of smooth, branchless trees. As he came near the place where the doors opened into Dome's Archives, he halted. The air held the retchingly sweet odor of decay, and as the light grew stronger he saw a grisly sight: two semidecomposed corpses lying where they'd fallen a few meters from the door.

The events of that hectic day flooded back as Treet re-membered their harried departure from Dome and the ensuing firefight. The moldering corpses offered a stark reminder, as had Calin's death, of the seriousness of his task.

Treet swallowed hard and moved toward the doors. He searched for and found the code lock with which he was to signal Tvrdy, but the mechanism had been blasted. Nothing remained but a scorched spot where the fibersteel had bubbled. There was no way to signal Tvrdy—if Tvrdy still lived and waited for his return, which he had begun to doubt. How would he get in?

He stepped to the great doors and saw that his entrance was provided: a third corpse lay pinched between the doors. The wretch had fallen on the grooved track, and the closing doors had crushed him. But not completely. The body had jammed the track as the doors ground shut, leaving a crack half-a-body wide.

Treet grimaced as he stepped over the corpse and wedged himself into the crevice. Darkness and panic swooped over him. His mind filled with doubt. What if Jamrog's men were waiting for him inside? What if Tvrdy had lied? What if he and his men had all been captured and executed?

He fought down the fear, and in a moment the darkness cleared and he saw himself standing poised on an imaginary line. He gritted his teeth and took one last look at the narrow band of blue sky and green hills glimpsed from under the landing platform.

"Now it begins," he told himself. Then, squeezing through the narrow way, he disappeared inside.

END OF BOOK ONE